ENEMY ACTION

BOOK THREE OF THE IMPERIAL MARINES SAGA

TERRY MIXON

YOWLING
CAT PRESS

Enemy Action

Copyright © 2022 by Terry Mixon

This is a work of fiction. All names, characters, places, and incidents are the products of the author's imagination, or are used fictitiously. Any resemblance to actual persons, living or dead, events, or locales is entirely coincidental.

Published by Yowling Cat Press ®

Digital edition date: 6/21/2023

Print ISBN: 978-1947376670

Large Print ISBN: 978-1947376687

Cover art - image copyrights as follows:

DepositPhotos | innovari (Luca Oleastri)

DepositPhotos | algolonline (Caroline Rosa Nicolette Atkinson)

DepositPhotos | vitaliy_sokol (Виталий Сокол)

Donna Mixon

Cover design and composition by Donna Mixon

Print edition design and layout by Terry Mixon

ALSO BY TERRY MIXON

You can always find the most up to date listing of Terry's titles on his Amazon Author Page.

Note: the links below (ebook only, obviously) redirect you to my website where you can click a button to go to Amazon. This allows me to participate in Amazon's associates program and earn a little more. Sorry for any inconvenience.

The Last Hunter

The Last Hunter

Bonds of Blood

Alpha Strike

The Enemy Revealed

Command Authority

The Grand Conspiracy

Shield of Humanity

Fog of War

Ships of the Line

Operation Liberty

The Empire of Bones Saga

Empire of Bones

Veil of Shadows

Command Decisions

Ghosts of Empire

Paying the Price

Recon in Force

Box Sets

The Empire of Bones Saga Volume 1

The Empire of Bones Saga Volume 2

The Empire of Bones Saga Volume 3

The Empire of Bones Saga Volume 4

Humanity Unlimited Publisher's Pack 1

Humanity Unlimited Publisher's Pack 2

Want to get updates from Terry about new books and other general nonsense going on in his life? He promises there will be cats. Go to TerryMixon.com/Mailing-List and sign up.

DEDICATION

This book would not be possible without the love and support of my beautiful wife. Donna, I love you more than life itself.

ACKNOWLEDGMENTS

I want to thank the folks that support me on Patreon. You got to read this book as I was writing it and that kept me working. You have my deepest thanks.

In particular, I want to thank those patrons that supported me at the $10 level:

Bryan Barnes
    Robert Broadly
    Tony Craven
    Bill Colston
    Dave Dolan
    Mark I Marcum
    Christian A. Michelsen
    John Page
    Keith Ramsey
    Carl Rumbolo
    Lisa Slack
    Dale Thompson
    Raymond Wang
    Clark Williams

Finally, I want to thank my readers for putting up with me. You guys are great.

1
―――――――

ndrea Tolliver did her best to ignore the people staring at her face as she stepped off the cutter that had brought them down to Seward. At this point in her life, she was resigned to the fact that everyone felt the need to gawk at the bird-of-prey tattoos that dominated her forehead and cheeks, but the attention still made her feel very self-conscious.

No matter how she felt, it wasn't something she could change. The predatory-bird tattoos of the Andrea Line were marked indelibly upon her skin, and she could never escape them, no matter how far or fast she ran.

What she *could* do was change her life into something she wanted to live, and that was why she was here. This was her first permanent duty assignment as an Imperial Marine. Not only had she finished basic training, but she'd gone through the advanced individual training required to turn her into a larval marine.

Her ability to assist in some of the training at the advanced school had even earned her a promotion to private first class. That honestly wasn't any better than being just a private, but it was one step further on her journey.

And at least her journey wasn't one that she had to take alone during this first stage. She still had her best friend, Diana, at her side. And Claudio, though he wasn't exactly much of a bonus.

"Man, it's cold here," he complained as he wrapped his arms around his torso. "Why couldn't they put the base in a more temperate zone?"

"Maybe they wanted to make it a little more challenging," Diana said as she stepped up beside him, her head even with his chest. "Exactly how tough would marines be if they did all their training in the bars at some urban center?"

Claudio's eyes narrowed as he stared down at the curvy redhead. "You're a real downer, Randall. Wouldn't you rather have *some* amenities in life? Do you want to live out in the boonies doing training forever? Your life doesn't have to revolve around being an Imperial Marine every single second of the day."

Diana laughed merrily. "Did that just come from the man that said I wasn't suitable to be a marine in the first place? How did *you* end up being the slacker in this crew?"

Six months ago, those words would've been all it took to start a brawl. Times really had changed because all Claudio did was grunt and shake his head.

"How many times do I have to repeat myself? I was wrong. You've got what it takes to be an Imperial Marine, but you just don't have to be one *all the time.*"

"But I *like* being an Imperial Marine all the time. Even when I go out drinking, but that's not going to be today. We need to report to battalion and get things sorted out.

"Aren't you excited, Claudio? This is it. We're at our first duty station. The generalized training is over, and now we get to train for war."

Andrea had been listening to their banter for the entire six weeks it had taken them to get from the advanced training base to Seward. Everything they'd said had been recycled several dozen times by now, but it hadn't gotten old.

All three of them were excited about what was happening. Andrea had trained for this day since she was twelve years old, and now she could dive headfirst into the only career she'd ever wanted.

And they'd never get to it if they didn't stop standing around like tourists. Time to get this show on the road.

"Enough chatter," she said firmly, cutting off their back-and-forth. "We've got to find a ride to battalion."

Diana mock saluted her. "Aye aye, Private First Class, ma'am!"

"It's just a stupid promotion," Andrea grumbled. "It's not like I'm any different than I was before. We're all still privates."

"Sure," Claudio said with a grin. "Just some of us are first class. Kind of like the senior line you used to be part of."

Even the thought was enough to make Andrea shudder slightly. "Do me a favor and never say that again. You have no idea what a nightmare that was."

Miraculously, Claudio did exactly that. Maybe he was learning the basics of being a decent human being. Diana was certainly an excellent role model.

The three of them made their way away from the landing pad, using the low-slung buildings to block as much of the wind as possible. While the temperature couldn't be called Arctic, it was by no means warm.

Considering this was the height of summer for this portion of the planet—she'd checked—that didn't bode well for them once winter was in full swing. Claudio would *really* hate that.

Once they got away from the pad, it was easy enough to find transport. This was where everyone arrived, so there were autonomous taxis waiting for them. Since they were reporting for duty, the taxi wouldn't even deduct the cost of the fare from their accounts this time.

They quickly loaded their duffel bags into the back of the taxi and stuffed themselves inside. That wasn't very difficult for the two girls, but Claudio was not small, so they made him sit up front by himself. Otherwise they'd have been squished against the sides of the vehicle.

The young man took the bump with surprisingly good humor. Maybe he really was growing up.

The drive to the 745th Combat Marine Battalion only took about twenty minutes, and they spent the time checking out the base that would be their home for at least the next decade.

Deployments for marines were stable unless they screwed up in some fashion. The people she met today would be the ones she'd be dealing with for years to come, so she needed to get this right.

Trouble started almost as soon as they arrived at battalion headquarters. This, too, was expected. These were combat marines, and many of them recognized what the tattoos on her face meant.

The Singularity and the Terran Empire had been at war—for certain values of the word—since before the Empire had existed as a political entity. Their covert battle had started when humanity was all part of the long-dead Terran Republic.

No one could really hold the complete history of the two nations in their minds, since it spanned more than ten thousand years, but there was plenty of bad blood to go around.

Thankfully this time—unlike the last two duty assignments—someone was waiting for them. A tall female gunnery sergeant, her face a deep brown and her uniform perfect, stood waiting at the base of the stairs leading into the building.

Apparently, she was specifically waiting for Andrea because her attention was laser focused on her when she stepped out of the taxi.

"Private First Class Andrea Tolliver?" the woman asked, her voice somewhat deeper than her frame suggested. "Privates Randall and Baker? I'm Gunnery Sergeant Ariel Singh, Delta Company's senior noncommissioned officer. Gather your gear and come with me."

Andrea didn't bother asking stupid questions. They'd tell her what she needed to know when she needed to know it. Gunnery sergeants were notorious for not taking crap, and she wasn't going to give the woman the slightest excuse to come down on her.

Apparently, Diana and Claudio agreed because they hustled to get their gear in record time. In less than fifteen seconds, the three stood with their bags over their shoulders, ready to go.

Singh led them away from battalion headquarters and deeper into the maze of buildings. One positive aspect of having her along was that she acted as a ward to keep others at a distance.

Andrea was drawing some negative attention from a number of marines who'd stopped to stare at her, but none of them dared approach. That almost certainly wouldn't hold true once they were fully integrated into their new unit, but that was a problem for later. Right now, she needed to figure out exactly what was going on.

Sadly, it wasn't something she could just ask. Singh would tell Andrea everything she thought she needed to know when she was damned good and ready and not one second earlier.

They arrived at a small building labeled Delta Company Headquarters, and Singh led them inside. Marines bustled about the interior of the building, performing their daily tasks, and many paused to look at Andrea's face as she passed. They didn't linger because Singh gave anyone spending *too* much time watching a stare that sent them packing.

It only took a minute to reach the company commander's office, and Singh went right in. When Andrea stepped into the room, she found herself in an orderly and meticulously clean environment. The desk behind which the company commander sat was immaculate and had nothing marring its polished surface.

The walls had framed pictures, and some held shelving with knickknacks, but everything was precisely placed, or so it seemed to her. If the room reflected the man's nature, he was a fastidious sort.

Delta Company's commanding officer was an interesting contrast of appearances. His skin was relatively dark, yet his hair was almost blindingly white. His facial structure also seemed to be fairly robust rather than slight. Despite all that, the man was handsome.

Not that she had any business thinking about the appearance of a senior lieutenant in the Imperial Marines. Instead, she snapped to attention and waited to be recognized, just like her companions.

Singh stepped over to the side of the desk and gave the lieutenant an unreadable look, raising an eyebrow in question.

The officer smiled at Andrea and the rest. "At ease, people. This might take a little while, and there's no need for you to be uncomfortable. I'm Senior Lieutenant Pedro van Buren, Delta Company's commanding officer.

"It's my duty and pleasure to welcome you to Seward. This is a nonstandard intake, but you'll forgive me if I say you're not exactly a standard greenie, Private First Class Tolliver."

He leaned back in his seat and examined the three of them. "I know more than enough about your history to realize there will be friction, Tolliver. Sadly, that's going to bleed over onto your friends as well. We'll do what we can to minimize it, but I hope you're ready to deal with it in a professional manner when it occurs."

"I hope so, too, sir," Andrea said levelly. "If I might ask, what exactly do you know about my history?"

The man smiled, showing off his pearly white teeth. "Oh, I don't know much about when you were in the Singularity, but I know a great deal about the kind of person you probably are. You see, I served with Grace Tolliver before she went on the raid where she retrieved you.

"I was the battalion adjutant back then, and she commanded Third Platoon of this very company. The same platoon that you're going to be assigned to, as a matter of fact."

Andrea found herself blinking in surprise. Out of all the possible scenarios she'd considered, that one had never occurred to her. The people here would've known Grace and Fei. Would that carry some weight in tempering their responses to her?

She had no idea, but obviously, someone else had thought it might.

Odds were good that it was Diana's father, J. Russell Macumber, Earl Still Water. The man was a roving director for Imperial Intelligence, and he'd been calling the shots about what happened with Andrea for years now, even though she'd only recently become aware of it.

"I can see you understand what I'm getting at," the man said, his smile widening slightly. "Your squad leader isn't going to be happy I'm assigning the three of you to the same fire team, but I've been aware of your imminent arrival for several months, and I've had time to prepare this company for what was coming.

"Expect to be brought up to speed as quickly as possible. You've got a lot to learn and many skills to hone. As deeply as we might wish for peace, the Empire is always involved in some skirmish or another, both internal and external. You three need to be prepared to do your part when the time comes."

He grimaced slightly. "You'll also have to be aware of some

obstacles to your success. You've got a strong advocate in both myself and the regimental commander, Colonel Jackson Grimsby. He was the battalion commander when Grace led her platoon into the Singularity. He's a good man to have at your back.

"Unfortunately, our battalion commander isn't exactly welcoming of your presence. I wouldn't say that Major Anatoli Bashir is exactly an enemy, but he certainly isn't your friend. He was a rival of Grace's and commanded one of the other companies back then. I think he was displeased that she was picked for the raid, and he wasn't."

Van Buren sighed. "It's not for me to speak ill of a senior officer, but the major's personality can be somewhat… challenging. To say he was less than pleased to hear of your existence—much less your assignment to his battalion—is something of an understatement. I'll try to shield you from his direct attention as much as I can, but there are limits, and I'd expect some type of confrontation in the future."

That wasn't exactly reassuring, but it could've been worse, she supposed. Having a person with an ax to grind was a lot better than having someone shooting at you. Some people would dislike her no matter what she did. It was a fact of life that she'd resigned herself to a long time ago.

"Whatever comes my way, sir, I'll handle it," Andrea said levelly. "I'm not responsible for where I came from, but I'll be the best marine I can be."

Van Buren smiled. "And that's all one can really ask of you. I realize this isn't an optimal situation, or even a fair one, but you at least have a friend in me. That won't get you any slack regarding your duties, but Gunnery Sergeant Singh and I will do our best to shield you from any official interference.

"I'm sure we'll have an opportunity to speak again, and I'd certainly like to discuss Grace at some point, but that's going to have to wait. Right now, I'll get you signed in remotely at battalion, and Ariel will see that you're introduced to Corporal Reed—your fire team leader—who will get you squared away. Off with you now."

Andrea stiffened back to attention before following Singh out of the office. This had gone better than expected, but she could already smell a storm on the horizon.

Lieutenant Van Buren would undoubtedly do his best to protect her from the major's attention, but if the major had an ax to grind with Grace, he'd have a *lot* more trouble with her.

And that didn't even count how much grief she'd get from her fire team leader, squad leader, and squadmates. She'd have to live with them every day of her life for quite some time to come, and if anyone was inclined to make her suffer, it would almost certainly come from that quarter.

Welcome to the glorious life of an Imperial Marine.

2

Sergeant Jerome Walker entered battalion headquarters feeling more than a bit uneasy. It was never a good day when the battalion commander summoned you to his office without an explanation.

Ever since he'd received the call, he'd been going over everything his squad had done and couldn't find a reasonable explanation as to why Major Bashir wanted to see him.

In the end, it probably didn't matter. It almost certainly wouldn't be anything good.

Not that he had anything against Bashir personally, but field grade officers were to be avoided when at all possible. The man had a reputation for being an ass, and Jerome didn't want to give the man any excuse to focus his attention on him.

The battalion adjutant waved him through, so Jerome walked into the major's office and came to attention in front of his desk. "Sergeant Walker, reporting as ordered, sir."

Bashir muted his computer's holographic display and focused his full attention on Jerome, steepling his fingers on his desk. The man considered him for a few seconds and then spoke.

"At ease, Sergeant. If you're worried that I've called you here to tear a strip off you, you can relax. I just need you to perform a task for me. One that requires discretion and attention to detail. Is that going to be a problem?"

"No, sir. Whatever you need, I'll make it happen."

Why would his battalion commander be contacting him directly? If the man needed something done, all it would've taken was a call to his company commander, who would then have passed it along to a platoon leader, who'd have selected someone suitable for the task. A major didn't call a sergeant directly, which set off even more alarms in Jerome's mind.

Not that he allowed his concern to show on his face. Whatever the man wanted, he was going to get it.

"Excellent," Bashir said, leaning back in his chair with a thin smile. "Your squad has three new people arriving today. One of them is of particular interest to me."

So that was what this was about. Jerome hadn't realized the new blood was due today. He already knew why Tolliver had attracted the man's interest since he'd been briefed about her. It also explained why Bashir had singled him out.

"Somewhat, sir," he said cautiously. There was no need to give the officer more ammunition. "I haven't reviewed their personnel jackets yet."

"Then allow me to pass them along so that we can discuss Private First Class Andrea Tolliver."

There was an inaudible ping in Jerome's implants as he received the files and brought them up. Experience and training allowed him to review their contents while still paying attention to what the major was saying, though the man wasn't speaking at the moment. It looked as if he was going to allow Jerome time to review the files.

Since his assigned task revolved around PFC Tolliver, he brought up her records first. The first thing he saw was the image attached to her file. Even though he knew what he'd see, her tattoos still sent a jolt of fury through him.

"It seems that our newest marine is a refugee from the Singularity," Bashir said. "She was supposedly vetted by Imperial Intelligence, but I wouldn't trust them to empty a field latrine."

"I've been instructed not to directly meddle, so I'm delegating that task to you. With your background, I expect you won't allow her any liberties. Keep an eye on her, and if there is any indication she's disloyal or has some hidden agenda, come directly to me with the information."

This was a nightmare.

Still, it made sense why the officer had selected him for this task. His older brother had died fighting the Singularity a decade ago. The loss still burned, and he felt nothing but contempt and rage when he thought about those bastards.

Even so, he had no business getting involved in trying to skirt Colonel Grimsby's orders to the major, even if he couldn't just tell the man no. He'd have to tread lightly if he intended to come out of this without having crap splattered all over him.

He couldn't allow his righteous anger to sway him into doing anything intemperate. All eyes would be on this girl, and he'd have to follow the book religiously, or someone would take their displeasure out of his hide.

Hell, they probably would anyway. He was screwed.

Jerome scanned Tolliver's records to see what else he could learn without directly answering what the major had said. A surprising amount of the data was classified and thus redacted. That made the already thin file downright skeletal.

Someone had wanted to make sure no one learned too much about her personal history before joining. Though, oddly, parts of her basic training record were also sealed. Very strange.

Her tattoos drew him back to her service image. While he had no personal experience with the Singularity, he'd heard stories. The only ones with tattoos were members of the warrior castes and the Singularity's leadership.

This girl hadn't been a peasant in her previous life, which meant that she had blood on her hands. The blood of people like his brother.

Jerome couldn't figure out why she'd chosen to keep the damned things. That seemed exceedingly arrogant to him. Which, on reflection, sounded just about right for someone from the Singularity.

After he'd seen what he could about Tolliver, he reviewed the other greenies.

Baker and Randall were much more pedestrian. That was good, since he didn't need more than one problem at a time.

As soon as he finished reviewing their files, he refocused his attention on the officer and nodded. "I can see why you'd want me to keep an eye on her, sir. I'll make it happen."

"I don't just want you to keep an eye on her, Walker," Bashir said, his tone more than a hint irritated as he leaned forward. "I want you to make damned sure she isn't a traitor. Is that clear?"

It was perfectly clear and probably the most dangerous set of orders Jerome had ever received that didn't involve directly coming under fire.

Still, he was the right man for the job. He couldn't bring his brother back to life, but he could make damned sure that one of those snakes wasn't worming their way into his beloved Corps.

"I'll make it happen, Major," he said grimly. "If there's anything questionable about her, I'll find out."

Bashir considered him for a few seconds and then nodded. "I'm going to want weekly reports about what she's doing. If she farts, I want to know how bad it smells."

"Yes, sir."

"And no word of this to anyone else. *No one.* Dismissed."

Jerome wheeled around and made his way out of the office and then to the field in front of battalion headquarters. Only once he was out of sight of the building itself did he allow himself to slow down and shake his head.

This was a crap job, and he knew it. Jerome wasn't a spy and had no experience determining someone's deep motivations. This task was almost guaranteed to be some form of goat rope. Bashir obviously wanted something concrete to hold over Tolliver, even though he'd never said those specific words.

Of course, he hadn't had to, had he?

Jerome wasn't quite sure if Bashir wanted him to manufacture evidence or just diligently look for it, but the officer had a particular outcome in mind. He could stick his nose into her business because she was in his squad, but if he got too aggressive about it, she'd have every right to go up the chain of command.

It wasn't his job to make her fail, he reminded himself. Just observe and report.

Still, part of him *wanted* to make her fail. She was literally the personification of the people who'd murdered his brother. No matter her story, it wouldn't be good enough to make up for that.

The thought made him smile coldly as he headed back to the barracks. By now, the new arrivals would already be in their fire team leader's hands. He had to let that play out first, and then he could find out why she was really infiltrating the Imperial Marines.

* * *

Diana let Andrea take the lead when Singh escorted them to the section of the barracks that would be their new home. Unlike basic training, it wasn't a full-scale bay but rather a large room capable of housing four people and their gear.

That gave them some privacy, and they even had a shared bathroom with a shower large enough for all of them at once. They would, of course, be responsible for keeping it in pristine condition.

A woman who was even shorter than Diana stood next to the only made bed when the four of them came into the room. She looked like she might have bitten into something sour for lunch, which likely didn't bode well for Diana and her friends.

"Corporal Simone Reed, these are the new people in Fire Team Two: Private First Class Andrea Tolliver, Private Diana Randall, and Private Claudio Baker," Singh said. "I understand it's going to be stressful to deal with their training simultaneously, but needs must when the devil drives."

Singh turned her attention to Diana and her friends. "Corporal Reed is very experienced, so I expect you to pay close attention to everything she tells you. She's undoubtedly displeased we've dumped you in her lap, but she'll be professional, and I expect you to act likewise. Give her one hundred and ten percent so that we can put this situation behind us as rapidly as possible. Understood?"

"Yes, Gunnery Sergeant," they all said simultaneously.

"Excellent. I'll leave the four of you to get acquainted."

And with that, Singh left the room and closed the door behind her.

Reed stared at the newcomers with more than a hint of displeasure. "Gunnery Sergeant Singh has understated the situation. Having my fire team taken away from me and distributed among the other fire teams pisses me off. I've spent years molding them to be my strong right arms. Now all I have is you greenies.

"I have no idea why someone decided it would be amusing to put you all in the same fire team, but all this will do is reinforce the weaknesses you already have and leave you with gaps in experience and knowledge.

"It falls to me to fill those gaps, and the process will be unpleasant for all of us. If I give you an order, I expect to be obeyed immediately. If you have a question, save it until we're done. There's only one of me and three of you."

With that, Reed gestured to the three unmade beds. "You can select any of those you like and get yourself set up. Once you've put your gear away, we'll go to supply and draw all of the other things you'll need.

"We are subject to inspection, so I expect you to keep everything neat and clean. It doesn't have to be laid out in any particular pattern, but don't lose your little minds with this newfound freedom."

Diana selected one of the beds and laid her duffel bag on it. She opened the locker and found folded sheets, a pillow, and a blanket. She pulled them out, set them at the head of the bed, and then loaded the wall locker with her gear.

When she was done, she made her bed quickly and neatly in the style that basic training had drilled into her. They might not want everything spit and polish here, but she could still make a mean bed.

Once she'd stowed the empty duffel in the drawer at the bottom of her locker, she turned and examined the corporal in more detail. The woman was eyeing Andrea with an expression that radiated displeasure.

Even though the lieutenant had said the company had been

briefed, Diana was surprised the woman hadn't directly questioned her friend about the tattoos that dominated her face. That seemed to be what everyone did when they first met her.

Though it was none of her business, Diana couldn't help thinking over the situation to figure out the odds of the various scenarios. With her father being a roving director for Imperial Intelligence, she'd had this type of problem solving drilled into her from a young age.

It annoyed her, but there wasn't anything she could do about it now. She was who she was.

The odds were high that her father had attached some kind of report to Andrea's orders to give her commanding officer a heads up. Since those orders would've arrived months ago, the officer had had an opportunity to get used to the idea and disseminate the critical details to those that needed to know them.

Of course, there were other possible scenarios, but she'd stick with her best guess until the evidence proved her wrong.

In the end, it didn't really matter. They were a thorn in the side of their new fire team leader, and she wouldn't be happy with anything they did.

That would undoubtedly grow worse before it got better. No matter how much effort the three of them put into learning what they didn't know, it wouldn't be fast enough.

Combat units were plum postings, and having someone assigned to one straight out of advanced training was unusual. To have three of them arrive and be stuck in the same fire team meant that they were woefully inexperienced and uneducated compared to everyone else.

Yep, the next few months were going to be fun.

Andrea was the next to finish getting her things squared away. The only thing left out was the box containing the really cool weapons the girl's guardians had given her.

Not that Diana didn't suspect her father had had a hand in it. No one got permits and permission to keep those kinds of weapons without serious pull, and that just reeked of her father's influence.

It would be interesting seeing how the corporal responded to something like this. Personally, Diana bet it would be with fireworks.

"Corporal, I need guidance on what to do with these," Andrea said diffidently.

"What are they?" Reed asked, taking a couple of steps over to look down at the box. Without asking, she opened it.

Her eyes narrowed as she looked back at Andrea. "Have you lost your mind?"

"I have permits and an Imperial exemption allowing me to possess and bear these weapons, even on this base, so it's not illegal," Andrea hurried to assure her. "This wasn't my doing, but I don't want to try to hide this from you."

"Let me see the permits and exemption."

The woman's eyes went unfocused for a few moments as she perused what Andrea must've sent her, and then they came back into focus, her frown deepening. "I don't know anything about Imperial exemptions or permits, but I do know someone that will."

Without asking permission, Reed closed the box and picked it up. "We're going to stop by the armory and discuss this with the armorer. I expect he's going to have a cow and impound these weapons. Then you'll have to argue with him, and it's your problem, not mine."

Diana almost smiled at her friend's scowl. It wasn't that Andrea necessarily *wanted* to keep the otherwise illegal stunner and flechette pistol on her person or in her wall locker, but her friend had a real problem with other people stepping on what she saw as her prerogatives.

Maybe that had something to do with how she'd been raised, but it would make for some excitement if the armorer put his foot down. Which he almost certainly would.

Well, she'd known the next few months would be fun, and it looked as if the party was about to get started.

3

ndrea had known the weapons were going to cause her grief, but she'd learned one lesson early in life. If you didn't want someone taking away everything you had, you had to stand up for the privileges you'd earned.

Besides, having weapons at hand when someone eventually tried to kill her wasn't a bad thing. And she was sure *someone* would try to kill her again at some point.

With her coming from the Singularity, making enemies was a trivial matter. Most potential foes would be satisfied with dark glares and slurs, but some would take their grievances further.

Considering that an Imperial noble had tried to have her killed during basic training, she'd be a fool to take anything for granted. Like Grace had always said, hope for the best and plan for the worst.

In this case, planning for the worst meant having access to weapons to defend herself with once the people that should have been her allies tried to kill her.

Those thoughts flowed through her mind as she followed Reed down the corridor and into the basement. That was where the armory was located because it was more secure underground.

Just like every other armory she'd seen to date, this one had a wide area where the marines could clean their weapons in front of what amounted to an armored cage where the armorer interfaced with them to collect weapons and perform other tasks.

The armorer's actual workspace was in the back, where they could work on the weapons without worrying about people looking over their shoulders. Or taking something. Inventory control was pretty critical when weapons like these were involved.

Reed walked up to the cage and banged her fist against the wire mesh. A few moments later, a man in dirty coveralls with sergeant's tabs stepped up to the counter. His blond hair was perhaps slightly longer than regulations allowed, but since the man worked out of sight, he could probably get away with it.

"Yeah?"

"Private First Class Tolliver has some personal weapons and seems to believe she has authorization to keep them in her quarters or on her person whenever she chooses, Sergeant Sherman," Reed said with a cheery smile. "I'd like your opinion on the matter."

With that, Reed set the box on the counter in front of the armorer, put her hands behind her back, and stepped to the side so she could watch the situation unfold.

Andrea found it difficult to read exactly what the woman was thinking. Either she had excellent control of her responses, or she just didn't care what the outcome was.

The latter was hard to imagine, but at this point, Andrea didn't know the other woman well enough to make a judgment call. She'd have to consult with Diana—her resident expert on reading people —later.

Sherman slid the wire barrier in front of the counter open, pulled her box inside, and opened it. As soon as he did, he sucked in a surprised breath and looked back at Reed.

"Do you know what you have here? These handcrafted weapons are undoubtedly worth more than both of us combined make in a year. I didn't think it was *possible* to make them this small either. These things are works of art and almost certainly illegal as hell."

He closed the barrier before going into his workshop for a scanner wand, which he proceeded to wave over the box.

"Definitely illegal. Neither one of these weapons shows up in the scan. If I didn't have them right in front of me, I'd never have known they were there. I can't begin to count how many regulations and Imperial laws the mere *existence* of these weapons violates.

"I also can't imagine any way these could be made legal or that anyone would be allowed to carry even the stunner on base. If you've got paperwork, PFC, I'd love to see it."

Andrea waited a beat to see if Reed would send the information to the armorer, but when nothing happened, she stepped up to the counter and forwarded the man the Imperial dispensation and permits.

She knew from having read them herself that they were brief and to the point. They acknowledged that the weapons were patently illegal in the Empire and yet gave her permission to both possess and bear them wherever she chose, other than in the presence of the emperor himself. That was the sole exclusion.

Sherman's eyes unfocused as he read everything, and then his eyebrows shot squarely up to his hairline. "Is this some kind of joke? There is no way the emperor or his sworn people would give *anyone* permission to carry this kind of weaponry wherever they chose. I think these are forgeries."

"There is information in the dispensation about how to contact the Imperial Representatives on any world and verify its authenticity," Andrea said. "You don't have to take my word for it, Sergeant."

"I also don't have to double-check on this nonsense either. I'm impounding both these weapons until an officer can make a determination. I'll issue you a receipt."

Her implants immediately pinged with an electronic receipt for the weapons and the storage box. Most people would've let the matter pass at that point, but Andrea wasn't most people.

"I'm afraid I'm going to have to insist, Sergeant. That's my personal property, and I have an *Imperial* dispensation allowing me to keep them. If you're going to dispute it, let's summon an officer and get this settled right now."

"If you've got a problem with me seizing these illegal weapons,

PFC, then you can trot your butt upstairs and talk to an officer yourself. This isn't my problem. It's yours."

And with that, the man picked up the box and walked back into the armory proper, slamming the reinforced door behind him.

"Well, that didn't work out quite the way you expected, did it?" Reed asked, seemingly amused. "As an interested observer, I have to say I'm invested in the outcome. Should we summon an officer and start your first day off with fireworks?"

That was the last thing Andrea wanted to do, but it looked like it would have to happen. Marching up to Van Buren's office was a little too dramatic for her taste, but she wasn't averse to sending him a summary of the situation and copies of the Imperial dispensation and permits.

She did so, not marking it as urgent. The man would get around to it when he had time.

"I've sent a message to Senior Lieutenant Van Buren," Andrea said. "He's going to make whatever decision he makes, and I'll live with the consequences."

Losing the weapons was a setback, but life didn't always go your way. This was one of those situations.

While her request worked its way through the chain of command, she still had gear to draw, and then she needed to meet the rest of her squad. A fire team was like a tight little family, but so was the squad as a whole.

There were going to be others besides Reed whose opinions mattered, and she needed to meet them and find out how they reacted to her.

Based on her experience, more than a few were going to be severely pissed off that she was there at all, and she wasn't going to rule out a fight. If that happened, well, it happened.

It was best to get any trouble out of the way as soon as possible anyway.

* * *

JEROME WAS surprised when he got a call from Eric Sherman, the Delta Company armorer, requesting that he come down and discuss something the man didn't want to talk about over the com.

It was unusual, but that didn't stop him from going down to find out what was going on. He had a little time to burn until Tolliver and the other greenies finished drawing their supplies and returned to their quarters.

When he walked into the armory, Eric was already waiting just inside the door leading deeper into the armory. With a gesture, his friend invited him in.

That was unusual too. Most armorers were extremely protective of their domains, Eric included. There were rules about who could be inside the armory and under what conditions.

"What's going on?" Jerome asked as soon as Eric closed the door behind them.

"First, I want you to take a look at these and tell me what you think," Eric said, leading him to a beat-up metal table with a wooden box on it. The lid was closed, but it looked like it held something valuable because the grain of the wood was luxurious and deeply polished.

At the man's urging, Jerome opened the box. Nestled into padded cutouts were a stunner, a flechette pistol, and three magazines/power packs for each.

He'd never seen examples of either weapon so customized. Each was significantly smaller than those used by the Imperial Marines or available on the civilian market in the case of the stunner. They were also much more finely crafted than anything he'd ever seen, almost qualifying as works of art.

"They belong to Tolliver," the armorer said.

Jerome grunted. He should've known.

"So, I can understand having a flechette pistol of her own is unusual, but what makes this something you'd want to talk to me about?" he asked. "Isn't this just a personal weapon being turned in to be held while she's on base?"

"Not even close," his friend said. "She sent me permits, and something she said was an Imperial dispensation that allowed her to carry either of these weapons—which are both highly illegal because they're not detectable by any scanner—wherever she wants, including here on base.

"I told her that was bull and confiscated them. Not a chance in hell I'm letting either of these things just float around unless someone orders me to."

Jerome blinked in surprise at his friend's outburst. "So she submitted a forged authorization to keep illegal weapons on the base? That has to be some kind of record, doesn't it? She only just got here."

"Some people think big, my man. She said she'd kick it up the chain of command, so she's not acting like they're forgeries. I shot a copy of everything to the lieutenant in charge of the armory too. I figure the brass will get it sorted out.

"I gotta say that I'm not sure what to think. First of all, why would she feel the need to carry a lethal weapon on base? Even a stunner seems paranoid. You'd think she was in danger of being attacked or something."

Maybe she was. Coming from the Singularity and flaunting those tattoos would earn her a lot of enemies. Most people would be satisfied with feeding her a knuckle sandwich, but it wouldn't surprise him if someone wanted to seek a more permanent solution to her presence.

None of this made any sense to him. Tolliver was drawing all the wrong kinds of attention to herself, and there was no way anyone was going to trust her with the kind of classified information that would make a difference to the Singularity.

As a spy—if that was what she was playing at—she was doing a terrible job.

The mystery of what the hell she was doing and why she was doing it was only getting deeper, and he was going to have to at least make some kind of initial assessment before he went crazy.

"I've already taken them apart," Eric continued. "Some real genius went into making these things out of materials that weren't going to trigger an alert. You can bet your ass I'm taking notes because a master weaponsmith designed and built these.

"They have to have come off the black market. There aren't any serial numbers or identifying information anywhere on them. They're beyond state of the art and completely untraceable."

Jerome nodded. "So, if they're not detectable, how did Reed get her hands on them?"

"Maybe she saw the box and asked questions," Eric said with a shrug. "Hell, as strange as the situation is, maybe Tolliver let her know they were there. The four of them would be living in one room, so there are only so many secrets they can keep from one another.

"If you want more details, you're going to have to ask Reed."

"That's not the kind of problem I wanted dumped in my lap, but I'll look into it," he said. "Let me know what the final decision is. If one of my people is carrying a weapon, I need to know about it."

"You got it."

Eric escorted him out of the armory, and Jerome found himself walking up the stairs already lost in thought. The girl had only been here a matter of hours. What the hell was she trying to accomplish?

He shook his head and cursed quietly. There was a lot going on under the surface here, and he needed to understand her at a deeper level. It was time to start doing some in-depth research on the Singularity.

A lot of the information would be classified, but maybe Bashir could shake some information loose that would put this in context. The officer would have to come through if he wanted Jerome to be able to do his job.

He quickly composed a note to the major, letting him know about the weapons and requesting as much information about the Singularity and the girl's tattoos as he could get.

That done, he headed for the mess hall. If he didn't get something to eat now, odds were the lack of calories would really screw him over before the day was done.

There would be time to confront his new problem child when he'd finished a quick meal. First, he needed to meet with his fire team leaders and get their thoughts on the situation and, if possible, get them on board with his secret mission without letting them know he had one.

4

It only took Diana about an hour to draw basic supplies and get back to their quarters. She kept expecting either the platoon leader or someone higher in the chain of command to call Andrea in to discuss those kickass weapons of hers, but nothing happened.

Based on the glances Claudio was shooting towards their friend, he was thinking the same thing. He eventually eased over to her while Andrea was talking with Reed.

"Do you think she's just trying to start trouble?" he asked in a quiet tone.

Keeping their voices down was smart, since their friend had a wicked sense of hearing.

"You mean with the weapons?" she murmured back. "Probably not. You've got to remember she comes from a very different society than ours. Even though she's been in the Empire for almost seven years, that kind of background is hard to overcome. You've never heard the full story of where she grew up, but it was a hellhole.

"I don't have time to tell you the entire story—and it's not my tale to tell—but I think you should ask her more about it. Now that you're not being such an ass, maybe she'll even tell you."

"I'm not an ass. I'm assertive."

She snorted. "The bottom line is that she had to put up with her crèche mates trying to kill her, as well as what amounted to psychological torture for the first twelve years of her life.

"Is it really paranoia when they're *actually* out to get you?"

Claudio compressed his lips and slowly nodded. "I suppose that's a valid point. It also probably explains some of her reactions to me and my sunny disposition. I have to admit that JR was right. She does kind of grow on people. Like a fungus."

Diana punched him in the arm and grinned. "She's working her magic on you. It sounds like someone doesn't have quite the same chip on his shoulder as when we first met."

He shrugged. "I may be slow, but even I can see there's more to her than meets the eye. I came into this with some preconceptions that turned out to be wrong. With more exposure, she's actually pretty cool.

"If we ever get into another fight, I know she'll be solid because she handled the thing on the training ship pretty well. I was wrong to think she didn't have what it took to be an Imperial Marine."

He grinned. "The jury is still out on you."

"Jackass," she said, giving him another punch. "You're turning into a big old softy. Besides, I know you like me better than you let on. Don't think I miss the way you stare in the shower. You think I'm hot, which is true."

That made the tall blond man blush, and he turned partly away from her. "We're not supposed to bring that kind of thing up. The marines are coed for a reason, and making a point of noticing I'm looking at you violates the spirit of that."

Diana laughed, not bothering to lower her tone now that they weren't talking about her friend. "And looking in the first place doesn't? Come on, I'll admit being naked in the shower with the boys was really uncomfortable in the beginning, but after a while, you just accept that you're going to see what you see.

"That doesn't mean you can't appreciate the view. It just means you have to keep the boners to a minimum."

He turned even redder, and then he laughed. "Now I know you're yanking my chain, but I'll admit you're not hard on the eyes. Don't think it means any more than that."

"You're not hard on the eyes either. Sand off a few more of those rough edges, and maybe we can talk about this again. What do you think about Andrea? Do you think she's pretty?"

"That's a dangerous subject to chat about with a woman you've just said you have some interest in, but I'm going to assume this isn't a trick. She's a little skinny for my taste, and it really takes a lot to look past those tattoos. I wouldn't go so far as to say that I'm attracted to her, but I can see that she *is* attractive.

"The fact that she can tie me into a pretzel is also a factor, though I'm not sure if it's a positive or negative one at this point. Once you get past her abrasive personality, I suppose she's okay."

That ridiculous statement made Diana laugh again, drawing attention from Andrea and Reed, though they didn't break off their conversation. She made sure to look as natural as possible as she turned her back towards the women.

"Since she doesn't have an abrasive personality, that's definitely trying to yank my chain, so I'll let the subject go. You know there are going to be confrontations as we integrate.

"There are three other fire teams in our squad, and someone will have a problem with her. Have you thought about how you're going to respond when they pick a fight?"

He grinned. "Hell, that's easy. I'll just stand back and let them get their asses handed to them. Say what you want about Tolliver, but she's more than capable of defending her honor all by herself.

"Not that I'm averse to little brawling if called upon, but I don't think she needs that kind of support. What she needs is us having her back. And speaking of backs, here she comes."

Diana turned and smiled at Andrea as her friend walked up to them. "Everything settled?"

"Hardly," her friend grumbled, "but that's out of my control. I'm a hell of a lot more concerned about a new problem. One that's so disgusting that I want to run into the bathroom and hurl."

That made Diana frown. What kind of problem could've become so serious in such a short time?

"Tell us about it, and we'll deal with it," Claudio said.

"Good. The two of you are the perfect ones to deal with it. You realize I can hear you flirting with each other, right?"

And with that statement, Andrea made a gesture like she was sticking her finger down her throat to force herself to throw up, making Diana laugh all over again.

"I wouldn't call it *flirting*, but I still think that falls under the category of none of your business. Unless, of course, you're interested in him as well, and then we should talk about it."

"No!" Andrea said as she raised her hands. "*Gods, no.* You two do whatever you're going to do and leave me out of it!"

"In any case, we're about to go meet the squad. Try to stop making lovey eyes at each other long enough for us to integrate, will you?"

And with that, her friend gave them an elaborate shudder and headed for the exit where Reed was already impatiently waiting.

Diana started for the door, glancing over at Claudio as she did so. "I'm not sure if we're actually flirting, but—her reaction aside—I don't think she's really that resistant to the idea. You have grown on her."

"I was just reacting to what you said, but I wouldn't object if we were to explore the idea a bit further, as long as it doesn't interfere with our jobs or our friendship. I'm finally settling into a good place with you two, and I'd rather not screw it up."

Diana nodded her agreement. She wasn't displeased with how the three of them had settled their differences and had no desire to screw that up either.

The future would bring what it did, but the most important thing was her friendship with Andrea. She'd have to talk to the other woman sooner or later about this and see what she really thought.

For now, they had enough problems on their plates. There would be conflict inside the squad as soon as they laid eyes on Andrea. How they settled it would set the stage for years to come, and she wanted to focus her full attention on that.

They couldn't afford for a single thing to go wrong in this meeting, which just about guaranteed there would be trouble.

* * *

As ANDREA WALKED AFTER REED, she thought about the bits and pieces of the conversation she'd overheard between her friends. Maybe what they'd been doing hadn't *quite* been flirting, but it was close. The relationship between the two of them had definitely changed over the months that they'd known one another.

Did the idea of that really bother her? She honestly wasn't sure.

Their potential love life wasn't any of her business, and she didn't want to interfere. Claudio had mellowed since they'd first met, and he had a *few* redeeming features. It turned out he was loyal to his friends, which she respected.

They *were* her friends, and she wasn't going to stick her oar in where it wasn't needed or wanted. If the two wanted a closer bond, more power to them.

At this point in her life, she wasn't the little girl that had been rescued from the Singularity anymore. She knew the differences between men and women now and even felt sexual desires, though she'd never had sex.

She even had to admit she'd snuck her own share of glances at both Claudio and Diana in the showers. She suspected all marines did something similar, no matter how used to coed showering they were. They were only human, after all.

Her guardians having a three-way relationship gave Andrea insight into the benefits of such an arrangement and the complications that could result from it. Just like any bonding, everyone had to respect everyone else and defer to what they needed to some extent.

In the case of Grace, Fei, and Kayden, it worked. Their personalities meshed on a level that had always impressed her.

Of course, there were problems, but the three worked them out like adults. Nothing was allowed to fester in the dark. If someone had a problem, they found a way to bring it up without being confrontational and worked it out.

If her friends decided they were going to take their relationship to a new level, she vowed she'd bring that same type of perspective to the situation. She wouldn't intrude, but if she had a problem, she'd let them know about it.

Thinking about that distracted her enough that she only belatedly realized they'd arrived at their destination. Reed took them through a double door and into a decent-sized gymnasium. It was filled with weight equipment and other gear to help keep marines in shape.

It also held the three other fire teams in the squad, who were busy working out.

Just like her group, they were obvious sets of four. There'd be a corporal or lance corporal in charge and three privates under their command.

She could isolate the separate groups at a glance because they were each working out together. One set was working on free weights, another worked on leg machines, and the final group used thick ropes to work their arms.

The twelve marines in the room were just as diverse as her fire team too. Male and female, tall and short, willowy and stout, dark-skinned and light. Just like the Corps itself, they were as diverse a group as could be imagined.

Everyone stopped what they were doing to stare at the newcomers. That wasn't the least bit intimidating.

"Listen up," Reed called out in a voice that carried throughout the large room. "This is my new fire team: Private First Class Andrea Tolliver with the tattoos, Private Diana Randall, and Private Claudio Baker. We'll be working together as a squad, so I want you to get to know them without breaking anything. Or anybody.

"Fire team leaders, Sergeant Walker has called for a meeting, so we'll leave our people to get acquainted on their own. Let's go."

Reed turned to face Andrea and her friends. "Remember, these people are going to be fighting beside you for the next five to ten years. This is your chance to introduce yourselves and find a place in the pecking order. Don't screw it up."

And with that intimidating advice, Reed and the other three fire team leaders left the gym.

The remaining marines surrounded Andrea and her friends. They didn't look very friendly, and she already had a bad feeling about how this would work out.

Nothing in life was ever easy, was it?

"Hi, I'm Andrea," she said with a nervous smile. "Please don't judge me by these tattoos."

It felt like groveling to have to say that, but otherwise, they wouldn't know how she felt.

It had to be said. Andrea wasn't defined by her tattoos, but everyone seemed to assume she was. In fact, they almost seemed to view their presence as her shoving her heritage in their faces.

That wasn't the case at all.

They said that people could never escape their pasts, but it was literally true in her case. The Singularity would always have its mark on her no matter what she did.

Almost in unison, the other marines looked to the largest man in the room as if seeking his guidance. That focused Andrea's attention on him, and she realized her initial assessment of him had fallen short of reality.

She'd seen the squat young man but hadn't quite realized the proportions of his body were even more extreme than she'd realized. He looked about a hundred and sixty centimeters tall and seemed almost as wide.

That wasn't really the case, but he was far broader and bulkier than Claudio, who wasn't a lightweight. The man's muscles had muscles. She'd never seen anyone so built in her life.

He was dressed in workout shorts and a torn-up shirt with the Imperial Marines logo that also said, "Marines do it in space."

Guy humor.

His dark curly hair was plastered to his skull from what must've been an intense workout. A glance over at the free weights showed an absolutely *ridiculous* amount on the bar. She was pretty sure she'd have had difficulty getting it off the stand, and she had musculature that was almost fifty percent more efficient than a normal human's.

Of course, she wasn't built like a stone monument either. As Fei had occasionally reminded her, quantity had a quality all its own.

"You don't like being judged by those tattoos?" the man asked in a voice so profoundly deep that she'd never heard anything like it. "Then why keep them?"

"They're built into the DNA of my skin. The only way I could get rid of them is by letting someone remove my face, and I'm pretty attached to it."

He looked at her with an unreadable expression. With a sigh, she prepared to fight.

"It turns out that I know something about being different too," he offered in a neutral tone. "I come from a world with almost twice the standard gravity most people have to deal with. People judge me by the way I look all the time, so I'm not going to hold your tattoos against you.

"I know where you come from, and our fire team leaders told us a little bit about your history. You'll get a fair shake here. If you carry your share of the load, you're going to find us willing to accept you."

Andrea felt her jaw drop slightly at the unexpected break. That had *not* been what she'd expected to hear.

She only just barely stopped herself from asking if he was sure. As Kayden had said, never look a gift horse in the mouth.

Andrea wasn't sure why looking at a horse's mouth was a bad idea, but the thrust of the saying was not to question good fortune that came your way. Something that happened far less frequently in Andrea's life than she'd have liked.

She stuck out her hand. "Deal."

He took her hand into his almost gently. "I'm Jeff Campbell. Welcome to the best damn squad in Delta Company."

5

Jerome watched his fire team leaders closely as they walked into his cramped office. He could tell at a glance that Reed wasn't pleased, and he couldn't blame her. After all, she'd just had three greenies dumped in her lap.

That didn't even include the waves caused by Tolliver's background. That had to be causing her some gas too. Gods knew it was causing him problems.

The rest didn't show much as they took their seats. He was sure they had their opinions because he'd led them for several years now and knew them well.

The best way to let this thing sort itself out was to lay everything on the table and see what they had to say. Once everyone was seated, he took the last remaining chair that wasn't behind his desk.

He hated that desk. It was something that came between him and his people, and he'd much rather be out doing things rather than paperwork.

Yet, one didn't stay in the military without getting promoted, and reports were part of that. One more thing to hate about not being a regular marine anymore.

"So, each of you has had a chance to see the new people—even if only briefly—and I'd like to know what you think," he said quietly. "Reed, let's start with you."

"This is utter bullshit," she said bluntly. "Whose bright idea was it to dump three inexperienced marines into the same fire team and expect them to perform up to spec? That's a recipe for disaster."

Straight and to the point, though it didn't actually touch the angle he'd expected to piss her off the most: Tolliver's heritage.

He kept his face neutral and nodded. "It's an unusual setup, but it wasn't my call. If it had been, I'd have split them up.

"As it is, we're all going to have to work hard to train them. It takes a village, as they say. Do you have any other thoughts about them?"

Reed smiled grimly. "You mean other than the fact that one of them has some highly illegal weapons that she'd prefer to keep in our quarters? Not really."

That caused everyone else to chuckle. Obviously, word of what had taken place at the armory had gotten out.

Still no comment on the fact Tolliver came from the Singularity. Interesting.

"I have to admit that surprised me too. I doubt anyone will consider letting her keep them, no matter what her dispensation says."

"Who even *gets* an Imperial dispensation?" Reed demanded. "This doesn't make any sense."

"Maybe it's because they expected someone to try to kill her," Corporal Dan Buckman said. "Those tattoos make her a target. It seems more likely for someone to punch her lights out, but under the right circumstances, I can see someone trying to kill her."

Corporal Elena Baranova, the leader of Fire Team Three, shook her head. "I'm still not sure whether that would excuse keeping a lethal weapon out where anyone could access it. The girl probably isn't even properly trained with something like that.

"That would make her a danger to everyone. I don't care what the officers end up deciding. I don't want her posing a threat to my people."

"Do you think she's a threat because of inexperience or heritage?" Lance Corporal Andy Dill asked quietly. "Being born in the

Singularity and having those things on her face is really going to cause her a lot of problems, especially in the Corps."

Finally, someone had mentioned the elephant in the room.

"The Empire is basically at war with the Singularity, even though it's not a hot one at the moment," Jerome said with a nod. "Hell, it's been going on as long as the Empire has existed. One of these days, that war is going to turn hot again. Can we trust her?"

"Someone certainly thinks so," Buckman said. "She wouldn't have been allowed into the marines if they hadn't thoroughly vetted her. She'd never have graduated basic training if they thought she posed any kind of risk. Are we supposed to second-guess the powers that be?"

"I think worrying about that would be a waste of time," Reed agreed with a dismissive wave of her hand. "Let's focus on the things we can control, like her training and getting to know who she is. Let's not assume she's an enemy simply because she's got those tattoos."

"Completely wicked tattoos, I might add," Buckman volunteered. "Does anybody know what they mean?"

Jerome shook his head. "Other than the fact that she has to be from one of the senior genetic lines inside the Singularity, I have no idea. I tried looking them up, but the information is classified. I'll have to meet with her at some point, and I'll ask point blank.

"No matter what you think, we need to do our own vetting. Whatever her history, we need to make sure she doesn't have a change of heart. Or that her heart was never in this to begin with."

No one responded to his words, so he pressed on. "I understand you might not agree with that sentiment, yet I want each of you to keep your eyes on her, and if she does anything out of line, I want you to report it to me at once. Is that clear?"

None of them were pleased with his directive, but nobody argued. Good. With more than one set of eyes on the girl, he'd find out that much faster if there was any strange behavior.

It was hard to keep the loathing he felt for the Singularity out of his voice anytime he spoke about the girl, but he had to at least maintain the illusion that he was being impartial.

Honestly, he didn't hate her personally. He just detested everything she represented. Her people had killed his brother, and he definitely wanted to make them pay, but he had to be very careful not to misjudge her because of how he felt.

Major Bashir had given him the job of making sure she wasn't a traitor, but even he hadn't said that he really believed she was one. At least not out loud.

Jerome actually pitied the girl. She was going to face suspicion for the rest of her life and never be fully trusted by the people around her. It was sad.

Well, that wasn't his problem. He had a squad to run, which meant that the new people had to be trained. It was their company's turn on standby for deployment, so if any issues popped up that required Imperial Marines in this sector, it was all too likely they'd be shipped out whether the new people were ready or not.

"Okay," he said, leaning forward. "We need to get the new people up to speed as quickly as possible, but it's not going to be quick enough, I'm sure. Let's start going over the critical areas first so that if we do get deployed, they don't drag us down."

And with that, he and his fire team leaders began constructing a training plan for the greenies. They wouldn't like it one bit, but that was tough. If they'd wanted an easy life, they never should've joined the Imperial Marines.

* * *

AFTER THE LARGE man had accepted Andrea as part of the platoon, the rest of the marines came in to shake hands and introduce themselves. Diana wouldn't go so far as to say they were friendly, but they seemed welcoming enough.

For her, it was relatively easy to make friends. She was outgoing and more than a little bubbly. Some people didn't like that, but they were few and far between.

To her amusement, Claudio seemed to be accepted almost instantly. The tall blond-haired boy just somehow seemed to fit right in. She had no doubt that the two of them would quickly make friends and become part of the group.

For Andrea, that would be more difficult. Her tattoos were often a barrier. No matter how close she stood to someone, they were always between them. They had to get to know her as a person rather than a symbol.

And, honestly, that was what Andrea was to most people: a symbol representing the Singularity. Or a symbol representing genetically modified humans. Or even a symbol representing genetically created human simulacra if the analogy were taken far enough.

Diana didn't think of Andrea as a fake human, but her genetics *had* been created from the ground up, only using human DNA as the base. Her roots were human, but it might be successfully argued that she wasn't. That was why the emperor had legally recognized her as such.

What she was shouldn't make one bit of difference, yet it did.

"Tell me about her," a deep, instantly recognizable voice said, making her jump slightly.

She turned and found Jeff Campbell beside her. It was kind of unsettling, like a hill had somehow walked up when she wasn't looking.

Diana stopped that thought instantly. She was looking at him just like people looked at Andrea. Like something other than human, and that needed to stop right this very second.

She smiled at the young man. "She's… complex. I'm not going to tell any of her secrets, but I get the impression the two of you might be a little more alike than the rest of us."

His smile widened slightly. "You mean because people don't quite see me as human? Yeah, that's something my people have faced for a long time. Still, we come from inside the Empire, so it's not quite the same."

"She was rescued from the Singularity during a raid when she was twelve," Diana stressed. "They indoctrinated her pretty heavily, but she was raised by retired marines and someone from the Singularity from what they called the lower orders. Basically, their regular people.

"They've fixed her view of the universe, though there is still the occasional landmine that pops up. She's a good person, and she cares about the people around her. Those tattoos make her seem aloof and distant, but that's not her. You've got to look past them to find the real Andrea."

"It's true," Claudio said, having snuck up behind her.

Diana jumped a little bit and then smacked him on the arm. "Don't sneak up on me like that!"

Claudio just grinned at her. "I have to admit Andrea and I didn't get along in basic. In fact, I was her enemy."

The squat young man crossed his arms over his broad chest and considered Claudio. "What changed?"

"I got past her tattoos, just like Diana said. She put her life on the line to save our training platoon."

That made Campbell's eyes widen slightly. "That's a pretty bold statement. Care to explain it in a bit more detail?"

"Somebody wanted to make sure she didn't graduate because that set an Imperial precedent. The emperor made a deal that she'd be legally recognized as a human being inside the Empire if she graduated from basic training.

"They tried to take her out and ended up killing a couple of people in the process. She led the way stopping the attack and got us out of the kill box. That's why she made it here."

"No," Diana said firmly. "She made it here because she's damned good. She was born to be an Imperial Marine."

Claudio shot her a look and shook his head. "Sorry, but she was born to rule the Singularity. Those tattoos mean she was designed to be one of the twelve ruling genetic lines there. Basically, high nobility, if one were to look at it the same as the Empire.

"That's a lot of baggage, but she's managed to carry it for the most part. All she wants to do is be seen as one of us. A lot of marines died on the mission that saved her, and she knows what they did to protect her. She wants to pay it forward, and I think that's remarkable.

"I should also mention that the platoon that went on the raid is the very same one we're part of now. All of us are stepping into the shoes of those that gave their lives to hurt the Singularity and save a little girl. For us, more than anyone else, that has to mean something."

Diana had to admit she was more than a little surprised at

Claudio's vigorous defense of Andrea. To say their relationship early on had been rocky was something of an understatement.

"I think that's a worthy aspiration," Campbell agreed levelly. "And we're going to give her a fair chance. If that's who she is, then she's going to be welcome here."

He smiled a bit grimly. "I won't say it's going to be easy because that would be a lie, but nothing rewarding comes without effort. All three of you will have to put in a lot of time and effort to carry your share of the load around here. She's going to have to put in extra, even though that's not fair.

"What she's *not* going to have to do is face outright discrimination because of her genetic heritage. This is one time when someone else has cleared the way for her. Anyone that might want to talk bad about tinkered genes has already had that discussion with me."

Diana smiled a little. She imagined those discussions hadn't gone well for anyone with a problem with the heavy-worlder.

"I don't think I've ever met anyone from a heavy-gravity world before," she said. "Why is that? Is the discrimination so bad that you just don't want to mix with the general populace?"

"Oh, it's not that bad," Campbell said with a shrug. "The problem is that when we leave home, it doesn't take us long to get out of shape. No matter how much effort we put into maintaining muscle tone and bulk, it falls off pretty quickly.

"I mean, take a look at me. I've been off my homeworld for six years now, and I'm nothing but skin and bones."

He followed that ludicrous statement up by flexing his arms and showing off an awe-inspiring amount of muscle. She had to admit that the view made her melt a little on the inside.

"Uh-huh," Claudio said with mock sympathy. "I can see how skinny you are. You should probably make another couple of passes in the mess hall to add some calories before you come in to work out."

The big man grinned. "Okay, so it's not quite that bad, but believe it or not, I'm out of shape compared to someone that lives on a heavy-gravity world full time. If I were to go home right now, it would take me six months to feel normal again.

"I honestly have lost some muscle, but you can keep your pity to yourself. I'll manage. Somehow."

He looked over at Andrea, who was talking quietly with some of the other marines, and grinned evilly. "And I think I know exactly how to welcome Tolliver into the squad with style and panache."

"Panache?" Claudio asked, frowning slightly. "What's that?"

"Watch and see."

"It's style and flair," Diana said, poking her friend in the ribs. "Something you wouldn't know anything about."

They watched as Campbell headed over to Andrea and interrupted her conversation by saying something and gesturing toward the mats set out on the floor.

Things were about to get interesting.

6

Andrea's breath flew out of her as she slammed into the sparring mat with bone-jarring force. She'd come at Campbell with everything she'd had, and he'd basically snatched her out of the air and smashed her down.

Hard.

She slapped weakly at the mat, signifying that she was out of it. As if that wasn't obvious.

The big man stepped back and watched her with a slight smile on his face. "You're a lot faster than other people. Stronger too. I'll bet that makes you a really tough opponent for just about anybody else."

"I swear I hit you as hard as I could, and you didn't even feel it," Andrea groaned. "It was like hitting a rock."

"Oh, I felt it, but they build us tough on Goliath. When the gravity is always trying to kill you, you have to be strong."

She sat up slowly and glared at him. "Just how high is the gravity there, and how do you take it?"

"1.69 Gs. It's not easy or forgiving, so people from other planets don't visit very often without some type of exoskeletal support. Those that do drop in don't stay long.

"You could make it, though. You're strong enough. Barely. You'd have to toughen up a bit, and it would be rough, but I think you could hack it."

She shuddered at the idea.

"In case you're wondering, my ancestors had some genetic tinkering too," he added in a cheery tone. "This was before the Empire existed, and it was only a modification rather than being created out of whole cloth like your genome was. Still, we face discrimination too.

"You can thank me for making sure nobody in this squad—or even at the company level—will make an issue about genetic modification, by the way. I'll have to have a few more words with them if they do. You're welcome."

"I'm not ready to thank you for anything just yet," she said as she levered herself off the mat. "I'm not the kind of girl that assumes a mountain is unclimbable just because she falls off once."

"That's the spirit! I'm not sure whether to be amused that you feel like you've fallen off a mountain or that you think you can climb me," he said with a chuckle. "Though I suppose it is flattering."

"I'd save the feel-good moment for now. There's still some ass whipping to be had."

He grinned and gestured for her to come at him as he dropped into a combat-ready crouch. "Big words for such a little girl. Why don't you make me?"

He was definitely the most challenging opponent she'd ever faced, but she doubted he was invulnerable. He might be bigger and stronger than her, but that didn't mean she couldn't use what he thought of as his advantages against him.

She hadn't just been trained in the combat style favored by the Imperial Marines. She'd learned half a dozen other styles, at least some of which favored those smaller than their opponents.

The key was going to be taking him down before he squashed her like a bug.

Fei's lessons about taking on talented opponents revolved around luring them into a sense of overconfidence. If they felt they had an edge, they weren't as likely to protect themselves properly against surprise attacks.

With his greater strength and size, Campbell had to be feeling pretty confident right about now. While Andrea had some edge against a normal human, the perks of coming from a heavy gravity world seemed to cancel them out.

It was time to play the wounded bird.

Andrea began circling her opponent, not coming into range to strike but being obviously wary about him attacking her. In addition, she added an almost imperceptible limp to her gait, as if she were favoring her left leg just the slightest bit.

She saw as he took her act in and watched his eyes narrow just the tiniest bit. Was that because he suspected what she was up to, or was he calculating some attack to take advantage of her perceived weakness? There was no way of telling until he acted.

Her plan was crazy when she really thought about it. It wasn't something that would work more than once with a competent opponent, but she was making a point here.

She wasn't to be taken lightly.

Andrea feinted at him to make him think she was testing his reactions and got a lot more than she'd expected when he exploded out of his crouch and charged her, his right fist swinging.

Here was where the benefits of her enhanced genetics came into play. He was big and strong, but he wasn't nearly as fast as she was when she dropped any pretense of holding back.

Andrea sprang to the side, nimbly avoiding his fist as it flew past her. Then she leaped at him, ready for the counterstrike with his elbow that she knew was coming, deftly interposing her leg as she climbed him like a squirrel did a tree.

The blow still hurt, but it didn't stop her.

She had no idea how squirrels had made it to DeSantis, but they'd somehow worked their way into the ecosystem, and she'd been delighted to watch them for hours when she'd been growing up.

There had been no living creatures in the crèche other than her line sibs and Keeper. The concept of an animal was exotic and mesmerizing. She'd wanted a squirrel as a pet, and only determined resistance from her guardians had stopped her.

She might not have gotten her way, but she'd learned a few lessons from the agile creatures anyway. Even as Campbell swung back around to grab at her, she scrambled behind him and clamped her arm around his neck in a chokehold.

She didn't hold back. This was one time she needed every bit of her strength and more. She put everything she had into choking him while hanging on for dear life.

For just a couple of seconds, the man seemed flummoxed by her attack and unsure of what to do when he couldn't pry her arm from around his neck, but then the trained reflexes of a combat marine took over, and he fell back, slamming her into the mat with his weight fully on top of her.

That landing was even more traumatic than being slammed to the mat the first time. Andrea really couldn't breathe now. She held on for all she was worth even as her sight began to dim from lack of oxygen.

Campbell struggled for another couple of seconds before tapping out. Andrea instantly released him, and he rolled off of her. She didn't bother trying to get up.

"I can't move," she croaked. "You've killed me."

He laughed even as he rubbed his throat and reached down with his other hand. "Whatever. That was great. Nobody else here is fast enough to pull that kind of crap on me. Now I'm going to have to worry about you figuring out some way to climb on top of my head while we're fighting.

"Sergeant Walker is usually the only guy that can take me, but he's been through the advanced course and knows all the dirty tricks. That isn't to say there aren't some people out there that can take him, though they're few and far between."

Andrea stood with his help, put her hands on her knees, and tried to catch her breath. She stretched a bit to make sure she hadn't actually screwed anything up. The marine nanites would do a good job fixing minor issues, but she didn't want to miss an actual injury.

"If he's been through the advanced course, how is it that anybody else can take him out?" she asked, playing for time.

Campbell leaned forward and lowered his voice. "A couple of years back, we went on a mission escorting a team of Marine Raiders. I know they're jacked out to the max with artificial enhancements, but they can turn those off and fight like regular folk.

"I saw one of them use a style I've never seen before. He wiped the mat with Walker. When he offered to do the same to me, you bet your ass that I said yes."

He grinned. "That man completely and utterly cleaned my clock. He was the most amazing hand-to-hand combat specialist I've ever seen. Honestly, it was as if my size and strength were a *disadvantage* fighting him.

"If you ever run into someone like Lieutenant Ned Quincy and they offer to fight you, do it. If you could pick up just a couple of their tricks, you could whip some serious ass."

Andrea had heard a bit about Marine Raiders. They were spoken of with such reverence that they were almost mythic. They were the ghosts that moved through the Empire, doing the emperor's bidding.

They had artificially enhanced musculature and graphene-coated bones, to start. That didn't count any of the supersecret stuff they supposedly had stashed away in their bodies. Or in their implants.

A fire team of Marine Raiders was probably more than equal to an entire platoon of marines. Maybe even a company. Who knew?

They were drawn from the ranks of the Imperial Marines, but there were so few of them that the chances of ever meeting one were slim indeed, so she wasn't going to count on that kind of blessing.

If she'd thought she had even a chance of being considered for their ranks, she'd have set that as a new life goal, but there was no way in hell anyone in the Empire would enhance someone like her to that level.

Pity.

"Well, what about a third fall to break the tie?" Campbell asked with a toothy grin. "You ready to rumble?"

Andrea put her hand against her forehead dramatically and fell back onto the mat, twitching and convulsing before letting her breath out in a death rattle.

That made Campbell and the rest laugh, and she felt like she'd finally come home.

* * *

Jerome had just created a rough draft of a remedial training program for the greenies when his implants pinged with an incoming call. It was from his platoon leader, Lieutenant Kenny Wong.

"Heads up, Walker, we've been called up. Looks like there's a labor dispute on one of the corporate worlds. The powers that be have decided it would be best to plant a company of Imperial Marines there for the next few months to make sure nobody does anything they're going to regret later."

The officer's words almost made Jerome snarl. He'd *literally* only had the greenies in his squad for a few hours, and they were already being deployed? Not good.

"What am I supposed to do with Fire Team Two, sir? I've got nothing but greenies there."

"We're not deploying into a combat zone, so you'll just have to make do. We'll set up a secure area once we get there and send folks out on patrol to wave the flag in everybody's faces. We'll just have to pick a safe location for Fire Team Two to be deployed into. We can work with this."

Jerome was far from certain about that, but it wasn't as if he had a choice in the matter. "Yes, sir. I'll get everybody ready to deploy. I'm going to have to run the new folks back through supply and pick up everything they'll need for a combat deployment."

"Copy that. Also, take Tolliver down to the armory to draw her personal sidearms. The colonel has decided that we have to bow to the Imperial dispensation.

"If we were staying here at the base, he might *ask* if she'd keep the flechette pistol in lockup, but when the emperor says something is allowed, well, we allow it. In any case, she's going to be armed while on deployment, so adding another couple of weapons to the mix isn't going to change the equation much."

The news didn't make Jerome feel any better, but once again, it wasn't as if he had a choice in the matter. "Yes, sir. I'll make it happen."

"Good man. I'm sure this will work out, even though we both have our doubts. Somebody trusted her enough to issue an Imperial dispensation, so we've got to run with that.

"I've got to call the other squads and get them in motion, so get ready to ship out in four hours. The troop transport in orbit is ready to receive us, but we're the last platoon heading up. Use that extra time well."

Once the call ended, Jerome headed for the gym. That was where his implants said almost everyone in the squad was, including Tolliver.

He walked through the door, ready to yell for everyone's attention, but found himself rooted to the spot as he watched Tolliver and Campbell circling one another on the mat. No matter how much of a hurry he was in, he wanted to see how this turned out.

Campbell was big and hellishly strong, but Tolliver was fast. Maybe the fastest he'd ever seen. Her reactions on the mat were like magic. She danced out of the way of Campbell's charges and seemed to just float away from his attacks.

That wasn't going to win the fight, but Jerome had never seen anyone resist the big man like that before.

To his surprise, a fair number of people were cheering her on. Campbell was well liked, so it wasn't that they were rooting against their friend, but it seemed Tolliver had gained a following.

The tattoos on her face were really striking. They made her seem severe and threatening, even though her actual expression was radically different. The girl was grinning as if she were having the time of her life.

Was that normal in the Singularity? Understanding women was difficult at the best of times, but trying to figure out someone from a completely different culture would probably make him crazy.

He wasn't sure how long this kind of fight could last, but he was sure how it was going to end. As soon as Campbell got his hands on the girl, she was going down. No one—no matter how they were modified—could stand up to strength like his.

And then, just like that, Tolliver did something completely unexpected.

In the midst of weaving all around Campbell, she dove underneath one of his swings and scrambled between the man's legs, wheeling around and planting her feet against the back of his legs even as he was grabbing for her. Since he had his hands right there, she grabbed his wrists and flipped the heavy-worlder end over end backward.

It was the most amazing thing he'd ever seen.

Campbell flailed wildly as he spun through the air before slamming face down on the mat. In an instant, Tolliver was on his back, yanking one of his wrists as far up the center of his spine as she could get it.

Admittedly, she didn't get it very far with all those muscles to work against. After all, Campbell wasn't the kind of man that could easily scratch his own back.

Yet it was enough. Campbell couldn't get the leverage to shake her off or even flip himself over without the potential of tearing muscles in his arm or shoulder. She had him pinned.

Jerome still expected Campbell to fight, but the man tapped out. That sent up a roar of approval from the crowd as Tolliver released him and stepped away, extending a hand down to help him up.

"I know you could've shaken me off, so I appreciate the gesture, but you're a better fighter than I am," Tolliver said loudly enough to be heard. "Thanks for an educational fight."

"Don't count yourself out, greenie. If this had been a real fight, I'd have shaken you off, but it wasn't. For sparring, this was a win."

Shocked to his core, Jerome still managed to step forward and clap his hands. "Eyes on me, everyone. Delta Company has been called up. I want all fire teams ready to deploy to orbit in three hours. Get your gear, and let's go serve the Empire. Tolliver, you're with me."

He gritted his teeth when the girl trotted up but extended his hand. "I'm Jerome Walker, your squad leader. I'd leave you with your team, but regiment has made a decision about your weapons, and we're going down to the armory so you can draw them."

"Thank you, Sergeant."

Without waiting for anything further from her, he left the gymnasium and headed for the armory. "I'd intended to have a conversation with you later today, but I'm out of time. I need to know more about your background, and I have to tell you straight up that the fact you come from the Singularity pisses me off."

"I appreciate your candor, Sergeant," she said as if his words weren't tinged with negative emotion. "I was twelve when the marines rescued me. I don't expect everyone to like me, but I want to have a chance to prove myself."

He smiled grimly. "Oh, you're going to have your chance at that. Even though we're going on a deployment, don't think I won't have my eyes on you. If I see anything out of line, you can bet your ass that I'll yank you up short. Do you understand me?"

"I do, Sergeant."

Well, this was turning into a singularly unrewarding conversation. He wanted to fight, he realized. That wasn't helpful, so he forced himself to shut up.

It was best if he got the weapons back into her possession and turned her over to Reed as soon as possible. According to the deployment orders the LT had sent him, they'd have almost a month of travel time for him to get into a better frame of mind.

If they were lucky, there wouldn't be any fighting on the other end, and they'd get this all sorted out. If he was unlucky, there'd be shots fired, and he'd have to trust a potential armed enemy of the Empire at his back.

Not the most pleasant of thoughts.

They reached the stairwell and headed down to the armory. Sherman was inside the cage, getting the weapons prepared for transport, when Jerome slapped his hand on the counter.

"Private First Class Tolliver is going to be drawing her private weapons," he said flatly. "Orders from regiment. Make the magic happen."

His friend looked less than pleased, but he brought the weapons and a sign-out form for them. She took the box and looked at Jerome expectantly.

"You're dismissed, PFC," he grumbled. "Go find Corporal Reed and draw the rest of the equipment you're going to need. Don't make us miss our ride."

Once she was gone, Jerome rubbed his face. Even with marine nanites, he'd discovered he could still get headaches, and this deployment was going to give him a migraine.

7

D iana hurried through the process of drawing her combat equipment and supplies. She needed to make sure everything was present and functional before being packed and shipped to the transport.

That meant going over everything she'd signed for under Reed's supervision and then packing it all back up again before moving on to the next item.

Somewhere during the process, Andrea came into the room, almost staggering under the weight of her own gear, and set it on her bunk before beginning the same task. She really should've made more than one trip, even with her strength.

Since her friend had been trained by former marines while growing up, she seemed to have a much better grasp of the process. That pleased Reed because she could focus her attention on Diana and Claudio.

Even so, it still took almost two hours to get everything set up the way the corporal wanted. They then carried it to the assembly area, where everyone else had already placed their gear for transport.

At that point, the fire team leaders vanished to get a briefing from Sergeant Walker. That left the squad with some free time, though they weren't allowed to go anywhere. They had to stay with their gear and prepare to load it when the pinnace arrived for them. Then they'd fly up to the transport with it.

"Any idea where we're going or what the situation is?" Andrea asked Campbell.

"A planet called Diorama," the big man said. "Some kind of corporate setup. They do rare mineral extraction and grow specialty medicinal crops for export. Apparently, the planetary government is controlled by the suits, and they've been making life a little tough on the citizens—or so they think—who also happen to mostly be their employees.

"So far, that's caused stuff like work slowdowns and sabotage, and the grand duke in charge of the sector decided to call in the marines."

"Why are we acting as the boot for the corporations?" Diana asked before her friend could respond. "If they're mistreating the people that live there, aren't we supposed to be helping them?"

Campbell shrugged. "I don't know enough to have an opinion yet. The Empire has pretty strict rules about the treatment of employees, dependents, and Imperial citizens in general. This isn't going to be some corporate hellhole, so there has to be more to the story.

"If the corporations are breaking the law, Lieutenant Van Buren is going to pick up on that, and he's going to take steps, I'm sure. We're not going to be the thugs enforcing the will of greedy corporations against the people they're abusing."

Andrea crossed her arms and nodded. "It's not like we're in a position to make any decisions. We'll get our orders when we get there, and we'll just have to trust our officers to do the right thing.

"I wish I knew more about the corporations running the planet and what they're doing. We might not have any control over the matter, but information is gold."

Diana was about to respond when her implants pinged for her attention. She turned her mental attention to them, expecting an incoming call or order, and found a notification instead.

You seem to be attempting to gather intelligence on a subject in one of your inactive databases. Would you like to activate the databases and query them for the information requested?

Diana frowned. Inactive databases? What the hell were those?

She tentatively sent an affirmative command to her implants. Maybe this was something that the marines had buried in there that she just wasn't aware of.

As soon as she agreed to activate the databases, she received a pop-up. Almost unsurprisingly, it was a note from her father.

*D*IANA,

I REALIZE *this will likely make you very angry, but I've taken steps to ensure you're as well equipped for your new life as I can. I've taken the liberty—and yes, I do realize it's quite the liberty and that you're undoubtedly displeased I've done so—to upload a selection of Imperial Intelligence files on a wide variety of subjects for your future use.*

This information is mostly classified, and I've broken a truly epic number of laws doing this, so unless you really hate me that much, please don't tell anyone you have access to them.

Basically, you have the data I typically carry around with me at all times, with select additions that I thought might prove helpful. A lot of it is general information about a vast number of worlds, but there are occasions when I need to either identify someone or get specific information and reports from other agents that have been on certain worlds, and these databases fill that need.

I'm sure you're wondering how I managed to place all this inside your marine implants. Just accept that I was able to use my influence to upload these files and make a single minor change to your software to allow you to access them. Nothing more.

Don't worry about them falling into the wrong hands because everything is deeply encrypted. Only you can access the contents of these files, and anyone else searching your implants wouldn't even know they were there.

I understand you have perfectly valid reasons to dislike many things about me. I've not been a very good father, and I regret that. Becoming an Imperial Marine is your way of striking out on your own and creating a life for yourself, and I don't want to interfere with that, but we both know that I'm the kind of man that loves to meddle in things that really aren't any of his business.

If you don't desire to use the information in these files, all you need to do is place the databases back to inactive status. Use this information if you think it might help save you or one of your friends. Or even just to make your job easier.

I wish you every success in your new life, and I love you.

Dad

WELL, that was irritating.

Part of her was furious that her father had screwed with her implants that way. He'd had no right to do that.

Diana started to deactivate the databases but stopped herself with a mental sigh. Dammit. He knew her too well. She was a puzzle solver, and those databases had information about the planet they were going to, which put her in a moral quandary.

Damn her father. Damn him for knowing her far too well.

With a sigh, she closed the notification, queried the databases, and started to read.

* * *

ANDREA NOTICED that Diana seemed distracted as she helped load the squad's gear into the pinnace, but she didn't have time to talk to her about it. Even though she could use her implants to communicate privately, she was just too busy to spare even that little bit of attention.

A lot of the equipment was heavy, and one distracted moment might mean an injury. So all she could do was file the information away and focus on the task at hand.

Since they were on a peacekeeping mission, she did ask Reed why they were taking so much combat gear. It looked like they were preparing for war.

The corporal smirked a little. "We *are* preparing for war, Tolliver. We hope we don't have to fight one, but intentions don't count for much if that's what's called for.

"I don't expect we're going to have too much trouble because the presence of Imperial Marines tends to calm most people down. I mean, really, who wants to fight a company of marines?"

The woman snorted derisively. "Not a bunch of civilians. They'd get their asses kicked. One of the corporations running Diorama? They do their fighting with lawyers. No one there is going to fight us toe to toe.

"Just think of us as a deterrent. The situation there might be simmering, but it's not going to boil over while we're watching."

Andrea nodded and accepted her answer. Reed knew more about this kind of thing than she did, so she might as well take advantage of the woman's experience.

If almost four hundred Imperial Marines couldn't deter a bunch of corporations and some grumbling workers, she wasn't sure what could. It wasn't as if these people could field anything that would threaten Delta Company. No matter what happened, they'd have the strategic and tactical advantage.

Since they were the last platoon going up, there was a little more pressure to make sure that everything was aboard. It was a lot like when Grace packed to go on a camping trip. She made sure that they had everything they might need because they wouldn't be coming back for it.

Andrea had always enjoyed camping. Having grown up in a sterile, artificial facility, she found the wilds incredibly exotic. Trees were far beyond anything she'd ever conceived of as a child. Swimming in lakes and streams, running through completely wild spaces, seeing animals in their natural habitat. It was all simply amazing.

Honestly, she couldn't think of anything more delightful than a camping trip. Maybe this deployment would be similar. And maybe hell would freeze over.

She cut herself off from that line of thought because it was a distraction. Under Corporal Reed's direction, she helped inventory everything while the noncommissioned officer checked the tally against a list in her implants.

That turned out to be a good thing because a couple of things hadn't made it into the load out. Campbell and his fire team were sent to retrieve the errant gear, and within five minutes, everything they'd need for this deployment was packed away aboard the pinnace.

With the back end of the pinnace filled with their equipment, that left just enough room for the platoon to strap into the seats that had been left aboard for them.

Once their platoon leader, Lieutenant Wong—a man that she hadn't had the opportunity to even meet yet—verified that everything was in order, he gave the order to launch, and they were on their way.

She sat in her seat and restrained herself from grinning. This was so exciting. She'd imagined doing things like this as an Imperial Marine since she'd been twelve years old, and now it was finally happening.

Honestly, she hoped the mission required nothing more than glaring sternly at the troublemakers because she'd killed before, and she didn't relish the idea of doing so again. Not unless it was needful.

But this was her first trip as a marine doing the business of protecting the Empire. Who wouldn't be excited about something like that?

"You're almost bouncing in your seat," Claudio said from her left. "You need to dial it back a little, or you're really going to earn some kind of nickname that you're going to regret for the rest of your career."

"Whatever you say, Tiny," she immediately responded, not quite catching herself in time to stop.

"Tiny?" Reed asked from Claudio's other side. "Now that sounds like a name that can stick to somebody your size, Baker. I'll make sure to keep it in mind."

"I can't believe you said that," her friend growled. "You promised."

"It slipped out," she said, more than a little ashamed. "Sorry."

"You're not sorry," he grumbled. "Not really. I'm never going to be able to get away from that damned nickname."

"Hey, you earned it," Diana said from Andrea's right. "We won't get into *how* you earned it, but you did."

Andrea turned to Diana, smiling just a little. "He did, didn't he?

It's weird looking back at how different we were. Have we really changed that much?"

"We were civilians back then, just starting to learn what it would take to become marines," Diana said. "Now we're out in the field, doing the work we wanted to do, but we've still got so much to learn.

"Yet we can't escape the people that we were back then. Not really. We'll change, but it's going to happen slowly, and there are links to our past that we either don't want to get rid of or can't escape. Our histories are the chains that bind us."

Something in her friend's tone made Andrea raise an eyebrow, but Diana shook her head. That was okay. She'd have plenty of time to figure out what was bothering her once they settled into the transport.

"I got a map of the transport," Andrea said as she sent the file to Diana and Claudio. "I realize something like that is old hat for everyone else, but it will be useful for us to know."

"What makes you think you're going to have that much free time, greenie?" Reed asked with a thin smile. "You three are sitting here talking about how you're finally doing marine business, but you don't have the training to do what needs doing.

"It's going to take us almost a month to get on station, and you can bet your ass that I'm going to be running you ragged the entire time. That still won't get you ready for what we need to do, but at least you won't embarrass yourselves and me in the process."

Andrea was certain that was true, so she didn't argue. "How long will it take us to learn the things that we need to know, Corporal?"

The woman compressed her lips and seemed to think about the question for a few seconds. "That honestly depends on how quickly you pick up things up. There are a lot of factors that go into training marines to do their basic duties.

"We'll focus on the skills that are most likely to be important during a deployment like this, so I'd say you'll probably be about half-trained for doing garrison duty when we arrive. To completely round you out as a marine, that's going to take years."

The woman shrugged slightly. "I understand you were raised by marines and even given some training on marine equipment, Tolliver. That might cut some time off for all of you, as long as you're willing to share that experience with your friends, but it won't have as much of an effect as you might like.

"A lot of being a marine is taking a skill and drilling it so completely that it becomes second nature. Working something so hard that you can't imagine failing to do it on command while drunk. It has to be that ingrained into who you are."

Andrea smiled a little. "Well, that's quite the evocative description. Are we going to spend much time drinking, Corporal?"

"Not over the next few months you're not," Reed said dryly. "You're just going to wish that you could. Now, sit back and shut up so that I can start figuring out what our training schedule will look like once we unpack aboard the transport. First thing in the morning, your asses are getting to work."

Andrea knew the words were meant to quell their excitement, but it had the opposite effect on her. This was what she'd always dreamed of doing, and she couldn't wait to start doing it.

8

F inally done seeing his squad squared away, Jerome met with the other squad leaders in the small briefing room set aside for their platoon's use aboard the transport. Timothy Healy of second squad and Andrew McLean of third squad quickly joined him.

Lieutenant Wong and Senior Sergeant Julian Derby, their platoon sergeant, came in a few minutes later. The pair had just been briefed by Senior Lieutenant Van Buren and Gunnery Sergeant Singh about the specifics of their upcoming deployment and were now about to pass that information along so the squad leaders could brief their fire team leaders.

As soon Wong settled himself at the head of the table, he laid it out for them. "Diorama is a corporate world under contract to extract rare minerals used to build flip drives and rare medicinal plants only grown on that planet. There are two primary corporations overseeing everything: Yi Holdings and Schuster and Associates.

"Over the last six months, they've reported a large uptick in worker unrest and sabotage at the mines. Yi Holdings claim that working conditions are good and the pay is excellent, so they're expressing some confusion as to why they're getting this kind of pushback."

He crossed his arms and leaned back slightly in his chair. "We won't know the truth of the matter until we get there, but it's always possible they're lying their asses off. It wouldn't be the first time, and we'll deal with them if that's the case.

"If they're telling the truth, this is something of a mystery. There's always a certain level of grumbling that takes place when a company owns everything, but this seems more serious."

"Medicinal plants?" Jerome asked, frowning slightly. "With medical nanites as widespread as they are and the excellent level of care that everyone inside the Empire enjoys, what kind of biological matter could be worth exporting?"

"I'm not really sure," Wong said with a shrug. "The brief doesn't cover what medicinal purpose these plants serve, but if someone is willing to pay for them, it seems that they must have some kind of value."

Jerome scratched his head and nodded. Deployments like this usually had a pretty obvious cause, but this one seemed a bit murky. They were going to have to figure this one out on the fly.

The lieutenant sent them the information he had on the two corporations and the world itself. Diorama looked like a beautiful place, with three overwhelmingly green continents nestled into oceans that covered about sixty-five percent of the planet's surface area.

The poles were covered in white and glinted in the images, and fluffy clouds covered swaths of the world. All in all, it was a beautiful planet that anyone should be happy to live on.

"What's the plan?" Healy asked. "Are we going to trust the companies far enough to land at the spaceport?"

"Until we have the lay of the land, we're not going to use the corporate spaceport," Derby said. "We'll select a point that's a reasonable distance from the corporate headquarters and the places they're doing the extracting and set up a garrison there.

"We'll get everything we need down in the pinnaces and build up a protected area that no one can threaten. Until we know exactly what's going on and who the bad actors are, we'll have to be careful of everyone. These people are supposedly prone to sabotage, and I'd rather keep any hostiles from mixing in with our personnel."

Jerome nodded. That made perfect sense. He'd focus on seeing his squad was situated and able to do whatever duties were required of them.

And speaking of duties, he needed to change the subject.

"That sounds pretty vague, but I understand we can't do anything about it," he said slowly. "We've got about a month of travel time to get there, and my people will be in decent shape to deploy except for Fire Team Two."

The other man nodded. "Your brand-new greenies. Nothing like having three people straight out of advanced training being dumped into the pot. How do you plan on bringing them up to speed?"

"That's just the thing, Senior Sergeant. We're going to be working them hard, but I don't expect they're going to be up to speed when we get there. Lieutenant Wong and I have already spoken about this a little, but there's no way that one month of training is going to get three greenies ready for garrison duty, much less a potential combat zone."

The lieutenant grimaced slightly but nodded. "You'll have to do the best you can. We'll shield them as much as we can and cherry-pick the assignments we send them on."

"They're going to feel like they've been run ragged, but you're going to have to tag the most experienced people in your squad to impart knowledge to them over the next month," Derby said. "That means they're going to get very little free time, but maybe—just maybe—they'll know enough not to screw up if the crap hits the fan.

"I realize they've only been with you for half a day, but do you have any first impressions yet? Particularly about Tolliver."

Of course she was going to come up, Jerome grumbled to himself. How could she not?

"I've literally only laid eyes on them for a couple of minutes, so I don't have any real impression yet, Senior Sergeant. What I *have* seen of Tolliver almost stopped me in my tracks, though. She was on the mat, going a couple of rounds with PFC Campbell."

The senior sergeant winced. "Ouch. I suppose we're lucky that she's still in one piece."

"Actually, I understand she won two falls out of three," Jerome said with a wry smile. "I watched her plant him on his face and jam him up pretty good in the final match."

The jaws of everyone in the room literally dropped. It was now so quiet that he could hear the disbelief swirling through their brains.

"I find that… difficult to believe," Derby said after a few seconds. "Campbell is formidable enough that even somebody with a lot of experience has trouble with him. I've seen the two of you fight, and beating him wasn't easy for you.

"How could a girl her age and size—even with her advantages—manage to take somebody like him? She can't be that strong or fast, no matter how her genes have been tinkered with."

"Let that be a lesson to you, Julian," Wong said quietly. "Tolliver's genes haven't been tinkered with. They were redesigned from the ground up.

"The classified report I read said that she was almost fifty percent stronger than anyone else her size, and her reaction speed is off the chart. She's bright, and she's had six years of being raised by retired combat marines. She has skills that no other greenie is going to have.

"Campbell learned a valuable lesson, and it's one we need to take to heart as well. We can't underestimate her capabilities."

The officer focused his attention on Jerome. "I want you to keep pressing her, Walker. We need to know exactly what she can do and what she can't. If that means she gets trained in different things than her friends, so be it. We can't afford to have a wildcard in our platoon if things drop into the crapper."

Jerome had already known this was coming, so he simply nodded. "Yes, sir."

It was going to mean a whole lot more work for him, but he'd make sure that at the end of the day, she was a lot more tired than he was.

* * *

It took almost twice as long to unpack as it had to pack, which didn't make much sense to Diana, but it was what it was. They finished securing everything and were released to grab something to eat.

Being aboard ship, the mess hall was significantly smaller than such a facility would be in a planetary environment, but they were marines and didn't mind crowding elbow to elbow to eat.

The food was excellent, and there was coffee, so she was good.

The entire time they were eating, even though she was engaged in conversation with Andrea and Claudio, part of her brain was still picking over the data she'd gotten from the illicit databases.

She had to admit the information seemed useful. That didn't excuse her father for what he'd done, but he knew her far better than she cared to admit. It was part of her nature to worry at puzzles, looking for solutions or unexpected outcomes, and his interference had played right into that.

When they'd finished eating, Claudio excused himself and headed for the gym. He'd made some new friends and was going to do some male bonding.

That suited Diana. Not only did she want her friend to build a network that accepted him—and by extension, her and Andrea—but she needed time alone with Andrea to discuss what her father had done and what she'd found out.

Unlike the fire team's room at the base, the entire squad was bunking in the same compartment for the trip to Diorama. They wouldn't get any alone time there, so she needed to find another place where she could have a conversation without being overheard.

Yes, she could have used implant-to-implant communications, but it was possible their superiors could monitor it. If so, that would be bad. Far better, there were no ears privy to this discussion.

Aboard a troop transport, that wasn't exactly easy to arrange, but it wasn't impossible either. The map that Andrea had given her earlier held a couple of potential locations. As the two of them walked out of the mess hall, she once again consulted the map and considered the various options.

The best one seemed to be a small study area set aside for continuing education. No one was going to be there at this hour because their schedules hadn't been settled yet.

"If you've got a few minutes, I'd like to show you something," she said to Andrea, tugging her down one of the side corridors and toward the study area.

Her friend raised an eyebrow but didn't object. "Sure. Something we can't talk about in the bunk room?"

"Exactly."

The map proved accurate, and they ducked into the study area a couple of minutes later. It wasn't large, only big enough for six people to sit at the tiny desks, but it was empty and had a hatch that she closed behind them.

It was always possible the room could be monitored remotely, but that seemed a stretch. Why would anyone want to watch marines read manuals or take higher education courses?

Andrea took a seat after swinging her chair around and rested her arms across its back as she stared at her friend. "You've been acting strangely ever since we lifted. What's going on?"

She took a seat across from her friend—sitting more traditionally—and clasped her hands in her lap. "In two words? My father."

Her friend shook her head with a sad smile. "What has he done now?"

Diana glanced toward the closed hatch and lowered her voice, even though she knew no one else was there to hear her. "He managed to get some kind of secret databases into my implants. When we were lifting off from the planet, and you mentioned wanting to know more about Diorama, my implants told me I had information in some inactive databases, and I found out everything he'd done."

Andrea took her hands into her own. "I'm so sorry. I know that has to drive you crazy. I can't imagine how I'd feel if my guardians meddled in *everything* I did. Just the little I saw of your father convinced me he was the kind of guy that manipulated things behind the scenes to get outcomes he wanted.

"It's great when you want the same things but not so good when you don't even have a clue what he's doing. Do you have any idea why he'd do something like this?"

"He said it was because the information might be useful at some point. I suspect he just wants to keep me safe, but I'm not convinced he hasn't made life more dangerous for me. Possessing those databases has to break a lot of laws."

"You could report their presence and let the chips fall where they may."

Diana sighed and shook her head. "He infuriates me, but I'd rather not see him rot in prison. If I don't say anything about them, no one will ever have reason to suspect they're there. I mean, seriously, who could possibly plant secret databases of classified information into marine implants? It sounds like something out of a spy vid."

Her friend smiled slightly. "It kind of does. So, if you've decided to keep using them, what kind of information do they have about our deployment zone? Or in general, for that matter?"

"I'll answer the second question first. It seems to have some information about a lot of places. It also has classified details that I shouldn't know about people, companies, and governments. We're talking actual supersecret data about them."

She lowered her voice even further. "I have contact information and ways to find agents working for Imperial Intelligence. I could even use those codes to identify myself as a member of the organization.

"Hell, it wouldn't surprise me if my father put me on the damned payroll. Do you think I could actually be an agent for Imperial Intelligence without knowing about it? Is that even legal?"

Andrea shrugged. "Probably not. I suppose you'll know if extra money starts showing up in your bank account. It wouldn't be labeled in a way that tipped anyone off. You know, like a stock dividend or something."

Diana blinked at her friend and brought up her most recent bank statement. She hadn't paid much attention to it because there hadn't been any need to. It wasn't as if she'd had much she could spend money on while in basic and advanced training.

Sure enough, there was an unexpected deposit labeled as a trust fund disbursement. Looking back, it started right after she graduated from basic training. It was a substantial amount too. Easily double what she was paid by the Corps.

"Dammit," she muttered. "I think he actually did it. I never signed anything, of course, but I'll bet a lot of agents don't work directly for

Imperial Intelligence and never signed anything either. How the hell did he draw me into his plans yet again?"

"You're just lucky, I guess. So what kind of information did you get about where we're going, Miss Superspy?"

Diana took a deep breath and let it out slowly. Being angry with her father wasn't going to make this any better. Besides, there was plenty of time to get mad later.

"I got the names of the primary corporations there and a list of senior-level employees working for them. There's also information about the rare elements they're extracting. They're used in building critical components in flip drives.

"There's also some kind of medicinal trade. They raise plants that provide an extract. I'm not sure what it does, but it's apparently lucrative enough to warrant being an official export."

Andrea nodded. "We're not exactly in a position to make decisions about what we do when we get there, but I think having access to that kind of information is going to prove helpful. Why don't you send me what you have, and we'll go over it together?"

"I'm concerned that private communications between marines could be monitored," Diana conceded. "I'd rather not send something that I know will get us both arrested. I understand that we could go encrypted, but that would raise other flags.

"For the moment, I suggest we just talk this out in a general way while we come up with a solution that won't get us both in trouble."

Her friend laughed. "You're overthinking this. We're just a couple of greenies. They have no reason to be monitoring what we send one another. If we lower the transmission power, there's no reason to expect anyone would even pick it up. You can't be paranoid about this forever."

Diana thought about that for a second and then nodded. "Fine. Let's step down our transmission power so it won't leave this compartment. I'll send you all of the information I have on Diorama, the corporations that run it, and any of the people mentioned.

"The data is about two years old, so there will probably be changes when we get there, but it's enough for us to start looking. You're right that we don't have any control over what happens when we get there, but it might save lives if we can spot something useful. Maybe we can find a way to get that information up the chain of command without incriminating ourselves.

"If it stops the need for shooting someone, it has to be worth it, right?"

"You bet it is," her friend said, squeezing her hands. "We have to be back in the bunk room shortly, or someone is going to come looking for us, so let's get to work."

9

Andrea was up bright and early the following day. As expected, she and her friends were the focus of attention going forward, and each was handed off to one of the other fire teams for focused instruction.

To her pleasure, she was sent to Campbell's fire team, and he was the one putting her through her paces. Apparently, someone thought they'd developed a bond that might make him more useful in assessing her than perhaps Corporal Reed would be.

She wasn't sure that was true, but he was a lot nicer to be around than Reed, for sure.

The first couple of hours involved the two of them sitting in the mess hall, drinking coffee, and going over what she knew. He seemed happy enough to let her do the talking, restricting himself to asking occasional questions.

His focus was on what equipment and procedures she thought she was familiar with. Though he likely disagreed with her assessment about what was an acceptable level of familiarity, he seemingly accepted what she was saying at face value for the moment.

Once they'd finished going through whatever checklist of items he had in his head, he rose and gestured for her to accompany him. They put their coffee cups in the rack to be cleaned, and he led her to the section of the ship used for weapons training.

"Shooting is one of those skills that's pretty easy to check, and you can't fake not knowing what you're doing," he said as he walked up to the armory. "We'll give you a quick run-through on the weapons and see if we can scratch them off the list.

"Honestly, the odds of us having to shoot anybody this time around are pretty low, but one never knows."

Sergeant Sherman gave her a sour look before turning his attention to Campbell. "What can I do for you, PFC Campbell?"

"We're doing a weapons check, Sergeant. I'll want both a flechette rifle, a flechette pistol, and ammunition for Tolliver."

"Why don't you let her use her own pistol?" the man asked in a snide tone.

Campbell raised an eyebrow and looked between the two of them. "I'm not sure what that means. Tolliver?"

She grimaced. "This isn't supposed to be public knowledge, but I have an Imperial dispensation to carry personal weapons. I have both a flechette pistol and a stunner."

The large man frowned slightly. "On you?"

She nodded. "They're miniaturized."

He took a slow breath and pursed his lips. "We'll test you on those as well, but I'm going to need standard marine-issue flechette weapons to do my verification.

"Sergeant Sherman will be more discreet about who he mentions this to going forward, I'm sure. It would be awkward if word got out that something that was supposed to be kept under wraps was just being blabbed about. Right, Sergeant?"

The man didn't look pleased at being told what to do by a private first class, but he didn't argue, simply nodding. "I haven't told anyone that didn't need to know, and I'll keep it to myself going forward."

Andrea would believe that when she saw it.

Once the armorer had retrieved a rifle and pistol, plus ammunition, and had her sign for them, Campbell led her to the firing line. The far end held targets and was backed by material she knew from personal experience would stop flechettes from penetrating.

He went over the safety procedures, so he was satisfied she understood what she was supposed to do and when she was supposed to do it. As the range safety person, he'd tell her when to load the weapons, when to make them ready to fire, and when to actually shoot them.

She'd done this plenty of times before under Fei's instruction, so she was confident that whatever he wanted her to do, she could perform to specifications. Shooting was something that she'd never had problems with. Not since she was twelve years old.

Step-by-step, Campbell ran her through the basic firing sequences, and she followed his directions precisely. Since this was supposed to test her skill, she didn't use her implants to link with the weapons, only relying upon her native skill to achieve what she considered excellent accuracy.

After running through a couple of magazines in both the rifle and pistol, Campbell nodded his satisfaction. "I think you understand how to use these weapons correctly. Did you link up with your implants to improve the accuracy?"

"No. It seems like cheating to use my implants to improve my fire control for a test."

"You know what they say. If you ain't cheating, you ain't trying. Going forward, if you have any advantages that you can add to the mix, do so. I want to see what your ultimate capability is, not what you do when you're giving yourself an artificial handicap."

Andrea picked the flechette rifle up and took a moment to link her implants with it. Once she'd done so, she waited for Campbell's signal and then raised the rifle and began firing. She swept the rifle from left to right, firing bursts at each of the targets as rapidly as she could bring the weapon to bear.

Considering her strength and neural response times, that was fast indeed.

Bursts of flechettes tore apart the targets' heads as rapidly as she could sweep from one to the next. In eight seconds, she'd killed ten targets. With more than a hint of a smile, she safed the weapon and set it down on the firing bench.

"That's just showing off," Campbell said as he put his hands on his hips. "I've been a marine for six years, and I haven't seen many people that can do something like that. Can you repeat it with the pistol?"

"I'm even faster with the pistol."

"Show me."

She repeated the process and put a single flechette into the heart of each target in less than six seconds.

The big marine whistled. "Okay, I'm not going to question your weapon proficiency going forward. Do you have any experience with other kinds of weapons?"

Andrea nodded. "Plasma rifles and neural disruptors. I've also gotten some use out of crew-served weapons, but I'm not very good with them at this point."

"But you *can* use them, which is better than a marine in your position should be able to say. Well done.

"So, let's see these personal weapons. If you're going to carry them, I want to be absolutely certain you're proficient with them."

She reached into her uniform and pulled the flechette pistol and stunner from their hidden holsters. Campbell blinked at them as she set them on the firing bench.

"Is this some kind of joke? Those aren't weapons. They're toys."

He picked up the flechette pistol gingerly and turned it over in his hands. It was tiny in his grip.

"I couldn't even get my finger through the trigger guard. Are you sure you can use this?"

She shrugged slightly. "It's not like I've had much of a chance to practice with it. I received them just after basic training, and they aren't the kind of thing I could just trot out at the advanced school."

"Then let's go through these a lot more carefully. Step-by-step, slow and easy."

She followed his directions and found that even though the weapons were small, they were inherently more accurate than larger ones. They interfaced with her implants just as seamlessly as the marine-issue ones had, and she was able to achieve even quicker times with the flechette pistol than she had with the bulkier marine version, shaving almost a second off her time.

The stunner behaved much like a neural disruptor, but it didn't have a lethal setting. She brought the internal menu up with her implants to verify that, since there was no switch on the weapon's exterior.

And she found out she was wrong.

The tiny weapon did indeed have a setting capable of killing someone, as well as stunning them. No one had ever called it a neural disruptor, yet that was precisely what it was.

She'd keep that information to herself. No need to get Sergeant Sherman all excited. If push really did come to shove, she might need that capability desperately someday.

Campbell shook his head. "I'm pretty impressed. If there are other skills you've learned to this level of ability, we might be able to get you further along than Reed thinks.

"Let's clean your weapons, get them turned in, and go grab lunch. I'm starving, and we can figure out exactly what we're going to do next while we eat.

"No matter how good you are, you're still going to be exhausted by the time we get to Diorama, but if we can hone some of your skills, maybe Corporal Reed won't be so hard on you."

Andrea laughed. "That'll be the day. She's going to run me into the ground no matter what I do, so I might as well learn something useful."

The big man clapped her on the shoulder, sending her staggering. "I like that attitude, Tolliver. Let's go do that."

* * *

JEROME KEPT an eye on what the greenies were up to remotely over the next few days and queried everyone working with them closely about their skill levels. While he was concerned about every single one of them, he had to admit his attention was focused on Tolliver.

Campbell had reported the girl was competent on the weapons

range and actually had a smattering of skills she'd need on this deployment. The big man didn't think she'd be completely ready for every task once they arrived on Diorama, but he thought she'd be able to handle most things with competent supervision.

That news irritated Jerome but also pleased him. The diametrically opposed emotions had to do with his conflicting orders. On the one hand, he had to keep an eye on Tolliver and make sure she wasn't a threat to his squad, the company, or the Empire.

On the other hand, he needed to make sure all his marines could handle whatever this deployment threw at them. If Tolliver could pull her own weight, that would benefit them all.

Randall and Baker weren't nearly up to that level of skill in anything, so they'd have to be suitably chaperoned the entire time they were on deployment, but there was nothing he could do about that.

They still had over three weeks until they arrived at their destination, so each of the greenies would get far more attention than they wanted. He looked over the schedules Reed had come up with and made notations to refine parts of their training.

They'd be doing double shifts the entire time they were en route, so he was sure they'd be cursing his name before this was all over. As long as they were alive to do the cursing, he'd be satisfied.

Once he'd updated the training schedule, he shot it back to Reed so she could implement it. Then he turned his attention to the scant information they had about Diorama itself.

They'd gotten an update in the last system about the two corporations, so that was something. Yi Holdings was a major corporation in this sector and had operations on multiple worlds. Schuster and Associates, on the other hand, was only present on Diorama.

Jerome wasn't sure how the second corporation had managed to worm its way onto the corporate world or if it had been there first, but that was certainly an unusual arrangement.

There was still no information about what was being harvested by the smaller corporation, which worried him. It had to be unusual, but no one seemed to have a clue what it was.

The other things they'd gotten—from commercial sources, by the way—were a few biographies of the senior corporate management on Diorama, though only for Yi Holdings.

The biographies were little more than names and a few paragraphs of information each, so the officers were going to have to talk with the senior managers and get a feel for who they were before they could start figuring out whether the problems on Diorama came from the corporations or the workers.

They'd pass through quite a few systems on their way to Diorama, so they'd hopefully get more information before they got there. Still, it probably wasn't going to be enough.

With a sigh, he went back to the recording from the range and watched just how devastating Tolliver was with the various flechette weapons. Her genetic modifications and the experience she'd picked up in the Empire had combined to make her an excellent shot.

At least that was one area where he didn't need to be concerned about her. Unless, of course, she was standing right behind him.

He cradled his face in his hands and growled at himself. She was a member of his squad, and he had to stop behaving like this.

Just because she came from the Singularity didn't mean she was a traitor. She hadn't killed his brother. If he kept behaving this way, he'd say or do something that compromised his ability to lead the squad, and that couldn't be allowed.

At least he'd gotten more information about her background from Senior Lieutenant Van Buren. Tolliver had been grown and trained to be a member of one of the twelve ruling genetic lines inside the Singularity. One didn't get much more powerful than that, he supposed.

The fact that she'd been rescued at the age of twelve and then deprogrammed—by professionals in conjunction with her guardians —meant that he shouldn't have to worry about her motives.

For God's sake, she'd killed Singularity troopers to help the surviving marines escape. Surely a little girl couldn't have been planted as a spy. He needed to get a grip on himself.

He rose to his feet and started pacing his cramped office. How could he accomplish Major Bashir's orders while not screwing up this deployment or his professional relationship with Tolliver?

The battalion commander had been clear that he had to keep his eyes on her as often as possible. While it wasn't possible to make reports about the girl's actions, that didn't relieve him of his duty to gather the information.

Yet how could he do that when she was so focused on the training he was heaping on her?

He shook his head. He wasn't going to be able to do anything until they reached Diorama. Even then, there was only so much he could be around her.

She was going to have to have someone watching over her at all times, though. That would be Corporal Reed for the most part, but if he paired her fire team with Campbell's, he could have more eyes on her.

The delicate thing would be getting reports about her behavior without tipping anyone off. He'd have to come up with a set of orders and guidelines that were generic enough yet allowed him to probe for more detail on her behavior.

No matter what he did, it probably wouldn't be enough for Bashir.

Thankfully, he had time to work out the details and get a feeling for what this girl was like before they arrived. He'd have to take the time to interview her in more detail, but he was going to put that off for as long as possible.

If she lumped him in with those that couldn't stand her because of where she came from, it would make her close up, and that would be the end of getting unfiltered information out of her.

Maybe he should just wait until they were on Diorama. He was buried in work already, and so was she.

He didn't like putting off a task, but in this case, waiting was probably better than rushing. Besides, after being worked hard for a month, she might let her guard down a little and say something she'd otherwise keep to herself.

He sat back down at his desk and began roughing out the instructions he'd eventually give to Reed and Campbell. They had to be exactly right, so he'd spend the next three weeks massaging them.

Then, once they reached Diorama, the real fun would start.

10

Diana and her friends finally got a break when they arrived in the Diorama system. Reed and the others had been pushing them hard—and she felt like they'd made a lot of progress—but it wouldn't do to deploy completely exhausted.

Of course, that didn't mean they could just lounge about. They still had to assist in loading the pinnaces for the initial drop to the surface. Still, that was like a leisurely stroll compared to running a sprint. It was almost relaxing.

Almost.

She and Claudio had made a lot of progress over the last four weeks, but even she had to admit they'd only scratched the surface of what they needed to know as marines. The level of competence exhibited by everyone else in the squad showed her just how far she still had to go.

To her annoyance, Claudio had made better progress than her. She'd never tell him so, but he was probably better suited to being a marine than she was. He seemingly picked up what he needed to know with just a couple of passes.

Oh, he was nowhere near Andrea's league, but he was making

better progress than she was. That only spurred Diana to work harder. She'd make the grade no matter what it took.

When they'd flipped into the Diorama system, everything kicked into high gear. The corporations supposedly knew they were coming —not that anyone had briefed lowly privates on that sort of thing— but now the situation had to be getting real for them.

For the workers, this was probably going to be the first time they'd heard that the marines were coming. Or maybe the corporations had been warning them for weeks that they had to stop their nonsense. Either one of those options made sense, so she'd have to wait to see which way it played out.

She and Andrea had had several skull sessions in which they'd gone over the information about the corporations and the planet itself. They were no closer to figuring out exactly what was going on, of course. The only way to figure out the circumstances would be to actually investigate, which would happen at a level far above them.

That was why she was surprised when her implants pinged her with a notification indicating that her databases had just been updated with new information on Diorama. She almost dropped the crate she was helping carry into one of the pinnaces in surprise.

In the time since she'd activated the damned things, they'd shown no ability to do that. She hadn't requested any kind of update, so where the hell had it come from? How could it possibly have gotten new information while she was still aboard the transport?

She firmly put that thought out of her head and focused on the task at hand. Trying to split her attention was a recipe for screwing up, and that was the absolute last thing she needed right now.

Once they'd finished loading the pinnace, Diana stopped in the study area so she could have some uninterrupted time to figure out what had happened. Sitting at the desk, she queried the databases about the update.

The response it gave her sent a chill down her spine.

The damned thing had been using her implants to interface with the communication systems on the transport and query each of the systems they'd traveled through. She didn't know who it was contacting—and it wouldn't give her that information—but it was getting new data and updating itself with every occupied system.

It hadn't been notifying her that it had been doing so either. Apparently, it only felt the need to let her know that she had new information about her current mission.

And that was what it referred to this as: her mission.

Since this new data had come in just an hour ago, it had to be from Diorama itself. Somewhere on or above the planet, something or someone had been gathering information and was ready to update any Imperial Intelligence agent that passed through.

That was terrifying.

What was even more frightening was the fact that her implants had been blithely forcing the systems aboard the transport to carry water for it. What if someone had noticed the transmissions?

Had the updates registered with the communication system and been logged? Why hadn't someone become curious about that and started asking questions?

The logical answer was that the marine systems had been modified not to notice or log the traffic. Maybe all Imperial systems had some kind of an exception to help shield the transmissions. That meant Imperial Intelligence was working in the shadows right in front of everyone's very noses.

How like her father.

Well, it wasn't as if she could stop the damned things from doing what they were doing. If someone noticed the transmissions, she'd have to answer some very pointed questions. Surely her father would've taken steps to make sure nothing like that occurred.

If he hadn't, there wasn't anything she could do about it. No amount of poking at the databases showed any way to turn the automatic updates off.

The purpose of the updates was obvious. Any time an agent traveled through a system, whatever updates had been propagated through the Empire for them would be added to their databases, so they always had the most current information possible.

Since her father was a roving director, he needed the best data he could get his hands on about a wide variety of things. And as she was using his databases, she seemingly received the same courtesy.

Did that mean her databases thought she was a roving director with Imperial Intelligence? Would it identify her as such if queried? That would be truly awkward if she ever met another Imperial Intelligence agent and had to identify herself.

She rubbed her face tiredly and checked the time. She could still get something to eat, but she needed to hurry.

A quick skim of the Diorama update revealed it had a lot more data about mining operations on the planet. It also had what looked like a complete employee list for Yi Holdings. Not just senior management but all the way down to the janitorial staff. Whoever had gotten the information must've been someone with complete access to their systems.

Or, more likely, there was some kind of program buried in their systems that forwarded the data to a central location where it was held for Imperial Intelligence. If that happened on every world, the spies were literally plugged into *everything*.

She wondered how they could operate at all, considering they must be buried under data. She'd read something about the spy agencies on prespaceflight Terra that suggested they often had the information they needed to make a given assessment, but it was buried in so much other data they just didn't know they knew it.

Certainly, modern computers would make that easier to deal with, but there were limits. If Imperial Intelligence collected vast swaths of data from every corporation and private organization—not to mention prominent individuals—just the storage requirements would be incredible.

No, it had to be something done on demand. Her implants must've queried the orbital network here at Diorama, and a program there had requested more specific information from the computers that had what she was looking for. It couldn't be anything else.

Interestingly, the data for Schuster and Associates hadn't changed at all. Did that mean their computer systems weren't significant enough to have the program? Or maybe they were small enough that they just weren't worth that kind of attention.

Well, she had more than enough new information to work with, so she headed out to get some lunch. When she had time, she'd update Andrea.

Again, there wasn't anything they could do about the situation, but it would at least help pass the time.

* * *

ANDREA GOT SO CAUGHT up in her work that she missed lunch and had to grab a ration bar to tide her over. She knew Diana was looking for her, but it would have to wait until things slowed down.

Her friend understood—in fact, she understood very well—because she hunted Andrea down and gave her a second ration bar because she knew Andrea needed the calories. Those thirty seconds were literally the only time the two had to talk.

The fact that her friend hadn't discussed anything with her over their implants meant that it had to do with the data she had on Diorama. So, while it might be interesting, it wasn't critical. After all, they were just a couple of privates, so there was nothing they could do about any discoveries her friend made.

When they'd finished loading the pinnaces going down on the first trip, she made a pass through the mess hall to get a real meal. It wasn't when everyone else was eating, but the cooks knew to expect her at odd times and had something that could be prepared quickly. That was one of the accommodations made for her heightened metabolism.

By the time she'd finished eating, the call was going out to gear up and board the pinnaces. As planned, she ended up in the seat between Diana and Claudio. Each of them was prepared for an actual combat drop, outfitted in their unpowered armor with a complete weapons loadout.

Not that anyone seemed to expect trouble. Apparently, the officers had already been in contact with the corporations running Diorama and received assurances that there'd be no issues with setting up wherever they chose.

Their leadership displayed admirable skepticism and were ready for trouble.

"How are you doing?" she asked Diana in a low tone.

"Good, but we're going to want to talk once we have a few minutes. It can wait."

Andrea nodded and patted her friend on the knee. "I'm sure we'll have plenty of downtime in the near future."

Diana laughed. "I highly doubt that. Maybe we can talk a little before we get some sleep, but that's not going to be anytime soon. We've got to build an entire facility to house us, and you can bet the command team wants it done before the sun rises."

"What time is it going to be where we land?"

"Someone said it's going to be just before dark. With the local planetary rotation, that'll give us a leisurely fifteen standard hours to get everything set up. I wouldn't count on getting any sleep."

"Fabulous."

That wasn't good news, considering how exhausted Andrea was, but it wasn't unexpected either. She was an Imperial Marine, which meant working long hours doing difficult tasks. If she'd wanted to sleep in, she should've become an accountant.

Or maybe accountants got even less sleep. She had no idea how bean counters lived. They were a mysterious lot that behaved by rules only they understood.

Andrea decided to take a nap while she had the opportunity. Falling asleep on command was a skill that all marines developed. One never knew when fifteen minutes of sleep might make a difference.

She was jolted awake when the pinnace detached from the transport and began dropping toward Diorama. Blinking to clear her vision, she checked her internal chronometer and saw that she'd been out for about twenty minutes. That was five minutes more than she'd planned on, so she'd count that as a win.

She tapped into the pinnace's cameras, and an image of the globe they were orbiting appeared in her mental vision. It was very much like the pictures Diana had shown her, but this somehow felt more real. They were actually about to land on this world, and she could watch it happen in real time.

Diorama was beautiful, with wide oceans of blue and continents seemingly covered in greenery. Oh, there were a few deserts and the ice-covered poles, yet it was a planet teeming with life. Even the clouds seemed to move around with a life of their own.

That was the kind of wishful thinking that would've gotten her in a lot of trouble if she'd been back in the crèche, but she indulged herself now and then. Imagination wasn't something to be torn out by the roots.

Keeper and her former line sibs might never understand how they'd crippled themselves by extinguishing that spark, but they had. She had no idea how it could be used against them, but she was much happier with the life she had now. Even if she'd survived the crèche, she'd have hated who she'd become.

The nighttime terminator was just ahead, and she could see dawn advancing across the surface of this world. A new day was coming, and she was watching it happen. Of course, that meant that the area they were landing at was on the other side of the world, but they'd get there quickly enough.

Her pinnace and the other three assigned to the transport ship would dive into the atmosphere shortly and swoop down on their predetermined landing zone without warning the locals they were coming.

It shouldn't be a problem because this was an area away from any large settlements. She wasn't sure how the command team knew they could use the land, but they'd have figured that out in advance.

Andrea had a rough idea where the mining was taking place and where the biologics were being grown and was able to put small glowing dots onto her mental map of Diorama to see just how far away they were from the proposed camp.

And she used the word "camp" specifically because the garrison base had been designated Camp Pyramid. If the name had any meaning, it wasn't clear to her, but it allowed them to refer to the base without getting confused with some other place on the planet.

According to the reconnaissance drones they'd sent down, Camp

Pyramid would be about a hundred kilometers away from a rural town. She had no idea what its population was, but none of the buildings rose above two stories.

It did have an area to transport livestock and frozen meat, since that was what the town produced. The livestock, according to their briefing, were Terran cattle.

She'd never personally seen anything like that before, but she'd seen pictures. She wondered how the creatures would stack up against her expectations if she were ever to come into contact with them.

In any case, the transport network might help them get additional supplies. Everything they could acquire locally would ease the drain on what they'd brought with them.

The pinnace dipped and began entering the atmosphere even as she thought about that. She imagined how she'd be controlling their flight path and wished she could look into the control area.

That wasn't authorized, so she had to make do with envisioning how she'd perform the operation if she'd been flying.

It would be a long time—if ever—before the Imperial Marines decided to train her on flying a pinnace. Those types of operations were almost always conducted by Fleet personnel. The fact that she'd actually logged time in the pilot's seat wouldn't convince them to make an exception to that tradition, she was sure.

Perhaps she could make a friend on the Fleet side that would be willing to give her some pointers, but that was for another time. For now, vessels like these would simply take her from point A to point B.

When they got to point B this trip, that was when all the fun started.

11

Jerome exited the pinnace as soon as it landed and began overseeing his section of the perimeter. He devoted his fire teams—except for the undertrained Fire Team Two—to the task, and they quickly spread out to make sure there were no threats in the area on his side of where the pinnaces had set down.

The sun was just above the horizon, and based on the briefings he'd received, he estimated there was less than a standard hour before darkness arrived. That meant they needed to secure the zone as quickly as possible.

The rest of Third Platoon was covering the other zones while the other platoons were working on the camp itself. Everything they needed had been fabricated in advance and packed away aboard the transport, so it was simply a matter of unpacking the crates, leveling the ground where needed, and putting the buildings together.

That wasn't to say that simple meant *easy*. He knew from personal experience that that wasn't the case.

Third Platoon would maintain the perimeter until about an hour after dark. At that point, another platoon would rotate into the prepared positions. Unlucky Third Fire Team had to dig two, since the greenies weren't there to do their part.

They'd lower the number of marines on watch once the weapons emplacements were set up and fully active. At that point, a couple of squads would be able to oversee security for the camp.

He tagged along with Fire Team One and stopped when they did. The four marines quickly began digging a temporary emplacement while he knelt behind them and checked the drones circling the area.

They'd been keeping continuous watch since they'd done the initial scouting run several hours ago. Their records showed no one had intruded into the zone during that time, though several animals had passed through.

Just to be thorough, Jerome reviewed the data on the animals and decided that while some of them were likely predators, human beings were too large to be endangered by them. Still, he tagged them for verification to be sure none were poisonous.

The area around Camp Pyramid was lush and green. It had been cleared at some point, so the marines had a commanding field of fire from the hill on which they were constructing the camp. The nearest forested area was about five hundred meters away at the closest.

The only reason he knew the area had been cleared by human beings was that there were the remains of some stumps in the vast fields. There was also fencing that separated the cleared area from the trees. That implied someone kept something in the cleared area on occasion.

As the locals raised Terran cattle, that seemed like a safe bet.

He pulled out a set of binoculars and began scanning the area in front of him. Electronic enhancement made distant things jump into precise focus as he carefully looked for signs of either people in the area or their recent presence.

After fifteen minutes, he was convinced that the area was clear for the time being.

The fire team had finished digging what amounted to a short trench during that time. They'd piled the dirt in front of the trench to give them protective cover and jumped into the hole they'd created.

This particular hole had to be somewhat larger than usual because Campbell was not a small man. Still, he more than made up for that by being the workhorse that had dug a good portion of the entrenched position.

Once they were in position, their fire team leader began dictating the zones each of them watched. They'd done this thousands of times before, and the process was worn smooth by experience.

They had everything settled in less than five minutes, which was good because about five minutes after that, one of the marines called out a thermal signature just above the trees in their area of responsibility.

Jerome brought his binoculars up and immediately spotted what the woman had seen. That was definitely a single-person grav vehicle, and it was headed their way. Someone had noticed the company's arrival and was coming to see what the hell they were doing.

"D-tac, Three Point Two Actual," he murmured onto the company tactical net. "We have an incoming grav vehicle at FT1."

As he was the leader of Second Squad, Third Platoon, Three Point Two Actual was him. Using the word "actual" was what declared him the leader of that group without using names.

"D-tac copies Three Point Two Actual," whoever was running operations said. "We're attempting to communicate with the vehicle, but they're not answering. You're authorized to *visually* engage the target and encourage them to land at your position."

"Three Point Two Actual confirms visual engagement only. Out."

Since he doubted the vehicle was making a bombing run, he stepped away from the entrenchment, pulled a flashlight off of his belt, and activated it to get the attention of the incoming vehicle.

It behaved just as he'd expected and began slowing and dropping in altitude until Jerome could see it clearly. It was long and slender, without an enclosed cab. An adult male rode the vehicle, using manual controls to fly while his legs gripped it as if he were riding a horse.

The vehicle had a landing skid that the rider adroitly brought it down on. He then stepped off the vehicle and strode toward Jerome resolutely.

The man was wearing a cowboy hat. Jerome had seen them used on the horse ranch his school had taken them to when he was a kid.

The man's clothes were dark colored and looked built to handle rough use, as were the battered boots he wore.

He was tall, weathered, heavily tanned, and had about four days' worth of growth on his face. He also looked extremely pissed off.

Jerome smiled and continued to let his weapon dangle off his harness while keeping his hands to his sides. Best not to be too provocative unless it was warranted.

"Who the hell are you people, and what are you doing on my land?" the man demanded as he stopped in front of Jerome, planting his hands on his hips.

"Imperial Marines. Delta Company, 745th Battalion. We've received permission from the corporations running this world to set up here."

"I don't give a damn what those bastards said," the man said as he spat meaningfully off to the side. "They may run this world, but they don't own it. I paid for this land, and it's mine. You can't just come in here and take it without my say-so.

"From what I can see, you're busy destroying one of my most productive grazing fields. You need to stop right this damned second."

Jerome shrugged meaningfully. "That's above my pay grade. I'm Sergeant Jerome Walker. Who are you?"

The man's eyes narrowed. "Here's another thing I don't care about: your pay grade. I don't know anything about the military, and I don't care to learn. I want to talk to the person in charge."

"Once you tell me who you are, I'll make arrangements to get you in front of the person you want to scream at, but you've got to cooperate with me a little first."

That got a lip twitch out of the man. "Men don't scream, Sergeant. They yell. And yeah, I intend to do a lot of yelling.

"I'm Craig Lindbergh, the owner of every bit of land you see around us. As far as I'm concerned, you're trespassers destroying what my family has spent years building. If you don't want me to head back to my place and get my rifle, you'll stop your bullshit and get me in front of the man or woman in charge of this outfit pronto."

Jerome had no idea what "pronto" meant, but the context suggested it meant "fast." That suited him just fine.

"I'm more than happy to get that done for you, Mister Lindbergh. Give me one moment."

He keyed his transmitter, making sure the volume was loud enough for the man to hear. "D-tac, Three Point Two Actual. I have Craig Lindbergh here. He tells me he owns the property we're setting up on, and he'd like to speak with Delta Actual."

"This is Delta Actual," Senior Lieutenant Van Buren said. "Escort Mister Lindbergh to the headquarters building, and I'll handle the situation. Make sure he comes on foot."

"Copy that, Delta Actual. Three Point Two Actual out."

Lindbergh grunted before Jerome could say anything. "Not only are you trying to steal my land, but you're also going to make me walk? Figures. Tell your people not to touch my skidder, or I'll take it out of their hide."

Then the man started up the hill at a determined pace. Yeah, he was pissed.

With more than a hint of a smile, Jerome started after him. This promised to be entertaining.

* * *

DIANA and her fire team were working with another to help level the ground where they were assembling the headquarters building. The flooring was in, and they were starting on the walls when Lieutenant Van Buren showed up with Gunnery Sergeant Singh to wait for something.

Or, as it turned out, someone.

A tall man dressed in an almost strangely archaic set of clothing walked up. His hat seemed to be made to protect his head from rain and sun. It was beaten and dusty, much like he was.

The rest of his clothing seemed to be made of a sturdy material favoring dark blues. His boots were oddly pointed, brown, and also well used.

The newcomer was accompanied by Sergeant Walker, so she focused intently on her work, though she had her ears peeled to hear what happened next.

"Which one of you is in charge?" the new man growled.

"I'm Senior Lieutenant Pedro van Buren of the Imperial Marines. I apologize for our presence on your property, but we obtained permission before we came down."

"Let me let you in on a bit of a secret, Senior Lieutenant. Most folks don't give two hoots or a holler about any of the corporate stooges that manage this planet. They're a bunch of stuffed shirts that don't give enough back to us to make up for the air they breathe or the food they eat.

"They might say what goes on in the capital, but they don't speak for anybody else. Hell, I doubt anyone outside the capital pays them even the slightest bit of mind."

Diana made sure that no one could see the smile on her face. Damn, the man knew how to tear somebody up. She made a mental note of some of his colloquialisms. She didn't know what they meant, but she was going to look them up. Two hoots or a holler indeed.

"I'm sorry you feel that way," Van Buren said. "Unfortunately, under Imperial law, we don't require your permission to be here, though, of course, we'll do everything we can to properly compensate you for our presence.

"We dislike intruding on you, but we've got a job to do, and we don't know that we can trust the corporations enough to set up anywhere they have control."

Diana risked a look over at the newcomer and saw that he had his hands on his hips and was scowling at their commanding officer. If he was the slightest bit intimidated, it didn't show.

"That's pretty much the first thing you've said that I agree with," their visitor said. "Those corporate bastards are a bunch of mealy-mouthed, weaselly sons of bitches. They'll tell you something to your face when everyone knows they mean something else. If they can trick you with a contract, they'll do it just to make enough money to pay for lunch. They'd lie when the truth would serve them better.

"I have to say I suspect why you're here. It makes me sick to my stomach to see those people call in the Imperial Marines to put their boots on the necks of the good people of this planet."

"That's not why we're here, Mister Lindbergh," Van Buren said seriously. "We're here to get to the bottom of the matter, and if it turns out to be the corporations causing the problems, they'll get the negative attention.

"Think of us like a damper rod inside an old-style nuclear reactor. We're just going to calm things down a bit to keep people from doing things that they might regret later."

"Those are pretty words, but actions speak louder. I can't say I know very much about what might be causing the corporations trouble, but they probably deserve it. They don't treat the people here right.

"And speaking of treating people right, we need to come to some kind of agreement because I'm not just going to let you tear up my property and squat here for God only knows how long for free. What do you say about that, Mister marine Lieutenant?"

"We're going to fairly compensate you for the inconvenience of having us here, but we'll be here until the problem is solved," Van Buren said firmly. "There's nothing you can do about that, and I'd rather not have that be a bone of contention between us.

"If I'd had any trust in the corporations, I'd have asked them who owned this property before we arrived and tried to come to an agreement ahead of time, but for the same reasons you've stated, I decided it was better to beg forgiveness than ask permission.

"In exchange for that, I'll pay the highest rate of compensation I can. We'll also pay for any actual damages and make sure that the property is restored as close to its original condition as we can before we're gone.

"I won't ask you if that's okay with you because honestly, you don't have much of a choice."

Diana could see the man didn't particularly like being dictated to because he crossed his arms over his chest and scowled at the marine officer.

While he mulled over what her commanding officer had said, she searched her databases for any information about him. What she found was shocking.

Craig Lindbergh was the descendant of a very prominent family —perhaps the most prominent family on the planet. When he'd said he owned the land they were on, he was severely understating the situation. He personally owned over five hundred square kilometers of land. His extended family owned adjoining property that more than quadrupled that.

While she could imagine how large an area like that was intellectually, the reality boggled her mind. How could one person own enough land to build a metropolis on? He personally had to be worth more money than the smaller of the two corporations that ran the planet.

And there was no way she could warn her commanding officer of that.

"Why don't you lay out exactly how much money we're talking about," Lindbergh said at last. "This is one of my best grazing fields, and under other circumstances, I'd have about five thousand head of cattle here in about a month. I'm going to make a wager you'd be pretty pissed if I set my cows loose in my own fields, wouldn't you?"

"Just about as angry as you'd be if I shot any that got too close to our perimeter," Van Buren agreed. "I think we can both avoid provocative behavior if we really try, Mister Lindbergh. I'll add that to the amount we're paying to compensate for the inconvenience.

"I presume you got other fields that you can put these creatures in because this one is definitely off-limits."

"I have one or two," Lindbergh allowed.

Talk about the understatement of the century.

To her amusement, the men then got down to bargaining. She'd never seen this kind of haggling before, but it was evident Lindbergh was no stranger to striking a deal. He fought as if the Imperial Marines were taking bread from the mouths of his starving family.

Another check showed he wasn't married. Talk about an eligible bachelor.

After a few minutes, a price was agreed to, and the men shook. Apparently, that was all it took, although Van Buren assured Lindbergh that he'd have a signed contract in his hands stating precisely what they agreed to tomorrow and that he'd pay up as soon as he got the man's banking information.

"Since you care so much about how the corporations are

maligning the people on your world, I wonder if I might ask you to assist us in our investigation?" Van Buren asked. "We'd be willing to compensate you for your time, but having someone provide an honest assessment of the people we're dealing with would be extremely helpful and might get us off your property that much faster."

Lindbergh scratched his chin. "I'm a busy man, but sometimes you have to set aside the things you'd like to do for yourself so you can do something for your community. Like I said, I don't know much about what's going on at the mines, but I hear there's some kind of trouble out there.

"I do know a few people at Yi Holdings, and a bigger bunch of snakes you'll never meet. As this would likely cause them great consternation, I'm inclined to accept your offer, but I'm afraid I have a stipulation of my own."

"And what might that be?" Van Buren asked warily.

"I find myself with a powerful thirst for knowledge. As I said to this young man beside me earlier, I don't know anything about the Imperial Marines. Turns out, that lack has bitten me in the ass.

"If I'm going to assist you in this matter, you can provide me with someone from your organization to answer my questions and to get my unvarnished opinion on whatever subject comes to hand."

A peek showed Van Buren nodding. "Asking for a liaison seems reasonable. Sergeant Walker would make a good choice, so I'll go with him."

"No offense to young Sergeant Walker, but he seems a bit set in his ways. Maybe it's just me being ornery, but you're inconveniencing me, so I'm going to select somebody that might be a bit inconvenient for you. Just think of it as me marking my territory, and let's move on, shall we?"

"I'll have to veto anyone that I think is unsuitable, but I'm willing to at least consider your desires. Should we draw lots or just have you wander around until you find someone that strikes your fancy?"

"No need to make things too complicated. Why don't we go with that girl who's been listening in on our conversation? Seems like she's good at keeping her ears open and her mouth shut. She can even bring her friend who's been watching us from the shadows behind her, so she's got company."

Diana looked over with a sinking stomach. Lindbergh was staring straight at her, as were Lieutenant Van Buren and Gunnery Sergeant Singh.

And a scowling Sergeant Walker.

This had gone pear-shaped in a hurry.

"You know, I think I can live with that," Van Buren said with a wry smile. "Private Randall, PFC Tolliver, front and center."

A glance over her shoulder showed a somewhat guilty-looking Andrea coming from around the corner of the headquarters building they were putting up. She hadn't even noticed her friend watching them.

The two trotted over to their commanding officer and braced to attention.

"I want the two of you ready to depart as soon as possible," the lieutenant said. "You'll accompany Mister Lindbergh. Whatever he's doing, I want you at his side, barring him shutting the door in your faces.

"We'll be heading to see the corporate government in the relatively near future, but it'll take a while to arrange the details. Until then, learn what you can and answer his questions as completely and truthfully as possible, leaving out classified or confidential material. Don't embarrass us."

"Yes, sir," they both said.

It only took one glance at the gunnery sergeant to realize she wasn't pleased with this turn of events because her eyes were narrowed. "Let me stress that you represent the Imperial Marines, privates. I expect you to perform this task thoroughly and well. If you don't, the three of us are going to have words."

Based on Walker's glare, he had a similar feeling. Well, this had turned ugly fast, and things could always get worse.

To make matters worse, Reed appeared at their sides from nowhere. "Tolliver, Randall, you're with me."

And just like that, the situation had gotten even worse.

12

Andrea followed Reed and Diana, not quite certain how she'd gotten caught up in everything. She hadn't been there for the start of the conversation between their commanding officer and the tall stranger, and she'd only been trying to figure out what was happening.

Somehow, this Mister Lindbergh had pulled Diana into whatever was happening, and now she'd been taken along for the ride. Not that she expected her innocence to save her in the end. Not with how pissed Reed looked.

The NCO took them to where their gear was stacked, waiting for the barracks to be assembled, then she turned on them, glaring.

"What the hell were you two thinking?"

"I didn't say anything, Corporal," Diana objected. "I was working, but they were talking right next to me. I couldn't help overhearing what they were saying."

"You were obvious enough about it that the man called you out," Reed countered. "That tells me that you aren't nearly as subtle as you think you are, and now I have the unenviable task of letting you and Tolliver represent Delta Company.

"And don't think I've forgotten you, either, Tolliver. Neither one of you is as clever as you think you are, and if you think I'm a bad person to have on your case, just imagine how deeply you're going to regret having Walker come down on you. Which he will."

"Corporal, that guy was looking to do something Lieutenant Van Buren didn't appreciate, and we happened to be handy," Andrea interjected. "If we hadn't been there, he'd have picked some random people. For all we know, that's exactly what he did."

The other woman looked like she wanted to argue, but instead, she sighed. "You might be right, but that doesn't change the seriousness of the situation. We don't know this man, and you two will be spending time with him away from the company.

"I want to get frequent updates on your status. Not necessarily about what you're doing or what you're saying but that you're okay and that the situation seems normal."

"Any time you change locations, I want to get a ping with your new location as soon as possible. You'll have your issue coms, and we'll have a drone in range to pick up your signal. If we have to extract you, we need to know where you are at all times."

She rubbed her face with her hands. "Honestly, this might be for the best. We needed a non-combat duty for you, though I don't like the idea of you being unsupervised. Gather your gear.

"You'll keep your sidearms but turn in your rifles to the armorer. You're not to use your weapons unless there's an extremely good reason, and if you lose one, you'll wish you'd been killed in an antimatter explosion."

The saying was a general threat in the marines, but Andrea vividly remembered the video of Anne Marie Scott—one of the marines on the raid where they'd rescued Andrea—being killed in a plasma grenade explosion. It had left nothing of her to bring home.

A sad and somber thing but part of the debt she'd joined the Imperial Marines to repay.

It only took a couple of minutes to find their packs and get their gear. After all, it wasn't as if they'd had an opportunity to unpack. In this case, all they had to do was slip their packs on, and they were ready to go.

Sergeant Sherman had set up a temporary armory near the

headquarters building and took their weapons without even his usual sarcasm.

Once that was done, Diana turned to Reed. "How are we getting to wherever we're going, Corporal?"

"If need be, we'll transport you, but I'd imagine Mister Lindbergh wouldn't have asked for two people to accompany him without some means of transporting them himself. Let's go find out what he has to say."

The three of them returned to the headquarters building, which actually had a roof now. The speed at which the marines could assemble these prefabricated structures was awe-inspiring. The camp really would be fully operational by dawn.

Lindbergh and Van Buren were still talking. Singh and Walker were gone. They were probably talking over the situation the squad leader would now be overseeing.

It was unfortunate that she'd gotten caught up in this because Andrea knew Walker already had it in for her. She knew it was just one more instance of her heritage coming back to haunt her. Only now, Walker had a valid reason to be pissed.

The men stopped their conversation as Andrea and Diana approached, and Lindbergh raised an eyebrow. "Do you think you've packed enough for a few days?"

"They're taking everything they might need in case something unexpected occurs," Van Buren said before they could respond. "You've been civil enough, and I do appreciate you giving me your identification so that I could verify your identity, but we don't really know you.

"I expect you to take care of them, but if there's trouble, rest assured that Randall and Tolliver can deal with it. They'll be on their best behavior, but I expect you to be a good host as well."

"We take hospitality seriously on Diorama, Senior Lieutenant," the tall man said evenly. "I've given my word that they'll come to no harm, and that's the way it'll be. When this is over, they'll be back with you without a scratch on them if I have anything to say about it."

"Good enough." Van Buren turned his attention to Andrea and Diana. "You two are representing Delta Company, and I expect you to keep that in mind at all times. Stay focused on your mission, and don't embarrass the Corps.

"It's your job to make sure we get information about the local situation. Talk to whoever you can and figure out exactly what's going on. Everything you hear is a rumor until it's proven, but the more we know, the better questions I can ask the corporations and miners when we get to the mining site.

"On the flip side, Mister Lindbergh is going to have questions about the marines, about yourselves, and about the situation as it pertains to our mission here. Unless something is classified, I expect you to be fully forthcoming. Is that clear?"

"Very clear, sir," Andrea said at the same time as her friend indicated her understanding.

Van Buren turned back toward Lindbergh. "Will you be able to transport them?"

"I can strap those packs to my skidder, and the two of them can ride behind me."

Andrea had no idea what a skidder was, and she was looking forward to finding out.

"Very well," Van Buren said. "I'll want updates in the morning, midday, and evening. Get what information you can on the corporations and their management in the morning, and send it to Sergeant Walker. I'll keep him with me when I head to the capital tomorrow."

"Yes, sir," Diana said. "We won't let you down."

"See that you don't. Dismissed."

Van Buren and Lindbergh shook hands, and the tall civilian headed out of the camp. The sun was down now, and the man pulled a flashlight off of his belt to illuminate their path.

"I won't say that I'm sorry I pulled you two into this, ladies, but I recognize this situation is none of your doing, and I promise to be a good host," Lindbergh said as they walked. "I suspect we'll get along fine.

"I know a fair bit about the corporations and the people running them, and I'll see that you get that information in the morning. I also have some people working at the ranch that might be able to share some insights about the mines."

"You'll find us good guests, Mister Lindbergh," Diana said.

"I think it's rude to call people by their last names, so I'd prefer it if you'd call me Craig."

"I'm Diana, and this is Andrea."

The man nodded and partly turned his attention to Andrea while keeping an eye on the dark ground. "When I saw you looking at us from around the corner, I noticed you had something on your face. I'll confess that's why I added you to this little round-up. I imagine you get asked about those tattoos quite a bit, but forgive my curiosity."

"Everybody stares at them, so you're not alone," Andrea said. "The whole story would take too much time, but the short version is that I'm a refugee from the Singularity. I'm an Imperial citizen now, but because of the techniques that were used to put them on me, I can't get them off."

"Can't say I know much about the Singularity, other than what I suppose everyone does, but I'm going to give you a bit of unsought advice. Based on your tone, you wish you could get rid of those tattoos. I'd imagine they've caused you quite a bit of grief.

"Here on Diorama, we're different than most people in the Empire, and we're not ashamed of where we came from or how we live our lives. That's partly us being ornery, but we don't let other people tell us how to live our lives."

He used the beam of light from his flashlight to illuminate a long, slender vehicle parked near an emplacement as they walked. That must be the skidder. She could see why it had that name.

"Never apologize for being who you are," he continued. "If someone has a problem with it, then they'll have to deal with it. It's their problem, not yours.

"My thought is that those tattoos are like scars. It sounds like you've earned them. Sometimes we need to be proud of our scars because they make us who we are. In some ways, they make us strong. Embrace that."

Andrea wasn't sure how to respond. Over the years, a lot of people had accused her of keeping the tattoos to rub her personal history in their faces. It sounded as if this man was saying that was what she *should* be doing.

It was a novel idea if nothing else.

The three of them stopped next to the skidder. Campbell waved but didn't get out of the trench. They'd obviously been briefed about what was going on.

"We can secure your packs at the rear on the right and left. These hooks have latches to make sure whatever's clipped in place can't come loose. They're meant for pulling and lifting things.

"There are two seats behind mine, and you can cinch a strap around your waist to make sure you stay on. It has stirrups, so if you've ever ridden a horse, it's not such a strange thing.

"There's an air shield, so it'll keep things relatively placid around us as we go. You won't have to worry about windchill or anything like that."

They secured their packs and mounted the skidder as he directed. He oversaw them cinching themselves down to the vehicle, and when he was satisfied, he climbed on in front of them and brought the vehicle to life.

Moments later, he picked it up off the ground and turned them around to head away from Camp Pyramid. They flew over the dark forest, and in just a couple of minutes, she couldn't see anything behind her.

It looked as if they were over completely unoccupied wilderness, much like places where she'd gone camping as a girl. This place seemed to have no human occupation.

Andrea wasn't sure what the population density was here in the wilds of Diorama, but it couldn't have been that high. She considered pinging Diana and asking for more details but decided that information could wait. The situation was what it was, and she might as well enjoy the ride.

And it was an enjoyable ride. She'd never ridden a grav vehicle like this, and it was completely different than flying inside an enclosed air car. It felt like she was part of the world around her.

It was a bit thrilling, and she wondered if she could learn to fly one.

She expected the trip to only take a few minutes, but they just kept flying. Ten minutes turned into twenty, which then turned into thirty. The planet's large moon rose into the sky, illuminating the landscape in a pale light. Where the hell were they going?

"I thought we were on your property," she said to Lindbergh, speaking loudly enough to be heard over the wind that made it through the air shield.

"We are. Don't worry, we're almost there. It's on the other side of that hill in front of us."

The tree-covered hill was too small to be a mountain but looked as if it would be one hell of a climb. Lindbergh took the skidder over it and revealed a surprise on the other side.

Spread out before them was an enormous, brightly lit ranch. Building after building covered a wide valley, and she saw a seemingly endless number of huge corrals, some holding cattle and others empty.

The scope of the operation blew her away. This wasn't some simple ranch. This was a massive operation, and there were probably hundreds of people working below.

They flew over the corrals and landed in front of what had to be the most elaborate ranch house Andrea had ever seen. It was breathtaking.

She'd grown up in a mansion. It wasn't that Grace, Fei, and Kayden had wanted something like that, but as a noble of the Empire, that was what the Duke had insisted Grace have. And it helped that there had already been one on the land he'd given her as part of her fief.

This house, though plainer, was *significantly* larger. It was wide and deep, holding uncountable rooms, she was sure. It also looked old but very well maintained. It had been here a long time.

Lindbergh stepped off the skidder and started helping them undo the cinches around their waists. "Welcome to the Big L Ranch, ladies. Grab your gear, and we'll get you inside. I'm going to assume you want adjoining rooms, and that's easy enough to arrange.

"By now, dinner has already been served for the hands, but I'd reckon we can get something whipped up for you. We can get to know one another while we eat."

Andrea had assumed Craig was a small landholder, but that was obviously not the case. There was more going on here than met the eye. A lot more.

The front door to the massive house swung open, and a woman with pale-red hair, wearing an apron, came out. "You should've called and told us we were having guests, Craig. Now I'm going to have to scramble to get a couple of rooms set up and get dinner on the table for you three."

"Diana, Andrea, this is my sister Rebecca. Rebecca, these young ladies will be with us a bit. I'll explain more while we eat."

Andrea hefted her pack and followed everyone into the house. This was absolutely not what she'd been expecting on her first deployment, but it looked as if it was going to be interesting.

13

Once they were relieved of their early evening watch, Jerome found a place near his squad to catch what sleep he could. He figured the odds were good that he was going to be up before dawn, and he'd need every advantage he could get.

His guess proved only too accurate.

Lieutenant Van Buren shook him awake almost an hour before dawn. At least he'd brought coffee. Jerome had slept in his uniform, ready for any problems that popped up, so getting up was as simple as taking the proffered coffee.

Breakfast consisted of a ration bar while the lieutenant laid out his plan. "Last night, I thought flying into the capital was the best idea, but after talking with the platoon leaders, I think it might be better if we lift off just after dawn and make our way in without giving them any advance notice that we're coming.

"They have mass transit to get from city to city, though it's as sparse as one might imagine. We can make our way to where one of those lines comes about a hundred kilometers east of Camp Pyramid and board a high-speed grav train full of cattle without anyone knowing who we are or what we're doing. I checked, and they do have passenger cars."

Jerome took a moment to look down at his uniform. "I think I might see a flaw with your plan, sir."

The man grinned. "Well, maybe they'll know who we are at the train stop, but unless somebody has an eye out for us, they're not going to receive a heads-up that we're on our way to the capital. We'll pick up some local clothing so that we fit in more naturally before we board the train."

"Why are we sneaking around, sir? Shouldn't we'd prefer them to know we're coming?"

Van Buren shrugged slightly. "I'd like to hear the kind of talk going on around us. We're coming into the situation blind, and I want to know what the man on the ground thinks.

"We'll get some information from Tolliver and Randall before much longer, but having multiple sources gives us a wider variety of thought. If the miners are acting this way because of actions taken by the corporations, I'd like to know before I start pointing fingers."

Jerome nodded slightly. "You think the miners were provoked, sir?"

"I'm not going to prejudge the situation, but we can't exactly sneak into the mine and ask them. One step at a time, Sergeant. Turn your rifle in and leave most of your gear here. We'll travel light."

"Yes, sir."

Once the lieutenant was gone, Jerome packed his gear into his bag and briefed his fire team leaders. They'd be able to handle everything in his absence, but he didn't like leaving them alone. They were his responsibility.

Once he'd turned his weapon in, he met a small party of marines near one of the pinnaces. It looked like the lieutenant wasn't going in with many people. In fact, once he saw who the individuals were, he realized that it was just the two of them and the flight crew.

Going in without support seemed risky, and he was about to caution his commanding officer that that wasn't a good idea when he stopped himself. This wasn't his business. Lieutenant Van Buren had made up his mind, so it was his job to keep the officer safe while whatever was going on happened.

How dangerous could it be anyway? It wasn't like they were

assaulting an enemy position. They were going into the city to have talks with senior management at two corporations. Corporations that had requested their presence on the planet, so odds were they wanted to make a good impression.

Once the lieutenant, the flight crew, and he had boarded the pinnace, everyone strapped in, and they made the quick flight to the small town nearest the train line. Being the experienced noncommissioned officer that he was, Jerome went to sleep as soon as they took off and only woke when the pinnace set down.

He blinked to clear his vision, unstrapped from his seat, and rose, shadowing Lieutenant Van Buren as he exited the pinnace. They were in a field next to a cleared, flattened zone that stretched from horizon to horizon across from a small, very rural town.

The path allowed a grav train to reach high speeds without worrying about running into anything. Because it utilized gravitic technology, it didn't need to touch the ground and flew above anything crossing the tracks. They were called tracks because trains had once used metal rails, and the name had stuck.

When the train was in motion, it traveled about five meters above the ground, more than high enough to miss any idiots that happened to be walking along the tracks or any animals that were crossing as they passed.

That wasn't to say that the shock wave from the high-speed passage wouldn't scare the crap out of them or cause minor injuries. If someone was stupid enough to walk along the tracks, they deserved what they got.

As soon as they were out of the pinnace, it retracted its ramp and turned to fly back the way it had come at low altitude. That should keep it off the flight control scanners, since they were made to be difficult to detect under the best of circumstances.

The town seemed like a reasonably sleepy place. There were people up and about and vehicles in motion, but it wasn't anywhere near what a person would see in a bigger city.

The roads were wide—wider than he'd have expected. Even with a few large cargo vehicles making runs this early, he couldn't imagine why.

There'd be a reason, though. People didn't make changes like this without a purpose.

"Let's get a move on, Walker," Van Buren said briskly. "No doubt the locals will be curious about what we're doing and where we came from, but let me do the talking, and I'll put them off. As long as we hold off getting tickets to the capital until after we get civilian clothes, word won't get to where we're going that a couple of Imperial Marines are on the way."

And with that, the officer began walking toward the town.

Jerome still wasn't sure this was a great idea, but it wasn't as if he had much choice. He checked his implant coms, but there weren't any reports from Tolliver or Randall at this point.

Depending on how long it took them to get any actionable intelligence, all he might get at first were simple messages that everything was going as planned.

He set up a warning to let him know when a report came in so that he could check it at once. He needed to stay on top of what the greenies were doing.

It really annoyed him that they were off doing things outside of his supervision because leaving greenies on their own was a recipe for disaster. At least they hadn't taken Baker with them. One day, the boy would make a good marine, but he was as subtle as a falling brick.

His secondary mission of figuring out whether Tolliver posed a threat was almost impossible under these circumstances. That wasn't going to please Bashir, but that couldn't be helped either.

This situation just kept getting more complicated. They'd only just arrived on Diorama, and things were probably going to get worse before they got better. Jerome grumbled wordlessly to himself and trudged after the officer. Whatever came up, he'd deal with it.

* * *

DIANA AWOKE EARLY, her implant alarm pinging. She rose from the overly large yet very comfortable bed she'd slept in and stretched before heading toward the bathroom. It, too, was large, though not exceptionally ornate.

Just like the house itself, her room was rustic. It wasn't meant to convey the impression of advanced technology or recent construction. Everything was functional, though crafted in a way that made it beautiful to her eye.

The floors, ceiling, walls, and furnishings were made of carved or planed wood, varnished until it glowed with an almost ethereal golden sheen. The outer wall was made of logs that were nearly as big around as she could reach with both arms.

It was homey, though she'd never seen anything like it. It was as if she was staying in a specialty lodge, like where people went skiing in the mountains. Everything was meant to convey a theme.

If she had time, she'd have to see if she could take a tour of the entire building. She suspected that the oldest portions had been built back when the ranch was initially founded and expanded upon as their needs grew.

The fact they needed so much space in the main house—not to mention all the outbuildings where the hands probably stayed—meant that this ranch likely had thousands of people living and working here.

She took a quick shower and was about to get a fresh uniform when she noticed there were clothes hanging on the back of the door. Someone must've slipped them into her room while she'd been in the shower.

Diana considered whether she should wear civilian clothes rather than her uniform and decided that it would be more polite to dress in the manner her hosts obviously expected, though she'd have to make some additions to carry out her duties.

The clothes were very much in line with what she'd seen Craig Lindbergh wearing yesterday. They were primarily blue, seemingly made to stand up to being worked in, and very functional. She noted with approval that the clothes had pants rather than a skirt.

Diana liked skirts and dresses, but having pants to protect her legs was almost a requirement in this environment. Giving her clothing like this was a sign of respect, and she appreciated it.

Someone had made excellent estimates of her sizes because the clothes fit. When she'd dressed, she saw a pair of boots beside the door. They were dark brown, relatively narrow, and came to a pointed end, just as Craig's had.

She suspected they were made this way to more easily work with stirrups. Rounded toes would be more challenging to fit into stirrups if someone was in a hurry, whereas something like this would slide right in. Once again, function trumped form.

The boots fit, too, so she wondered if someone had come into her room while she was in the shower, checked her marine-issue boots, and then left boots sized for her. If so, she appreciated the courtesy.

She went to the bedside table and picked up her holstered flechette pistol and stunner. They weren't made to be concealed like Andrea's tiny little weapons, so she'd just have to accept they'd be on display for anyone that cared to look.

If they didn't like it, tough. She was an Imperial Marine and on duty.

Diana put her flechette pistol on her right-hand side and her stunner on her left in a cross-draw configuration. That meant she had the choice of which weapon to go for with her dominant hand, but the way the weapons were situated meant she could grab either with her off hand, even if it was a bit awkward, and get it deployed.

She put her spare magazines on the belt near the appropriate weapons and stepped into the hallway. From the sounds coming from downstairs, breakfast was already underway.

Just a couple of steps brought her to Andrea's door, where she knocked. When her friend called for her to come in, she opened the door and stepped inside.

She found Andrea just pulling her boots on. Her clothing was similar to Diana's, if slightly darker in tone. Her friend looked good, though her tattoos kind of clashed with the cowgirl image.

"They're already eating," she said. "We should get a move on."

Andrea stood and double-checked her weapons. She had them in the same configuration as Diana, except her stunner wasn't in a cross-draw position. If needed, she could draw it with her left hand. One of the benefits of being ambidextrous.

Together, they went to the wide wooden staircase and took it down to the main floor. The noise was coming from the left-hand side, so they made their way in that direction. That brought them to a large dining room that held a long wooden table with roughly forty people seated around it.

There were platters, plates, and bowls everywhere, and it seemed that everyone was talking. They were chatting with the people next to them and making comments to the people across from them. Everything seemed so cheerful.

Craig Lindbergh rose from his seat at the head of the table and gestured for them to come over. She saw that he had seats open on his right and left sides.

When they reached him, he put two fingers in his mouth and blew one of the most piercing whistles that Diana had ever heard. That killed the conversation almost instantly.

"Listen up, you yahoos. These two are our guests, and you'll extend them every courtesy. Both of them are Imperial Marines, so mind your manners, or they might break your ugly faces. That's the boys. You ladies have pretty faces, but they might break those, too, if you push them. You will note they're armed, so be polite."

A wave of chuckles went down the table, and Diana noted that roughly two-thirds of the diners were male. All of them were dressed similarly to her, so she was definitely picking up on a theme. These were work clothes, and these were working people.

"On my right is Diana Randall, and on my left is Andrea Tolliver. I'll say this one time, and I expect you to pass the word along to your people in the strongest of terms. I don't know of anybody that might have a problem with someone coming from the Singularity, but that's what her tattoos mean.

"If someone has a problem, I expect them to speak up, and we'll send them to work in one of the outbuildings today. There's not going to be any trouble because if there is, I'll take a personal interest in making sure that the matter is settled. Is that clear?"

Craig sounded like Lieutenant Van Buren when he was making a point. He was in command, and he said how things would be.

"I don't think you'll have much trouble," Rebecca said from the tail end of the table, where she occupied the end seat like Craig. "Not many of our people would've ever had contact with anyone from the

Singularity, and everyone respects you, Craig. That girl will get a fair shake here."

"That's just what I'd expect. Ladies, if you'll take your seats, you're a couple of minutes behind, and you're going to need to pack away some calories expeditiously. Today's going to be a busy day. I'll be happy to tell you everything I know, but we'll be doing it on the move."

Diana sat, feeling a little self-conscious at being the center of attention, but quickly found herself digging into the delicious food. Whatever came today, she'd make sure she was well stoked to deal with it.

A glance at her friend showed that she was feeling more self-conscious. Apparently, having her tattoos called out in front of a room full of people was a new experience for her.

Well, she'd have to get used to it eventually, so she might as well start now.

14

A ndrea hadn't expected Craig to mention her tattoos quite so publicly, but on reflection, he seemed like a direct guy, and it made sense for his personality. Everyone around the table snuck a look at one point or another, and it was hard to focus on the food rather than the attention.

Luckily for her, she loved breakfast, and this meal had all the things she liked most about her favorite meal. Plenty of bacon, pancakes, eggs fixed just the way she liked them and coffee by the gallon. There was even orange juice. Who could ask for more?

There were new foods that she'd have to consider too. Grits, for example. The jury was still out on them, but they weren't terrible.

She focused her attention on the meal and stuffed food into her face. When the pancakes were gone, she reached for the biscuits and buttered two of them. They were flaky, moist, and delicious. She'd just added a new favorite item to her fantasy breakfast list.

"This might be none of my business, but you sure can pack it away for such a little thing," Craig said just loudly enough to be heard over the constant roar of conversation. "How in the world can you keep a decent figure when you eat so much?"

Well, the lieutenant had said to be forthcoming.

She took a drink of the surprisingly excellent coffee to clear her mouth and looked up at the man. "Most people don't realize it, but anyone from the Singularity with these tattoos is from a specialized line. Either warriors or managers at the upper-middle end of the spectrum and higher.

"I was created from an optimized DNA template that had been cleaned out of things the designers thought undesirable. I don't know much about DNA, but while mine is *based* on human DNA, it's been enhanced in a number of ways."

The man's eyes narrowed just the slightest bit, but he nodded. "Such as?"

"My metabolism runs hotter than just about anybody else I've ever met. My muscles are about fifty percent denser too. Odds are good that I'm stronger than anybody at this table, no matter our relative sizes or gender. And my nerves operate faster too.

"Those are just a few examples of the Singularity's alterations to people like me. I've got to put away a lot of calories to feed some of those modifications, and perhaps one of the only benefits is that I get to keep my girlish figure."

That was something of a joke, considering her figure ran more toward the boyish than the girlish. She'd developed breasts, but they were nothing to write home about. Neither were her hips. No hourglass figure for her.

Of course, she'd grown up with Keeper as a living example of *exactly* what she'd look like as an adult. In just a few more years, the transformation would be complete, and she'd look precisely like every other adult of the Andrea Line.

Which was depressing.

"I see," Craig said. "Well, don't eat so fast that you choke. We can take a few extra minutes to make sure you get enough."

Andrea took advantage of that, lowered her head back to the proverbial trough, and continued devouring the delicious food while Craig talked with Diana. She listened with half an ear to their conversation and several others.

Her enhanced hearing and faster neural processing meant that she could discern individual threads, figure out who was talking to whom without looking, and segregate those discussions in her mind so that she could generally follow along with maybe half a dozen different conversations simultaneously.

The process wasn't easy, but it wasn't impossible either. She hadn't realized she could do something like that until she'd arrived at basic training, listening to other people talk in the mess hall. Why the Singularity wanted their people to be able to do this, she didn't know. Perhaps it was only a side effect of something else. It wasn't as if she could ask anyone.

Most people were done eating and heading out within ten minutes, either individually or in small groups. Five minutes after the exodus had begun, only Craig, Rebecca, Diana, and herself were left.

Andrea was down to just a few things on her plate, so she sped up, cleaning it off and drinking down the last of her coffee.

That had been some really good coffee.

She used her napkin to make sure she hadn't splattered food all over her face and then stood. Craig was still talking with Diana about horse riding, which it seemed her friend had some experience in, so Rebecca stepped over to her with a smile.

"It wasn't easy for me to see from the other end of the table, but I think you might've enjoyed breakfast. I'm glad that you liked my cooking."

Andrea looked at the remnants of food set out for over three dozen people and raised an eyebrow. "You cooked this all by yourself? What time did you get up? Hell, did you even sleep?"

The other woman laughed. "I do have help, but I was up about two hours ago. Things happen early on a ranch, and there's always somebody needing food somewhere. Eating breakfast every morning with the various supervisors makes sure Craig and they stay on the same page.

"To change the subject, I realize it's none of my business, but I wanted to ask why you keep your tattoos so visible when it's obvious they make you uncomfortable," Rebecca said quietly. "If you don't want to talk about it, just say so. Craig is about to leave and take you girls to see what the operation looks like, so we can't talk about it in detail now in any case."

Andrea sighed and quickly explained how the tattoos were linked to her DNA, and they couldn't be removed. It was a story that she told enough times that the words just fell out of her mouth in the right order. She didn't have to think about them anymore.

Rebecca crossed her arms and frowned slightly. "I can understand that, but what about covering them?"

"Covering them? With what?"

"What do you know about makeup? I see that you're not wearing any, but that doesn't necessarily mean you're ignorant about the use of it, and I don't want to make an assumption."

Andrea shrugged. "I never really saw much point in makeup. If I did anything with my lashes, no one would notice because of the tattoos. People rarely see my face because of what's on it."

"What if you could use makeup to cover the tattoos in such a way that it left your skin the way it would've looked without them? Maybe that's not something that appeals to you, but perhaps there are times where you'd like to go somewhere and do something without having them be the center of attention. You do realize that's possible, right?"

Andrea blinked at the woman. She heard her words, but they didn't seem to make any sense. "What?"

Rebecca smiled. "Craig is about ready to head out, so why don't we talk about this when you get back for lunch? Like I said, I'm not suggesting this because I think you should cover them up all the time, but there might be moments in your life where you'd prefer to be seen without them. I'll do some research to make sure, but with modern technology working inside the makeup, that's not out of the question."

Andrea tried to say something in response, but her brain couldn't seem to formulate a complete thought. She'd gone through the painful process of having the tattoos removed after she'd arrived on DeSantis, only to have them come back within a few months. With them gone, she'd felt euphoric. Learning she'd had no choice in the matter had been crushing.

Grace wasn't one to wear makeup, and maybe that was why the suggestion had never come up. She was an adult now. Did she really want to hide who she was? Or was that falling into a trap in which the tattoos defined her?

She'd have to think about this, but she already knew she'd try it if the other woman came up with a solution. Just once, she'd like to see what her options were.

It would make her life much easier if everyone wasn't judging her because of the tattoos, but she didn't want to set aside something that made her who she was.

What to do? That was always the question, wasn't it?

"If you're ready, we can head on out," Craig said. "It's going to be a mite chilly this morning, so we'll grab a couple of jackets at the front door, and I'll give you a tour of what we do here at the Big L Ranch."

"Thank you for your offer, and I think I'll take you up on it," Andrea told Rebecca. "I'm going to have to think about whether it's something I'd want to do long term, but I really appreciate your help."

The woman pulled her into a brief hug and then released her. "It's my pleasure. Now, I want you to be very careful not to fall off any horses. My brother is well known for not taking people's riding skills into account."

Craig rolled his eyes. "One time, and I'm marked for life. I promise I'm not going to put anybody on a horse they can't ride. Do you have any skill in the saddle, Andrea?"

"I've *seen* horses. At a distance."

He chuckled and smiled. "Then we'll find you somebody gentle and get you trained up right quick. Come on, ladies, the cattle wait on no one."

And with that, he headed for the door, and Andrea fell in beside Diana in his wake. This should be interesting.

* * *

JEROME STEPPED out of the clothier's shop, looked up and down the street, and felt utterly ridiculous. He'd swapped his marine uniform for something that looked like it belonged on a trail ride. The clothes were called western style, though he didn't really understand what that meant. West of what?

The worst part had to be the boots. They rubbed his feet

differently than his marine-issue boots, and that was going to take some getting used to. Still, if he thought he looked bad, the lieutenant looked worse.

Somehow, the officer had let the shop owner talk him into a huge hat and belt buckle to go along with his outfit. He didn't look like he was on a trail ride. No. He looked like a tourist enthusiastically *thinking* about taking a trail ride.

Jerome had tried to talk Van Buren out of going that far, but he'd been unsuccessful. He'd even pointed out that the hat the man had chosen was fifty percent larger than any other hat they'd seen with no success.

Frankly, he was almost convinced they were getting just as much attention from people passing on the street as if they'd stayed in uniform. Maybe more.

Just as he'd been telling himself for most of his adult life, this was one more thing he couldn't control. Officers would do what they wanted, and you couldn't talk common sense to them. Sadly, this time he wasn't sure how he could mitigate the situation either.

About the best he could hope for was that when word arrived in the capital that strangers might be coming, they wouldn't be associated with the marines but some lost tour group.

Jerome hefted his new bag over his shoulder and followed the officer back to the small station serving the train line. They'd checked and still had a few minutes until the next train arrived.

Getting tickets was as simple as declaring their destination, paying, taking the printouts, and having a seat to wait for the train. For once, something went right, and it came in pretty much precisely on schedule.

A loud whistle in the distance announced its approach, and Jerome watched as the long series of interlinked cars lowered down from their standard traveling height and cruised into the station.

The passenger cars were at the front of the train, while the animal cargo was kept to the rear. That made a lot of sense, considering the smell. If the positions had been reversed, the passengers would've had to deal with the stench for the entire trip, whereas the smell of the cattle would be whisked away in transit, leaving the passengers unbothered.

An older gentleman was checking tickets as the few new passengers boarded, and all it took was presenting the printouts to him, and they were welcomed aboard. He'd expected there to be some kind of weapon scan, but there obviously wasn't, since no alarms rang when he crossed into the car.

They'd taken the precaution of putting their weapons into his bag so that they didn't draw unwanted attention. Well, *more* unwanted attention, considering the looks the LT was getting. Getting the weapons out in an emergency might be a little dicey, but they didn't anticipate fighting on this scouting mission. He only hoped that assumption wouldn't bite them on the ass.

There were three passenger cars linked together just behind the grav locomotives. The passageways between each were open, and the seating was left to the passenger.

He'd expected the cars to be almost empty, but the seats were almost half-full. It seemed that a lot of people were making a trip to the capital. Out here in the wilds of the planet, he'd expected to see more men than women, but the opposite was actually true. The passenger ratio was about sixty percent female.

However, that didn't mean they were dressed any differently than the men. Surprisingly, the kind of clothing most of them wore was virtually identical to what he was wearing. He'd thought he'd been turned into a caricature, but in fact, the clothier had been telling him the flat-out truth the entire time.

Well, there was a first time for everything, he supposed.

Of course, *nobody* in the train was wearing a hat anywhere near as large as Lieutenant Van Buren's, and that shiny belt buckle the size of a dinner plate really did stand out—and not in a good way.

The officer was drawing a lot of stares as they walked and more than a few chuckles. If that bothered him, it didn't show. In fact, there was no evidence that he was even aware of the ridicule, which made no sense because the lieutenant was a very savvy guy.

After passing through the rearmost passenger cars, they arrived in the front one, which was, in fact, a dining car with seating so people could eat and drink while watching the scenery go by.

This was for people who wanted a little socialization. That made it perfect for them because they'd have more options in an open area like this when it came time to talk to people.

Van Buren chose a relatively large table with a decent view of the town. Someone from the bar came over and dropped off a couple of menus. The selection of food and drink items was limited, but they weren't here for the cuisine.

Since it had been a long time since he'd had a real meal, Jerome ordered breakfast and coffee. Lieutenant Van Buren did the same.

By the time the food was delivered, the train had lifted off the ground and accelerated toward the capital. The compensators were pretty good because while he could feel the motion, it didn't really tug at him that much. That was probably more to protect the cattle than the human passengers.

Within a few minutes, the train was running at full speed and floating high enough off the ground to give a decent view of the scenery blurring past them. Jerome wasn't sure how fast they were moving, but it was a sprightly clip.

The officer wasn't that talkative as he ate, so Jerome tucked into his own meal. Within twenty minutes, all that was left were empty plates and their coffee. Those came with free refills, which was good, since he'd be drinking as much as humanly possible. Coffee was marine fuel, and he needed a recharge.

He was about to ask Van Buren what their plans were when he caught motion out of the corner of his eye and turned his head to see a couple of men approaching their table. They were dressed similarly to everyone else on the train, but something about them set off little alarm bells in Jerome's head.

"What party are you coming from?" one of the men asked, more than a hint of a sneer coloring his voice. "Don't see many hats like that outside costume parties. And why aren't you eating off of that dinner plate around your waist?"

Lieutenant Van Buren simply smiled back at the man. "I thought they looked nice, so I figured I'd pick up a set. It's a great conversation starter, don't you think? Got you over here, didn't it?"

The man seemed less than impressed, and his friend leaned forward just the slightest bit. "Are you trying to make fun of us? I don't know who you are or where you come from, but some things in life leave a lasting mark. If you think you're going to make fun of the people around here, it's going to be a painful lesson."

"I'm not looking for a fight," Van Buren said easily. "Remember, you came over here to make fun of me, not the other way around. Why don't you boys sit down, and I'll tell you who we are?"

Jerome half expected the man to throw something at his officer's head and was tensing to react when the first man laughed. "Well, I can't say you're wrong. If you buy the coffee, I'll sit down and listen to your story before I decide whether to toss your pretty ass off this train or not."

And just like that, they had their first customers.

15

D iana accepted the jacket Craig offered her, but she didn't think it was really cold enough to warrant it. Still, it wouldn't hurt to have it with her, and it did serve one useful purpose. It covered her weapons, so she looked like the rest of the hands wandering around the ranch in the early-morning light.

As this was something of a frontier area, she was a bit surprised she didn't see more people openly wearing weapons. Some people were armed, but they were the exception rather than the rule.

She suspected there were probably more weapons to be had in an emergency, but they weren't ubiquitous during everyday operations.

Craig led them out of the main house and toward one of the nearest corrals. Unlike the majority of the ones they'd seen flying in, this one had horses in it.

Riding horses suited her fine, and she was looking forward to seeing exactly how Andrea reacted to being put on one of the large beasts. She didn't expect her friend to have much difficulty learning to ride, but the comedy potential was definitely there.

Honestly, she wished Claudio were there too. She suspected he had no experience with horses and would've loved to see him fall on his face. It was small of her, but she could live with that.

The sun was only just barely over the horizon, yet there were people everywhere performing tasks she'd likely never know the reason for. Her guess that the ranch had a lot of people was borne out.

"So, I understand you're going to ask me questions about the situation here on Diorama, but I need to ride out to one of the satellite corrals this morning. This first part will be slower than I'd prefer, but we need to bring Andrea up to speed with walking before taking her up to a trot.

"Ignore everything my sister said because I know better than to give her a horse that's going to cause her problems. I've got a very gentle soul in mind, so you don't need to worry."

"I'm not worried," Andrea said levelly. "I'm a quick learner, and I'm not afraid of them. Whatever I need to do to control one, I'll figure it out."

"I like your spirit," the man said with a smile. "Still, we're not going to make this too challenging. Let's head into the barn and grab saddles, and I'll show you what needs to happen to get your horse ready to travel."

The barn was made out of wood just like the ranch house, but where the living space had been made pretty and smooth, everything here was rough and sturdy. Several saddles sat off to the right-hand side as the group entered the relatively dim space. Beside them were bits, reins, and the rest of the gear for riding, which was collectively called tack.

Craig stepped over, grabbed a saddle, and hefted it on his shoulder. "Grab some tack and a saddle."

Having done this before, Diana grabbed the closest saddle, lifted it to her shoulder, snagged the tack, and watched her friend. Andrea grabbed her tack and saddle a little more clumsily but had no difficulty carrying it. One of the benefits of being freakishly strong.

In the corral, Craig narrowed his eyes and scanned the herd of horses. Diana had always been impressed by the relative intelligence of horses. They might not be able to talk, and they certainly weren't sentient, but they weren't stupid either.

"There she is," the man said with a smile. "See that roan bay off to the right-hand side? Her name is Celia, and she's going to be your ride today, Andrea. She's older and very placid by nature. If you do something wrong with her reins, she'll most likely just ignore you. She knows what to do and how to do it."

Andrea stared at the horses with a look of confusion. "I don't know what those words mean."

"Sorry. Roan means the horse has a pattern of white and reddish-brown hair on the body."

"Okay, I think I see her."

He turned his attention to Diana. "You can take the black mare just off to Celia's right. Her name is Cyclone, but don't let that fool you. She's actually relatively sedate. When she was a colt, she had a lot of fire, but she's mellowed over the years."

And with that, he led the two over to the horses and showed them how to put blankets across their backs and then saddle them. When that was done, he gave them a brief lesson on how to cinch the saddles tight and make sure the horse wasn't holding her breath.

"That's a trick horses will pull on somebody that doesn't know any better, so you'll want to watch for it. Even though the saddle strap doesn't hurt them, they don't like having something constricting them, so they'll hold their breath. That means the saddle ends up loose and can slide to the side, dumping you on the ground."

"Well, that would certainly suck," Andrea said as she eyed the horse warily.

Ten minutes later, with Craig's assistance, they had the horses saddled, the bits in their mouths, and Diana was on her mount, getting a feel for how she moved.

As she'd told Craig, she'd ridden before, so she wasn't going to have trouble as long as they didn't try anything complicated or dangerous. She used her hand to shield her eyes from the sun and tried to figure out which direction they were going to go without success.

Failing that, she turned her attention to watching Craig help Andrea mount and walk her through how to control the horse using her reins. Her friend was frowning in concentration but nodded as each instruction was given and then promptly demonstrated her understanding. Though her seat was terrible, she could maneuver the horse.

Craig nodded in satisfaction. "As your friend can tell you, the first time you ride is going to be less than pleasurable. The muscles in your legs and back aren't going to appreciate being used in ways they've never been stressed before.

"I understand you have advantages in muscle density, but I doubt that's going to save you from feeling stiff and sore when this is all done."

Andrea grinned. "Maybe not, but the medical nanites we have should help. The marines have some that are a grade above what you civilians have access to."

"Lucky you. Let me know how it works out for you in the morning."

"Did you girls forget something?" Rebecca called out from the corral fence. When Diana looked over, she saw the woman holding two hats similar to Craig's. That would certainly be useful in keeping the sun out of her eyes.

Diana carefully maneuvered her horse over to the fence and took both hats, thanking the woman and choosing one at random to stick on her head. It fit well enough, so she handed the other to Andrea.

Her friend looked utterly ridiculous, but Diana wasn't sure she looked any better.

With them finally outfitted, Craig opened the gate so they could walk into the yard. Then he mounted his own horse and slowly led them to an area clear of people where he could continue Andrea's education.

Her friend was picking up the details really well and taking instruction on how to sit much better than Diana had when she'd been a girl. Of course, she'd been mesmerized by the power of the horses and only given the instructor half an ear.

After roughly half an hour of making sure both girls knew enough of the basics to get by, he led them away from the main ranch area and seemingly off in a random direction. There was no sign this was a common path, but then again, there weren't a whole lot of those to be seen either. She suspected the ranch hands made sure they didn't follow predictable paths so the grass didn't get worn down.

"We've got a couple of hours of riding ahead of us, so we've got plenty of time to begin going over the information you need," Craig said. "I'm going to make the assumption you've already let your superiors know you're up and about. I'll make sure that by lunch, you have a basic rundown of the corporations as I know them."

Diana had already sent a ping to Sergeant Walker, letting him know she and Andrea were up and traveling today. A nearby drone was retransmitting her com signal. She and Andrea knew how to locate and use it if need be, but it would keep circling the area around them on its own.

Walker had told them to keep him in the loop but that he was going to the capital with Lieutenant Van Buren. Reed would be their primary point of contact for now.

"I've done a bit of reading about the corporations and Diorama from our briefing materials and what little I could find on the public data net," Diana lied. "That's potentially slanted, so I'd rather you assume we know nothing. With the corporations running things, it wouldn't surprise me if they had their own propaganda arm inside the information net."

Craig grinned at her from where he rode easily beside them. "You'd be wrong. The information net and news organizations on this planet are privately owned and relatively skeptical of our government. That's not to say the corporations can't put pressure on them and sometimes get things changed, but on the whole, you're not going to find many outright lies.

"The biggest of the corporations is Yi Holdings. They have the primary contract here, except for what Schuster and Associates was already doing when they arrived. They make most of their money mining the rare elements used for flip drives. It's a lucrative trade, but mining it on a planetary surface isn't exactly the safest of endeavors, so there are expenses."

Diana nodded. "But they've been doing this for a couple of hundred years, and they haven't had any labor issues before, so something must've changed. Any idea what?"

Craig shook his head. "I've heard rumbling for a couple of years about the working conditions, but some of our hands used to work in the mines and dispute that. Now, don't get me wrong, the company has cut corners where they can, but they pay the miners relatively well, and the safety conditions have always seemed to be a priority.

"That isn't to say that the managerial team wouldn't like to change things. Anytime they can save money, that means more profit for the company and likely bonuses for them. Hell, with senior management owning stock, if they do well, they're going to reap the benefits too."

Diana didn't answer right away because they'd just crested the hill they'd been climbing, and she had a tremendous view of the rest of the valley laid out ahead of her. Much of the land had been cleared, but it must've been done a long time ago because the grass was smooth and lush.

The hillier sections and some of the flatlands had tall trees, many of them looking like they were hundreds of years old. They speared high in the sky, and their canopies were wide and thick.

They looked like Terran transplants, but she couldn't identify what kind. Most newly colonized worlds imported invasive species from Terra to make themselves more comfortable. Right or wrong, that was just how it was done.

Since the Empire had been expanding for ten thousand years and the Terran Republic for another five before that, their handiwork had had a lot of time to spread on worlds touched by humans.

"You were saying a lot of negative things about senior management when you spoke to Lieutenant Van Buren," she said eventually. "Who were you talking about, and what kind of people are they?"

"The Yi Holdings CEO is Massimiliano Sticchi, a fat cat out of the core worlds. He never goes far without his hatchet woman, Kate Geller. When he wants dirty work done, she's the one that carries out his orders. If anyone is directly messing with the mine, it's going to be her or someone under her."

"But they don't run the mine itself, do they?" Andrea asked. She was riding on Craig's other side and seemed to be keeping pace reasonably well.

"No. I'm not sure who the manager at the mine is, but they'll be more familiar with operations underground. From what I understand, all the management there came up through the ranks and spent their time underground.

"I understand that Sticchi tried to replace them with toadies he could control when he came here about five years ago, but that got shut down pretty damned fast. The people at the mine are tight with one another, and when you start attacking one of them, they'll present a united front. They like their management, and they'll go to bat for them."

Diana consulted her databases and came up with the name of the mine manager: Ismael Nieto. His biography indicated he'd been a miner there for almost forty years. He'd risen through the ranks and joined management about twenty-five years ago.

There was a notation that he was well-liked and considered evenhanded. How the secret Imperial Intelligence computer program gathering the data would know that, she had no idea.

She also looked up Sticchi and Geller. The information on him was very illuminating. He'd been accused of stock fraud and corporate malfeasance a total of five times in the last three decades, though no charges had ever been brought or proven.

Those were from before he'd been hired to run Yi Holdings and hadn't been enough to scare off the Board of Directors. Or maybe that was what had interested them. Who knew?

There was no information about why they'd replaced their previous chief executive officer, but they must've been unsatisfied with them in some way. Considering some of the things that Sticchi had been accused of, odds were they wanted to squeeze more profit out of operations here.

Underneath him was a circle of people that ran other operations around the planet. The company apparently did more than mining and was somewhat more successful in cutting corners there.

Interestingly, none of the sabotage and grumbling that had brought the Imperial Marines to Diorama was coming from those quarters. It was all at the mine.

She skimmed Geller's file, but it was pretty sparse. The woman was dark-haired and had a face that looked vaguely familiar, but that couldn't be because Diana knew her. She had to look like someone Diana had met at some point, but it wasn't ringing any bells at this point.

Her work record was vague, to say the least. She had a list of employers from before she'd arrived at Diorama, but details were lacking. Each was just a brief entry in her biography without more than a job title.

Over the next couple of hours, she let Craig fill her in on what he knew about Sticchi and Geller. Some of the things he said were mentioned in the databases, but most were not. His primary sources were people working for him who once worked for Yi Holdings.

She compiled everything into a concise report and shipped it off to her superiors just as they came around a large copse of trees and arrived at their destination.

Unlike the other bits of the forest they'd passed, it looked like the ranch hands were actively logging here. Someone in the trees was using chain saws and axes to fell some of the massive trees by the sound of it. The wood was being processed out in the open, and they were creating what certainly looked like a new set of corrals and outbuildings.

As the saws and equipment used power packs, they were surprisingly quiet. Not silent by any means but more subdued than she'd have expected.

"Welcome to our new calving pen," Craig said as he pulled his horse to a stop. "This is where we'll bring pregnant cows so they can give birth and be seen to. Our old pens just aren't big enough to handle everything anymore, so we're expanding."

Andrea had opened her mouth to respond when a shrill scream

sounded from somewhere deep in the woods off to the right. Then the workers began fleeing out of the woods. Diana was wondering what the hell was going on when something bestial in the woods roared.

"Ah, hell," Craig said as he kicked his horse into a gallop. "We've got a pack of dire wolves attacking the camp!"

16

Andrea prodded Celia into motion, using what Craig had taught her to indicate she wanted to go faster. When the horse broke into a trot, she kept urging more speed and quickly discovered that going faster than that was a completely different rhythm and almost fell off the horse.

Luckily for her, the saddle was secure, and she held on, guiding Celia toward the chaos erupting in front of her. Even in their panic, the people running from the confrontation deeper in the forest were able to dodge out of her path and give her a clear shot right to the edge of the forest.

When she arrived, she managed to extract her feet from the stirrups and jumped down to the ground, pulling her marine-issue flechette pistol from its holster and racing into the woods through the quickly thickening brush.

Her enhanced hearing tried to catalog everything around her, but the noises were mostly unfamiliar and chaotic. She'd have to handle this on the fly.

By the time she'd gotten ten meters into the forest, she'd realized she was now the point person. Everyone else had fled except for someone shouting up ahead and the sound of a flechette rifle discharging.

Andrea changed course and dodged an old fallen tree. She kept her attention focused around her, though. Just because there was a threat ahead didn't mean there weren't others off to the sides.

Her paranoia paid off when she circled a large tree, and the sound of something scrabbling in the undergrowth to her left made her pivot just in time to see something that looked like a monstrously huge and vicious black-furred dog leaping out of the bushes toward her.

With her pistol already out and ready, she was able to fire multiple flechettes into the creature's body. The wounds had to be fatal, but the animal was already in the air, and momentum was a bitch.

The big hairy beast slammed into her, knocking her down and almost making her lose her pistol. It didn't attack her further because it was thoroughly dead, but it stank to high heaven and was bleeding all over her.

Her increased strength came in handy as she rolled the beast off and surged to her feet. That got her up just in time to see two more dire wolves racing out of the woods behind the first.

One of the first rules of combat she'd learned was that if someone was attacking you, it was always best not to be where their attacks were landing. She dove to the left, rolling as she hit the ground and firing as soon as she had a stable platform on one knee. The leftmost beast took four flechettes and, by some dark misfortune, was still able to turn and bite her before it collapsed.

Its teeth clamped onto her right forearm and went deep. Burning agony shot up her arm and made her see red. She tried to free her arm, but it was well and truly caught.

With no other options, she pulled her marine-issue knife with her left hand and jammed it into the side of the third wolf's head as it snapped at her. The hull metal blade and monomolecular edge drove it in to the hilt, and the last beast died, falling away from her and ripping the knife's grip out of her blood-slicked fingers.

It hurt like hell for her to pry the dead wolf's mouth off her arm, but she got free. Not wanting to waste a single second, she transferred her flechette pistol to her left hand, ignored her profusely bleeding arm, and continued deeper into the forest, staggering slightly as she tried to focus on what she was doing.

She'd trained for many different forms of combat but never against animals. Having to worry about some kind of beast trying to rip her arm off was definitely a new and unpleasant twist.

She could hear Craig somewhere behind her, yelling for her to wait, but she didn't. Those three beasts wouldn't be the only ones in the woods, and the screaming in front of her had stopped. That couldn't be good.

Pushing aside some brush with her injured arm, she broke out into a small clearing that had been turned into a charnel house. Two more of the beasts lay dead, and a young man with a flechette rifle stood protectively over a fallen woman, his eyes wild with fear and adrenaline.

He swept the rifle over toward Andrea but yanked it up before the barrel lined up. "Watch out! There's more in the woods!"

Before Andrea could respond, Diana came racing out of the woods with her pistol out and sweeping for targets. Craig came out behind her with a rifle in his hand. It wasn't the kind that shot flechettes, so it must be an old-style slug thrower. She hadn't seen him carrying anything like that, so she wasn't sure where it had come from.

Diana snatched the rifle out of the boy's hands, holstered her pistol, and turned slowly, scanning for threats. If another dire wolf came out of the forest, it would be dead before it got to any of them.

Craig raced to the unconscious woman's side and looked at her injury with a grimace. "Get me a medical pack, Leroy. If you can find a medic, I need them too."

"Diana, cover him," Andrea ordered.

Her friend looked uncertain for a moment but raced after the boy. He needed her protection more than they did.

Andrea stepped over beside Craig and the woman, turning slowly in place and using her enhanced hearing to try to discern any threats coming their way before they arrived. Now that she was on defense and didn't have to run through the forest, she could pay more attention to what was going on around her.

"How bad is it?" she asked.

"They tore her leg open pretty bad, but as long as I can stabilize it, we can get someone out from the ranch house with more skill. She's not bleeding too bad now that I've got pressure on the wound, so that's a good start."

He glanced up at her arm. "You're bleeding an awful lot out of that arm. Come closer and let me use a hand to slow the bleeding."

She ignored his offer. "I'll live. How many of these things travel together?"

"Between half a dozen and a full dozen. They're not stupid, so they'll retreat now that they've lost the element of surprise. They want a handy meal, not a fight to the death."

The sound of movement in the woods in the direction Diana and the boy had run told her that someone was coming, but she still pivoted her weapon to cover the break in the forest anyway. That ended up being a good call because a dire wolf that looked to be half again larger than the ones she'd seen thus far bounded out, snarling.

Even with her enhanced reflexes, the damned thing was in the air before she could fire. Since she couldn't do anything about it landing on her, she took a moment to line up her shot perfectly and fired a single flechette that caught the thing right between the eyes and blew the back of its skull off.

A heartbeat later, it slammed into her with the full force of its momentum, dragging her along the forest floor as it slid, already dead. Again, she rolled the creature off and stood, looking for more threats.

"Well, any thoughts I had that you weren't an Imperial Marine are now thoroughly gone," Craig said in a strangled voice. "I couldn't even grab my rifle in time to shoot."

"All in a day's work," Andrea said as nonchalantly as she could. Her right arm was throbbing badly because the beast had jarred her wounds and dragged them through the dirt and leaves. She would have to get them looked at as soon as they had time because, as good as her medical nanites were, they weren't *that* good.

They had a minute of tense waiting before a dozen men and women armed with pistols and rifles ran into the clearing and surrounded them. The workers must've had weapons somewhere, but they hadn't had them easily accessible.

Either that or the people with them had run at the first sign of trouble, which wasn't what someone with a weapon was supposed to do. It was their job to run *toward* danger.

If she'd been in command, she'd have ripped a strip off them. No matter what had happened, someone had screwed up.

Well, that was Craig's problem.

It took another minute for the medic to arrive and begin looking at the wounded woman's leg. She hadn't regained consciousness, but Craig seemed confident she'd survive.

"I think you can put that up now," he said as he stepped beside her. "Safe your weapon, and let me holster it for you."

"I got this," she said, activating the safety and awkwardly reaching around to holster the weapon, having to slide her hand under the jacket to make it work. "Sorry about the clothes."

"Screw the clothes," he said bluntly. "People matter, not things. Let me clean some of the gunk out of your arm. It looks like you'll need some stitches, but I'll leave it to a professional so they can finish cleaning that out and give you shots for the bite."

"Are dire wolves venomous?"

He smiled grimly. "No, but their mouths are filthy, and deep punctures like this might give an infection a foothold in your arm. I'll take your word about your medical nanites being better than average, but best not to take chances."

She gritted her teeth and ignored the pain as he irrigated and cleaned the wounds. There were tears in her flesh, but they looked *relatively* minor. As long as she didn't have any significant injuries, she could still keep using her arm, at least for now.

"I don't need to tell you how crazy running into the woods by yourself is when dire wolves are around," he said quietly. "Nevertheless, you probably saved two lives today.

"If the last of the pack had gotten to them, they'd have killed them both. Thanks for being the shield between them and certain death."

The momentary vision of Anne Marie Scott sacrificing her life for her squad briefly filled her mind. "I'm an Imperial Marine. It's my *job* to stand between the innocent and certain death."

"Maybe so, but everyone at this ranch owes you a debt of gratitude because this could've been a tragedy. You've bled for us, and here on Diorama, that means something. Don't think we'll forget it anytime soon."

The adrenaline that had kept Andrea moving was finally bleeding out of her system, and she took the opportunity to sit down. "You'd do the same for me. Let's not make this into something bigger than it has to be."

He grinned as he pulled a sterile pad and some gauze from the medical kit. "Did I ever mention that if someone saves the life of someone on Diorama, we have to serve them until we die?"

She scowled. "Don't yank my chain."

Craig laughed. "It's not true, but the look on your face makes it worth trotting out. Still, we believe if someone does us a service, we owe them one in return. Debts here are paid promptly and in full.

"Once we get you back to the homestead, you need to sit down with young Leroy. He used to work at the mines, and if anyone can tell you what's going on there—even things he's not supposed to talk about—he will. You saved his sister, and he loves her more than life itself."

He held up a hand to stop her reflexive response. "And before you object that you didn't save her, he's not a stupid man. When he finds out you killed three dire wolves in the woods on your way to him, he'll understand those monsters were coming for them both.

"Hell, you saved my life, too, since I couldn't get my gun up in time when the pack alpha came flying out of the woods. I can't believe you shot him right between the eyes while he was in the air.

"That's the kind of thing that'll end up being told around campfires for decades to come. Young lady, your story will become part of the lore of the cowboys of Diorama. And trust me when I say those stories are only going to grow in the retelling."

He chuckled a little. "Considering that it's already a damned miracle, I can only imagine what they'll attribute to you once they start embellishing it. You'll be two meters tall and have killed one of them with your bare hands."

"Thanks for reminding me. I need to get my knife out of the head of one of those beasts before we leave. They'll charge me for it if I lose it."

He blinked at her and then narrowed his eyes. "You killed a dire wolf with a knife?"

"I didn't really have a choice, since the other one was chewing on me."

"I'll be damned."

A loud whine over their heads made her look up just as a wide-bodied grav vehicle flew over the construction zone at high speed, already turning for what looked like a hasty landing. It was no doubt here to pick up the injured, a category she knew they'd lump her into.

She rose to her feet. "It was a pleasant ride out here but just a little bit more exciting than I thought it was going to be."

He gently clapped her on her uninjured shoulder. "Never a dull moment on the Big L Ranch. Let's get out of the way so the medics can get Beatrice out of here, then we'll find your knife and go back with them. Someone else will have to bring the horses in."

Once even more people ran into the clearing, he led her back the way they'd come, shaking his head with wide eyes as she retrieved her knife, wiped the blood off on one of the dead dire wolves, and sheathed it.

She suspected the stories around the campfires would start out being hard to believe. Who knew what they'd sound like in a few years?

Andrea sent a message to Diana to stay here while she returned to the ranch house to get her wound looked at. If there was a second attack, having an Imperial Marine on hand was the right call. Her friend would have to come back with the horses or on a later flight.

She'd eventually have to report the attack and that she'd been injured, but she was going to hold off on that. She needed to see what information Leroy might have for them, and if she said something that made Corporal Reed pull her and Diana out, they'd lose the opportunity.

That would probably piss Reed and Walker off when they found out she'd delayed reporting it, but she could live with that. It wasn't the first time she'd done something that pissed other people off, and it certainly wouldn't be the last.

Thinking about Sergeant Walker made her wonder how he and Lieutenant Van Buren were doing. Hopefully, their mission was a lot less stressful than hers was turning out to be.

17

Much to Jerome's relief, the LT set his hat aside and grinned at the men now sitting across from them. "As you might've guessed, my friend and I are from off planet. We intended to take a little tour of the backcountry just to see what was going on out there but didn't realize exactly how far the train would take us.

"The hat and the belt buckle are a bit exaggerated, I'll admit. It's what tourists do, and to be fair, the shopkeeper had them in stock, so don't blame me for buying them. What about you boys?"

The men glanced at one another before the one who'd spoken earlier took the lead. "Just a couple of ranch hands going into the city. Nothing big, but the wives wanted us to pick up some stuff. Shipping to the backcountry isn't as smooth and easy as you might think. I'm Daniel Paci, and this is Nick Parada."

"Pedro van Buren," the LT said. "This is my partner in crime, Jerome Walker. If it seemed that we were being disrespectful to you folks, I apologize. Maybe we can buy you something more than coffee to make up for it. We've just finished eating, but if you'd like something, I'd be happy to put it on my tab."

The offer seemed to mollify the two men, but they quickly refused.

"We appreciate your hospitality, but taking your food for a misunderstanding doesn't seem right. We'll order something and chat with you for a bit to make up for being a little belligerent."

The LT waved the man behind the bar over, and he quickly took orders from the men. He poured everyone coffee before he left.

"I'm a bit surprised to hear that things are hard to get when you got this train line," Jerome said when the LT nudged him under the table. "I understand it's used to take cattle in, but surely they can bring cargo out."

"You'd think," Paci said with a snort. "Yet that's not how it works these days. All the trains that come out seem to only have a few cars for parcels and cargo tacked on mostly as an afterthought. If you want anything shipped outside the capital, you'll pay through the nose for it."

Parada nodded. "For something relatively small, it's cheaper to get a ticket and make the trip yourself than to get it shipped. Significantly faster too. It's those damned corporations."

The LT leaned forward, his expression interested. "I can't say I've been to many corporate worlds, so I don't have any experience to judge by. Is this Yi Holdings really that bad?"

"Didn't used to be. It seems like it's only been in the last five years or so that things have gotten bad. I'm not exactly sure what changed, but it really does seem like the priorities of the corporation have changed.

"Used to be they cared about making sure people here were relatively happy, but since the new guy came in, it's been all downhill."

"The meat we produce goes to the capital, and it's the same in other large cities on Diorama," Paci said after he took a sip of his coffee. "None of it gets exported, so it doesn't really benefit the corporation that much. Still, they get something for moving it, so that's where they squeeze us.

"There have to be hundreds of little things—for a corporation the size of Yi Holdings, anyway—that they do to eke more money out of us that just makes life miserable. That and they're starting to intrude into everyday life in the cities."

"That's definitely new and unwelcome," Parada grumbled.

"Probably won't be long before they try to do something like that in the backcountry. You can bet that won't go over very well."

"I thought their contract was to work on the mines," Van Buren said with a hint of a frown. "I really didn't look at the information about the planet all that closely before we got here, since it was only a layover. Apologies for that."

Paci grinned. "Hell, you're just passing through. We get that. As for squeezing money out of the economy, they find other ways to get what they want. This lack of getting cargo out to the boonies is a way of making us pay more for the privilege of having what we used to have for close to free.

"It wouldn't cost them much to put cargo cars right behind the passenger cars. They'd be empty going into the city and add very little weight to the train. Coming out to the country, they'd be packed to the brim, but the cattle cars would be empty. It would all balance out."

"Now they'll only start doing that again if we pay a premium on the weight of the packages coming out," Parada grumbled. "I'm surprised they haven't raised the prices for people and limited what kind of luggage we can bring along. Honestly, I'll bet that's coming."

"Is it just the one corporation doing this, or is the other one involved?" Jerome asked. "I've already forgotten its name."

"Schuster and Associates," Parada said. "Kind of a strange name, if you ask me, but then again, Yi Holdings doesn't exactly scream mining, either, does it?"

"Yeah," Jerome said with a nod. "That's them. What exactly do they do? Are they causing you trouble too?"

Paci shrugged. "They do some kind of organic extraction. I can't say I ever recall hearing specifics. I understand they have a stake in what happens here, but they're really quiet."

"They are that," Parada agreed, taking a sip of his coffee. "They keep a low profile, but so long as they don't mess with us, I'm happy to let them do whatever they're doing.

"People that grow things for a living are a little odd."

The bartender came back over with the food for the other men. Jerome decided to order some toast and bacon because he was still hungry, and the conversation moved to general things as the train continued along.

By the time everybody finished eating, they were fairly close to the capital. The train was going a lot faster than Jerome had given it credit for. It was still going to be early morning when they started looking around.

He still didn't have any idea what the LT was curious about, but if he wanted to do some recon and get more information about the corporations on their own ground, Jerome was willing.

The arrival at the station was anticlimactic. The train slowed and pulled into a platform to let the passengers debark. He imagined the cattle would be taken farther up the line and herded into a slaughterhouse.

The LT left a big tip on the table—more than enough to pay for all the meals—but only after the other men had paid and headed back into the other passenger cars.

Since they didn't have any luggage other than the bag over Jerome's shoulder, he and the LT could exit directly from the dining car.

The crowd on the platform was significantly larger than Jerome had expected. Maybe they were going deeper into the city. Why waste a train going somewhere else when it had passenger cars handy?

His guess was proven correct as the passengers waiting to board began doing so. The LT scanned around and found a handy exit leading down to the street, and the two of them started in that direction.

Jerome noticed a pair of men in uniform watching everyone leaving the station when they were about halfway there. They didn't seem concerned about the people entering, but everyone leaving the platform was getting some scrutiny.

That was odd and concerning. His eyes flicked down to their waists, and he saw they were armed with stunners. Police of some kind, then, or maybe corporate security. He didn't know what they called themselves here.

They took an interest in the LT's hat, proving Jerome's concern to have been a valid one.

The man on the left stepped in front of the officer and held up his hand. "Identification, please. What brings you into the city?"

Van Buren frowned at the man. "Excuse me? This is the Empire, and I don't have to explain myself to you."

The security officer seemed unimpressed. "If you want to avoid being detained, then you'll start cooperating."

Things looked like they would get problematic in a hurry, and now Jerome was thinking about the weapons in his bag. The men obviously hadn't scanned them, or they wouldn't just be talking. Sadly, it meant that the two were unarmed versus a couple of men with stunners.

Worse yet, they'd have com units. If they needed assistance, it would only be minutes away, at most.

Maybe it was time to identify themselves. The corporations knew they were there anyway, so what did it cost them?

He almost suggested that, but the security officer confronting his commander decided to act first. The man grabbed Van Buren's arm while reaching for what were probably handcuffs at the small of his back.

Van Buren might be an officer, but he was trained in hand-to-hand combat, so he had no difficulty breaking the man's grip and punching him in the gut, sending him staggering back into a short railing that he promptly flipped over. The security officer fell into the grass, writhing and trying to breathe.

The second security officer went for his stunner, but Jerome drove his fist into the other man's jaw before he could do anything, sending him sprawling on the plascrete.

The fight got the civilians around them riled up, and everybody started screaming and running in various directions. Van Buren took advantage of the chaos and headed down the stairs toward the street below. His plan was obviously to get lost in the street crowd.

Jerome started after him, but apparently, he hadn't knocked the security officer out completely because the man grabbed his leg. He quickly shook off the man's grip and kicked the stunner out of his hand before he could bring it to bear, but that delayed him for a few seconds.

Long enough for the officer to reach the street and be speared with a blue stunner beam right in front of Jerome's eyes. The LT went down hard, and Jerome started swinging his pack off his back to get his weapons.

"They already have him," Parada said from right next to him, holding a hand out without touching him while Paci kicked the fallen security officer in the gut.

"I can't leave him here," Jerome argued.

"Security is going to swarm this place before you get to him. We know another way out, but they're going to catch you unless you come with us."

Jerome waffled for two full seconds before he heard whistles blowing down below. That would be security officers responding to the incident. If he didn't want to get picked up with the lieutenant, he had to leave now.

He didn't want to do it, but it wasn't as if they were going to actually arrest Van Buren. The man commanded a company of Imperial Marines who'd be knocking on their door, demanding his immediate release.

Of course, that was only true if Jerome could let them know what had happened.

As much as it galled him, he turned and walked away with the two ranch hands as they led him toward a small door set on the side of the train station. He figured it had to be locked, but they opened it right up and sauntered through as if they owned the place.

He followed directly behind them with a prayer and closed the door behind him, locking it to make sure no one could easily follow them. The LT was on his own until he could call for help.

* * *

DIANA WATCHED as the big grav vehicle carrying the wounded lifted off and headed back toward the ranch house at high speed. It had Andrea, the wounded woman, her brother, and Craig. She hadn't gotten a good look at her friend's bloody arm, but it didn't seem to be doing more than inconveniencing her.

She tagged the recon drone they were using as a signal booster and had it sweep the area. It was more than capable of identifying large creatures like the dire wolves, even deep in the forest.

They should've been using it to scout the area as they rode, and she was sure that Reed would point out that lapse when she had the chance. They'd deserve the criticism, too, because this was a rookie mistake.

Within ten minutes, she knew there were no other serious dangers in the area and passed that information along to the person in charge of the construction effort.

The woman didn't seem convinced, but that wasn't Diana's problem. A little paranoia was probably a good thing. She wasn't the only one who'd learned a hard lesson today.

The task of protecting the construction site discharged, it was time to gather the horses and head back toward the ranch house. With Andrea injured, she wanted to get there as quickly as possible, but she had to do so in a safe manner. That meant she needed somebody better trained than herself to make sure the horses—and she—arrived safely.

Diana turned the weapon she'd taken over to the work crew and asked for someone to escort her. Ten minutes later, she had a lanky man named Clint riding along with her, leading the horses by their reins while she rode alone.

The man wasn't much of a talker, but that suited her just fine. She was going over everything that had happened and trying to figure out precisely what they'd done wrong.

And make no mistake, they'd done something wrong. They should've gone in as a team, but Andrea had raced ahead at a faster pace than Diana could keep up with.

Was that her fault for being too slow, or was it Andrea's mistake for not holding back just a bit to allow the rest of her team—Diana—to keep up? Her friend wouldn't like the answer because Diana was sure that Andrea hadn't even thought about her when she'd gone running headlong into danger.

At the clip they were moving, it didn't take them long to get back to the main ranch house. She saw no sign of the grav vehicle, so it must've already dropped off its passengers and departed.

Diana sent the drone ahead and had it make a pass around the ranch house, confirming that Andrea was inside via her com unit, though she didn't contact her.

She headed toward the corral holding the horses, but Clint took her reins from her. "I'll see your horse gets taken care of," he said when she protested. "Go check on your friend."

"Thank you."

She headed up the stone steps and considered knocking on the door, but that seemed ridiculous. Dozens of people—at least—lived in the place, and they were always going in and out.

Diana pushed the door open and stepped inside, trying to figure out where she'd find her friend. She stopped long enough to hang her coat where they'd gotten it from and hooked the hat over the top of it. She'd grab them later if she needed them.

It seemed a safe bet that Andrea would be in the room she'd been in earlier. Her injuries weren't bad—relatively speaking—so Diana would go there first and expand the search only if needed.

She found her friend and Rebecca in Andrea's room, as she'd guessed. They'd gotten Andrea out of her bloody clothes, and she'd showered. That was good because she'd been covered in gore, including her hair.

Rebecca had a tray of first-aid gear and was busy putting the final touches on several stitches in her friend's arm. The wounds looked pretty ugly. Both women looked up as she came in.

"Is everything okay back at the corral?" Andrea asked, visibly tensing.

"It's fine," Diana said. "I used the drone to scan the area and came up clean. They should be safe enough, but I'm certain they'll be more careful going forward. How's your arm?"

Her friend shrugged slightly. "It hurts, but it's not that bad."

"Stitches will do for now," Rebecca said, "but if we had a regenerator, I'd suggest we use it. It's been something I've gone back and forth about getting because it's not an insignificant investment, but I think we'd best have one on hand for the next incident."

"I'm glad the two of you were there because I'd have hated for something to happen to Leroy and Beatrice. Those two are some of the sweetest people you'll ever meet.

"Dire wolves don't usually come this close to the ranch, but you can bet Craig is going to send riders out to make sure there aren't any more lurking out there."

"How is Beatrice?" Diana asked. "I only got a quick look at her wound, but it looked pretty bad."

"The medic agreed, and Craig took her and Leroy to the nearest town with a real doctor. Now, let me repeat what I just said. You both saved two lives today, which means a lot to us. Thank you."

Diana grinned a little bit. "That wasn't me. Andrea got too far ahead of me, so she's the one that did all the cleaning up. That's four dire wolves by my count, one by knife. I'm pretty sure that's impressive."

Rebecca stopped putting away the first-aid kit and stared at Andrea. "You killed *four* dire wolves by *yourself*? And one with a *knife*? Are you kidding me?"

"Just the idea of one person facing down a single dire wolf by themselves is pretty much a death sentence unless they get very, *very* lucky."

Diana sat on one of the chairs, relaxing for the first time in what felt like hours. "Andrea told you how much different she is than the rest of us. She wasn't kidding."

"That's bull," her friend said as she moved her arm to see how the bandaged area felt. "If it'd been Diana in the lead, she'd have killed at least two of them and probably the third in the clearing.

"That one with the knife? Maybe not, so I'm glad it was me."

Diana laughed. "I still have a lot to learn to be a frontline marine. Maybe Sergeant Walker could've taken all four of those dire wolves, but I couldn't. I'm certainly not as good with a knife as you are."

Rebecca shook her head. "The two of you are crazy. When I saw Andrea come through the front door covered in blood like that, I thought she was a dead woman walking. I'm probably going to have nightmares about that."

"Sorry," Andrea said, just a hint contritely. "I'll pay for the damaged clothes."

"Don't be ridiculous," Rebecca scoffed. "Those clothes—and you —were damaged in service to the Big L Ranch. You don't owe us one damned thing.

"It's the other way around. You can bet your ass there's going to be a big dinner tonight or tomorrow, and you're going to be the guests of honor."

Rebecca rose to her feet. "I've got to get something for Andrea, so I'll be right back. Diana, we'll have lunch in a bit, but I'll send something up because I want Andrea to have time to decompress without everyone hounding her."

Once the woman was gone, Andrea hung her head a little. "You're right. I got caught up in the moment and forgot you were behind me. That could've cost me my life."

"Delaying might also have given the dire wolves enough time to kill two people," Diana countered. "This is one of those situations where being impetuous might actually have saved the situation. Trust me, I'm sure Corporal Reed will point out exactly where we screwed up in the after-action report."

"As will Sergeant Walker," her friend said with a sigh. "This wasn't what I had planned for our first day here, but at least we got some decent information, and I'm told the man I saved used to work at the mine. If anyone can tell us what's going on or has contacts there, Craig said it would be him.

"When they get back, I'll have to talk to them. That might be later today, or it might be tomorrow if they decide to keep Beatrice for a while."

The two of them were quiet for a bit. Feeling restless, Diana rose and walked to the window looking out over the corrals in front of the house. This place had been nothing like what she'd expected, but she liked it.

Too bad they weren't on vacation. They had a mission to carry out, and they couldn't do anything more until Craig Lindbergh returned.

What she *could* do was start compiling a report of the incident with the dire wolves. As much as she suspected Andrea didn't want to mention the fight with the dire wolves and her injury, Diana had to blow the whistle.

She'd emphasize that her friend's injuries were minor, but that might still draw a response from Reed. If it did, it did. They were part of a team, and sometimes they didn't get to make the calls about what happened next. This time, it was going to be up to the corporal.

As she was staring out the window, she saw the big grav vehicle come in for a landing at a much more sedate pace than it had demonstrated itself capable of. It quickly settled to the ground, its ramp extending.

Craig Lindbergh and the young man that had been protecting the injured woman walked out. Based on their expressions, nothing had gone terribly wrong, but she hadn't expected to see either of them for quite a while yet.

"Looks like our potential contact just got back from town," Diana said. "Rebecca apparently still has something she wants to talk with you about, so I'm going to leave you here and see what this Leroy has to say about the mines. That information might be useful very soon."

And with that, Diana headed out the door and toward the stairs leading down to the ground floor. She saw Rebecca coming down from the third floor with a tray covered in tubes and makeup brushes.

She frowned slightly at the sight but didn't let that stop her from continuing down. Solving mysteries and gathering information was what she lived for, and this was her opportunity to shine.

18

Diana had barely left when Rebecca arrived bearing a small tray holding several tubes and small brushes. Andrea frowned for a moment before realizing it had to be the makeup the woman had referred to earlier. The stuff that had the potential to cover up her tattoos.

The idea of doing something like that still felt subtly wrong, but she wanted to see how it worked. Her only memories of life without the tattoos were those of a twelve-year-old girl. This was the face she would wear for the rest of her life, and she wanted another look with an adult's sensibilities.

Rebecca closed the door and set the tray onto the chair that Diana had used earlier. "I can see from your expression that you're still of two minds. Let me reassure you that this comes off just fine. If this isn't something you want to pursue, it's all gone in less than five minutes. No muss, no fuss.

"On the other hand, if this isn't something you'd like to try at all, just tell me to mind my own business, and we'll forget about it."

Andrea shook her head. "I don't know if it's something I want to do, either, but I have to see what I'd look like. The last time I saw my face without these tattoos was when I was a child. I don't know what's right, but I have to see. I really do appreciate you taking the time to introduce me to this concept. It means a lot to me."

The woman made a shooing gesture and smiled. "This is just girls talking about makeup. We can do this every dang day, and you still wouldn't owe me a thing. Now, I want you to sit here on the edge of the bed while I figure out exactly what the right mixture is.

"I've got to get the tone right, so I'll have to play around a bit. Also, this doesn't have to be heavily applied. You see, there's a technological trick buried in it that's used for a purpose very similar to what we're doing right now."

Andrea scooted to the edge of the bed and tilted her head to the side as she looked at the other woman. "What does that mean?"

"This particular brand of makeup is made to cover scars. Sometimes people get hurt, and they don't want to have a scar that's visible to God and everyone. Medical nanites are a rarity here in the backcountry. That'll probably change in time, but the price that Yi Holdings charges for them are fairly hefty."

Andrea froze. "The corporations *charge* you for medical nanites? I mean, more than just some nominal sum for installing the hardware? I'll admit that I don't have a lot of experience, but I thought that kind of thing was available for everyone."

Rebecca grimaced. "Maybe that's true elsewhere, but the medical establishment here works directly for the corporation, and they charge a premium for something like that. My brother and I—as well as a number of the supervisors—have them but not everybody.

"If it was up to me, we'd go ahead and spend the money to give everybody that kind of benefit because Beatrice is going to take a while to recuperate from that injury, and medical nanites would certainly improve the speed and quality of her recovery."

"You do realize that you could import medical nanites and install them yourselves, right? I don't know the details, but it should be possible, as long as you have a doctor trained in the procedure."

Rebecca shook her head. "They're on the restricted list. One more way to make sure the corporations control what happens here and squeeze the largest amount of profit out of everything that happens on Diorama.

"Unlike most worlds, you pay fees and taxes for just about everything here. They nickel-and-dime you to death. In case you're not familiar with what nickels and dimes are, they're small bits of money used back on prespaceflight Terra in a country called the United States of America.

"The saying means that someone will take a little here and a little there to make their profit, and it all adds up to quite a bit of money when taken together."

"That has to be the most reprehensible thing I've ever heard of. Have you tried complaining to the Imperial representative?"

All the while that they'd been talking, Rebecca had been mixing the contents of several tubes and eyeing Andrea's face. The end product didn't quite look the same color, so Andrea wasn't sure how this would work.

Rebecca nodded. "I have, and he couldn't care less. Everybody knows the man is on the take, and there isn't going to be anyone coming out here to audit what he's done."

The woman took a small brush and picked up some of the cream that she'd mixed together. "Now, let's start on one side and see how it dries. The color will shift a little bit as it does, so it's impossible to get it precisely like your normal skin on the first try, but as long as I get close, I can blend it in."

Rebecca lightly brushed the cream over Andrea's left temple and sat back to examine the results for about sixty seconds before she added something else to the cream and mixed it up again. Then she reapplied it over the same area and expanded downward by about the same amount before waiting again.

"I think I've got it pretty close now, so we'll give you the full coverage and let it dry."

It took about fifteen minutes for Rebecca to put it across Andrea's entire face, all the while talking about the things the corporations did on Diorama that she wished would change. Intermixed with that, she spoke about the makeup process itself and how once someone had the exact shade they were looking for, it could be premixed in larger quantities. The final product could also be applied with a makeup pad.

According to her, applying it to Andrea's entire face with a pad would take less than five minutes from start to finish, including drying time.

"Just how hard is it to get this stuff off?" Andrea asked. "If I wash it with soap and water, will I ruin it?"

"People are out working in the rain, and they get soap and other cleaners on themselves all the time. The designers wanted to ensure it didn't come off when it wasn't supposed to, so it requires a specific cleaning agent. With that, it'll come right off.

"Now, that doesn't mean it doesn't wear off. The technological component has a limited power run, and once it stops working, it'll stop blocking what's underneath. This kind of makeup is meant to be applied daily, and while it will last for more than a full day, it won't last two.

"You might be able to get thirty-six hours out of it, but that would be pushing it. There'd be failures of the coverage around that point, most likely."

Andrea frowned slightly. "So it doesn't fail all at once?"

Again, Rebecca shook her head. "I've never seen it pushed to that point, but the instructions I read said there would be spot failures, so maybe the part over your cheekbone would stop being covered and then the part on your forehead."

The woman leaned back and nodded. "Why don't you take a look in the mirror and tell me what you think?"

Andrea rose and walked into the bathroom. She stopped in front of the mirror and stared at herself, sucking in a deep breath.

She was unrecognizable.

A moderately tall woman with dark hair and slightly pink skin stared back at her from the mirror. She could see her dark eyes clearly, and her expression was one of shock.

It was a woman that Andrea had never seen before.

Rebecca stepped up behind her. "I think I did a decent job, but I'd take a picture in good light to make sure when getting a batch made, so it was perfectly tailored. You're a beautiful girl, both with your tattoos and without them, but that's undoubtedly two different experiences.

"Seeing you with your tattoos is a bit intimidating. Seeing this girl, people would admire you going down the street but wouldn't give you a second thought. No one would ever associate you with the Singularity."

Never taking her eyes off her own reflection, Andrea reached up and touched her face delicately to see if she messed up the makeup. It was dry and didn't smear. She rubbed harder. No effect.

The final test was lathering her hands with soap and water and vigorously washing her face before toweling it dry. Once again, there was no indication that there was anything there. It was spooky.

Andrea shook her head in shock. "I never thought anything like this was possible. I honestly don't know if this is right for me, but I appreciate having the option.

"Your brother told me that my tattoos were like scars, and sometimes those had to be worn with pride because they were part of who we were."

Rebecca made a dismissive noise and shook her head. "Men are strange creatures that sometimes revel in their own injuries. There might be something to what he says, but I wouldn't take Craig too literally. The man loves his metaphors, but he can take them too far.

"While those tattoos can be part of who you are, they don't always need to be. Everybody needs a break. Maybe you keep the tattoos when you're at work but cover them up if you're going out on the town. In the end, only you can make that decision, and it has to be what's right for you."

The woman had given Andrea a lot to think about. She wasn't going to make a decision today. Hell, she probably wasn't going to make a decision for weeks or months. Maybe years.

"Now, let me walk you through removing the makeup and applying it yourself. I'm going in to see Beatrice later, and there's a shop right down the way that can make a premixed batch. I'll pick up enough that you can use it—or not—as you choose for quite some time to come. That's my gift to you for saving Beatrice's life."

"It was my honor and duty to save her life," Andrea objected. "I don't need payment for that."

"And yet, here we are. I can't make you take it with you when you leave, but I can make sure you have it with my gratitude. Personally, this is nothing compared to what I expect my brother will do when he gets around to it. Debts are something he takes *seriously*."

Andrea sighed, imagining how uncomfortable that would be. Maybe if she just kept her head down, he'd get focused on other tasks and wouldn't embarrass her.

Yeah. Even she knew that wasn't very likely. One more problem to be dealt with when the time came.

* * *

JEROME FOLLOWED the men deeper into the dim room on the other side of the door, looking left and right for threats while also trying to assess what purpose the space served. As near as he could tell, it was some kind of storage, perhaps for lost luggage or other misplaced items.

The shelves contained a wide variety of bags and other things, including a stuffed animal. It looked like some kind of dog but more ferocious. It was also larger than he would've expected for a child's plush toy.

He wanted to ask the men where they were going, but they quickly reached a circular staircase that went down, and he found himself hurrying after them. They weren't waiting around to answer questions, and he couldn't blame them.

Things had gone terribly wrong back on the train platform, and he still wasn't quite sure how the situation had spun out of control so quickly. Whoever those goons had been, they'd been looking for someone, and Lieutenant Van Buren had fit the bill.

Had they really been watching in case any marines tried to sneak into the city? Surely that kind of behavior wasn't standard on any Imperial world. People had the right to free passage, even on a corporately owned planet. Something just wasn't right here.

Even as he descended into darkness, Jerome took the bag off his back and dug around inside until he found a stunner. There really wasn't a place for him to have it easily accessible, but the short jacket he wore was of sufficient length that he could tuck it into the small of his back, and it wouldn't be immediately obvious that he was armed. It would have to do.

Jerome found it wasn't completely dark when they reached the bottom of the stairs. There were dim lights stretched out in front of them, and he quickly realized they were in a tunnel of some kind.

The walls were made of cracked and flaking plascrete that hadn't been prepared correctly. There were pipes and conduits of different colors running down the length of the tunnel, and the dim lighting over their heads was spaced out far enough that there were pools of darkness in between.

The men broke into a sprint. They were obviously concerned that someone was pursuing them, and Jerome couldn't argue they were wrong.

These people obviously weren't who they'd claimed to be. Cowboys coming in from the backcountry wouldn't have known how to get into the station and the tunnels beneath it. Someone had had to unlock the door, probably while the confrontation between security and the lieutenant was blooming.

Whoever Paci and Parada were, they had unexplained depths that he would have to figure out before deciding whether he could trust them. They were allies of convenience, but he didn't know what their endgame was. That would have to change *very* soon.

His implants told him they were heading south, but he didn't know what lay around the train platform. They traveled about five hundred meters before the tunnel ended with a familiar set of spiral stairs leading upward. The men raced upward, and he followed.

The building they came out into seemed to be some kind of warehouse. Admittedly, it was still part of the train network because there were a number of grav train cars set side by side in the dim light.

They weren't cattle or passenger cars, so he assumed they were made for cargo. These would be the ones the men had spoken of. He supposed that was one bit of evidence supporting some of their tale.

Rather than question them now that they seemed to be somewhat in the clear, he watched closely to see how they behaved. They knew precisely which exit they were going to, and they were keeping an eye on their surroundings as if they were trained to watch for threats.

The interesting thing was they weren't behaving like marines. Their threat sweeps weren't quite the same, but they definitely weren't cowboys.

He doubted they'd been aboard the train before Lieutenant Van Buren and he had boarded. They'd been in town, waiting to see if any marines came their way. Or they'd been monitoring Camp Pyramid and followed them when they'd gone to town.

The details would come out when he started asking pointed questions, and he'd be asking a lot of those very soon.

The exit they chose from the warehouse was made for small vehicles rather than people, but they were able to lift the metal door and slide under it as if they'd performed the action a thousand times. Paci held it up for Jerome, and then the three of them walked off down the street as if they didn't have a care in the world.

The people in the city were dressed somewhat differently than those out on the frontier but not as much as one might assume. Their clothing was still somewhat more functional than the average Imperial world, but not everybody wore boots or hats. Regular shoes were more prevalent, and people went around with bare heads. He and his companions didn't *quite* stand out, but it was close.

"I don't know what the hell is going on, but we need to get out of sight and change clothes," Jerome said in a low tone.

"Just hold your horses," Parada said. "We've got one more block to walk, and then we'll be out of sight and out of mind. Stop looking around. You're going to draw attention."

Jerome wanted to grab the man, shove him up against the building, and demand answers, but sometimes being direct wasn't the quickest way to get what he wanted. This time, he'd keep following along until he got those answers, then he'd figure out what needed to be done to rescue the lieutenant.

The two led him to an alley where one entered a code on a keypad beside a locked door, and they went in. This new building had a cramped hallway that led to a rickety set of stairs leading up.

As soon as he saw the central area and the stairway, Jerome

realized they were in some kind of apartment building. They'd come through a service door in the back.

They went up four flights of stairs to an apartment for which Paci produced a key, unlocking the door and letting them all in. The apartment was plainly furnished and not in a cowboy theme. It looked like a city dweller's place, but there was a slight layer of dust over everything that indicated it hadn't been used in some time.

Before anyone could say anything, Jerome drew his stunner and covered the two men. "I appreciate what you've done for me, but I'm tired of being lied to. Who the hell are you people, and what the hell is going on?"

If being threatened with a weapon was disturbing for them, it didn't show. Parada went over to the window and opened the blinds slightly so he could look out.

"No sign of security on the street, so I think we got away. It'll take them a while to figure out exactly what happened on the platform. They'll take your lieutenant to the security holding cells and start asking him pointed questions, but they're not going to hurt him too badly right off the bat."

Considering that neither he nor the lieutenant had ever mentioned that they were Imperial Marines or what Van Buren's rank was, that statement confirmed his guesses about the two.

"It seems like you know who we are. Who the hell are you?"

"We already told you our names, and they're accurate enough. They're not the ones we were born with, but they're the ones we're using here. What we didn't tell you, Sergeant Walker, is that we work for the Imperial Security Services."

Before Jerome could respond, his implants pinged with an incoming communication. Somewhat skeptically, he reviewed the transmission and found it contained encrypted identification for both the individuals in front of him that identified them as members of the Imperial Security Services.

The transmission used Imperial protocols, so he had no reason to doubt its veracity, though he wasn't sure what to believe at this point.

The Imperial Security Services filled a peculiar role inside the Empire. In a lot of cases, Imperial facilities were guarded by marines

—but not always. There were times when it was either inconvenient or inappropriate to have marines looking after something, requiring another organization to handle the work.

That was where the Imperial Security Services came in. They weren't precisely police—though they had limited police powers—and they definitely weren't military. They filled a role inside the Imperial Department of Justice, and there was absolutely no reason for them to be on Diorama.

Yet here they were.

Reluctantly, Jerome lowered his weapon slightly. "That doesn't explain what you're doing here. You obviously knew we were coming and at least guessed at the kind of reception we might receive, so I think it's story time. What the hell is happening?"

"We might as well have a seat," Parada said. "This is going to take a while. We'll chat while Paci keeps an eye out for trouble."

19

Diana came down the stairs at a trot and walked out the front door just as the grav vehicle lifted off. The two men were headed toward the ranch house but stopped as soon as they saw her. Craig nudged Leroy, and the two of them continued up the steps until they stood in front of her.

"The doctor says that Beatrice is going to be okay," the older man said. "The damage to her leg is pretty extensive, but he was able to get everything back where it needed to be, and she's in the regenerator. We'll go back in the morning, and if everything is still good, she'll come home to recuperate."

The young man extended his hand to Diana. "Leroy Cavanaugh. I want to thank you and your friend for saving my sister and me. If the two of you hadn't come into the woods in spite of the danger, we'd be dead, and that puts me in your debt.

"Craig says you have some questions about the mine. While that won't clear what I owe you, I'll be happy to tell you everything I know."

"You owe that debt to Andrea, not me," Diana said with a smile as she shook his hand. "You can tell her that yourself in a little while, but

Rebecca is looking after her arm at the moment, so I'll avail myself of your kind offer."

"Whatever you need."

Craig gestured toward the door. "Why don't we go in and get more comfortable? It's still too warm for a fire, but we can set up next to the fireplace."

The three of them went into the ranch building and off to the side of the ground floor that Diana had never been in. That opened into a rather large area with a lot of comfortable seating and a *ridiculously* large fireplace.

As in large enough for her to lie inside it and not have the soles of her feet or the top of her head touch either side.

She stopped, turned to Craig, and raised an eyebrow. "Are you kidding me? What the hell do you need with a fireplace like that for? And what do you feed it? Whole trees?"

He smiled wryly and nodded. "It is big, I'll grant you, but it was built by my ancestors as part of the original house. If you think it dominates this room, you should've seen what it looked like in that much smaller structure.

"As for fuel, it does eat trees. Thankfully, we can cut them into pieces first, so we don't have to cart the entire trunk in at once. With the big cast-iron grate we've got inside it, we can use split pieces about a meter and a half long without any grief and still have plenty of space for cooking pots on top."

"You cook on *that*? When you've got a fire going, it will incinerate everything."

He shrugged slightly. "There is a particular skill that comes to cooking over a fire, I'll admit, but it's not impossible. You've just got to keep what you want far enough above the coals. If you've got a roaring fire, it better be the dead of winter, or this entire floor will feel like a sauna.

"Grab a couple of chairs, and I'll get us some tea. It feels like it's already been a long day, so I'll grab something for lunch as well because I have the feeling this conversation might take a while."

And with that, the man turned and headed back the way they'd come. Leroy walked nearer to the empty fireplace and gestured to one of the chairs. Once the two of them were settled, she reached out and put a hand on his leg.

"I'm really glad your sister is going to be okay. She looked pretty rough when we got in there, and I was worried."

He grimaced and shook his head. "We didn't think there were any dire wolves in the area. It's not the season for them to be down this far from the mountains, and even though it was a small pack, one of those things can kill anybody they put their teeth into.

"Living out on the frontier, you always have to keep an eye out for danger, and I was right there with the rifle, but I was still too slow to save her. I took out the wolves in the clearing before they could finish her, but the rest of the pack would've gotten us both. Your friend—and you—saved our lives."

"Like I said, all I did was run into the clearing looking pretty. I didn't even have to fire my weapon. If you want to talk to somebody that's death on two feet, that would be Andrea."

The young man nodded. "That doesn't reduce my gratitude to you for putting yourself at risk for us. You can rest assured that I'm going to thank your friend for everything she did for my sister and me, and I'm going to start by answering every single question you have about the mines and the operations there.

"Everything is on the table. If you want to know the foreman's secret peccadilloes, I'll tell you. He'll be pissed, but I can live with that."

She had to look the word up, and it almost made her chuckle. "I think we can probably do without knowing anybody's secrets unless they're relevant to the troubles at the mine. The Imperial Marines were sent here because of the sabotage and unrest. It's our job to figure out who's causing it.

"I'm not really worried about the personalities involved. The miners may have valid reasons for being angry, and we just have to dig down to find their grievances. We don't want to punish the wrong folk. If the corporations are doing something to drive the miners to this, we need to know."

Craig came back in with a small platter of sandwiches and tea before the man could respond. He set the glasses of ice out and filled them.

"Here on Diorama, we serve unsweetened tea. You can add whatever you feel necessary to the deal, but that's on you. We've got some ham and cheese sandwiches with mayo and mustard right here, if that's your go-to condiments. Why don't the two of you stoke up before you really get into this conversation?"

Since Leroy had busied himself adding sweetener to his tea, she did the same. Then she selected a couple of sandwiches, added mayonnaise and mustard, and topped them off with fresh lettuce. The ham was nice and thick, and the cheese was really sharp when she took a bite. It was going to be an excellent set of sandwiches.

Her desire to question Leroy about what was going on faded as she ate. It was hard to ask questions with her mouth full, so she devoted herself to the sandwiches. The tea wasn't bad either, but the sandwiches were some of the best she'd ever had.

The bread was interesting too. It wasn't quite sourdough, but it wasn't very far off either. It looked like it was freshly cut, so it had probably been baked in this very building. Hell, the ham might've come from pigs raised at the ranch, as might the lettuce.

Could they make cheese?

Probably. They already had cattle, so imagining there were milk cows around wasn't much of a stretch. The idea that these people were so self-sufficient that they could make everything necessary for sandwiches, other than the condiments, was damned impressive.

Or could they make the condiments too?

She had absolutely no idea what went into making mustard and mayonnaise, but it seemed that if they could grow the right plants, it might be possible. If so, that was amazing.

It took them a couple of minutes to do justice to the food, but soon enough, Diana was left nursing her tea while the sandwiches were utterly demolished. Leroy was eating a little slower than her but not by much.

Craig watched the two of them silently. Obviously, he was letting her run the show, and she appreciated that.

When Leroy finished the last of his sandwiches, she let him drink some tea and then leaned in to start the questioning.

"Like I said before, I'm not looking for anybody's secrets. I just want to know the story behind the sabotage and what's causing the people to do it. If that's the corporations pushing the miners into acting, so be it, but if the destruction has a different cause, I just want to know what it is."

Leroy scratched the side of his head and grimaced slightly. "You see, that's the thing. I left the mines about two years ago, but I still have lots of friends there, and we talk all the time.

"It's not the miners having an excuse for sabotaging things that we should be talking about. It's the fact that there's *not* any sabotage going on.

"So far as I know, the people at the mines are just as confused by your arrival as everybody else on the planet. Operations there are going smoothly with zero unrest or sabotage, no matter that rumors of it keep getting around."

Diana opened her mouth to respond but closed it again. Then she narrowed her eyes. "Is this some kind of joke? Why would the corporations call in the marines if that were true?"

The young man shrugged. "I haven't got the damnedest idea. All I can say for sure is that unless all of my friends are lying to me—which I don't believe for one second—there's no trouble at the mines. As for why the corporations would call you in when nothing was going on, I couldn't begin to imagine."

"If you'd like to take a look, I'll get Leroy, Andrea, and you up to the mines," Craig said. "I'm not sure if that would step on your commander's toes, but he can't get inside like Leroy. Say the word, and you're in like Flynn."

Diana had absolutely no idea who Flynn was or what he was getting into, but she *was* interested. The idea of exploring this mystery appealed to her, but if she did something like this without running it up the chain of command first, there would rightly be hell to pay.

"We've been authorized to accompany you and ask questions," she ventured. "If Leroy was to take *you* up to the mine for a tour, we'd be happy to go with you, but we couldn't conduct an investigation on our own."

Craig laughed. "That's sneaky, but if you think it's going to save your ass from young Sergeant Walker when he finds out, you're wrong. Still, I've got a sudden and intense hankering to see what's happening at the mines. I think we should take a little trip up there before dinner. What do you two think?"

Leroy smiled. "I'm game."

"I'll need to talk with Andrea to be sure, but I don't expect she's going to have any objections," Diana said. "We should probably get some food into her and then figure out how we're going to explain who she is when we get there."

Craig crossed his arms over his chest and smiled smugly. "I happen to know for a fact that my sister is having a discussion with her about something that might come in real handy right about now. Why don't we head back to the kitchen and make her some sandwiches and tea to eat while we discuss the situation with her?"

Diana rose to her feet and grabbed her plate and tea glass. "Sounds good. I could do with another sandwich myself."

20

A ndrea removed the makeup and was oddly relieved to see her tattoos once again covering her face. For something that had caused her so much trouble over the years, it was unsettling how bereft she felt with them gone. Theirs was definitely a complicated love-hate relationship.

Under Rebecca's direction, she washed her face and dried it thoroughly. She took a second towel and hit it again to be sure. Any residual moisture would probably cause problems, which wasn't what she wanted. If she was going to use this stuff, she wanted to use it correctly.

The woman presented her with a pad and directed her on how to apply the makeup while looking in the mirror. She pointed out that it wouldn't be the same color as her skin until it had thoroughly dried, which took about sixty seconds. It would be darker until that point.

Ignoring the differences in skin tone as she applied the makeup, Andrea focused on making smooth, even strokes. There were portions of her face that didn't need any makeup, but since it was her face, she didn't want bare areas to look different from the rest, so she covered it all.

Because she had no experience in applying makeup, she made mistakes. Rebecca pointed them out and gave advice on how to correct them. The first application was a bit uneven, and Andrea could see where the makeup stopped and her bare skin started, even after she attempted to blend the two areas together.

Rebecca told her that she'd get better with practice and had her remove the makeup again and apply it more slowly as she gave directed advice on technique and application. Andrea managed to do a better job, focusing on the task at hand, though nowhere near as good as what Rebecca had done. Still, it looked serviceable.

The tattoos were covered, and while she could still see where the makeup ended, Rebecca helped her with some final steps to further blend the transition between the two. The process wasn't complicated, but it would take some practice to make sure she knew exactly how to do this in the future.

If she decided it was something she wanted to do.

Because she was something of a perfectionist, she removed the makeup and put it on again. This time she went slowly and methodically, performing the tasks she'd seen Rebecca do and trying to mimic the style the woman had used.

She paid close attention to the color of the makeup as it was applied and at least made sure that it was consistent as she went. She might have the wrong shade when she was done, but at least it would be the *same* shade this time.

When it was dry, it wasn't that far off from her regular skin tone, so she listened again as Rebecca walked her through blending the two zones together, so they seemed continuous unless someone looked carefully.

Even then, if they weren't looking for makeup covering her entire face, they might very well miss what she'd done. After all, didn't women apply makeup to their faces all the time? She was overthinking this.

When she finished, Rebecca clapped her hands delightedly. "Oh, that's excellent. You can improve your technique, but no one would know if you walked out into the house right now. Considering that most people never look past your tattoos, I doubt anyone would recognize you. Well done."

Andrea put the makeup pad down and took the time to store the remaining makeup in a jar that Rebecca had brought for just that purpose. There was probably enough for three or four applications, which was far more than she expected to use anytime soon, but it would be there if she decided there was a purpose to be served.

She stared at herself in the mirror, still amazed at the ordinary person that looked back at her. The view of her unblemished face was both spooky and yet really beautiful. This was what the girl inside her had grown into.

It was also what Keeper looked like without her tattoos, though the woman was older.

The authoritarian despot of the crèche wasn't nearly as intimidating without her tattoos. Andrea could see the human being now rather than the hardline ruler she'd known during her early years. The tattoos definitely had an effect because they changed the perceptions of everyone that saw them. It didn't matter what the person underneath looked like, so long as the tattoos had the desired effect on the viewer.

This was a lesson she'd known all her life but only now really understood.

There was a knock at the bedroom door, and it opened before she could say anything. Rebecca headed out of the bathroom, but Andrea took a moment more to stare at herself in the mirror before following.

Diana had returned, and she'd brought Craig and Leroy with her. Craig—who was holding a tray with sandwiches, glasses of tea, and condiments—took one look at her and smiled. He didn't say anything, but his eyes told her that he'd known this was happening.

Leroy and Diana, though, blinked at her in confusion. They'd just found a stranger in Andrea's room and were trying to figure out exactly what was going on.

Diana opened her mouth to say something but froze. The realization in her eyes was obvious, and it made Andrea grin.

"No way!" her friend almost screamed. "You found some way to remove your tattoos? Let me take a look at you!"

Without waiting for Andrea to respond, her friend grabbed her by the shoulders and stared at her face from just centimeters away. "No. You've just covered it with makeup. I had no idea there was anything powerful enough to hide tattoos like yours."

"What do you think?" Andrea asked, more than a little nervous about what her friend thought.

Diana smiled. "I think you're flat-out gorgeous, that's what I think. I also think no one who knew you before would recognize you now. The only reason I did was because I knew this was your room, and I'm your best friend. If you walked past Claudio in a bar, he'd stare at your ass and whistle, but that would be the extent of it. He'd never recognize you."

"Ewww." Andrea held her hands palm out in rejection. "No, thank you."

Her friend laughed. "This is the most amazing thing I've ever seen, and it makes what I have in mind a whole lot simpler. We've brought you sandwiches and tea, so why don't you stoke up while I explain what I think we should do next?"

Andrea sat on the edge of the bed, took the tray from Craig, and set it beside her. There was enough for both Rebecca and herself, and the two women began serving themselves as Diana began explaining what Leroy had told her and what they were going to do next.

She was blown away by the news that there was apparently no sabotage or unrest at the mines. Her brain circled around the subject even as Diana was talking, but she couldn't figure out any possible reason why Yi Holdings would be doing that. It just didn't make any sense.

Still, if it was true, somebody was playing a deep game that would have very serious repercussions when Lieutenant Van Buren found out. This needed to go right to the top, even if they didn't have any proof it was true.

"I'll send a message to Lieutenant Van Buren letting him know what's going on," Andrea said. "He has to take this into account, even if it doesn't prove to be accurate—apologies, Leroy."

The young man shrugged. "I understand covering your bases.

You'll find out soon enough, but your superiors need to be prepared. Do you think they'll tell you not to go?"

"There's only one way to find out."

Andrea quickly composed a brief message outlining what they'd discovered and forwarded it directly to Lieutenant Van Buren. The transmission was boosted by the com gear on her belt and then again by the drone circling around the ranch house.

She received a response from Camp Pyramid that the message had been received and forwarded to the lieutenant. She'd marked it as high priority, and that was the best she could do.

If he didn't like the idea of her going to the mines, he'd send something back ordering her not to proceed. Unless she received orders to stand down, she'd assume he was good with Diana's plan.

That done, she devoted herself to preparing her sandwiches and eating. She'd always adored good food, and this was delicious. Even the tea was great, though it needed sweetener.

As a kid, she'd had innumerable sandwiches, but these were something to remember with their thick ham and sharp cheese, as well as the spicy mustard and smooth mayonnaise. Even the bread was delightful. All together, it was an amazing meal.

When they'd finished eating, Rebecca began gathering the detritus left over from the meal. "I'll take care of this while you head for the mines. If there's nothing going on, I suggest keeping things low-key. There has to be a reason for someone to fake this kind of trouble, and they won't want their secret getting out before they're ready."

"I've already called for our ride," Craig said. "Once we have a little more information, we can make a better call about what needs to happen next.

"I doubt very seriously that anyone is going to cause trouble. If they're concerned about the marines, they'll be watching for them to make an appearance. With that makeup on, Andrea isn't going to stand out, and Diana won't either. They'll both easily fit in as hands from the ranch."

"And what will you be visiting the mines for?" Rebecca asked, raising an eyebrow. "It's not like you're building a flip drive."

Her brother shook his head and smiled. "No, but there are other things there that might be useful at a ranch. They recover quite a bit of iron ore as part of the mining process, and our blacksmith could certainly use a larger supply. If I can pick it up in bulk, that'll save me a good bit of money and time. At least that's the story I'm going to run with."

"That's a good idea," Leroy agreed. "They recover a lot of iron ore, but most of it is dumped into the slag heap, since it's not worth hauling anywhere. If you come down and pick it up, they'll probably be happy to let you have it cheap, particularly with me smoothing the negotiations."

"Well, then, I suggest we head on out and see what's afoot at the mine," Craig said, turning toward the door.

Andrea took time to hug Rebecca and thank her again for everything she'd done. Going out in public like this felt a little strange, but it was definitely going to be an experience to remember.

"What about our weapons?" she asked as they headed for the stairs. "Are they going to be a problem?"

"Make sure your jackets are long enough to cover them," Leroy said. "If they've got a problem, we can check them in. I don't expect they will, but one never knows."

Even if they demanded they turn them over, Andrea still had her undetectable weapons. Besides, she was a lot more dangerous unarmed than most people assumed, and so was Diana. If there was trouble, they'd handle it.

"Let's do this," she said, heading after Craig. "I'll need a new coat and hat. I kind of ruined the first ones."

Hopefully, she wouldn't end up covered in blood this time.

* * *

JEROME GRABBED a bar stool from the divider between the kitchen and the living area and sat, keeping one foot on the floor and his stunner in his lap. He wasn't willing to give the two men the benefit of the doubt, even if they had sent him their identification. There was just too much going on for him to feel comfortable doing that.

For their part, Paci and Parada seemed happy enough to park themselves on the couch, keeping their hands in their laps while they explained the situation. He was sure—based on their earlier movements—that they'd continue to check the windows to be certain no one was massing around the building.

He was willing to allow that, so long as they didn't make any strange moves. The odds that the couch had weapons hidden in it was pretty high, and if they moved their hands in a way that he didn't like, he'd stun them on the spot and sort it out later.

Parada led off. "You're probably asking yourself why someone from the Imperial Security Services would be working on Diorama. There's an Imperial project here that the corporations aren't aware of.

"That means I can't tell you precisely what it is, either, but it gives us a reason to be paying attention to what's going on. Like you, we've heard about the unrest and sabotage at the mines. That's why the Imperial Marines are here, right?"

Jerome was willing to give them a nod. It wasn't as if it was really a secret.

"We've put out feelers to see if we could determine the cause of the disruption, just because we'd rather not have any waves in our little pond," Paci said. "Seriously, getting any firm information about what's going on at the mines is almost impossible. No one there wants to talk about the situation, so we have to assume negotiations are still taking place to settle whatever differences the workers and Yi Holdings have.

"I suspect your arrival has set everything on its ear. Now whatever clandestine talks were taking place, well, those are probably shot. We know for a fact that Yi Holdings is busy clamping down on information going off-planet because of supposed technical failures that coincidentally started as soon as you arrived in the system."

Jerome felt his lips tightening. "Why don't we bring up the elephant in the room? You knew security would have an eye out for anyone that looked like an Imperial Marine sneaking into the capital.

"Why would they be doing that, and how did you get onto us first? For that matter, why didn't you just tell us the truth while we were on the train? Playing spies isn't exactly the most effective use of our time and energy, don't you think?"

The two men shifted a bit uncomfortably. "Technically, we shouldn't even be telling you any of this. After we left the dining car, we had a talk and decided that if you didn't make it through, we should intervene.

"It's one thing to stop our communications from going in and out, but it's a completely different thing when an Imperial corporation begins taking action against the marines. That tells us something very wrong is happening, and we're going to need your help figuring out what that is."

Doing this kind of work wasn't Jerome's forte. He really needed to let Delta Company know what was going on. He was certain communications in and out of the capital were restricted. He had his military com, but it wouldn't interface with the local network. Even if it could, he was sure that somebody was taking steps to ensure that no messages made it back to his comrades.

He'd have to be clever to get a warning out, and these people could probably help him after they answered one more question.

"How did you know who we were?" he asked. "You never heard my rank or the lieutenant's, but you knew."

"We can query your implants for an ID without them telling you we've done so. That's not a general police power, but we have extra leeway. We can't get anything else, but that was more than enough to know who and what you were."

Well, wasn't that just peachy? Still, there was nothing he could do about it. Might as well move along.

"I've got a couple of problems that need solving pretty damned fast," Jerome finally said. "They've got my commanding officer, and I've got to get him back. It seems insane that they think they can just take him and get away with it."

"What makes you think they'll admit to doing so?" Parada asked. "If they get their hands on you, there's no evidence they have him at all. As for what they hope to gain from keeping him, that's a mystery and one of the reasons we're helping you. Whatever game Yi Holdings is playing, it's a lot more serious than we'd bargained for."

"They're going to have your officer locked up in some kind of security setup that isn't public," Paci said. "That means he's not just going straight to jail, he's probably already in a secure facility directly under the corporation's control.

"The three of us won't be able to breach anything like that, and even if we could, the risk to Lieutenant Van Buren would be exceptionally high. They can't let him talk now. They've taken a step too far."

"They're also not going to let you send a message back to the rest of the marines," Parada said. "I've already checked, and the local com network is down due to 'technical difficulties.' It's happened a few other times, and they're busy blaming sabotage for it. Big surprise, right?

"You can also bet they'll be triple checking anyone leaving the city, particularly going in the direction of your camp. We're not very far from the train station, and I feel confident they're already surrounding this area to start going door-to-door."

"It's not going to be hard to identify us, since they'll have our pictures from the cameras at the station," Jerome grumbled. "Real soon, every security officer in the city is going to know what I look like and probably you too."

"They'll know who you are because of the body cameras on the security agents," Paci said. "They're not going to know us because we put the cameras at the station on a loop before the train arrived. Standard procedure for us to make sure they never get any good images of our faces.

"This is the first time they've had security on the platform itself, so there was nothing we could do about them. As for being in danger here, it's true. Sooner or later, somebody will come knocking. They're not going to take silence for an answer either. They'll be able to tell the apartment is occupied, and they'll kick the door in to get to us."

"Which is the reason we're not going to be here when they arrive," Parada said. "As soon as we figure they're getting to this general area, we're going down to the subbasement, and we'll make our way clear from there. We'd have already done so, but we needed to convince you that we're trying to help and that we need your help in turn. Whatever's going on here, we need to join forces so we can settle this."

Jerome thought about that but wasn't so sure. This could be some trick, and the men in front of him might be working with the corporations. Or the corporations might not be involved at all in whatever was going on.

That was unlikely but still possible.

"Before I decide, I've got to get a message back to my people. If you can help me do that, I'm willing to believe what you're doing enough to help."

The two men glanced at one another, and Paci shrugged. "I think we can get you a military-grade transmitter capable of reaching your camp or the ship you have in orbit. It's not going to be easy to get to, but it shouldn't be *too* heavily guarded.

"We'll have to break into a warehouse and steal something quite valuable to make this work. Even if we return it after the fact, you can rest assured the owner will not be happy. If you're willing to take those steps, we're willing to help you do this."

Jerome considered the pitch for all of three seconds. "It's not like my situation could get much worse, could it? Let's get the hell out of here before security finds us.

"Once we've got a couple squads of Imperial Marines to back us up, we can take a little trip to Yi Holdings and demand they return my commanding officer. We can also start asking pointed questions with armed and armored marines backing us up. They won't have any choice but to cooperate."

He could tell they didn't completely agree with his assessment, but they did get up off the couch.

"We've got some weapons in the apartment and some other gear that would be helpful for breaking and entering," Parada said. "Are you willing to trust us with something like that?"

"Trust? No. You'll just have to deal with the fact that I'm watching you. Cross me, and you'll deeply regret it."

Paci grinned. "I think I like you, Walker. Let's get what we need and get the hell out of here before we have unwelcome visitors."

Jerome wasn't sure he was making the right choice, but it wasn't as if he had a lot of options. He needed to get back into contact with Delta Company, and he needed to do it now. Every minute he delayed was time for Yi Holdings to do something bad to Lieutenant Van Buren, and he wasn't going to let that happen.

Not on his watch.

21

As they flew toward the mines, Diana couldn't take her eyes off Andrea. Her friend looked utterly, *radically* different with her tattoos covered. Seeing her friend as a regular person was a shock.

She'd had more than half a year to get used to her friend the way she was, and now she had to accept her as something different. All this time, Andrea had been saying the tattoos didn't define her, and Diana had agreed, yet here she was thinking differently about her friend when the tattoos weren't in evidence.

Based on how Andrea kept touching her face, Diana wasn't alone in feeling that way.

Whatever her friend did, she'd support her. The presence or lack of tattoos did not change who Andrea was, and it wasn't going to change how Diana felt about her.

Still, it might very well change how other people saw her—and not necessarily for the better. Those who knew she had the tattoos would now start questioning why she'd covered them up.

Those would be the same people that said she wore them only so she could wave the Singularity flag in their faces. There would be no winning an argument with people that wouldn't be satisfied no matter what Andrea did.

For example, her friend had a very prickly relationship with Sergeant Walker. The man went out of his way not to engage her about her background, but Diana wasn't an idiot. She could see he had a serious problem with her, even though he struggled to keep it under control. She didn't know what had happened in his past, but it had scarred him in a way that made him difficult to read.

It was almost as if he had conflicting desires. If he'd been given free rein, he might very well have landed on Andrea like a ton of plascrete, but there was some kind of mitigating desire that had him watching her like a hawk and restraining whatever urges he felt.

The odds of that being something good were low, but she had nothing to base any guesses on. All she could do was keep her eye on events as they happened and try to make the best assessment she could.

All of them were sitting in the back of the large grav vehicle that had taken the wounded back to the ranch house after the dire wolves had attacked. It was obviously a multipurpose vehicle, built to carry cargo, people, and occasionally livestock, depending on how the interior was configured.

In a lot of ways, it was like a marine pinnace. You could pack it full of seats and carry a large number of marines, you could strip out the seats and pack it full of cargo, or you could mix and match like they'd done on the way up to the Fleet transport on Seward.

If the goal was transporting cargo and livestock commercially, something like this wouldn't have made sense, but she could see where it would be useful in taking smaller loads of cargo and particular groups of livestock from one location to another.

It definitely beat having a couple of dozen ranch hands do the work using something on the ground, because it could get to places that ground-based transport couldn't and do it faster.

In a pinch, it could take them all the way to the mountains where the mines were located. That would've taken days for something on the ground, even if there had been cleared paths to get there, which there weren't unless one counted the grav train tracks.

The raw ore was moved by train, according to her databases. It was taken to the capital and shipped out to special refining complexes in other systems.

That was interesting but not really important right now. Three things had her attention at the moment: her friend and how she interacted with the rest of the marines, the supposed trouble at the mines, and the overarching problem where the corporations were behaving strangely.

That last item was still very murky, and it had only come to light because the mines supposedly had no trouble going on. If there wasn't any sabotage or widespread disaffection, there would've been no reason to call the Imperial Marines to Diorama.

Yet, the corporations running the planet had done precisely that. What was their real reason?

The only way to solve the mystery was to get more data. The Imperial Intelligence databases didn't have enough information to make any guesses as to what was going on, but that might change as they started adding to the list of people they were keeping an eye on.

Right now, the only players she knew were the chief executive officer of Yi Holdings, Massimiliano Sticchi, and his attack dog, Kate Geller. They'd seemingly come on board with the company around the right time for whatever was in progress to be laid at their feet, but without any kind of guess as to what they were doing, Diana couldn't figure out a motive or even the process that was playing out around them.

"We're coming up on the mines," the pilot called out. "We'll be landing just outside the general parking area for regular grav cars, so the landing might be just a little bit rough. Ignore any rocks or debris slapping up against the hull."

Less than a minute later, the grav carrier settled to the ground, and there was a fair bit of rattling against the hull. As soon as the vehicle began shutting down, Craig stood and lowered the ramp.

"You stay here and watch our ride, Barry. I don't think we're going to be too long, but it's best not to have you walking around the mine and falling down a hole or anything."

"Thanks for that vote of confidence, boss," the pilot said dryly.

"I'll just stay here in this seat so I don't accidentally trip over anything."

"You do that," Craig said with a grin as he headed down the ramp with Leroy at his side. Andrea and Diana fell in behind them, already playing the roles of ranch hands.

Diana wondered how much turnover the Big L Ranch had. Would somebody familiar with the place recognize that she and Andrea didn't belong?

Just inside the regular parking area was a grav transport made to skim along the ground. It had a number of seats and no top. Standing beside it was an older, rotund man with stringy brown hair that clung to the fringes of his head.

He was dressed in light-gray coveralls that looked sturdy and wore work boots. He grinned and pulled Leroy into a hug. "Damn, boy, it's good to see you again. How's your sister?"

Leroy hugged him tightly and then grinned back. "Is that the only reason you're glad to see me, Ray? You'd like another shot at my sister? I thought we'd already discussed that."

The other man laughed. "While your sister is indeed a fine woman, my wife would object. Besides which, I'm old enough to be her father. I understand society is more accepting of that kind of thing these days, but she's not interested in an old coot like me.

"So who are your friends, and what brings you back to the mines? I was pretty sure we'd seen the last of you, considering how fast you left."

Leroy held his hand to his chest as though he were wounded. "That hurts! I just wanted to see some sunlight for a change."

"Isn't that the damned truth? Makes me glad not only to see you today but to be out here in this pretty weather."

Leroy gestured at Craig. "This is my boss, Craig Lindbergh, the owner of the Big L Ranch. Andrea and Diana are a couple of the new hires he's taking around today. Craig, this is Ray Reeves, my old shift supervisor and now part of the management team.

"Tell me, Ray, is this is an example of screw up and move up, or did you actually show some talent for a change?"

The balding man laughed as he shook Craig's hand. He barely spared a glance for Diana and Andrea.

"I have a real talent for bossing slackers like you around, that's for sure. Everybody pile into the scooter, and we'll head for the mine. The offices are just inside the underground area, and everything's been completely reinforced, so no hard hats required."

They climbed into the grav vehicle, and Ray quickly had it turned around and headed back up the mountain. They didn't have to go much higher elevation-wise, but they did go around a spur of rock to get to the entrance to the mine itself.

Diana wondered why they'd chosen to dig into the mountain away from where they'd parked, but as soon as she saw the area where they were doing the mining itself, she understood. Right around the corner of the spur, there was a considerable drop-off down into a valley far below. It looked as if they were using that giant crack in the earth as a place to dump the things they didn't need.

It probably wasn't the most environmentally friendly thing to do, but there was no river running through it and nothing but rock all around, so maybe it was okay. It undoubtedly also depended on exactly what they were throwing out. She'd have to do more research to be sure.

Ray took the vehicle through the entrance to the mine itself but curved off to the left-hand side and into a tunnel that went up rather than down. He stopped in a parking area and led them to a lift that took them up.

The area they came out in looked like the inside of an office building, with carpeting, good lighting, and office workers dressed like they were working in the city. Not at all what she'd expected for a mine.

"Why don't we talk in my office about what you're looking for, Mister Lindbergh, and let Leroy take your new hires on a little tour of the mine? He'll get them hard hats and make sure they don't go anywhere dangerous, so I don't have any objection to them poking around."

"That's mighty kind of you, and I think that sounds like an

excellent idea," Craig said. "You three stay out of trouble and be back here in an hour. I can't imagine it taking longer than that to set up something interesting with Ray."

Leroy led Diana and Andrea back to the lift. Diana started to say something when they got inside, but Leroy shook his head. He pressed one of the buttons near the bottom of the panel, and the lift car dropped deep into the ground. Only once it reached its destination and the three of them stepped out into a much dimmer area did Leroy say anything.

"I figure it's better not to say something that might catch security's attention inside one of the lifts. If anything is monitored, it's going to be the lifts. Grab some hard hats."

There were several racks of equipment near the lift, including hard hats, flashlights, and other safety or mining gear. There was lighting strung up over their heads, but it had the feel of something temporary.

She took a hard hat and a flashlight. Andrea and Leroy followed suit.

"This is one of the lowest levels for the lift, but the mines go much deeper. We'll go down on a second lift and hit one of the break rooms near the active areas where I know some of my friends will likely be, and then you'll be able to ask some questions without worrying that management is listening."

"Wasn't Ray one of your friends?" Andrea asked as they started moving. "He sounded friendly."

"He's a nice enough guy, but he *is* management. If you want to hear the real skinny about what's going on, we need to talk to your average miner. Come on."

Diana fell back to the end of the single-file group and looked around curiously as they walked. She had no idea what they'd learn, but the experience was really interesting.

It turned out there were special lifts used inside the mine itself that were definitely not suitable for anything going to an office. They were dirty, their floors covered in grit, and she was afraid to touch the walls because she'd become immediately filthy.

"As the mine goes farther down, they extend the shaft for these temporary lifts," Leroy said, seeming not to notice as the lift bucked and groaned slowly downward. "They use them for carrying equipment and personnel, not the ore itself. Those have different, larger lifts that get them from level to level."

"If it doesn't carry the ore, why is everything so dirty?" Andrea asked, eyeing the walls.

The young man grinned. "Mining is dirty work, and if you spend any time down here at all, you're going to look like you fell into a hole and rolled around for an hour. There isn't any getting around that."

The personnel elevator took them deep into the mountain, though not as far as the buttons indicated it could go. The mine was significantly larger than Diana had imagined.

She knew mining for the materials used to create flip drives consumed a lot of regular material because the stuff was rare, but she hadn't realized just how much ground they had to chew through to find what they needed.

When they exited the elevator, the tunnel they were in was extremely rough and definitely made for people moving lots of heavy material without real concern for how they made a hole through the mountain. The floor of the passage was *relatively* flat but far from smooth.

The walls? Rough didn't begin to cover it.

Spaced out every five meters or so were supports to ensure no cave-ins. At least that was what she decided the beams must be for.

Since there were no signs, she wasn't sure exactly how Leroy intended to get wherever he was going, but the man acted as if he were going somewhere familiar. Since he'd worked down here for years, odds were good they weren't lost.

At least she hoped not.

She had to challenge that assumption when they came around a corner and found themselves face-to-face with a couple of miners standing in front of a barricade blocking off the tunnel in front of them.

One of the men held up a hand and frowned. "This area is closed. You'll have to go around."

Leroy started to reply, but the man's gaze swept past him, briefly floating across Diana and Andrea before he did a double-take and stiffened.

"I'm sorry about that, ma'am," the man almost groveled in apology. "I didn't see you right off. Go right on through."

At a gesture, the other man—whose eyes were just as wide—opened the barricade and gestured for them to go on.

Leroy gave the men a strange look but said nothing as he continued into the mine.

Andrea edged over to Diana and spoke in a low voice. "What the hell was that?"

She shrugged slightly. "I haven't got the slightest idea. It didn't seem like they wanted to let us through. Based on what he said, I think he was looking at you when he changed his mind."

"That's not the only thing," Leroy said. "Did you get a good look at their coveralls? Even Ray's had a little bit of something on them. Those guys? Clean as a whistle. They aren't miners."

They were speaking quietly but weren't very far away from the barricade they'd just passed. Far enough that a low conversation was safe, but Diana was really concerned that something important was happening, and she didn't understand it at all.

Andrea stiffened for a moment and then caught up with them, her stride having to hitch a little bit to match back up. "Sound in these tunnels is a little weird, but I caught part of what they were saying after we passed. Most of it was garbled, but I caught a familiar name: Geller.

"Seems odd they'd be referring to the Yi Holdings CEO's hatchet woman. I think we might have our first real proof that the corporations really are up to something."

Diana nodded and brought up the file she had on Kate Geller again. She started to read, but her attention jerked back up to the image she had for the woman. She'd seen it before, of course, but it hadn't meant anything to her then.

That was no longer true.

"Andrea, we've got a big problem," she said softly. "I just checked the file we have on Kate Geller, and I know exactly why they just let us pass."

She sent the image to Andrea, and her friend stopped dead in her tracks, her eyes widening.

"Holy crap!" Andrea whispered urgently. "Geller is a member of the Andrea Line with her tattoos covered! The Singularity is here!"

22

Andrea's mind was racing in circles. They had to get this information to the company as soon as possible, but they had a big problem. They were buried deep under the mountain, and their communications equipment wouldn't work under those conditions. Their military com units wouldn't connect with the civilian network used in the mine, either, so they needed another solution.

They'd brought the recon drone along with them, but it was in the grav vehicle they'd arrived in. With the amount of rock surrounding them, they couldn't send a warning unless they left the mine.

That meant their first priority had to be getting out without tipping off the bad guys that they'd made a mistake. In a perfect world, they'd get back out, and Geller wouldn't even be aware they'd found out her secret, but Andrea knew they couldn't count on that.

Far from it, in fact. The clock was ticking, and they needed to be in motion.

"You know the mines," she said to Leroy. "How can we get out without passing those same guards? We can't count on them letting us go without getting suspicious."

"There are several ways out of this area, but it's going to depend on what we're looking to accomplish," Leroy said. "The central part of this area is where the miners go while off shift, or at least they used to. It has a break room and a couple of bunkrooms.

"I seem to remember there being a couple of other ways out of the area, but they don't lead back to the elevator we just used. One of them goes deeper into the mine and the other to the ore extraction area. If we're going back up to the offices, we're going to have to get past those guards or others just like them."

"We can't waste this opportunity," Diana said. "Whatever they're doing here, they definitely don't want anyone to know they're doing it. We're inside their guard, and we need to get to the bottom of this before we escape."

Andrea waffled for a couple of seconds, but she eventually decided Diana was right. They had one chance to find out what was going on. If they didn't take advantage of it, they wouldn't get a second opportunity.

"Okay," she said, holding her hand out to forestall any objections. "It's obvious we're not going to find the people we were hoping to talk to, so we're going to make a high-speed reconnaissance pass through this area to determine what we can.

"As soon as we do that—whether we succeed or fail—we need to get out of here by the most expeditious route possible. We'll send a message to Craig to break off whatever he's doing and head back to the grav vehicle if we can, but we need to get out of here before all hell breaks loose."

She turned to Leroy. "I don't think most of the miners are involved in what's happening, but some of them have to be. There's no way these people could just move in down here and set up shop without *somebody* covering for them. At least we know your old boss is clean. He didn't even give me a second look."

The man didn't look pleased but didn't argue either. "If we keep going straight, we'll end up in the break room. The bunk rooms are off to either side, and there's also some storage available for supplies.

"It wouldn't surprise me if the first set of guards have already sent word that we're on our way in, and if one of these new people realize you aren't Kate Geller, all hell is out for noon. We need to be ready for that."

Andrea drew back her jacket to reveal her weapons. "Diana and I are more than ready for trouble. Can you use a stunner?"

The young man shook his head. "The only things I've ever used were flechette and slug rifles for hunting and protection while on the range."

"The stunners aren't much different. We don't have much time, so help me move these over to him, Diana. If push comes to shove, I'd much rather have three armed people than two."

The young man frowned. "If you give up your weapons, you're not going to be much help. You're trained, so you should keep them."

"I have my secrets," Andrea said somewhat coyly. "Let's make this happen before somebody starts wondering what the hell we're doing."

Unclipping her holsters and moving them to his belt only took thirty seconds with the two of them working on it. Thankfully, they didn't require removing the belts to make the switch work. Once Leroy had the weapons settled around his waist, they made sure his jacket covered them.

She then relocated her concealable flechette pistol and stunner to her belt. They wouldn't be hidden if she had to go for them, but they'd be more accessible in the new locations, and seconds counted now.

Never having seen them before, Leroy gawked at the tiny weapons. "You're chock full of surprises."

"That's what my guardians tell me. Now, let's get a move on."

Leroy set off. They made a couple of twists and turns, but there were no side passages that they could've gotten confused with.

She recognized the break area when they came into it because it was a much wider space, though still very cramped. It was filled with break tables and a couple of machines to make coffee and tea. There were three men and a woman in the break area, already on their feet.

The woman stepped forward and looked at Andrea, her expression more than a bit suspicious. "Miss Geller, I didn't expect to see you again so soon. Is something wrong? And why are you dressed like that?"

Andrea gave the woman a chilly smile. "Sometimes, when you're doing something with a certain group of people, it benefits you to dress similarly. As for seeing me so soon, I wasn't aware that I needed to explain myself to you."

She was channeling Keeper as she spoke, just on the off chance that behaving like the woman would help her disguise seem more authentic. They were already operating at a disadvantage because they were dressed in cowboy-style clothes, and she needed every advantage she could scrounge up.

The woman stared at her for a few seconds and then looked away. "Of course. We haven't made any progress since you were last here, and I don't anticipate doing so without utilizing more force than you've authorized thus far. If you've come looking for a breakthrough, I'm afraid we don't have it yet."

"That's disappointing, but I suppose not so surprising," Andrea said, trying to parse what the woman had said. "I've been thinking about the results thus far, and I'm wondering if we couldn't change the parameters a little bit. Run down the major points for me again so I can update my plans."

One of the men frowned more deeply before shaking his head slightly. "Your man is already doing everything he can to make her talk, but I'm not sure he can get anything from her without taking it up a notch.

"She's got some kind of drug resistance, so he can't dope her to get the answers you're looking for. What are you thinking? Cutting off her fingers until she starts telling him what you want to know? That might work, but it's kind of permanent."

Well, that was grotesque. These people were sick bastards.

So, they had a prisoner down here. There was no telling who this woman was, but if the Singularity wanted her, then it was worthwhile to extract her. Anything that somebody from the Andrea Line was interested in was automatically interesting.

The question was, could they get their hands on this woman without starting a fight that was going to bring every bad guy in the mine down on their heads?

The answer was almost certainly no, and they had no idea how many bad guys were in the area. There could be dozens in the bunk rooms to either side of the break room. The prisoner had to be somewhere close, too, but Andrea didn't know where yet. It would be essential to get that information before making any irrevocable moves.

Sadly, she had no idea how to make that happen, and she was already out of time. The people in front of her were looking for answers right now, and she needed to pick a plan and run with it.

She opened her mouth to do that, but before she could speak, the doorway leading to one of the bunk rooms opened, and a tall man with a hatchet-thin face stepped out. His eyes swept over everyone in the break room and settled on Andrea.

"Why have you returned so quickly, and why are you dressed in that ridiculous clothing?" he demanded.

Andrea had no idea who the man was, but he didn't seem the least bit afraid of her.

Before she could make up an answer, Diana drew her stunner, shoved it in front of Andrea, and fired it on wide beam. Everyone in front of them—including the new man—was within the weapon's arc and dropped.

"He wasn't buying what you were selling," her friend said. "We need to get a move on. Leroy, cover the exits. Andrea, you go low, I'll go high."

Andrea drew her stunner and hit the doorway that the man had just come through, crouching and swinging in to cover the room from the bottom half of the door while Diana did so from above her. A stunner beam flashed through the doorway, but the two marines had already fired. The four men and women inside the room dropped like puppets with their strings cut.

Whatever they'd been expecting, it hadn't been an outright attack. The rapid assault had come as a surprise, and they hadn't even gotten to cover.

The room was otherwise empty, so Andrea turned in place just in time to see Leroy fire the marine-issue stunner—which she'd set to wide beam—at the other bunk room doorway, taking out the two men who'd rushed through it.

They went down hard, but a third person inside the room stuck an arm around the corner and began firing a flechette pistol. His aim was execrable, so he missed hitting anyone, but that could change with a single unlucky shot.

Andrea ran around the side of the break room, taking herself out of the direct line of fire and racing toward the doorway from an angle where the man couldn't see her coming. When she was close, she dove through the door and fired as soon as her weapon was clear, even as she skidded into the room, losing her hat in the process.

Her shot took the man squarely in the face, and he dropped. Wide beam stuns were less effective than pinpoint accuracy, but the man had eaten virtually the entire beam, so he was going to be out for a while.

Diana came racing through the door, swinging her weapon around and covering every angle only to discover that the room was otherwise empty.

Andrea still made a pass through the room while Diana returned to the break room.

Her friend searched everyone quickly, collecting their personal belongings, since they might have usable intelligence. Most had com units, but one had a larger, specialized unit.

Thus far, no one outside their little area seemed to have heard anything. That was good news, but luck like that wouldn't last. They were on the clock, and they needed to get the hell out of there as quickly as possible.

Andrea went to the man who'd spoken to her and searched him, removing his com and other things from his pocket to throw into the bag.

He had a picture of a woman in his wallet. What made it interesting was what was written on the back. It was a woman's name, which was normal enough, but it was written in the Tongue, the language used inside the Singularity.

That wasn't proof of anything, but it made him a desirable prisoner, so they'd keep him if they could.

As soon they finished sweeping the bodies for intelligence, Diana moved over to the storage room at the rear of the break room. That would be where things like coffee and other supplies were stored for use by the miners.

Andrea covered her friend as she opened the door, and they quickly discovered the room was being used as a prison. Some blankets were tossed on the floor, and an unconscious woman lay there, not having been roused by the fighting.

"Check her," Andrea said as she stepped back out into the main room and covered the exits with her stunner. There were two ways out, and Leroy had the first one, so she'd make certain no one came their way through the second.

"She's out cold," Diana said. "She may be drugged. What do we do?"

"Leroy, go get her. You'll be in the center of the group. I'll keep watch on the back and carry the guy. Diana will take point, so direct her on where we need to go."

The young man gave Andrea a look and frowned. "Shouldn't you carry the woman? That guy weighs a lot more than she does."

"You must not have gotten the word," she said with a chuckle. "I'm a lot stronger than I look. Just grab her and try to keep up."

Andrea went over to the man and took the precaution of giving him another shot from her stunner. She'd take no chances that he'd wake up at an inconvenient time.

Once that was done, she slung him across her shoulder and got him settled as well as she could. By then, Leroy had emerged from the storage room with the woman across his shoulder.

He stared at her in surprise. "I guess you are stronger than you look. We need to take the exit we didn't come in through. It'll take us deeper into the mine, but we'll have an opportunity to go right or left in about fifty meters. If we go left, it'll take us to a lift for ore that we can use to go at least partway back up if we choose.

"I don't recommend that we go down because they'd have us pinned. We need to get as high up the mountain as we possibly can if we're going to try to evade them."

"And what happens if we go to the right?" Diana asked as she took the lead.

"That takes us to a series of ramps we can use to go up or down.

The miners use it to get between levels without taking the lifts. They'll go all the way up."

"Both of those tunnels are going to be guarded," Andrea said. "Time is not on our side, so let's move out."

The three of them weren't running, but they weren't walking either. It was only going to be a very short while before someone discovered what they'd done, and they needed to be elsewhere when that happened.

As if to emphasize that point, the com unit she'd confiscated from the guard chose that moment to come to life. "Guard point one checking in." A few moments passed, and whoever had spoken repeated themselves.

Andrea took a chance and activated the com unit. "Copy that."

"Excuse me? What the hell does that mean?"

"Crap," Andrea muttered. "They were expecting some kind of specific response. We're screwed."

"Guard point two, this is guard point one. Send someone to check the break room and the prisoner."

"Here we go," Diana said. "Sounds like there's only one other guard post, probably at the fork. We'll have to take them out and backtrack to get the first guard post. We don't want to have somebody close behind us. I'll take the front pair. Andrea, you have our friends back the way we came."

Andrea dropped her prisoner next to Leroy. "You stay here and let us handle this."

Taking all the guards was a smart move. If they didn't know where they'd gone, it would take a lot longer to pin them down. All she needed to do now was take out the bad guys without getting herself shot.

23

J erome followed the men into the subbasement once they'd changed into clothes that blended into the city better and discovered why they'd felt so confident they wouldn't be followed whenever the corporate security forces finally entered the building.

They had a fake wall in the subbasement, leading to a disused sewer tunnel. Once they were through it and the doorway was closed behind them, there was no reason for any searchers to continue to look in the area. After all, the apartment building they'd just left lacked any reason for the searchers to believe they'd ever been there. His old clothes were in his bag with his uniform just to be sure they weren't found.

The stench in the tunnel was definitely noticeable, but it wasn't as overpowering as he'd have expected. Apparently, whatever biological material was present had had a long time to decay. He'd still want to shower when everything was done, but at least he could breathe.

He had no idea how far below the surface they were because they were going down and even came into a small substation of some kind with a corroded ladder that took them even deeper beneath the surface.

It came out into a dark tunnel that was not part of the sewer system, for which he was thankful. There were light fixtures on the ceiling, but there was no indication they had power. Whatever purpose this area had once served, it was dark now.

The men had brought lights, so they could see where they were going. Jerome followed behind them with his stunner in his hand. He didn't really expect they were going to do something to him at this point, but if they were so inclined, this would undoubtedly be an excellent place to make it happen.

They left the strange series of tunnels about fifteen minutes later, moving back into what looked like a drainage tunnel. There was a lot going on underneath the capital.

Jerome suspected most major cities had networks of similar tunnels, but very few people knew about them. If one had a good map of them, they could move an army underneath the city without anyone being the wiser. Something to keep in mind.

In all, it took them almost an hour to reach the destination the two men were heading for. It was a bricked-off tunnel that wasn't nearly as bricked off as it first appeared. In fact, the entire wall was actually a façade covering a hatch that they opened, shifting the whole wall on almost silent hinges to allow them access to what lay beyond.

Unlike everything else he'd seen so far, this had taken quite a bit of work to put in place. It wasn't simply repurposing what was there for another task. It involved disassembling something to get those bricks and then mounting the hatch strongly enough to support the weight without making any noise.

The men had turned their lights off before they'd opened the hatch, so he listened. There was the sound of something moving in the distance, but he couldn't quite place what it was. He could feel movement in the air, which probably meant it was some kind of subway system.

They proceeded through the hatch and closed it behind them.

"You guys want to tell me why you have secret passages hidden underneath the city?" he asked as they walked through the darkness. "You didn't build this in an afternoon, so there has to be a purpose to it."

"Need to know, my friend," Paci said. "Let's just say that the mission we're supporting requires something like this as a bolt hole in case things go bad."

Jerome's next surprise was when they came to a much wider tunnel that was obviously used for the subway service. There were some lights overhead, but they didn't dispel the deep gloom in which they stood.

Parada checked his chronometer. "We've got about fifteen minutes to wait. We'll have a passenger train go by first, so let's keep the lights out. They'll be going fast enough that no one should see us in the shadows, but why take chances?"

"Fill me in on exactly where we're going, what we're stealing, and who we're pissing off," Jerome said. "If I'm about to make enemies, I'd really like to know if it's worth it."

"There's a collector living here in the city that used to be in Imperial service," Paci said. "She's retired but still a force to be reckoned with. As for what we need, she's got quite a selection of equipment, and that almost certainly includes something with a long-range transmitter that can reach orbit or the Imperial Marine encampment."

"If she's ex-Imperial service, why don't we just ask to borrow it? Why do we need to go through this convoluted scheme to break into wherever she's keeping this equipment and take it without her knowing? Why wouldn't she help us?"

Parada shrugged. "She might be cooperative, but are you willing to take that chance? As things sit right now, if she decides she doesn't want to get involved in whatever's happening, she can make one call and have us picked up. She's not really the kind of person we want to cross, but needs must when the devil drives."

The answer didn't satisfy Jerome, but once again, he wasn't in control of the situation. He didn't know who this person was, where they were located, or even what kind of equipment they had. The two men wanted to play it this way, and he really didn't have a choice about playing along.

A few minutes later, the passenger train they'd spoken about came racing by, buffeting all three of them with the wind of its passage.

Since it wasn't linked to the ground via tracks, there was no roaring sound to mark its passage, but it was well lit and almost hypnotically blinding as it raced quietly past.

They waited another ten minutes, during which Paci pulled a device out of his jacket. Jerome considered asking what he was doing but decided he'd find out soon enough.

The next train arrived in an unusual fashion. It actually slowed down and stopped so they could board it. Either the man had called it, or he had some means of controlling it remotely. If it was manned, that meant someone would be aware that something strange had happened, so he hoped that wasn't the case.

The car they boarded was made for cargo and completely full of crates. There was a passage for an inspector to walk through the center, and that was where they stood as the train began moving again.

"This particular train is automated, and it didn't register the stop," Parada said. "I'll boost the speed a little bit to make sure it arrives on schedule, so it'll get us across the city without anyone knowing we've even been here.

"We'll get off on the other side pretty much the same way we got on board and walk to a place where we can access the surface. Once we get up there, we're going to be less than four blocks away from the warehouse where the equipment is stored, according to the map I have."

The trip across the city worked just as advertised, and they disembarked exactly the same way they'd boarded. They were in a tunnel off to the side, but it didn't have a hidden hatch this time. It simply led to a ladder that let them out behind a locked door on a subway platform.

Dressed as city dwellers now, they easily blended into the population and made their way up to street level without raising any eyebrows, even when they went past a couple of security guards chatting near the entrance.

They watched the people going into the subway but barely glanced at the three as they exited. Not that Jerome relaxed until they were well clear of the station.

The section of the city they were in now definitely looked more commercial in nature and became a series of warehouses almost as soon as they left the main street. Twenty minutes later, they were staring at a dingy, rusted warehouse.

"That's the place," Parada said. "We have no way of knowing if she's in there or not. We're going to be taking a chance by breaking in, but it's one that we can't really avoid. If she catches us, don't do anything intemperate. I'd hate to see anyone get hurt."

Jerome stared at the man with narrowed eyes. "Let me ask you two again, exactly who is this that we're about to piss off?"

"If we don't have to tell you, it's better that you don't know. Believe it or not, her identity and presence here are classified. She's not really in the game at this point, but people like her never really get out."

"That doesn't reassure me," he said with a sigh. "If we get busted, this is your fault."

"And if we have to explain it, we will. The security system on this warehouse is probably top-notch, so it will take time for us to break in without triggering any alerts. Let's get busy."

The three of them went around the building to a personnel entrance in the back. There was a keypad and sensor for the security system. The two men quickly got to work, with one partly disassembling the panel while the other kept watch over the street.

Jerome decided it was in his best interests to help keep an eye out for trouble, so he looked in the other direction.

Their plans went wrong just as quickly as he'd feared when the door leading into the warehouse swung open unexpectedly, revealing an old woman in battered coveralls holding a very functional-looking flechette pistol that covered all three of them quite handily.

"I suggest you boys keep your hands right where they are," she said with a drawl that made it apparent she was either a local or had been here long enough to pass for one. "If you don't, I'm going to chop you into hamburger, and then I'll have to explain things to security. I hate paperwork, so let's not complicate matters, shall we?"

"I know this looks bad, Mrs. Kolstad, but I can explain," Parada said. "We didn't want to involve you in what's going on, but this is a class one emergency."

She eyed the man suspiciously, and the bore of the flechette pistol didn't even twitch. "I'm not inclined to be generous, so I suggest you speed this explanation up before my finger gets tired."

"My name is Nick Parada, and this is my associate Daniel Paci. We're with the Imperial Security Services, and we're on Diorama in an official capacity. One that I can explain if you'll just give me a moment. Here is our identification."

The woman's eyes narrowed even further. "While those do seem to be authentic, you're busy breaking into my warehouse, so you'll forgive me if I have concerns. Who is the third guy?"

"Sergeant Jerome Walker, Imperial Marines," Jerome said, eyeing the weapon held professionally in her grip.

For the first time, one of her eyebrows twitched. "You're from the company that just landed?"

"Yes, ma'am. I don't know these two, and I don't trust them any further than you do, but corporate security took my company commander into custody when we came into the city, and they sprang me out of a trap.

"I don't know what's going on, and I haven't got the slightest idea who you are, but I *really* need to tell Delta Company what's going on. Forgive me for intruding like this."

She eyed the three of them for a moment and then stepped back into the warehouse. "I'm going to *provisionally* accept what you're saying. Step inside and give me more details before I change my mind."

Jerome stepped into the dark warehouse behind the others, making sure to keep his hands in plain sight and not make any hasty motions. The woman could kill all three of them with a squeeze of the trigger, and all of his training would be for nothing. She had the drop on them fair and square.

A second after the door closed, the overhead lights came on, and he blinked in surprise at what he was looking at. Sitting in the middle of the warehouse was an older-model marine pinnace with what were obviously some customized modifications.

It had to be at least the previous generation and more probably the one before that. It was old but looked serviceable. Who the hell was this woman?

"Let me see some identification, Sergeant Walker," the woman in question said.

Jerome sent her his identification. "These two jokers won't tell me anything other than there's a way for me to get a hold of either the Fleet transport in orbit or my company in this warehouse.

"I told them I thought breaking in was a bad idea, but they seemed to think it was the only way to get what I needed. As I said, I don't know who you are, but I'm asking you as an Imperial Marine to help me save my commanding officer."

The woman considered him for a few seconds before nodding. "I suppose a bit of explanation is in order. I have something here that can contact either of those locations, but I'm afraid it's been broken for years. I should be able to get it fixed relatively quickly but not immediately. It wasn't a priority, you understand."

She safed the flechette pistol and stuffed it into the back of her pants. "As for me, I used to serve the Empire like you back in the day. Senior Sergeant Susan Kolstad, retired Marine Raider."

Jerome blinked in surprise. Marine Raiders were the absolute best that the Empire had to offer, and they had a level of medical nanites that kept them young for a lot longer than standard marine medical nanites, much less the ones used by the civilian population. Just how old was this woman?

She smiled a little. "Don't you know it's rude to ask a lady how old she is?"

"I wasn't asking, just wondering."

"I didn't get the medical nanites they use these days. I've actually been retired for almost eighty years. I was getting a bit creaky by that point and decided it was time to settle down, so I came home to Diorama."

She gestured toward the pinnace. "I picked up some surplus equipment here and there, and I've been tinkering with it over the years. It keeps me active.

"Now, I was a marine before I became a Marine Raider, and I'm much more inclined to care about your problem than theirs, Sergeant Walker, but I want to hear their story too. Spit it out, gentlemen."

Paci stared at Walker for a long moment and then sighed. "There's a facility on Diorama that grows biomedical matter. It's owned by Schuster and Associates, which is a cover organization owned by the Imperial Department of Defense.

"THEY MAKE the ingredients for Panther here. Somebody kidnapped one of our lead scientists, and we think the trouble that's going on at the mines is somehow related to that."

Jerome frowned slightly. "Panther? What the hell is that?"

The old woman rubbed her face and sighed. "It's serious trouble, that's what it is. Panther is an *extremely* classified drug used by the Marine Raiders during combat operations. If they're making both parts of it here, and someone is trying to get the formula, that's something I can't ignore because it puts the Empire at risk.

"It looks like I need to get busy repairing the transmitter on this pinnace. I don't suppose you know anything about com equipment, do you, Sergeant Walker?"

"A little," he admitted.

"Then let's get to work."

24

They had to get out of the mines fast, and Diana knew they needed to roll over any resistance as quickly as possible. To do that, she'd have to take out a pair of guards on the way to the ramps.

She was sure Corporal Reed would've advised a careful advance using available cover so the marines could cover one another while leaving the enemy exposed. Sadly, they didn't have enough marines for that, so she'd just have to bull her way through the obstacle.

At least one of the guards from the checkpoint would advance to see what had happened at the break room. If they were smart, the other was alerting their superiors that something was wrong. That meant forces would probably be moving to cut them off shortly.

All of that went through her mind in the two seconds it took for her to come into contact with the first of the guards in front of her. The woman came around the corner with her stunner up, but she wasn't expecting to have Diana in her face so soon. That cost her.

Diana fired on narrow beam and took her out before she could even bring her weapon to bear. That done, Diana didn't even slow down as she jumped over the woman's twitching body and caught sight of the guard post at the tunnel fork ahead.

The man there looked in her direction while talking on a com unit. He didn't even have time to squawk before she'd stunned him.

Circling the area to be sure she hadn't missed anyone, she snatched the com unit he'd dropped off the ground and listened.

"You broke up during that last transmission, Mike, but I think you said the intruders are heading your way," a man said. "Withdraw from the guard post and keep watch when they leave if you can. We've only got two dozen people here, and it'll take at least an hour to get additional people on site, so we need to manage this fast.

"If they've got the prisoner, we need to know that too. Can you handle that?"

Diana cleared her throat and moved the com farther away from her face. When she spoke, she did so in a low voice. "Understood."

She pumped her fist silently in the air when she didn't get a suspicious response.

She doubted either of the guards she'd stunned had much of value in their pockets, but she searched them even as she called out for Leroy to come join her.

As expected, she didn't find anything all that exciting, but who knew what was on the electronics? That was why they took everything from enemies when collecting potential intelligence.

When Leroy trotted up with the woman over his shoulder, Diana gestured toward the tunnel leading toward where he'd said the ramps were. "The person on the other end of this com said they had about two dozen people at the mine. If we're lucky, we just stunned more than half of them, but we can't count on luck.

"We have to send them looking in the wrong area. How can I get the best bang for my buck in misleading them?"

She had no idea what a buck was or why someone needed to get the largest explosion from it, but it sounded like a great phrase for a marine, and she'd picked it up.

"If we go lower, it'll leave us trapped," the young man said. "If we can go up a couple of levels, I think we can move laterally to where the ore is processed."

"Is there going to be an exit there?"

He nodded. "I doubt it's one you'll like very much, but yes. You saw where they were dumping the scree? We can go through there and use an emergency lift to get us down to a path leading to a disaster rally point. After that? I have no idea."

Andrea came trotting up with their male prisoner slung over her shoulder. "That sounds like an excellent plan. I stunned both of the guards behind us.

"I had the captured com on, and they never gave away any details about me looking like Geller, so with them heavily stunned, it'll be at least four hours before they can possibly squeal. You sounded great, Diana. That guy had no idea he was talking to you."

"Get started up the ramp, and I'll be right behind you," Diana said. "I'll tell them we're going down."

She waited until the two had gone down the tunnel before activating the com. She continued her deception, moving the unit nearer and farther from her mouth as she spoke to help disguise her voice.

"They just went past. Two women and one man. They had two unconscious people with them, a man and a woman. They went down."

The information cost her nothing and might add some believability to her report when they had someone really look through the break room.

The other party started to respond, but another voice cut them off. "This is the roving patrol. Guard post one was down, and I'm in the break room now. The prisoner is gone, and I'm not seeing that military interrogation guy. That must be who they have with them.

"I'm heading back to the personnel lift, so I'll coordinate with our remaining people to block the lower levels. We should have them sealed down there in about ten minutes, but there's no way we can do this without stunning every miner we come across."

"The boss ain't gonna be happy about that, but it's either that or lose the prisoner and the military guy that she said was so important," the first man said. "Do it. Mike, follow the intruders slowly and make sure they don't try to double back. We'll stop them here, but the boss will have to kick off her plans right the hell now. Hope she's got everything in place."

Diana made sure the transmitter was off, raced down the tunnel to the ramps, and headed up. She edged her way around the other two and took the lead with her stunner out front. "How many levels do we need to go before we exit?"

"Exit at the next level," Leroy said. "There's going to be a series of passages, and I'll lead you through them. If we run into anybody, we're going to have to decide if we're talking or shooting pretty fast."

"If you think they're bad guys, shoot them," Andrea said. "If you're not sure, just do the best you can. Diana is going to be right behind you."

Diana followed Leroy through the door. Nobody was there, and they dodged through the passageways and to the lift that moved the ore without being spotted. A lift was already in transit, so Leroy hit the call button to stop it at their level.

She went through their captured gear while they waited and collected all the com units. It only took a minute to remove their power units. Now they couldn't be traced, but they could dig into them later for intelligence.

It wasn't going to be long before the bad guys figured out they'd been tricked and spread out looking for them. When that happened, they needed to be the hell away from this damned mountain.

They had to get word to Craig and the driver. They also had to warn Delta Company of the Singularity threat.

When the lift car arrived, it was full of ore. That wasn't very helpful, but there was still space enough to fit inside. The first half meter of the car was empty, and the pile was secured behind a wooden barricade to keep it from shifting.

They stuffed the unconscious people on top of the pile while they stood in front of it. Moments later, the lift doors closed, and they were on their way.

"If somebody opens the door, you're going to have to make an immediate decision whether to stun them or not," Andrea said. "If it's a single person, take them out, Diana. If it's multiple people, I'll take them out with wide beam. We won't shoot the miners themselves, but we have to take down anybody we aren't sure about."

"Look at their coveralls," Leroy said. "If they look like they were just taken out of the packaging, you're probably looking at bad guys. If the person in front of you is dirty, it's a miner."

That sounded like good advice, so Diana readied herself with the stunner's focus turned to its most precise setting. Somewhat to her surprise, no one interrupted their ascent. When the doors opened again, it was at the level the car had originally been on its way to.

A couple of miners were waiting for the load in small vehicles with mechanical scoops. Their coveralls were almost entirely black, and so were their surprised faces, so they weren't bad guys.

Diana exited the lift and holstered her stunner, gesturing for the miners to back up. She didn't bother explaining what was going on because nothing she said would make sense to them. All they'd see were a bunch of armed strangers coming out of the ore lift with a couple of unconscious people.

"Leroy?" one of the women asked, her eyes wide. "Is that you? What the hell is going on?"

"It's me, Eva," Leroy said as he came out of the lift and grabbed the unconscious woman. "I can't explain, but there's trouble down in the mine. There's a bunch of strangers in here with stunners shooting people. They can't know we came this way. Understand?"

The woman nodded jerkily. "If you say so. Where are you going?"

"We're going out through the dump. If anybody asks, you never saw us."

"You got it. Let me go run it for you. Who are these people?"

"No time. You're just going to have to trust me."

The woman hopped out of her machine and led them down a wide passage. Leroy and Andrea—once her friend had grabbed the unconscious woman—followed closely, with Diana bringing up the rear.

Once they reached the end of the tunnel, it opened into a massive chamber holding piles of ore and rock, as well as sorting machines that probably sifted the valuable materials from the dreck.

Their guide ignored the people staring at them curiously and raced to the big opening that showed the sky ahead of them. An open lift car that went down at a substantial leftward angle was bolted to the outside of the mountain. It also followed a steeply dropping slope rather than going straight down.

The wind gusted hard, and Diana almost lost her hat before grabbing it. She followed up by getting Andrea's and Leroy's hats in hand as well. They might need them later.

Even though the lift car was open, it was surrounded by wire mesh, so they weren't really in danger of falling out. It was heavily reinforced along the top in what she suspected was a safety measure to ensure that no debris or rocks fell onto the people inside the lift.

Based on the size of some of the rocks she'd seen down in the valley, that might not be enough if something truly sizable came their way.

The woman—Eva—opened the lift car, and the three of them quickly got inside. So did she, hitting the controls that started the car downward.

"What the hell is going on?" the woman demanded. "Why are you carrying those people? What happened to them?"

Since the woman was speaking to Leroy, Diana left the explanation to him. Now that she was out from under the mountain— even though there was a huge spur of rock between her and the grav carrier—she tried to connect with the drone inside it. The signal was weak, but it was there.

Afraid that she'd lose the connection before she could get a warning out, Diana sent a priority com request to Corporal Reed. A couple of seconds later, the woman was on the line.

"Reed. Go, Randall."

"I might lose connection at any minute, but we're at the mine. We've got proof that someone from the Singularity is on the planet and has been for at least five years. There's no sabotage or disaffection here. It's all a smokescreen. We've got people after us, and they're shooting."

"Hold one."

Moments later, Diana's implants lit up with an alert warning of possible imminent enemy action. She imagined that everyone at Camp Pyramid was now scrambling to defensive positions. It was smart of Reed to get the warning out as quickly as possible.

"Details, Randall," Reed demanded. "What is your current status? I'm getting a combat team ready to extract you."

Before Diana could respond, there was a low thump from the other side of the spur, and her connection to the drone vanished. That was bad news, but at least she'd gotten enough information to the corporal to put the company on alert.

Even if whatever the enemy was planning to do was put into motion right this very second, the Singularity was going to find it difficult to take an entrenched company of Imperial Marines when they were on their guard.

"It looks like they just took out the grav carrier and our drone," Andrea said. "I was using the external speaker and microphone to warn Barry so he could tell Craig what we were doing. He couldn't connect with him and had headed to the mine on foot. I think he got clear before the grav carrier went up.

"I saw that you contacted Reed. Does she know what's happening?"

Diana made a waggling gesture with one hand. "I told her the Singularity was here, but I didn't get a chance to warn her about Geller. She knows we ran into hostilities at the mine, and there is no sabotage. She said she was scrambling a combat team to extract us. We'll just have to hope that's enough."

"Even at max speed, they won't be fast enough to save us unless we can get away from the general area. If they can blow up the grav carrier, they can get us too."

Leroy finished his abbreviated explanation to Eva as the lift car finally reached the mountain's base. There was a path off to the right-hand side that led clear of all of the material being dropped out of the mine, and he didn't hesitate to head in that direction.

"Remember, Eva, you never saw us. If they think you know anything, they're going to mess you up, and I don't want to see that."

The woman nodded her head jerkily and swallowed hard. "Get the hell out of here before they come looking with an air car. If you can get into the trees, you might be able to hide until they're gone."

"You've done us a great service, and the Empire thanks you," Andrea said. "Now, get the hell out of here before someone sees you."

With the three of them out of the lift car, the woman quickly had it rising back up the steep face of the mountain. Diana hoped she was going to be okay.

"We're about three hundred meters from the edge of the forest," Leroy said as he carried the woman as fast as he could down the path. "We'll be out of sight once we get under the canopy."

"That'll only work until they get some infrared scans on the area," Andrea said. "We need to increase our distance from the mine as quickly as we can. For now, they think we're trapped on the lower levels. That'll change when they get reinforcements. Let's go."

Diana moved to the front of the group, and they headed for the trees at a quick trot.

25

B y the time they got under the cover of the trees, Andrea was really feeling the weight of the man over her shoulder. She might be stronger than an average human woman, but she'd been carrying this guy for a while, and it was wearing on her. Her injured arm was throbbing.

Even as she jogged down the rough path, her mind was racing, trying to figure out some means of escaping the bad guys before they got reinforcements. They'd already proven their resolve by blowing up the grav carrier, so they'd have no qualms about burning down the entire forest to get them if that was what it took.

It wasn't even going to take that much, honestly. If anyone had a decent set of infrared binoculars, they'd be able to pick them out within half an hour. There were only so many ways they could get away from the area, after all.

Escape and evasion were taught to all marines, and there were methods to shield one's infrared signature, but she had none of her equipment with her. Everything was back at the ranch.

That was an oversight she felt confident Corporal Reed would take pleasure in pointing out. In fact, the after-action report on this entire mess was going to be a disaster. She'd done so many things wrong that they'd chew her ass right off.

Still, she'd take that if that meant getting away. Being torn up by one's superiors for doing a poor job was a lot better than being taken prisoner by a society that thought she should've been executed as a failure.

In fact, Andrea had no doubt that was precisely what would happen if they caught her. A flechette to the head would be the best she could look forward to in their hands.

The path under the trees led directly to a clearing with a temporary building set in its center. It was obviously the rally point Leroy had indicated the miners would retreat to in case of disaster.

It likely held all kinds of survival equipment and rescue gear. If they could find something to help them escape inside, it might make the difference between survival and death.

She was about to use her knife to force the door open when Leroy simply tapped a code into the lock and opened the door.

"Every miner knows the code to get in," he said. "When somebody's life is on the line, you can't wait for a supervisor to get here. You need to access the rescue gear as quickly as possible."

"Thank God for common sense," Diana said fervently. "Let's find something that might help us. There won't be any way of getting us out of here faster, but maybe there's a long-range com unit."

Andrea wasn't going to hold her breath. Not only was there no need for one, the bad guys probably already had the area jammed. It was what she'd have done.

Besides which, exactly who were they going to call? The planetary government? Since the woman masquerading as Kate Geller was from the Singularity, her supposed boss was either in on what was going on, or she was manipulating him, neither of which was helpful to them.

It was a shame Diana hadn't been able to let Reed know the specifics about Geller. Without that information, the company was operating in the dark, even though they'd been tipped off in a more general way.

Of course, Andrea still didn't know what Geller's plans were.

Somehow, the woman thought having a company of Imperial Marines on the planet was desirable, so it probably wouldn't be good.

Even as she thought about what that might mean, she scanned the equipment and supplies laid out in the building. There were packs of climbing and rescue gear, medical kits, and everything else that might be useful in a natural disaster or accident. There was also plenty of stuff for digging deeper into the mine, likely to rescue trapped miners, but that wasn't going to be helpful right now.

Andrea was already tired, and if she had to carry that man through kilometers of heavily wooded forest, she was going to need a recharge.

Thankfully, there were survival rations here, so she tore one open with her teeth and proceeded to devour it while stuffing more in her pockets.

"What are our options?" she asked as the others searched through the equipment, looking for things that were quickly and easily available. "Is there anything in the area that would be of assistance to us?"

"There is a train line about ten kilometers away," Leroy said as he slung a pack over his shoulder and cinched it down tight against his back. "It has a spur that comes to the mine to pick up ore. It terminates about three kilometers from here, but the ground is pretty rough between us and it, or so I've been told."

"That's not very helpful," Diana said. "Since it's cleared like a road, that's going to be one of the first places the bad guys check. Besides, even if we got there, it's not exactly like we can wave a train down. We don't even know the schedule, and those things move really fast."

"Is there anything else in the area?" Andrea asked. "A town? A village? A nature preserve that might have facilities where we could hide?"

"Not really," Leroy said as she grabbed one of the rescue packs for herself and slung the male prisoner over her shoulder again. Now she was *really* weighed down, which would be problematic in a hurry.

Diana, the lightest of the three, grabbed what had to be the biggest pack. It had rope strapped to the outside, a pick for digging, and other underground rescue gear. Andrea wasn't sure what she intended to use it for, but if her friend thought it might be useful, then she was probably right.

The three of them exited the building, and Leroy picked the woman back up and locked the door behind them. Before they could move any farther, Andrea heard a whine in the distance and looked up in alarm.

Coming over the trees to the left-hand side of the building was a beaten-up air car that was smoking from the left-hand side and seemed to be shimmying as it plummeted from the sky toward the clearing.

"Incoming!" she shouted.

She scampered around the side of the building, dumped her prisoner, and drew her flechette pistol. Leroy and Diana followed a few seconds later.

Andrea expected someone in the air car to open fire, but they didn't. Instead, the vehicle managed to avoid slamming into the ground—barely—and shimmied three-quarters of the way around before it came to a halt just above the grass.

The right-side door popped open, and someone stuck an empty hand out. "Don't shoot! It's Craig Lindbergh."

"Come out with your hands up," Andrea said. It sounded like him, but she had to be sure. Even if it was him, he could be under duress.

Somewhat to her relief, Craig exited the car with his hands up. "Barry's with me. We got away from the mine. They opened fire on us, but the air car is still about halfway functional. I don't know what you did to piss them off, but it looks like you've kicked over a hornet's nest."

Diana advanced, holstering her flechette pistol and drawing her stunner. She looked inside the vehicle and then holstered it again. "All clear."

"Can that thing even fly?" Andrea asked as she stepped away from the building and put her own weapon away.

"Depends on your definition of the word 'fly,'" Barry said from inside the vehicle. "We lost some of the grav modules, and it's pretty flaky, but the emergency backup systems are working now that I've overridden the safeties."

"Will it get us very far?" Diana asked suspiciously. "Or is it going to crash and kill us?"

"You pay your money and take your chances just like everybody else," the driver said. "We've got room for everybody, including whoever those people are, but if we're going to get out of here before they organize a chase, I suggest we get moving right the hell now."

"Where the hell did you get this, and how did you get here so fast?" Andrea asked.

"I hotwired it. Used it to run into the grav sled that blew up my grav carrier. Hope I killed the bastards."

"There was some kind of alert in the mine," Craig said. "When Ray ran off to deal with it, I decided I should head back outside just in case. Got out just in time for Barry to pick me up in this flying wreck."

The wreck in question had three rows of seats, so they could sit the unconscious people in the back. It was possible the woman would regain consciousness soon, but the man would be out for hours still.

As soon as everybody was in the vehicle—with their new packs beside the unconscious people—Barry lifted off the ground. The grav modules made a hideous whine, and Andrea was certain they wouldn't last very long.

"I can't get very much height, but I *should* be able to stay above the trees for a little bit," Barry said. "Where are we going?"

"There's a train spur a couple of kilometers around the mountain," Andrea said. "Head that way, and we'll figure out what we need to do once we get there. Can we call anyone from this thing?"

Craig shook his head as he looked at them over the front seat. "Somebody's jamming communications. We tried calling planetary security but couldn't get through."

"I'm not sure that would've done much good anyway," Diana said. "Kate Geller—the personal assistant to the man in charge of Yi Holdings—is working for the Singularity. We don't have time to get into the details of that right now, but it's almost certain the problems here on Diorama were set up by her."

"That doesn't sound promising," the man allowed. "Do you have any idea what's going on?"

Andrea gestured toward the two in the back seat. "The woman back there was their prisoner. We haven't had a chance to look at her, but I think she's been drugged. The man was working with them and is somehow connected with what I'm going to guess is the Singularity ground forces. They called him an interrogator.

"Sounds like whatever they're planning, they've already taken Delta Company into account, so I'm afraid this entire situation is a trap. Honestly, isn't that what the Singularity does best anyway?"

"If they've got enough military force on the planet to deal with a company of Imperial Marines, then this isn't some little scheme," Diana argued. "This is one of their raids into our territory."

"How the hell would they get enough people and equipment across the border to do something like this? It's one thing to send a disguised freighter with maybe a platoon of fighters, but if they're planning on going toe to toe with a company of Imperial Marines, you can bet they've got at least twice as many people on hand."

Andrea certainly hoped not because that would be *really* bad news.

The air car acted as if it was going to crash into the trees at any moment, but it managed to make it all the way to the train spur and dropped down closer to the ground in the cleared area, which seemed to ease its ability to fly. It was too bad the thing was damaged because being able to take off in any direction would've definitely increased their odds of escape.

As things sat now, they were pretty much limited to the train line. If the bad guys figured that out, it didn't matter how far they got because they were eventually going to get caught.

Maybe they could get a couple of dozen kilometers away and hide the air car well enough to escape. She suspected it wouldn't be that easy, but one could always hope.

"Does anyone have any idea what the train schedule is?" Craig asked. "I understand they're not going to the mine, but could we expect a train passing by anytime soon?"

"Without a functioning com unit, there's no way to know," Barry said. "Maybe we could find a place to lay low until one does. If so, what would we do?"

Even as he spoke, they arrived at the main train line and turned right.

"Uh, I know when the next train will be here," Diana said before anyone answered the driver.

"When is that?" Andrea asked, suspecting that her friend had checked the databases her father had loaded into her implants. It seemed strange that they would have train schedules, but who knew what spooks thought was important?

"Right now!" her friend said grimly. "It's coming up behind us right now!"

Andrea turned in her seat and stared out the rear window, where a grav train was approaching with frightening rapidity. It was going to be on top of them in seconds!

26

J erome had to admit he was somewhat surprised when Kolstad let Paci and Parada leave, though she made them put her security system back the way they'd found it first. Personally, he didn't trust the men out of his sight, but she seemed to be a little bit more blasé about the situation.

"What are they going to do?" she asked when he mentioned it as they headed toward the ramp at the back of the pinnace. "Turn us in? I don't think corporate security would welcome them with open arms."

"Look, the Imperial Security Services don't exactly have a sterling reputation, but they're not Imperial Intelligence by any stretch of the imagination. Aren't you being a little hard on them?"

"Aren't you being a little easy on them?" he asked in response. "They broke into your warehouse."

"So did you, but I'm cutting you some slack, aren't I? Look, Walker, I've been around a long time, and after a while, you get a feel about people. You seem like a straight shooter, and while those other guys don't, there's a certain amount of covert behavior that goes into what they do.

"Their IDs check out, so I'm going to give them the benefit of the doubt. If they come back and cause me problems, *then* I'll shoot them."

"A woman after my own heart," he said with a smile as they started up the ramp. "Where did you get this thing? It's an antique."

"I took it with me when I retired," she said, giving him the eye. "Did you just call me old?"

"You *are* old. I'm just wondering whether the pinnace is in better shape than you."

She laughed. "You're a firecracker. We used this pinnace on our last mission, and it got beaten up pretty good. They were going to scrap it, but I talked my CO into letting me take her as a fixup project when I retired.

"Getting her here was something of an adventure, but I've had a lot of time to work on her. I don't get much call to take her out for a spin anymore, but she can still fly. She doesn't have any weapons systems, but the old generation stealth materials still do the trick. They're not nearly as good as what the Raiders use nowadays, I'd wager, but they're still probably better than what you guys use."

He grunted. "The Imperial Marines don't get much call for sneaking around. So what's wrong with your transmitter?"

"I have no idea," she said as they walked through the bay in the back of the pinnace, which was empty of seats or cargo. "It showed up red on one of the self-tests a couple of decades ago, and I never got around to hunting the problem down. There were always more important things to do, if you know what I mean."

"A couple of decades," he said with a raised eyebrow. "Just exactly what was more important than fixing this particular problem over the last twenty years?"

She waved a hand breezily as she stepped into the control area. "A man, of course. I was seeing someone back then, and trying to track down exactly which component had failed didn't seem like it was all that important at the time.

"Still doesn't, though I'll admit that the man didn't work out, either, so I'd have been better off making the repair. That's the problem with being a civilian. You have to try to find people you can actually get along with, and you never really fit back into society once you've been in the military. That's true for being a marine and worse for a Marine Raider."

He looked around the control area and was surprised by how neat and clean it was. Everything was old and covered in a thin layer of dust, but it looked like the interior had been completely restored.

Kolstad wedged herself into the pilot seat and began activating systems. The consoles powered up cleanly, and everything seemed to be in working order at first glance. He wasn't a pilot, so he didn't really know for sure, though.

"All primary systems are green, except for communications," she said. "Let's open up the avionics compartment and see if we can spot anything obvious."

When she pointed out where it was at the side of the control compartment, he got down on his hands and knees and undid the mechanical fasteners to gain access. When he opened it up and looked inside, he had to smirk a little.

"So, if all systems are green, exactly how did something get in here and make a nest?"

"What? Let me take a look at that."

She was able to squat a little and tilt her torso enough to see inside.

"Damned Iniri," she grumbled. "They're a local species that fills a role similar to that of birds on Terra. There isn't any external access for the avionics compartment, so one of them must've gotten aboard while I had the ramp down and set up a nest.

"That was a really bad call, since I haven't been in here in forever, and it had nothing to eat. It always makes me sad to see an animal get itself trapped somewhere and not be able to get out."

Now that he looked, Jerome could see that the nest had a skeleton in it. It really was kind of sad.

"Well, get me some gloves, and I'll start cleaning this out," he said. "It probably tore some wires or pulled a chip loose, so that might be an easy fix."

"Or it bled or defecated on something important and shorted it out," she countered. "That'll be harder to fix. I might be able to scrounge up something from one of the other bits of salvage I've got stashed in here. If not, I'm going to have to buy something.

"Maybe your friends will be back by then, and I can send them off on a shopping trip."

Since she knew the interior of the pinnace better than he did, he let her get him some gloves and started pulling out feathers—or something very much like them—and bones, dumping them into a bag she held open for him.

Once he'd gotten everything he could by hand, she gave him a portable vacuum, and he cleaned the area of debris. When he'd done that, he took a rag she'd found somewhere and began wiping everything off, working carefully so as not to damage anything while picking up anything that was dried to the components. He ran the vacuum across the area again once he was done to get the last of the detritus.

She went back to the control console and shook her head. "It's still down. Try pulling out the components and reinserting them. Then we'll check any exposed wiring."

One at a time, he plucked the removable components and eyed them. When the contacts seemed a little dirty, he used a clean part of the rag to polish them before reinserting. He also sniffed each piece as he pulled out to see if he smelled anything burned. It'd been twenty years, but he might get lucky.

He hit pay dirt on the third component. The contacts were a little charred. It looked like something fluid had gotten in there.

There was surprisingly little odor to the whole thing. Neither the dead animal nor the burned equipment really smelled like much after twenty years. The sewer had been worse.

He set the damaged piece out on the deck and continued to work through the rest until he'd finished with everything he could remove and reinsert. Nothing else seemed to be out of whack.

That done, he sat up and held up the piece for her inspection. "I think this is probably the culprit. Looks like it got something juicy down in the contacts and shorted out. You have anything in your salvage that'll do the trick?"

She took the component from him and turned it over to look at it from various angles. "Maybe. I'll have to rummage through the bin and see if anything pops. You're welcome to join me if you like."

"Actually, if you have somewhere I could take a shower, I think that might suit me better."

She led him out of the pinnace and to one of the corners of the warehouse, where there was indeed a shower and clothes cleaner. He began stripping off even before she turned and walked back deeper into the warehouse. One of the benefits of not having any body modesty.

He tossed his borrowed clothes into the unit and had it start working on them while he got into the shower and cleaned off. He was an efficient man, so he had himself scrubbed clean in short order.

Jerome pulled his marine uniform out of his bag, got dressed, and equipped himself with his weapons. If someone came looking for them at the warehouse, he wouldn't be able to run and hide in the general population, but he didn't feel like running anymore.

He got one of his ration bars out, slung his bag over his shoulder, and headed back toward the pinnace. The sound of the exterior door opening made him put his hand on his stunner and watch as Paci and Parada came back into the warehouse.

Neither of them looked very pleased. Of course, they hadn't looked pleased about *anything* since he'd met them. Still, they looked less pleased than usual.

"What's wrong?" he asked.

"Not sure," Parada said with a frown. "It just seems like there's a lot more activity from corporate security than I'm used to seeing. The little buggers are swarming, but it's not like they're looking for us. I'm not sure what's happening, and that worries me."

"They're going to a higher state of alert," Paci said. "I'm not sure if they're planning on defending the capital from someone or launching an even bigger manhunt for us. I've never seen anything quite like it."

"What about you?" Parada asked. "Were you able to get the communication unit working again?"

"We found what we think is a bad part," Jerome said. "We might be able to get it back up and running if Kolstad can find something in her spare parts bin. If not, we might have to send you guys out on a shopping trip."

The Imperial Security Service agents grimaced in unison. Obviously, the idea of going back out into whatever was happening was not high on their to-do list. He respected that.

Too bad if that was what they had to do.

"I think I found something that'll work," Kolstad said as she walked up to them. "It's not quite the same, but I believe it's compatible enough to do the job if I play with the configuration settings. If not, well, we'll have to try something else."

The four of them trooped into the pinnace with Kolstad in the lead. Jerome got down onto the deck again, took the piece from her, and pushed the replacement part into place until it clicked. On general principles, he put the access panel back on, secured it, and stood.

Kolstad had sat in the pilot seat and started working on some type of configuration screen using the main console. It seemed to be giving her a little bit of trouble because she was muttering curses but smiled after about thirty seconds.

"There we go," she said, patting the console. "You're a good girl."

After a few seconds, she grunted. "I'm picking up some traffic, but the encryption I have is ancient. Can you make sense of this, Walker?"

He tried to connect to the pinnace, but it rejected him. "You'll have to give me access to the network so I can get the raw feed."

She brought up a new screen and tapped something. "Try it now."

He tried again, and his implants connected this time. That done, he tapped into the com feed and found himself listening in to the Fleet transport and Camp Pyramid talking while his implants decrypted the transmissions.

Based on the clipped language and requests for more precise data from the area around the camp and the mines, something was up.

He didn't get any personal updates because he hadn't announced himself. To do that, he'd have to transmit. That meant he'd have to upload more than the basic marine encryption to the pinnace.

Kolstad was a Marine Raider—he'd insisted she share her ID

earlier—so he was willing to take that risk, but it wouldn't stop the bad guys from knowing they'd sent something from within the capital. Maybe even tracking them down.

That was a problem he hadn't fully considered. It was a mistake he'd add to his private after-action report.

"I think we have a problem," he admitted. "As soon as we transmit, corporate security is going to come swarming if they can pinpoint us."

Kolstad leaned back in her chair and scratched her chin. "True, but I have some hardwired communications links I had installed back when I bought the warehouse. There were times when I moved data I didn't want anyone to know about.

"I paid some city workers to wire me into the system in such a way that it couldn't be traced back to me. Then I installed my own hardware into the line to make absolutely sure of that.

"If we can break into one of the city transmitters remotely, we won't have to use the transmitter on the pinnace at all. We'll still have to encrypt the final product for retransmission, though."

That sounded overly complicated to Jerome, but he wasn't a communications specialist. He just wanted to get this over with, but if they made a mistake now, it would waste all the effort they'd gone through to make sure they didn't get tracked down.

Lieutenant Van Buren's life was probably on the line, and he couldn't afford to drop the ball.

All the while they'd been talking, he'd been processing the com traffic in the background. He heard the moment something changed and frowned. The transport had cut off in midsentence, and Camp Pyramid was attempting to get them to respond without success.

"Boys, I think we've got a *big* problem," Kolstad said as she tapped the console. "My passive scanners just detected a big fusion explosion in orbit."

Jerome's blood ran cold. What had just happened?

"Set up whatever you need," he said through clenched teeth. "I think we just got dropped into the crapper."

27

Diana stared at the train bearing down on them, certain they were about to die, only to be yanked sideways when Barry jerked the air car as far to the right-hand side of the cleared path as he could get. It was *just* enough.

The grav train thundered by, the wind of its passage threatening to crash their car into the trees or the ground as it passed at high speed. She had no idea how long the thing was, but it seemed to stretch on forever.

"Increase our speed as much as you can!" Andrea shouted. "This is our chance!"

"Our chance to what?" Craig asked incredulously.

"We have to get on board that train."

"That's crazy," he said, almost sputtering. "We do some dangerous things here on Diorama, but that's by far the most insane suggestion I've ever heard. There's no way we could do anything like that without killing ourselves."

"Have you got any better ideas?" Andrea demanded. "Those people are going to find and kill us unless we do something drastic. You're going to say no to the one chance that almost literally falls in our laps?"

She didn't wait for him to answer, pulling her knife from her belt and jamming it through the ceiling of the air car. She used the monomolecular edge with her strength and sawed a hole in the air car that was big enough for them to go through.

It only took ten seconds, and suddenly the part that was being cut out ripped off the air car and flew back, slapping the side of the train and flying off into the woods like a Frisbee thrown by a mad god.

"We're still going too slow," Andrea shouted over the now-roaring wind. "Juice this thing harder, Barry. We need to match the train's speed for a little bit."

"If I do that, it's going to burn out the grav modules pretty fast. Are you sure this is the right thing to do?"

"It's the only chance we have to survive. I'll make the jump to the train, and then everyone else will have to come across on a rope. Getting the unconscious people across is going to be really hard, but we can do it if we try."

Diana had been looking out the front window of the air car and saw just a hint of blue where the grav train was going to pass.

"I think I see a river ahead," she said. "If we can do this right, we might be able to dump the air car into it. If we can, the people pursuing us won't find a wrecked car to tell them exactly where we went."

She turned to Andrea. "If we've got to hold on until the last possible second and then turn the air car into the river before someone makes the final jump, that's going to have to be you. Only you have the strength and reflexes to make this work. If any of us try, we're just going to die.

"I'll go across and secure the rope so we can start bringing people over. We'll have to do it fast and start with Leroy. Then we'll bring the unconscious people and finally Craig and Barry. We'll have to wait until we get right on top of the river for you to make the final move."

Even as she said the words, Diana knew she sounded insane. Just getting on the train from a moving air car that was bound to fail at any minute was crazy, but her plan was certifiable.

Yet it was the only chance they had.

She retrieved the climbing pack from the back of the air car, grabbed a coil of rope, unspooled as much as she could, and tied one end around her waist. This was one time when she was glad the marines still taught knots because everything would be over if she got this wrong.

"Make sure to secure your end really well," Diana said as she unhitched a small pickax from the pack. "If I miss this jump, that rope is how you get me back into the car."

Rather, it would be the way they retrieved her body. She couldn't afford to make a mistake.

She levered herself up, and the wind snatched her hat off her head. She'd forgotten she was even wearing it.

The air car was going almost as fast as the train, but they were still losing ground. A glance toward the train's rear showed they didn't have very many cars left before they ran out of options.

"The end of the car is coming," Andrea shouted. "Barry, you need to give it everything you have when we get to the back of the train, and Diana has to jump. I'll help shove her over so my strength can be added to hers, but we're only going to get one chance at this, so we can't afford to screw it up."

No pressure.

Diana let her friend help brace her as she climbed onto the roof of the air car and watched as the final car on the train came even with them. Barry goosed their speed, and she almost slipped, but Andrea's grip held her steady. The air car also rose a little bit, giving her just a little bit of a boost toward the train.

She put one leg on the roof and jumped.

Andrea shoved her feet as she leaped and gave her just enough extra momentum to land on top of the train. She immediately began sliding and jammed the pickax through the ceiling to arrest her motion. It felt like it was going to rip her arm off when she jerked to an abrupt halt, but she managed to maintain her grip.

It was difficult to see with the wind and grit in her eyes, but there was a roof hatch, maybe half a meter to her left and a bit behind her. It was secured with a sturdy-looking lock, but she was able to pull her marine knife from her belt and cut through it with a couple of hacks.

She wasn't nearly as strong as Andrea, but the knife made the work easy.

She tried to put her knife away but lost her grip, and the wind ripped it out of her hand, sending it tumbling back along the train roof and off. She hoped it missed the air car.

It took every ounce of her strength to hold onto the ax while she used her left hand to open the hatch. It had a pneumatic assist, and the opening was toward the rear of the train, so it could go up even in the face of the wind.

Now came the tricky part. She had to let go of the ax in order to get a grip on the hatch frame. She took a deep breath, grabbed the hatch frame with her left hand, and let go of the ax.

The wind almost ripped her off the train, but she held on for all she was worth. Once she was shielded by the hatch cover, she was able to climb into the train itself.

"I'm inside the train," she said over her military com. "I see a sturdy support post I can tie the rope to. Five seconds."

And that was about what it took for her to secure the rope. Once it was thoroughly tied down, she climbed back up onto the roof and used the handholds there to climb back to the rear of the train.

Maybe everybody would think it was funny later. She could see the hilt of her knife sticking out of the center of the reinforced windshield as the air car bobbed behind the train.

"Send Leroy," she said, holding onto the rope and train for support.

To his credit, the young man immediately climbed out of the air car and up the rope toward her. He'd been smart enough to leave his hat in the air car.

He was probably frightened, but he didn't let it show. He had a rope of his own tied around his waist as he came across, and she realized it must be to help pull the unconscious people across.

The thing that concerned Diana the most was the amount of smoke coming from the air car. It had increased dramatically. Whatever was going on in its engine compartment was coming to a head, and that vehicle was going to fail shortly. They had no time to waste.

As soon as Leroy reached the train and she'd showed him where to hold on, he tugged on the rope at his waist, and Andrea pushed the male prisoner out of the air car.

She'd found something to clip onto the rope and had secured that to the man's body. He jerked around a bit in the airflow, but they were able to pull him up the rope and onto the top of the train successfully.

When he arrived, she saw that he'd been secured by one of the special rings used in climbing that allowed for movement on ropes while still securing oneself. She'd used them but only vaguely remembered what they were called. D rings?

She and Leroy were able to get the man to the hatch, remove the rope from around his waist, unclip him from the main rope, and lower him inside.

That meant dropping him a couple of meters to the floor, but she didn't feel bad about that.

They returned to the rear of the train, and Leroy fed the rope holding the D ring back to Andrea, who adroitly caught it and ducked back inside the air car.

A few moments later, they repeated the process with the unconscious woman.

Thankfully, getting her into the train was just as straightforward as the man had been, though Leroy leaned as far into the train car as he could to cushion her fall.

They'd finished the most challenging part of the extraction and were down to three conscious and motivated people. Getting them over shouldn't be too difficult.

Relatively speaking.

The next person was Craig Lindbergh. Andrea had secured him with the D ring, and so they just tugged him across the rope until he was on the train. He tried to assist them, but that proved to be his undoing, and he lost his grip and almost fell before Diana snatched his wrist in her free hand.

The sudden tug of him falling almost yanked her off the train, but she managed to maintain her grip until he could find another hold. Then the two of them scrambled up to where Leroy was, and the two of them got Craig down into the train car.

"That last one was too close," Diana said to her friend. "Tell Barry not to help. Just let us move him."

"Copy that. Can you see how far away from the river we are?"

Diana leaned to the right side of the train as far as she safely could while still using the hatch cover to block some of the air, and she saw that they were a lot closer to the river than she'd have guessed. At this rate, they'd be there in less than a minute.

The other thing she saw terrified her. The grav train apparently didn't need a bridge to cross the river. It looked as if the thing was going to fly across the open gap and just act as if something was supporting it.

Maybe it was the momentum that got it across, or maybe there was enough strength to the grav modules that they could support the train from a greater height. She didn't know, and it didn't matter, but the air car wasn't going to be able to maintain its altitude when it reached the river.

"New problem," she told her friend. "There's no bridge. Looks like the train doesn't need one. You've got to get off before we get there."

"Sending Barry across now. Once we get there, I'll jump out of the air car, and you're going to have to pull me over. The air car isn't going to be able to support the height, and it'll fall into the river."

Diana wanted to argue with her friend, but she knew Andrea was probably right. They were committed at this point, and no matter how crazy her plan sounded, Diana was just going to have to do her part to make sure it worked.

"Leroy, tell Craig to be ready to cut the rope when I signal," she said. "We'll have one shot at this."

He nodded and moved to the hatch to shout instructions down to the other man. Once finished, he waited there to relay the call.

Moving Barry across was similar to moving one of the unconscious people. He didn't try to help them, and they were able to tug him where they needed him to go and then get him into the train car, where Craig assisted him down.

Only one more extraction to go. The one most important to Diana. She had to make this work.

Before she could fully play the rope out, they ran out of time. The train arched over the river, and the aircar started falling.

Andrea shot out of the air car and grabbed the loose rope. She slammed back into the falling air car but maintained her grip. Barely.

"Cut the rope!" she shouted to Leroy.

He must've already given the signal because the rope flew past her as the falling air car plunged into the white water below them. It disintegrated on impact, flipping end over end before being swallowed by the rapidly moving water.

Diana and Leroy got Andrea on top of the train just as they reached the far side of the river and went into the trees.

Once she was sure her friend had a secure grip, they made their way to the hatch, basically shoving Andrea in first because Diana wasn't going to see her friend slip at the last possible second. Leroy went in next.

Diana took a chance, wrapped her left hand around the loose rope, dropped the free end to the people inside the train car, and stretched out far enough to grab the handle of the pickax. It took a little bit of wiggling to get it to pop free, but she didn't want to leave a clue sticking out of the top of the train.

Andrea helped pull her in and then closed the hatch behind her as Diana slumped to the floor and tried to avoid collapsing entirely.

Unbelievably, they'd pulled it off.

"Is that the kind of thing you Imperial Marines do every day?" Craig asked with a grin as he clapped a hand on her shoulder. "You guys are a lot tougher than I gave you credit for. Hell, you might even be cowboy tough. Guess those campfire stories are going to get even more unbelievable."

Diana laughed, trying to keep a hysterical edge from seeping into her voice. She wasn't nearly as good at playing tough as Andrea because she wasn't really that badass.

"All in a day's work," she said shakily. "Is everybody okay?"

"I didn't think we were going to be when that knife flew into the windshield," Barry said. "That scared a year out of me."

"Sorry about that. It slipped."

"All's well that ends well," Craig said firmly. "We made it out alive, which was a damned miracle. Now we just have to figure out what to do next."

"Who are you people?" a faint voice asked.

Diana looked over and saw the woman they'd rescued was sitting up against the side of a crate, blinking and trying to focus her attention. She was awake. Sort of.

Her timing was excellent. If she'd woken up while they were getting her to safety, she'd have lost her mind.

"I'm Private Diana Randall, Imperial Marines," Diana said as she crawled over to the woman. "We rescued you from the mine."

The woman opened her mouth and closed it again, blinking furiously. "The marines are here? Oh, no. That means it's already started."

Diana had no idea what that meant, but it couldn't be good.

28

Andrea knelt beside the woman and took her hand in hers. "You're safe now."

It took the woman a few moments to focus on Andrea's face, and then she recoiled. "It's you!"

"It's not what you think," Andrea said quietly. "Kate Geller is genetically the same as me, but she is *not* me. We rescued you from the people she had holding you."

Diana knelt at the woman's other side. "I know you don't know us, but what my friend is telling you is true. She escaped the Singularity as a child, and now she's an Imperial Marine, just like me. We only arrived on Diorama a few days ago, and we've gotten caught up in whatever is happening.

"We figured out that Geller's pulling the strings inside Yi Holdings, and she wanted to get a company of Imperial Marines on the planet, though we don't know why. We managed to warn our company, so they're on guard until we figure out what's happening. You're safe now, at least if we can manage to get away from the pursuit."

"They're chasing us?" the woman asked as she rubbed her face. "I don't know whether I should believe you or not, but at least you don't sound like them."

Craig squatted down beside them and nodded at the woman. "My name is Craig Lindbergh, and I own the Big L Ranch. I don't know who you are, but it's always possible you know who I am. I can vouch for these young women.

"They've only been here two days and have already caused more trouble than anyone I can think of. They picked up a prisoner when they rescued you, so maybe that'll count for something."

He followed up the last with a gesture toward the unconscious man.

The woman managed to focus her attention on the male prisoner and blanched. "He's really knocked out? You're sure he's just not playing? He's beaten me a lot, and I'd rather not have to go through that again."

"He's not going to be beating anyone again," Andrea assured the woman. "My name is Andrea Tolliver, and I'm a Private First Class in the Imperial Marine Corps. This is my friend Private Diana Randall."

"Darcy Gilbert. Tell me exactly what's going on, and prove to me that this isn't some kind of trick."

"I'm not sure how I can do that when I look exactly like that woman," Andrea said slowly. "We come from the same genetic line inside the Singularity. I don't know precisely who she is, and I've never met her. I'm using makeup to cover the tattoos on my face just like she is."

"Tattoos? What kind of tattoos? Why do you wear them on your *face?*"

Andrea smiled sadly. "They put them on me when I was twelve, and I can't take them off. They're tied into my DNA, so even if I had them erased, they'd come back. It's the mark of one of the twelve leading genetic lines inside the Singularity.

"If they had any idea I was still alive, I'm pretty sure they'd send a lot of people to kill me. They really don't want their secrets getting out, and they wouldn't be happy I was working for the Empire."

Leroy walked over to the male prisoner, hauled back one hand,

and slapped him as hard as he could. The man's head flew to the side, but there was no other reaction.

Diana leaped to her feet. "What the hell are you doing? He's a prisoner! You can't beat him!"

"I'm not technically beating him," Leroy said with a grim smile. "I'm proving to our friend that he's really unconscious. We stunned him when we rescued you, and he hasn't had a chance to wake up yet. He's probably got another couple of hours of being completely out. Does that help?"

"Maybe," the woman said grudgingly. "Do you have any water?"

Andrea shook her head. "It's a long story, but we couldn't bring anything with us other than you. Trust me when I say you'd be glad you weren't awake for the process."

"There might be some water somewhere in here," Leroy said. "Let me look around and see what I can find."

The woman seemed to be becoming more aware of her surroundings, and her speech was less slurred. Whatever drugs they'd put into her system were wearing off.

"Why did they have you at the mine?" Andrea asked. "And why does the arrival of the Imperial Marines mean their plan has kicked off? Are they crazy? Even with the Singularity involved, they can't take on a company of Imperial Marines."

"They disagree," Darcy said. "They gloated about how they were going to kill a bunch of Imperial Marines when they finally arrived. That was just the kickoff to carrying out their full plan, though, which I can't tell you about."

The woman rubbed her eyes and looked over at Craig. "I've heard your name bandied about, Mister Lindbergh. I can't say I recognize you by sight, but you're something of a local institution. Is there anything you can tell me that might convince me to share more information?

"The problem I have is that the bad guys—including a woman that looks just like your friend—have been trying to get me to tell them things about what I do for over a week, and they've not been gentle about it."

The man rubbed his chin and shook his head. "I'm not sure I can.

Maybe if we knew one another, I could give you my word, and it would mean something, but for all you know, I'm part of their plan and just playing this part.

"What I will ask is if there are things you can tell us about what they want that the bad guys already know. If they are already clued in, repeating the same information isn't going to harm you in any way. We're lacking information about what's going on, and it's tough to make decisions when we're working in the dark."

The woman thought about that for a moment and nodded. "I suppose that makes sense. Let me start off by asking where the hell we are. I can tell we're on a vehicle of some kind, but I don't think I've ever been inside of anything like this. Is this a cargo truck?"

Lindbergh shook his head. "It's a cargo car on a grav train. We hitched a ride from the area around the mine after we escaped. It's moving pretty fast, so if they don't realize we're on board soon, they're not going to be able to intercept us before we at least get away from the mine.

"My young friends apparently caused quite a ruckus and stunned a number of people that were holding you. They tried to shoot us up as we left, but they didn't have anything handy that could chase us down after we took out the two that were trying to keep us from taking off."

"Maybe some of the intelligence stuff we gathered would help," Diana said. "I put it in a bag and tied it around my belt. I didn't have any other place to put it while we were running."

Andrea watched her friend take the small bag from around her waist and was astonished that it had survived all of the abuse they'd given it. Diana dumped its contents in front of Darcy.

The woman pawed through what was there and nodded at some of the identification. "I recognize a few of these people as guards. I suppose this could still all be faked, but it seems kind of ridiculous when they were getting close to breaking me. Why switch things up when you're about to get what you want?

"The truth is, I work for the Empire as a lab manager at a classified project on Diorama. The bad guys already know the truth of what we're doing, but they're looking for the specifics in order to be able to use it themselves. The Empire uses Schuster and Associates as a cover for our work."

Andrea considered that and nodded. "I've heard the name of the company but almost no details about it. Did they predate Yi Holdings here?"

"Yes. They were set up here before the rare minerals used to make flip drives were discovered. It was too much trouble to stop the other company from coming in to recover the materials, and the Empire needed them, so someone worked out a compromise, but I'm not really privy to the details.

"Things have changed since then because Yi Holdings runs everything now. That kind of started maybe fifty years ago when they wanted to make more money off of the general population. I suppose that's just the nature of corporations.

"It really got bad about five years ago when new management came in, but I didn't realize it was worse than greed and corruption until a week ago."

Leroy came back holding a bag that looked like a medical kit, but he'd obviously retrieved a sealed canteen of water from it. "I found this at the front of the train car. Must be for emergencies."

Darcy took the canteen from him and drank a few gulps before grimacing. "This tastes terrible." She then proceeded to drink even more of it.

"Easy," Diana said, slowing her down. "If you drink too fast, you might get sick."

The woman nodded but continued drinking fairly steadily until the canteen was empty. Andrea wasn't concerned about finding more water. If there was water in this car, there would be more in the others.

"So, Schuster and Associates are working on something that the Singularity wants," Andrea said slowly. "If the Singularity has been here for five years, that means they've been aware of what you're doing for longer than that. Why did it take so long for them to act?"

The woman shrugged slightly. "I'm not sure. If they intended to take on a company of Imperial Marines, maybe it took them a while to get what they needed to the planet. Smuggling it into the Empire without being detected couldn't have been easy.

"I suppose since they already have some of the information, I have to at least make sure you understand exactly what's at stake. The project I work for grows plants and other biological materials used to concoct a highly classified drug."

Andrea frowned. "That's pretty vague. Could you be even a little bit more specific?"

The woman shook her head. "Not about the drug. That's what they want information about. They want to know how we mix the various components together to get the final result. If it was just a matter of taking everything and figuring it out on their own, they'd fail.

"While we have everything we need to manufacture the drug here, there are certain processes that aren't straightforward or intuitive. It would take decades to figure out how to do it without our knowledge, and that's only if they had all of the biological material they needed, which isn't a given, considering this is the only planet that one of the major ingredients natively grows on."

"I can't imagine there's anything in existence that can't be grown somewhere else using advanced technology," Diana argued. "Why keep everything here if that's the case?"

"You'd think it would be easy, but you'd be wrong. The vast majority of what goes into this drug could be manufactured anywhere, but there's one specific part that's native to Diorama. It's impossible to grow anywhere else.

"And that's the problem. It has to be in large quantities because this particular ingredient has to be distilled down quite a bit, so it's unrealistic to expect anyone is going to be able to duplicate this drug without a lot of time, money, effort, and access to a lot more raw materials than they could rightly expect to have."

"If they've been trying to get the specifics from you so they can grow what they need once they leave Diorama, that means they have a plan to take everything with them when they go," Andrea said grimly. "We got a warning out to Delta Company that things were going down at the mine, and they've gone on the defensive. Whatever attack the enemy hopes to drop on their heads isn't going to be so easy now.

"We need to get more information about what's going on with your secret project if we're going to have any chance at all of thwarting them before they strike there."

Diana nodded. "And now that they know you're loose, it's going to make them strike sooner rather than later. If Geller isn't already mobilizing to go in and take what she wants, I'd be shocked."

"How can we stop her if we don't know anything at all? We can't drop a platoon of marines into the middle of your secret project to fend her off without details you're not willing to share because you don't trust us. How do we overcome that in time to save your friends and associates? And make no mistake, people are going to die if we don't act."

Darcy sighed. "I know that, but you're saying the same things that the bad guys would say. If there was any way at all you could prove more of what you're saying, I'd tell you things I'm not supposed to tell anyone. I just need to be sure I'm not helping the enemy."

Andrea opened her mouth to argue, but a loud thump on the roof of the train startled her.

"We've got company," she snapped, drawing her flechette pistol and gesturing toward Darcy. "Get her under cover."

She and Diana picked opposite sides of the train car and covered the hatch in the roof. While it wasn't strictly necessary for the bad guys to come through that entrance, it was likely. When they did, they'd get an exceptionally hot welcome.

Her com unit pinged with an incoming message. It was from Corporal Reed.

"We're on the roof of the train car. Is it safe to enter?"

Andrea let out a sigh of relief and holstered her pistol. "It's safe. We're glad to see you, Corporal."

"We'll see about that after the ass chewing takes place."

The hatch levered open, and Claudio dropped into the car, sweeping around with his stunner. Moments later, half a dozen marines dropped in and quickly scoured the car from one end to the other, eyeing the civilians with suspicion.

Corporal Reed dropped in once that was done, followed by Campbell. It looked like the corporal had brought two fire teams to rescue them, and Andrea was grateful.

"What the hell is going on, Tolliver?" Reed demanded as she stepped up to her, frowning. "Apparently, your actions have precipitated an all-out attack on the company. And what happened to your face?"

"It was my doing," Craig said from where he stood nearby. "I was going to the mine for something else, and one of my hands that used to work there gave her a tour. I'm not exactly sure what happened, but they found a lot more than they bargained for."

He gestured toward Darcy. "This young lady was apparently their prisoner, and that unconscious guy over there was one of the captors. Were they supposed to just leave her there? She was drugged and tortured."

"I don't know, and it's above my pay grade to decide what was appropriate or not, but you kicked over an anthill, Tolliver," Reed growled. "It's a good thing Randall warned us because the company is now under attack. I'm not sure precisely what they're facing, but it looks like Singularity troops.

"The news isn't all good, though. They took out the Fleet transport, so we don't have any fire support other than what we brought with us. We need to know what the hell is going on and turn the tables on these bastards fast. That means you need to start talking."

A young woman stuck her head down into the train. "We've got incoming, Corporal. The pilot says a couple of air cars are coming from the mine, and they're catching up. They must be pretty damn fast."

"Those aren't going to be friendlies," Diana said. "It's going to be someone looking for their former prisoner and us."

"Then we need to get the hell out of here," Reed said. "Who's going to tell me exactly what the hell is happening while we do?"

Andrea looked over at Darcy. "Are a couple of fire teams of Imperial Marines in a marine pinnace enough proof that I'm not Kate Geller?"

"I think so, yes."

"What's this?" Reed demanded. "Why would she think you're whoever that person is?"

"If we're going to evade the air cars, I'll have to tell you while we move, Corporal. The little bit of information I got from Darcy tells me we don't have much time to turn this around.

"The Singularity is on the move, and we haven't seen all their cards. You can also bet they've got an escape plan they're going to execute if things don't work out. We can't let them get away."

The woman considered Andrea for a long moment before nodding. "I'm going to get the full story out of you, Tolliver. If you've screwed up, you can bet I'll bust your ass down to private."

"You'll probably have to stand in line for that," Andrea said glumly. "Let's get a move on. Our dance partners aren't going to wait forever."

29

Jerome rubbed his eyes tiredly. He and Kolstad had been working for hours, and he'd finally become convinced they were never going to be able to transmit any kind of message to his compatriots. At least not anytime soon.

It wasn't because he thought they couldn't overcome the technical hurdles to access a transmitter, but somebody was jamming Camp Pyramid. There wouldn't be any signals going in or out of the marine encampment until this was settled.

Paci and Parada went back out to tap some of their intelligence resources. Somebody knew what was going on, and he desperately wanted to find out what that was. Unknown forces had just destroyed a Fleet transport and killed a lot of people. From everything he could determine, those same people were attacking Camp Pyramid, and he had no idea what their situation was.

From his point of view, the worst part of this was that he'd lost his commanding officer. Lieutenant Van Buren should be out there running the company. Instead, he was locked up somewhere in this damned city, waiting for Jerome to spring him.

He probably didn't know that was what he was waiting for, but it was true. If anyone was going to get the officer back into the game, it had to be Jerome, Kolstad, Paci, and Parada.

A less impressive team was hard to imagine. A decrepit—relatively speaking—retired Marine Raider, an almost unarmed marine, and two Imperial Security Service agents to take on an entire corporate security apparatus.

Things did not look promising.

Nevertheless, they had to find a way to make this work. His only hope at this point was those slippery ISS bastards and whatever tricks they still had up their sleeves.

All he had with him were his sidearms. He didn't even have any unpowered combat armor. While Kolstad might have something in the warehouse, it would almost certainly be shaped for the female form and probably not that useful to a big guy like him.

While he'd been brooding, Kolstad had been trying to pierce the jamming and gather what information she could. It turned out she still had a pair of stealthed drones she could send on autonomous missions, so she dispatched them to scout the area around Camp Pyramid.

He'd worried that the neighbors might have seen something for a while, but no one came sniffing around, so they'd gotten out without a hitch.

It took them about three hours to make the trip, and they weren't able to get any information back once they'd arrived, so he and the rest had to wait until one or both of the drones came all the way back.

Or failed to return. That would be information, too, though less helpful.

Since that was going to take about six hours before they could learn anything at all, he took the opportunity to catch some shuteye in the flight engineer's jump seat on the pinnace. It wasn't comfortable, but he was used to sleeping in odd places.

He woke when somebody bumped him on the shoulder. Kolstad was standing over him. "One of the drones made it back. You're going to want to see what it spotted."

He levered himself to his feet and stretched. "What have we got?"

"I've got good news and bad news. Since I'm a Marine Raider, we thrive on bad news, so you get that first. It looks like your camp was assaulted by an extensive force with heavy armament.

"The good news is that it looks like your people repulsed their attack and handed the enemy heavy losses. There were some pretty significant craters on the perimeter and even in the camp itself, so I'd anticipate the bad guys tried a sneak attack that failed."

"Show me," he ordered.

She sent the recon footage to his implants, and he proceeded through it quickly. It wasn't quite as detailed, or even in the same format, as he was used to, but it was enough for him to pick up the information she was talking about.

Camp Pyramid seemed mostly intact, though it had taken some damage from explosive munitions. A dozen crashed grav vehicles were scattered across half a kilometer around the camp perimeter.

Some areas near the destroyed vehicles were heavily peppered with casualties dressed in some type of combat fatigues, but he didn't recognize the style. They might be mercenaries, though they were idiots for trying to engage a prepared marine company if that were the case.

A more comprehensive look at the area showed a number of armed grav vehicles still circling around Camp Pyramid at a distance, exchanging fire with the marine emplacements. Whoever they were, they were moving professionally and keeping the marines pinned down.

More concerningly, there was a significant force set up about ten kilometers away from the camp behind a rather large hill. They seemed to be preparing an attack.

If the marines had any drones out, they'd know about them. That wasn't a given, though. If the enemy had taken out all the eyes in the sky, they might be able to proceed without being spotted until it was too late.

"Just how stealthed is this drone?" he asked.

"Quite a bit," she said. "It's old Marine Raider tech, so it's not cutting edge by their standards these days, but it's still tough to spot.

"Even so, it looks like whoever this is spotted the other drone and took it out. You know what we're looking at down there, don't you?"

"Mercenaries?"

"That might be what they want you to think, but those are Singularity ground troops. They're not using standard Singularity equipment, but I've studied how they move and fight, and I have no doubt that's who they are."

He blinked in surprise. "Singularity ground troops? Here? Diorama isn't exactly the kind of place to draw that kind of attention, especially considering how many troops we're looking at.

"Hell, they have something in orbit that took out a Fleet transport. Why would a Singularity warship come to a place like this?"

"I doubt very seriously that we're looking at a real warship," she said, leaning back against the pilot's chair. "Whatever's up there took out a Fleet transport, yes, so they're no pushovers, but they haven't followed up.

"If we were looking at a warship, we'd be seeing strikes from orbit by now. Not directly but with pinnaces strafing the camp. Since we're not, they're operating with what they have on the planet's surface. I'd wager they took out the transport with a surprise attack at close range. The attacker might not even have survived the return fire."

She scratched her nose and grimaced. "If we're looking at a raid by the Singularity, they smuggled each of these people here and probably modified civilian craft for their purposes. That couldn't be done quickly or easily, but it *is* possible. I should know, since I trained hard to do something similar to them when I was on active duty."

He pursed his lips and shook his head. "I'm not buying that. There's absolutely nothing worth that kind of effort on Diorama. The only thing of interest here—that they know of—is the mine where they extract the rare elements for the flip drives.

"And while that's valuable, it's not exactly uncommon. The loss of the mine wouldn't even put a damper on ship construction in this sector. That's a lot of troops down there, so what justifies bringing them here?"

"They're not interested in the mine," Kolstad said firmly. "It's a smokescreen. They have to be here for the formula and ingredients for making Panther. If so, that means they've known about it for at least a decade. They'd have needed that long to plan the raid.

"I think your company is just a secondary objective and maybe a distraction. If they vaporize the Panther facility, and there was no indication that it was intentionally attacked, it might be written off as collateral damage. One big bomb might be written off as bad luck."

Jerome considered her theory and couldn't dismiss it out of hand. What was evident to him was that something was going on that they hadn't been aware of when they'd arrived.

No matter what the draw for the Singularity had been, he had no doubt the controlling corporations on Diorama were somehow involved. The corporate security forces had been waiting for a delegation of marines to arrive in the capital.

If they'd come in force, they might've been met with force. As it was, someone had decided to simply take them into custody.

There was still a lot he didn't understand, but it was more critical than ever to get his lieutenant out of custody. If, of course, he could figure out where the man was and develop a viable plan for springing him.

"That's fine deductive reasoning," he finally admitted, "but there's nothing we can do about it. Even if your pinnace was armed, the two of us couldn't effectively use it to help defend Camp Pyramid or even the secret Panther factory.

"Honestly, I'm not sure the marines even need our help directly. Maybe we could take out the jamming, and that would make a difference."

She shook her head. "You're looking at this wrong. The odds are excellent they originally meant to split you up into smaller groups and attack you individually. None of the forces I see down there look like they're going to be sufficient to beat your people as a unit. Whoever's in command of the marines will turn things around shortly no matter what we do.

"The question we need to be asking ourselves right now is, if they don't have a chance of victory, why are they even attacking? The smart thing to do would've been to call everything off when their plan went to hell. Instead, they're going full bore. Why?"

Not only did he not have enough information to answer that

question, he also wasn't sure figuring out the enemy's motivations was even really possible. Who understood the Singularity?

Well, he supposed Tolliver did, at least to a degree, but she wasn't even in camp. Instead, she was off at a ranch. If she was smart, she'd stay there until the attack was over. Two marines with just their sidearms were not a threat to the attackers.

Frowning, he brought up the view of the area around Camp Pyramid. A lot of exploded ordnance that had struck the camp looked like it had impacted their landing field, and the remains of three pinnaces sat there burning.

There should've been a fourth. Where was it?

One more question that he wasn't going to get an answer for.

"Knock knock," Paci said from the compartment behind them.

Jerome turned his attention to the men as they entered the control area and was surprised to see they both had smiles on their faces. That was unusual and perhaps a bit unsettling.

"Don't you two look like the cat who caught the canary?" Kolstad asked. "I take it you have good news."

"Maybe not the best news in the world but pretty good," Parada said. "We've found where they're keeping your lieutenant, Sergeant Walker. And with all the hubbub, it looks like getting to him isn't out of the question."

"Really?" Jerome asked, not ready to take that at face value. "That is good news. Any idea why corporate security is losing their little minds here in the capital?"

"They think they're going to be invaded," the man said as he leaned up against the bulkhead. "More specifically, they're confident you Imperial Marines have come to take charge of the entire planet and imprison the corporate leadership.

"I'm not sure *why* they think that, but I've talked to enough people to be relatively certain they're not just blowing hot air. Their leadership seems convinced."

Paci shrugged. "In the end, their motivation doesn't matter. The place where they're keeping your lieutenant is located inside the city center, and the guard force is smaller than it would typically be, as well as being distracted."

"I believe it's possible to gain access to the building and spring your lieutenant without too many people being aware that we're doing so until we're gone."

"Just the three of us?" Jerome asked warily. "We're talking a city full of corporate security, and you think the three of us can waltz into a secure location, spring my lieutenant, and then just wander back out without raising any eyebrows? I can't wait to hear your plan."

Paci laughed. "You've really got that tone down, don't you? I've seen actors playing grizzled marine NCOs that sound *just* like you."

"We have someone that can help us get into the building and even up to the floor where your lieutenant is being kept. Getting him out of the room they're keeping him in might be a little bit tricky, but it's not out of the question."

"Let's say I believe that," Jerome countered. "How do we get back out again once we've stirred up the hornet's nest? You know that place will be flooded with people the moment the alarm goes out.

"I don't know about you, but I'm not a vid hero. I run out of ammunition, and I can get shot just like anybody else."

Parada grinned. "The trick to avoiding that is using a different exit strategy. If the information we have is accurate, Lieutenant Van Buren is being kept in one of the executive suites at the Yi Holdings corporate building. It looks like their CEO wants to question him personally and has him on ice until he has the time to do so.

"There's a shuttle pad on the roof. That would make things fairly easy for someone with a hard-to-detect aerial vehicle to pop out of nowhere and land long enough for us to scurry aboard before they take off. Once we're gone, tracking us would be a lot harder."

"How did I get dragooned into your crazy scheme?" Kolstad asked, holding up a hand. "I'm done with assaulting prepared positions and shooting people. I'm retired."

"I thought Marine Raiders were adrenaline junkies. This planet is in the middle of an insurrection. I have no idea what else is going on, but it's not going to be just corporate security in the capital losing their minds. Their leadership is panicking.

"How long before they trot Lieutenant Van Buren out as a hostage? If they send a message to the Imperial Marines telling them to stand down or they'll blow his head off, we all know what's going to happen.

"The marines won't bow to that kind of pressure, and they'll come in hot. The only way we can save a lot of innocent people—relatively speaking, as we're talking about corporate security—is to take that option off the table."

Personally, Jerome agreed with that assessment, but the argument wasn't aimed at him. No matter what happened, he already knew he was going to sign off on the final plan because there was no way he'd stand by and leave his lieutenant in the lurch. Not a chance in hell.

The real wildcard here was Kolstad. If she decided she was in, her skills—as rusty as they no doubt were—and the equipment at her disposal could make a big difference in their chances for success.

Still, she'd have to make that decision on her own. This was an all-volunteer mission.

The old woman glared sourly at the Imperial Security Services agents. Then she sighed. "Dammit."

"I take it that means you're in," Paci said. "We thought that might be the case, so we stole all the information we could about the building and the surrounding area. It's in a governmental zone, so there really isn't any air defense to speak of. It's not like this planet was designed to stand off an invasion.

"The tricky part is going to be timing everything so that we can get in, get the lieutenant on schedule, and be on the roof when you're ready to pick us up. If we're too early, the reinforcements will pin us down. If we're too late, someone's going to come along and force you off the roof. Timing is going to be key."

Kolstad smiled sourly. "Believe it or not, I think I know a guy that can help us with that. Now, let's have the information so we can plan. We probably need to execute this sucker within the next few hours, so we're going to have to nail down as many details as we can up front."

Jerome let his breath out slowly. Her acquiescence at least made this mission survivable. There wouldn't be a second bite at the apple, though, so they'd have to snag Lieutenant Van Buren on the first try.

Piece of cake.

30

Once Diana had helped Darcy onto the train's roof and into the pinnace, she secured the woman in one of the seats and sat next to her. She then tapped into the pinnace's tactical network and downloaded everything she could about the situation back at Camp Pyramid.

There wasn't much to see. It looked as if the entire area was blacked out, and there were no communications with it at all.

Going back through the sequence of events in the log, she could see that the camp had come under sustained attack shortly after the pinnace had taken off and left the area. Missing a pinnace in the attack probably hadn't been in the Singularity's plan, but it was good luck for her and her friends.

One thing she hadn't counted on was the destruction of the Fleet transport. That was a horrific tragedy that had undoubtedly cost hundreds of lives. It also made the job of turning this thing around significantly more difficult, but the decision-making portion of their involvement in these events was over.

Corporal Reed was the senior noncommissioned officer, since they weren't counting the pilot in the marine command structure. She'd decide what needed to be done now.

She felt sorry for the pilot. They'd have come from the transport, and all their crewmates—barring any at Camp Pyramid—had just been killed. That was going to be hard to live with.

Well, if she couldn't make the decisions going forward, she could at least solve the mystery of exactly what was going on. It was time to get answers.

"What is the Singularity trying to steal?" she asked the scientist. "We need to know enough to stop them with the forces we have available. That's eight marines and this pinnace."

The woman looked torn, but she eventually nodded. "Everything I'm about to tell you is extremely classified. Even under the circumstances, I'm probably going to get into trouble for telling you about it, but you're right.

"What we've got is a small facility that collects and grows a lot of biological material and then follows a strict recipe of condensation and distillation to get everything to the precise dosages needed. There are other steps, but I'm not divulging them. The end result is a two-drug combination used by Marine Raiders to enhance their combat abilities."

Diana blinked at the woman in surprise. She wasn't sure what she'd been expecting, but that hadn't been it.

"Marine Raiders are already augmented to ridiculous levels," Diana objected. "Why do they need combat enhancement drugs?"

"What you're thinking of are physical enhancements. They've got graphene-coated bones, artificial musculature, and even a protective web installed underneath their skin that keeps them from being stunned. If you didn't know about that, it basically grounds the stun beam before it can take them down.

"All of those things make them powerhouses in a combat environment, but if you've ever heard rumors about their performance when push comes to shove, they're much more effective than even that. One of the reasons is a drug called Panther."

The woman paused for a few seconds to let that sink in before continuing. "It's the two-drug combination I mentioned earlier. One part of it speeds up the reactivity of the human nervous system, so there's almost no delay in transmitting an order from the brain to any part of the body. It might seem like that isn't necessary because nerve impulses travel really fast, but there's a difference between fast and almost instantaneous.

"The second drug speeds up neural processing in the brain itself. Once again, you'd imagine that happens almost instantly, but it's just not true. Under the effects of the second drug, you have what feels like all the time in the world to think about what you want to do and how you want to do it."

The woman smiled a little and shook her head. "With those working in concert, a Marine Raider moves like a ghost dodging between things that most people couldn't even see in time to react. In conjunction with their physical enhancements, that makes them dominant on the battlefield.

"Imagine if all Singularity troops could do that. We can't allow this to fall into their hands."

That was a lot to think about, and Diana was sure that she was missing some of the implications, but that didn't matter. The Empire couldn't afford to lose this secret.

"I assume you've got some means to prevent it from falling into their hands that they must've been working to circumvent," Diana said. "They won't be able to walk into your facility and take what they want, will they?"

Darcy shook her head. "All our equipment is subject to a self-destruct order. There's no way they can get into the facility fast enough to seize everything they need, at least in a perfect world.

"My concern is they've been working on a way in that no one has thought of. They picked me up right off the village street, and I had no idea that any of us was in any danger. There's a real chance they can get inside the facility and take the equipment intact if they eliminate the people that could initiate that self-destruct. There aren't that many of us."

After a few moments of thought, Diana nodded. "Then we have to assume that's what they're going to do. They've had years to plan, and it wouldn't surprise me if they've managed to slip some people into the facility or turned someone that's already there.

"Those people might not have all of the necessary clearances to do anything on their own, but they'd know who has what they need. They'd also know how to take care of anyone that's a threat to their ability to carry out this operation."

"What can we do about it?" Darcy asked, her face a mask of worry. "Until a few hours ago, they had everything going their way, but now that I've escaped, they have to know their plan is in jeopardy. That means they're going to act immediately. How can we stop them?"

"The first step is to convince Corporal Reed that we have to help. If we can't get her on board with whatever plan we come up with, then it's not going to happen. She's the decision-maker, and if she says we're not taking the mission, we're not going.

"If you can convince her this is what we need to do, she can give the orders, and we'll go in hot to make certain we at least keep the Singularity from taking anything away from the facility. That might mean the total destruction of your lab, but I think that's better than its loss to the Singularity, don't you?"

The woman looked torn but nodded. "Keeping it secret and safe seems like a lost cause at this point, so we have to do what's necessary to protect the Empire. Do you really think eight marines can make a difference?"

Diana smiled coldly. "Under the right circumstances, a single marine can make a difference. Also, if we act quickly, we've got at least one ace up our sleeves. The fact that Andrea looks exactly like their chief may give us an edge getting into the building and turning the tables on them. They're going to see her and think it's the other woman."

"That's creepy," Darcy admitted. "I can tell it's not her now that I'm really awake, but they're almost identical. How is that possible?"

"Genetics," Diana said. "They have the exact same DNA. Whoever crafted the template for the Andrea Line trimmed and tweaked it to get the precise results they wanted, and now they grow people that are indistinguishable from one another.

"Geller is a little older than Andrea, and that's the reason you're seeing a slight difference in their appearance. Give Andrea another half-dozen years, and she's going to be fully mature and look *exactly* like that woman."

She smiled a bit sadly. "It's even truer when she's not wearing the makeup that's covering her face right now. She's got the tattoos that the Andrea Line uses to mark their members across her forehead and cheeks. There would be no mistaking her for anything else if she took it off."

Darcy frowned. "Do you think Geller will take her makeup off? That might make things more complicated, since we don't know which state she's in. If any of her minions see your friend, and they don't look the same, they're going to start shooting."

The question set Diana back a little, and she closed her eyes to think it through. After a few seconds, she shook her head. "Taking off the makeup gains her nothing at this point. They've gone to a lot of trouble to make sure they have deniability. She's going to have her tattoos covered."

She rose to her feet, unsecured the other woman, and pulled her to her feet. "We've got to talk to Corporal Reed. I haven't got the slightest idea where your laboratory is, but the clock is ticking, and we've got to get there ASAP.

"We can't just land directly on top of it either. We're going to have to come in from some distance away so that we don't warn them we're there. Come on."

She led the scientist to Reed, who was debriefing Andrea. It didn't look like a pleasant process, but her friend would survive. It wasn't as if they'd done anything truly wrong.

Even if they hadn't been supposed to go to the mine, their presence there had revealed the entire plot. That had to count for something.

Reed looked over at her as she approached and frowned. "I'm a little busy here, Randall. Wait your turn."

"This can't wait, Corporal. This is Darcy Gilbert, and she's a scientist at a classified Imperial research project here on Diorama. She says the Singularity is trying to steal an Imperial secret from there that we can't let them have."

The noncommissioned officer turned her attention to Darcy.

"That's a bold claim. Who exactly are you, and why should I believe you?"

"I'm the lead research scientist at the Panther Project. That name is classified too. Here's my authentication and an official request for Imperial assistance."

Reed frowned even more as she processed whatever the scientist had just sent her. "That looks valid to me, but it leaves me in a bit of quandary. Assisting you means we can't help defend the rest of Delta Company. Is this really that important?"

Darcy nodded firmly. "I don't know why they're attacking your company, though I'm sure the prisoner you have strapped in over there could probably answer those questions if he were so inclined.

"What I can tell you is that the loss of what we do at my project would severely damage the ability of the Empire to conduct operations and give the Singularity a boost that might change the dynamic of how well they fight.

"I'd rather not destroy the entire facility, but I believe the woman going by the name of Kate Geller is on her way there right now or is perhaps already there. She's going to take the equipment, all of the raw supplies, and attempt to recreate what we've accomplished with the forced assistance of scientists she'll kidnap. That cannot be allowed to happen."

"Geller," Reed said with her lips pursed. "She's the one that looks like Tolliver, right? She's a high muckety-muck inside the Singularity. She's here for this?"

"From what we know thus far, Corporal, she's been here for at least five years undercover as the assistant to the CEO of Yi Holdings," Diana said. "That means whatever is going on has been aimed at getting the contents of this lab.

"She's probably been using that time to infiltrate the facility and get people in place that can prevent them from using any kind of self-destruction protocols. She'll have identified anyone that would be worthwhile to kidnap, like Miss Gilbert.

"The attack on Delta Company has to be a secondary objective. As good as it would be for them to win that particular fight, the secret has to be the real primary objective."

She considered Andrea. "Considering the timing, this might be meant to get some payback for the raid you were rescued on. The first operation would've been in the planning stages, so someone higher up could've made the call to bleed the marines while they were at it.

"Ballsy in my opinion but not out of the question. That'll be something for the higher-ups to figure out. We have more immediate problems."

Reed held up a hand and began pacing. She did so without interruption for thirty seconds and then turned back toward them. "From what I can guess about the Singularity, if there really wasn't any sabotage or dissension at the mine, that meant they were trying to draw elements of the marines out to different areas of the planet.

"They'd probably have preferred to do so over a period of a couple of months, so they could strike us while our strength was at its weakest. That means they're probably ill prepared to take on the company in a dug-in position.

"Your warning about their presence probably saved a lot of lives, Randall. Well done. That doesn't excuse you from going to the mine when you knew better, but apparently, I'm going to have to set that aside for right now and deal with the situation at hand."

She focused her attention on Darcy. "I need to know everything about the layout and location of your facility. If you have maps of the general area and the interior, I'm going to need them too. We only have two fire teams, so that means we've got eight marines to make the magic happen.

"What exactly do you make there?"

Darcy explained what Panther was, and Diana could see Reed pale. The noncommissioned officer didn't argue after that.

"We can leave a marine aboard to provide fire support, but the only one of us really trained in the use of shipboard weapons is me. Corporal Buckman from Fire Team One isn't quite as good at that sort of thing, so he'll have to lead everyone inside."

She grimaced. "I've got three greenies in my fire team, so that means there will only be four fully trained marines in the assault. We have no idea what kind of force the enemy brought to the table, but it has to be more than that. How exactly are we going to win a fight like that?"

Diana grinned coldly. "For them to be successful, they have to get everything they need: equipment, formula, and personnel. We just need to deny them any part of that, and they're screwed."

"That still doesn't give us great odds, but I suppose you're right," Reed acknowledged. "I'll need that information about the facility now, Miss Gilbert."

Each of their implants pinged with an incoming transmission, and once they'd accepted, they found themselves in possession of a number of maps.

The first was a very general area map locating the area they needed to get to. It wasn't far away from the capital, which Diana wasn't sure was actually a positive from their perspective. The enemy could likely get reinforcements in short order, and they could escape and evade much more effectively in an environment like that.

On the positive side, the laboratory itself was in a small valley dedicated to growing crops in tiered ledges all along the hills surrounding a very picturesque little village. It was gorgeous, but more importantly, it was relatively small.

The benefit of that was that they could quickly get from the hills to any place in the valley. How well that would work in practice, she wasn't sure, but it was better than having a facility where they could see the marines coming from kilometers away.

As it was, the marines could disembark outside the valley and come in on foot. If they timed things well and didn't get spotted, they might get very close indeed.

The last map they received was one showing the facility itself. It was located directly under the village, which meant almost everyone in that small community either worked for the laboratory or knew it was there.

In a way, that was bad. When the bad guys decided to come in force, everyone they rounded up would know something about operations inside the facility. They could use force or drugs to compel people to turn on their comrades and loved ones and wring every bit of information they wanted out of them in a very short amount of time.

What person would resist when bad guys started shooting loved ones? And, from what she'd heard about the Singularity, they wouldn't hesitate to do that or worse.

Diana was about to say something along those lines when her implants pinged for her attention. A moment later, she watched in amazement as the facility map updated, adding new details and a few areas that hadn't been there before.

The valley map also updated, showing two hidden locations accessing tunnels that led to the facility.

There was also a priority message from the Imperial Intelligence databases, a new and frightening turn of events.

CATEGORY ONE EMERGENCY DECLARED. Extraordinary access to Project Panther facility data granted. The agent is now tasked with stopping the loss of any data from the facility and securing the product, equipment, and personnel at all costs. Any and all measures needed to carry out this mission are authorized.

Access to Imperial computers in the facility is granted. Priority access codes are available to the agent for the duration of this emergency. The Empire also requires the agent to report this emergency as soon as practical to the nearest Imperial Intelligence field office.

IT NOW LOOKED as if she didn't have a choice about revealing her undesired status working for Imperial Intelligence. That was just perfect. How would she even know where to report the emergency?

Her databases responded by providing a listing of systems where she could find an Imperial Intelligence field office. It was unlikely she'd be able to get to any of them, though she supposed it wasn't out of the question.

She queried the databases about Seward. It did have an Imperial Intelligence field office, but there was no telling how long it would take the company to get back there.

Well, the outcome of that problem wasn't within her control.

Completing the mission was. Best to focus on the things she could affect.

"That's everything I can give you," Darcy said. "I've highlighted the areas inside where the critical computer systems are located and the distilling and formulation equipment. Those are critical for this process. The hills around the village are where we grow everything we need to produce Panther, hidden among more mundane crops.

"Some of it can only be grown on Diorama because of specific nutrients and other elements in the soil itself. Every time someone has tried to move it off-planet or grow it in an artificial environment, they've missed some aspect of what was needed, and the plants died or failed to produce the requisite effects when distilled.

"There's still a bit of art to this science, and we haven't been able to figure out the specifics of making it work in another environment even after hundreds of years of trying."

"Is this a complete map?" Diana asked. "Are there other ways in that might not be on it?"

"To the best of my knowledge, it's complete. I suppose it's always possible there are areas I'm not cleared for, but if so, I don't know about them."

"Everybody listen up," Reed said. "We're going into a facility to stop the Singularity from getting something they cannot be allowed to have. According to my calculations, it will take us about two hours to get to the valley, and we need to be ready to jump on this as soon as we get there.

"Gather round, and let's start hashing this out. We've only got the eight of us to make this work, and I'm going to have to stay on the pinnace to provide fire support when the time comes. It's a big task for two fire teams, one of which doesn't have the necessary training for this type of operation, but we're the ones that have to pull it off. Understood?"

Everyone crowded around and nodded at the corporal's words. This wasn't going to be an easy job, but it was a critical one. The very security of the Empire was at stake, and that knowledge showed in their expressions.

The damage would be incalculable and irreparable if they

couldn't stop Geller and her Singularity goons. Diana would have to take some real chances here if she wanted to give them a shot at success.

She couldn't just reveal the information she was privy to without blowing her cover completely, though. Any trust the rest of them had in her would evaporate the moment they decided she had a connection to Imperial Intelligence, so to make this work, she'd have to find a way to present the information without looking as if she'd done so.

Diana accessed the pinnace's systems and began setting up something inside the scanner system to add anomalies that would reveal the secret passages leading into the facility. If she could make it look as if the scanner suite had picked up the information on its own, it would protect her cover.

Of course, it wasn't that simple. That type of tampering wasn't an authorized activity, and the system blocked her. With a sigh, she tapped into her Imperial Intelligence databases and requested their assistance with the matter, explaining in brief what she wanted to do and why it was essential to protect her cover by doing so.

The databases—which seemed to have components that were decidedly more than simple databases—seemed to ponder that for a few moments and then presented her with an access code. She transmitted it to the pinnace, and the locked systems suddenly opened for her.

Well, that was terrifying. It meant that an Imperial Intelligence agent could—under the right circumstances—manipulate the data their equipment presented to them. No wonder everybody was suspicious of them.

And here she was doing precisely the same thing. Talk about shades of gray.

Over the next fifteen minutes, she added just enough data to be presented in the initial scans of the valley to make Reed look at the areas she needed her to examine a bit closer.

If the corporal didn't find the tunnels, Diana could pretend to be going over the data herself and bring the anomalies up, but she'd

TERRY MIXON

prefer not to be associated with this at all. She was as deep in the shadows as she could get, and she wanted to stay that way.

Andrea would be an excellent proxy to "find" the anomalies if that was what was called for. Her friend already knew where she'd have gotten the information, so that would be her backup plan.

Looking at the maps of the facility, she saw that some of the hidden areas weren't connected to the two access tunnels, so there was more going on than they'd been cleared for. Or Darcy had decided they didn't need to know about them and had cut them out of the map she'd provided them.

Maybe she'd had a reason to do so, but Diana wasn't going to let this mystery pass unsolved. Since she was in this up to her eyebrows, she might as well sink in over her head.

One way or another, she'd understand what was being done at this facility before they finished.

If, of course, she survived defending it.

31

———

By the time the pinnace finally arrived at the valley that held Project Panther, Andrea had found some combat fatigues that fit her and unpowered armor in one of the storage lockers. She'd also drawn a rifle from the arms locker. She felt a lot more prepared now and knew Diana did as well.

There'd been talk of pretending to be Geller, but that was just too dangerous. They had no idea how the woman was dressed, who she would be with, and what people knew about her.

It was far better to just go in hot and take them out the old-fashioned way.

It was dark when the pinnace made a low-altitude pass outside the valley, but that didn't inhibit its passive scanners. Andrea piggybacked on those and took a good look as they mapped the area. Knowing the terrain would be crucial when they went in.

The pilot kept them out of sight while Corporal Reed then used drones to map the valley in more detail. The entire valley was blanketed by jamming like the capital and Camp Pyramid, so the drones went in on preprogrammed courses and then returned with their scanner haul.

Andrea doubted it was a coincidence the valley and the capital were both being jammed, though she didn't understand the reasoning for the capital. Why did the city matter?

The marines couldn't communicate with Camp Pyramid, and the enemy had destroyed the Fleet transport, so why block com traffic from the capital?

Yes, Lieutenant Van Buren was there with Sergeant Walker, but what could they do by themselves? They couldn't communicate with anyone, and they were probably already in custody or dead.

So why jam everything? There had to be more going on that they just weren't aware of yet.

Once they had a complete map of the valley, they'd make their final plans. Just looking at the village, it didn't seem as if anything was wrong. There were no fires, so it seemed unlikely that a general attack had taken place, but she also didn't see any people moving around in the early evening dark, which seemed strange and ominous.

"We have to assume they're here and proceed accordingly," Reed said grimly. "Now that we've got the actual layout of the valley, we need to plan the best approach into the village. We know where the entrance to the facility is, so we'll have to take that into account and try to minimize contact with anyone there."

Andrea was about to nod her agreement when she got a private communication request from Diana. She accepted it at once.

I've got something for you to pass on to the others, but I need you to keep the information as low-key as possible because it could lead back to my little secret, her friend said. *Basically, there are two tunnels leading into the facility that we can access on the valley's periphery.*

I planted some anomalies in the drone's scanner readings. It doesn't look like Reed spotted them, so I need you to point them out. The highlights are visible only to you.

Got you covered, Andrea responded.

She went back over the drone data and quickly spotted Diana's anomalies pulsing in her vision. Other than the planted anomalies, nothing stood out. Whoever had done the construction had made sure they were undetectable from a distance.

She only hoped that wasn't the case for targeted scanning because Reed would need to confirm that something was there.

"Corporal Reed, Corporal Buckman, I'm seeing something odd in the scanner data," Andrea said, marking the two fake anomalies. "Here and here."

The two noncommissioned officers put their heads together and seemed to study the scanner feed, probably communicating back and forth privately like she and Diana had done.

"Those might be something," Reed allowed. "I'll send the drones back in to have a closer look. It's always possible we're looking at hidden ways to get out of the facility. If so, that would save us a lot of time and trouble."

Andrea looked over at Darcy and raised an eyebrow. "Are there exits that we don't know about?"

The woman was frowning and examining the data herself. Corporal Reed had granted the woman access so she could see what they saw. "I've never heard anything about escape tunnels, but I suppose that would make sense. Maybe only the facility coordinator knows about them. Or perhaps a few people on his staff."

"If so, I'm surprised I wasn't brought in on something like that. As the lead researcher, I should've been read in on the full plans."

It took Reed a few minutes to have the drones make runs on the anomalies with low-powered active scans. One came back sooner than the other, and Reed examined the data more closely. "Yeah, that sure as hell looks like a concealed exit. If the other ends up being the same, we'll either pick one to go in or split up the teams and go in separately."

Andrea looked over at Diana to see if she had a preference, but her friend didn't say anything. Maybe she didn't know where the damned things led inside the facility.

Well, she didn't have to wonder. She could just ask.

Do you have any idea where the tunnels come out in the facility? Since the official map doesn't show them, it would be really helpful to know.

Her friend responded almost at once. *There are some areas inside the facility that don't show on the map she shared. Either she doesn't know about them, or she's playing her cards close to the vest.*

The map I have shows them, but it doesn't explain what they're for. Bottom line: I can't tell you which entrance is better or if we should split up.

That wasn't as helpful as Andrea had hoped, but it was what it was. In the end, without any way to pass the information along—even if she had it—the corporals would have to make the call.

Once Reed had determined the other "anomaly" was an entry point to a separate tunnel, she made a decision. "I really don't like splitting up the fire teams, but without knowing where either of these tunnels goes, we're going to have to probe both of them.

"Buckman, your people are experienced, so I'll ask you to lead the greenies. Are you good with that?"

The male corporal nodded. "Campbell, take lead of our fire team and make sure our people don't get into any trouble. We'll go with stunners unless there's an overriding reason to use lethal force.

"Our goal is to stymie the intruders if they're there. It's always possible we've beaten them here or that they're not coming at all. Expect to run into facility security if that's the case."

"What about me?" Darcy asked. "Once you get inside the facility, we can use my access codes, or I can at least identify who I am to our people."

Reed shook her head. "This is a combat situation, and we can't take that chance. You've been missing for a week, so it seems likely your codes have been deactivated. If you tried to use them, all that would do was set off alarms. You stay with me on the pinnace."

Obviously, the news didn't satisfy the scientist, but Andrea knew it was the right call.

My databases gave me access codes for the facility, Diana sent privately. *We won't know what things are where, but we should be able to do some unexpected things when we get inside.*

"What's our game plan when we get inside?" Andrea asked aloud.

"We have every indication this facility is either going to be attacked or has already been attacked," Reed said. "Once inside the facility, you'll move to make contact with whoever is there. If it's still in friendly hands, let Buckman make contact with their leadership.

"If it's not in friendly hands, you're authorized to secure the facility. I'd rather not hurt any noncombatants, so only use the level of force that's appropriate. Stay safe and make the other guys take the hits."

The pinnace entered the valley low and fast, setting down near one of the concealed exits. Campbell and his people exited, and Andrea watched as they searched for and located the concealed exit.

It was actually pretty damn clever the way it was hidden, but even though it was in an outcropping of rock, it was still possible to tell it was different by looking closely.

That didn't mean they were able to open it, though.

"I'm not finding any way of getting into this damn thing," Campbell said after a minute. "I've located the receiver that should trigger the door, but I can't even get it to respond. Just how destructive should our entrance be?"

"Corporal Reed?" Andrea said. "Diana has some skill at dealing with access points like this."

"Does she, now?" Reed asked almost rhetorically. "It's not like it's going to cost us anything to have her look. Go see if you can open that thing up, Randall."

Diana headed down the ramp at a trot and made her way to the concealed entrance. She did something to the wall, and it sank back into the rock outcropping and then dropped out of sight, revealing a regular lift.

"Well, that's a *very* handy talent," Reed said, eyeing Andrea. "I'll want to know more about it at some point. How did she get in when Campbell couldn't?"

"Everybody has their strengths, Corporal. Sometimes we just have to accept that we're not the best at everything."

"Words to live by, I suppose."

Diana came back into the pinnace, and it picked up immediately and headed around the valley even as Campbell and his team entered the lift. It only took a minute to get to the new location, and Buckman, Diana, Claudio, and Andrea exited the pinnace to hunt for their own way into the facility.

Once again, Diana used her magic access codes to force the lift to open. Andrea certainly hoped it also shut down any security alarms because there had to be something to notify the facility if someone was coming through their back door.

The pinnace took off as soon as the hatch opened. Corporal Reed would be heavy fire support if they ran into the Singularity deep inside the facility and had to make a run for it.

Or if they broke the backs of the enemy and sent them scurrying out like cockroaches when the lights came on. At Buckman's nod, Andrea pressed the button to take the lift down. It was time to turn the tables and confront one of the monsters that wore her face.

32

J erome wasn't a big fan of the rescue plan as it began unfolding, but that was simply because he didn't know enough about it. Kolstad refused to tell him exactly who their contact was— which he thought was damned shortsighted—but there was nothing he could do to force her to cough up the information.

The building where corporate security was supposedly holding Lieutenant Van Buren was a big one, taking up an entire city block in an area of the city that was very upscale. It rose like a mountain into the sky, towering over the buildings around it. He really hoped the contact had been correct about exactly where the LT was because if they had to search for him, it would be impossible.

Their contact met them at a service entrance at the rear of the building. He looked furtively in both directions to make sure no one was watching, but he didn't seem concerned about the security camera directly over their heads.

Jerome almost asked about that but decided that it didn't matter. They were already committed, and it might draw unwelcome attention if he made a big deal about it. The best thing to do at this point was to keep going and hope for the best.

He'd brought his weapons and those for the lieutenant, but he didn't intend to use the stunner unless he had no other choice. Breaking his commanding officer out of his cell was important, but he wasn't going to kill someone that didn't have it coming. The best outcome would be if he didn't have to shoot anyone at all.

Fat chance of that.

Neither the Imperial Security Service agents nor the contact said a single word as they proceeded to a service lift. The man pressed one of the buttons and tapped an ID code into a pad just above it, but he didn't stay inside the lift with them. He headed down the corridor without looking back. They were on their own.

As the lift rose into the building, Jerome eyed the interior, looking for the cameras. Security would have a way of seeing who was in the lift, and if they decided the three of them looked sketchy, they could stop the lift wherever they chose and hold it in place. That would be a disaster, but it wouldn't be entirely unexpected.

"Don't worry about that," Paci said, noting his gaze. "Kolstad said our friend has disabled the cameras covering the entrance we used, the lift, the floor we're heading to, and the roof. All security sees is a playback of what was going on an hour ago.

"That'll stay in place for another half hour, so if we don't dawdle, we should be able to get in and out before anyone even knows we're here."

Jerome nodded silently and followed the men when they exited the lift on the level that supposedly held Lieutenant Van Buren. The corridor wasn't empty, and it was obvious several of the people present were guards because they were standing outside the room the three were heading for.

Other than the guards, people that looked like functionaries came and went through large double doors at the end of the hall. If Jerome had to bet, that would be where the chief executive officer worked.

One of the functionaries coming in their direction literally glared down his nose at the three of them. "How did *you* get in here? Do you have an *appointment*? Where is your *escort*?"

Ignoring the man, Jerome leaned to the right and extended the stunner he'd been concealing under his jacket far enough to strike everyone in the hall, including the arrogant talker, but leaving his companions untouched.

Everyone dropped, but that didn't mean there were no consequences. Somewhere in the ceiling, an alarm began sounding.

"The security scanners picked up the weapons fire," Paci said. "Let's get your lieutenant and get moving. We'll be a little early to the roof, but there's nothing we can do about that now. We'll just have to improvise."

"You get him," Jerome said as he sprinted down the hall. "I'm not going to pass up an opportunity to get some intelligence and a prisoner."

He raced through the double doors and found himself in an office filled with expensive furniture, art, and various knickknacks that looked like they were made of precious metals or other valuable material. The wide desk sitting in front of the large windows looking out over the city was made of wood that almost glowed in the light striking it.

It was damned nice, but he was sure it was built on the misery of others. Blood money and worse.

A corpulent man was already on his feet behind the desk, frantically rummaging in a drawer, almost certainly for a weapon.

There were also three other people in the room, one of whom looked like a secretary and two additional functionaries. Blasts from his stunner took them all down.

Time was limited, so he holstered his weapon and raced around the desk. Since the man had conveniently unlocked the open desk drawer for him, Jerome grabbed a case of data chips sitting right there next to the weapon the man had been going for—a flechette pistol—and stuffed both into his jacket pocket.

None of the other drawers were locked, so he gave them a quick pass and found nothing of immediate interest.

Jerome eyed the large man and sighed. Why couldn't he have been skinny?

He grabbed the man, slung him over his shoulder with a grunt, and staggered under his weight. Jerome wasn't out of shape, but no one really trained to carry somebody this large. Maybe Tolliver would've had better luck, but she wasn't here.

"Let's get a move on, marine," Lieutenant Van Buren called out from the hall. He was free and now holding a stunner confiscated from one of the guards.

His face was bruised, so it looked like someone had beat him up. The thought of that enraged Jerome, and he considered kicking one of the security guys as he went past, but he was afraid he'd fall down under the load he was carrying if he tried.

"Stairs right here," Parada said. "Security is on their way, so we need to get a move on. Our ride isn't going to be ready, and we'll have to hold the roof until she gets here."

The four of them piled onto the stairs, with Paci watching the rear and Parada leading the way. This was a special staircase serving only this floor, the penthouse above it, and the roof, so they didn't have to worry about guards from below catching up with them as quickly.

There might be some guards in the penthouse, but Jerome suspected not. The CEO didn't seem like the kind of person that trusted unaccompanied people in his home. Odds were that they'd only need to worry about guards chasing from behind or already on the roof.

The lieutenant helped Jerome shoulder part of the load and grunted under the man's weight. "Thanks for coming for me. I'm still not sure exactly what the hell is going on, but this moron seemed to think we were an invading force that was going to kick him out of his job and take control of the planet."

Jerome blinked. "Seriously? He's the one who called for us?"

"Never underestimate stupidity."

He and the lieutenant staggered up the stairs and through the door leading onto the roof with their burden. There was no one there, which was a relief. Sadly, Kolstad hadn't arrived yet either.

With communications being jammed across the city, they weren't going to be able to call her. She was supposedly keeping watch over the general area, so she should be able to adjust her plans at least a little.

Sadly, it wasn't quick enough to stop security from trying to come through the door they'd just used. Paci and Van Buren stunned them from cover before any of them fired.

That was a good thing, since the idiots were using flechette pistols. If they'd opened fire, they'd have been indiscriminately spraying lethal projectiles over a wide arc of the city, threatening uncounted people with injury or death.

"Heads up," Parada said. "Our ride is here."

Jerome only spared a part of his attention for the marine pinnace that came roaring in from their left, flaring to land even as the ramp came down. Van Buren helped him get their prisoner inside even as Parada and Paci covered their retreat, firing their stunners at new threats that must've come through the roof door.

There still weren't any seats in the back of the pinnace, so Jerome dropped his prisoner to the deck and grabbed something to hold onto as the pinnace lifted off and tilted hard to the left, diving off the side of the building and taking itself out of the line of fire.

To Jerome's relief, Paci had managed to get the ramp closed, so none of them were going to fall out. He took a few moments to find something to secure the prisoner because having him roll around loose during heavy maneuvering was an excellent way to end up with a dead body in very short order.

By the time he reached the control area, Lieutenant Van Buren was already in the copilot's seat, talking with Kolstad. "I don't know who you are, but thanks for coming to get us. The Empire is in your debt."

The old woman grinned. "The Empire's been in my debt for a lot longer than you've been alive, kid."

"Lieutenant Van Buren, meet retired Senior Sergeant Susan Kolstad, late of the Marine Raiders," Jerome said.

"Very late," the old woman agreed. "I'd rather not have gotten mixed up in this business, but the people you're here to disrupt have involved themselves in a very secret Imperial project, and I'm afraid we need to make our way there and stop whatever's going on right now.

"You're not going to like hearing that because your company is under attack even as we speak, but this is a class one emergency, and you're just going to have to trust your people to fight without you."

Van Buren's eyes narrowed. "I'll be the judge of what I need to do. Sergeant Walker, what the hell is going on?"

"The two men that came with me are with Imperial Security Services. They're attached to something called Project Panther. They make a combat drug of the same name for the Marine Raiders, and the Singularity is trying to steal it.

"I'm not sure why any of this is happening, but the company is under attack by what we suspect is a Singularity raiding force. They've managed to destroy the Fleet transport, so we don't have any support. The capital and the company area are being jammed, so we can't even let them know what our situation is."

The officer grunted. "That's not good, but I know what Panther is. We can't allow the Singularity to get it. What's the plan?"

"We'll get out of the city as quickly as we can," Kolstad said. "Once we're clear, they won't be able to pursue us because their communications are just as jammed as ours. The Imperial Security Service agents gave me the coordinates of the facility, and we should be able to get there fairly quickly.

"I've got weapons and unpowered armor in the lockers—I guessed on sizes—so get yourselves ready to go. If you can fly this thing, I'll swap out with you and armor up myself."

The old woman grinned. "It looks like I have one last fight to wage for the Empire. It's time to kick some ass."

33

D iana led the way down the concealed tunnel with her senses alert and looking for trouble. She and Andrea had found uniforms, rifles, and unpowered armor for themselves in the pinnace, so they were just as ready for trouble as everyone else, but she really hoped that they didn't find any.

It had taken some work to convince Corporal Buckman that she should lead the way rather than him, but she was actually pretty good at convincing people to do what she wanted. In this case, it was necessary because she was the only one that had access codes that could control any security system they might chance across.

She hoped she'd disabled them all when she'd ordered them to shut down at the secret entrance because otherwise, Campbell and his people would set something off without her there to mitigate the situation.

The security systems inside the facility itself were down. She couldn't tell Buckman or Claudio that, but she passed the information on to Andrea. Whatever was happening ahead of them wasn't going to be a cakewalk.

And what the hell was a cakewalk anyway? The saying didn't

make any sense. Was walking with cake really that easy? How could it be? One slip, and you'd drop the damned thing.

This was just another instance of picking up some weird saying she really didn't understand. All that mattered was that they would have a difficult time of it, and they needed to be ready.

She had her stunner out but didn't expect to find anyone in the secret tunnels. If anyone inside the facility actually knew about these tunnels, they'd have either used them by now or were unable to do so.

It took the four of them about fifteen minutes to reach the inner security doors. According to the maps Diana had, they let out into a secret section of the facility that wasn't on the map that Darcy had given them.

Thanks to her earlier commands, the security door at the end of the tunnel was unlocked, so Buckman ducked out into the room first. It led into a storage area with racks of carrying cases.

She stopped long enough to open one, revealing a padded interior filled with small vials labeled *A*. That letter was on the outside of the case too. The other rack held cases labeled *B*.

Since this facility only produced one thing, it had to be the two-part drug called Panther.

It looked as if someone was building a stockpile in a location that wasn't on any of the maps. Since Imperial Intelligence knew about it, that probably meant it wasn't some type of scam or crime, just a way of storing extra amounts of the drug without it being general knowledge even inside the facility itself.

As she passed by the end of the rack, she found special autoinjectors with two cavities that could dispense the drug. The autoinjector cavities were labeled, so the dosage was important. Something to remember if it came to using the drug. Since marine Raiders had pharmacology units, this was a way to have someone other than a Marine Raider use Panther.

On a whim, she grabbed one of the autoinjectors and seven vials from the A and B cases while Andrea and Claudio followed Buckman out into the facility. That was enough for everyone in the attack teams if needed. She closed and latched the cases to keep her actions under wraps if anyone came looking.

She'd probably get into trouble for poaching these if she revealed that she'd done so, but if it turned out they needed that kind of edge, she had no compunction about using it. After all, her instructions said to stop the theft by any and all means.

Diana followed the rest out of the hidden storage room and quickly discovered the situation inside the facility was a lot more clear-cut than she'd thought it would be. Sprawled out just on the other side of the hidden door was a man in a lab coat.

He hadn't been stunned. He'd been shot with flechettes at close range, and his blood was sprayed all over the hidden door they were coming through. Based on the fact that the blood hadn't yet dried, the murder had happened very recently.

The Singularity was definitely inside the facility.

Before she could make up her mind what the best course of action was, there was a scream from just outside the room they were in and the sound of a flechette weapon discharging. The scream cut off abruptly, and Diana knew that someone else had just been killed. They needed to get into action.

Buckman obviously agreed because he trotted over to the door, holstered his stunner, and prepared his flechette rifle. Andrea opened the door at his gesture, and he stepped out, pivoting in place and firing a short burst.

The rest of them followed him out and saw that he'd shot someone in nondescript body armor. There was another body in the corridor. A woman in a lab coat lay dead against the wall, freshly murdered by the intruder.

If the bad guys had a list of people they wanted to take alive, she obviously hadn't been on it. Or maybe they weren't taking anyone alive. They wouldn't know for sure until this was all over.

First, though, they needed to turn the tables on the intruders and start trying to take the facility back. Buckman made a gesture with two fingers, and Andrea came forward with her rifle at the ready. She'd go left around the corner ahead of them, and he would take the right.

Claudio would back Buckman up with his stunner, and Diana

would do the same for Andrea. Once they were sure the corridor ahead was clear, Buckman would decide which direction they'd go.

They all pivoted around the corners at his signal, and Diana immediately had two targets. She fired her stunner on wide beam, but neither of the armored men fell. Their armor had to be shielded.

They raised their flechette rifles to fire, but Andrea fired faster. Neither of them was hit by the wild burst one let loose as he died, but it wasn't a good morning for taking prisoners.

Once the two were down, Diana holstered her stunner and unslung her rifle. This was going to be a fight with lethal weapons today.

She turned to see how things were going on the other side and found a disaster. One or more of the flechettes that had missed them had struck Corporal Buckman in the back. His armor had mostly held, but it was apparent that something around his neck had failed because his head had been blown almost entirely off.

Claudio was kneeling beside the corporal and shook his head. Their ad hoc fire team leader was dead, and they were on their own.

* * *

ANDREA CURSED when she saw that Buckman was dead. His armor should've stopped that kind of hit, but it must've caught him just right and gone through the area where his helmet and shoulders met. Just bad luck.

Bad luck that left her responsible for keeping her friends alive.

Buckman and Reed had worked out a plan to sweep the facility. All they had to do was keep the enemy from getting certain things like the computer files, the machinery used to concentrate and formulate the drug, and the key personnel who had the knowledge to do the work.

Under Campbell's command, Fire Team One was going for the machines that concentrated and formulated Panther. She and her people were tasked with ensuring that no one got any information from the computers.

Both groups were responsible for making sure they liberated any prisoners they found. With just six marines in the building, that wasn't going to be easy.

"Wait a second," Diana said. "We're going to need every edge we can get. Bare your arm."

"Excuse me?" Andrea asked.

"Just do it. You, too, Claudio."

Not sure what the hell was happening, Andrea opened the seal on her armored forearm and exposed her wrist. To her shock, Diana produced an autoinjector from a pouch at her waist, inserted two small vials, and injected the contents into her arm.

"What the hell is that?" she demanded. "What are you giving me?"

"You know what it is," her friend said. "I'm giving us an edge that we desperately need."

Even as Diana replaced the empty vials with fresh ones and did the same thing to Claudio and herself, the world seemed to change. Weirdly, it began slowing down. Or at least it kind of seemed that way. Andrea wasn't quite sure how to describe it.

Panther was supposed to speed nerve reactivity and the brain's processing speed. The latter was probably why everything seemed to be going so much more slowly.

She really wished her friend had run this plan past her first. What if she overcompensated for something under pressure?

Well, this could be a big mistake, but she was kind of committed now. She'd just have to make it work.

She took a deep breath and waited in place until the world seemed to stabilize around her. With no one but her friends standing beside her, it didn't seem things were all that different, but she still felt as if she had an eternity to plan things out before her body had to get into motion to carry out her instructions.

It felt bizarre, but they needed to get moving. The people running this facility wouldn't be happy about the level of destruction they were about to cause, but it was necessary. Now that its location and purpose were compromised, everything had to go.

Since she was tasked with making sure the computers were destroyed, and the enemy didn't get any critical data, she really hoped the researchers had backups of everything important. If not, they had a lot of work ahead of them.

She gestured for her friends to back her up as she headed down the corridor with her rifle at the ready. It was a shame the bad guys were in armor that protected them from stunners because it would've been nice to take more prisoners. Maybe they'd get lucky and end up with some in a damaged but alive condition before this was all over.

They made it four turns before they ran into the first resistance they'd encountered since they'd been treated with Panther. The fight was a real eye-opener for her.

She was already fast compared to the human norm, but Panther took already fast reaction times and made them almost instantaneous. Add in the quicker thought-processing speed that came from the other half of the drug, and she felt as if she had all the time in the world to make the magic happen.

Which was damned useful when she spotted a large cluster of men and women in nondescript body armor like the other intruders just outside of the computer center. She quickly gave instructions to her friends, and they all leaned around the corner as one and opened fire.

Diana came in from the left side of the group and Claudio from the right. Andrea started in the center, and since they had the drop on the enemy, she went for head shots. The armor was lighter there because the area was usually harder to hit.

In what felt like going to the range and taking carefully aimed shots at each person, she shot four people in the time it took her friends to fire twice. The enemy was so slow that they barely seemed to have time to react before they died.

Yet die they did.

The single survivor of the ambush managed to get through the doorway, even though Andrea was pretty sure she'd hit the woman in her trailing arm as she'd ducked out of sight. Panther made a *huge* difference in her ability in a fight. They couldn't allow the Singularity to get their hands on this.

The three of them raced down the hall, intent on following up their attack as quickly as possible. They didn't know how many people were inside the computer center, and they were going to have to take care of business in a hurry.

Andrea found the woman she'd shot lying on the floor, clutching at her shattered and bleeding arm, when they burst in. She'd lost her rifle but was going for a weapon on her belt, so Claudio shot her dead.

There were maybe a dozen people in the room. Two-thirds of them were in civilian clothes and being held at gunpoint, so they were most likely members of the facility staff. Three more were armored in the same nondescript unpowered armor as the people they'd been fighting thus far.

The final person was Kate Geller. She was in civilian clothes with clamshell armor across her chest. Her head was uncovered, and strangely, Andrea felt happy that she was wearing a helmet that protected her identity from the woman. Geller didn't know she was dealing with someone else from the Andrea Line.

The tableau ended abruptly as one of the guards began shooting at her and her friends. They returned fire and dodged for cover. It was a lot harder to hit them with friendlies in the area, but Andrea took one of them out, and her friends got the rest.

Geller ducked behind the computers in the chaos, and when Andrea followed her, she found an emergency exit door swinging shut. She started to charge after the woman but spotted the plasma grenade spinning on the floor just in time.

"Grenade!" she shouted as she threw herself backward.

The blast picked her up and hurled her into the wall, but it was a glancing blow. She staggered to her feet and stumbled after Geller. The exit door was blown wide open, and the race was on to capture her before she escaped.

Her friends would have to deal with the computers and the civilians. She had no time to waste.

34

Jerome searched the pinnace and found what looked like Imperial Marine combat armor from roughly a hundred years ago that would fit him. Whether or not it would actually still deflect flechettes that might otherwise kill him after all this time, he didn't know. He'd have to hope for the best.

He also found some flechette rifles and even a few plasma grenades. With those, he got himself fully outfitted for combat. Then he saw to scrounging up something for the Imperial Security Services agents. They didn't get any grenades, but he found flechette rifles and combat armor for them.

He and Lieutenant Van Buren had argued quietly about whether the lieutenant would be going with him during the assault. Unsurprisingly, he lost that fight. Van Buren insisted he was a fully trained combat marine, and he wasn't going to be left behind in an unarmed pinnace.

Kolstad had armor that fit her perfectly, an improbably large squad support flechette rifle, and a bandolier of plasma grenades. She looked ridiculous with her helmet off, but he knew that was an illusion. This wasn't someone's grandmother running off to fight. She was a Marine Raider whose age probably only barely slowed her down.

Once everyone was fully outfitted for combat, they were less than ten minutes away from the valley housing the facility. They weren't coming in very quietly, but they weren't exactly advertising their presence, either, so he was somewhat surprised when they detected a marine pinnace rising to meet them.

With the jamming still in place, they couldn't communicate with the other vessel, but Lieutenant Van Buren made the judgment call that it was probably one of theirs rather than something brought in by the Singularity.

The fact that the other vessel hadn't already opened fire was supporting evidence to that theory, he supposed. It was unrealistic to expect the Singularity could get their hands on something like that.

Van Buren pulsed their scanners at the pinnace, and the return confirmed his guess that it was almost certainly one of those assigned to the company. That meant other marines were on site, and they needed to identify themselves before they were fired upon.

Apparently, the best way to do that was to set down and act non-threatening. That was kind of counterintuitive, but it was Van Buren's best plan for avoiding being shot out of the air. Once they were on the ground, he took off his helmet and stepped outside, and waved at the pinnace as it circled.

That quickly confirmed his officer's guess because the pinnace landed next to them, and Reed came running down the ramp. "Sir! Camp Pyramid is under attack, but there's another situation going on."

"I've already been briefed," Van Buren said. "My pilot is a retired Marine Raider, and we've got two Imperial Security Services agents aboard as well. They say that there's a factory that manufactures a drug for the Marine Raiders, and the Singularity is trying to steal the ability to manufacture it. We've got to stop them at all costs."

Reed nodded. "We've already infiltrated two fire teams into the facility through hidden escape tunnels. We rescued the head research scientist who was being held prisoner at the mines.

"Actually, to be fair, Tolliver and her friends did. We dropped

Mister Lindbergh, his driver, a ranch hand, and the research scientist off at a safe place because I'm providing fire support if our people need it."

"Any word on what's going on inside the facility?" Jerome asked. "If they went in through the back door, maybe the lieutenant and I should go through the front."

"That's complete and utter bull," Reed said bluntly. "Lieutenant Van Buren is more than capable of manning the heavy weapons on our pinnace. It's not an officer's job to run into a firefight. The company will need him once we kick the Singularity's ass here.

"One of the other things we discovered is that the assistant to the Yi Holdings CEO is a member of the Andrea Line like Tolliver. She's using something to cover her tattoos. Tolliver has the same thing on her face right now, so you need to be careful because you may come face-to-face with either or both of them. Tolliver is in uniform, armored, and with her fire team."

Van Buren scratched his chin and nodded. "I'm beginning to see a pattern to all of this. The moron running Yi Holdings—who we have aboard our pinnace—was certain we'd come to take him into custody and terminate the contract his corporation held over the planet. If he didn't know what his assistant was doing, she might've been playing him as well."

"From everything Tolliver and her people were able to discover, it doesn't look like there was ever any sabotage at the mine, sir," Reed said. "Honestly, I think Delta Company was a secondary objective. If they could pull an Imperial Marine company onto the planet and get us split up into smaller groups, the raiding force they have would've been sufficient to take us out.

"Since we're onto them, they're not strong enough to cause us too much damage, although it looks like they destroyed three of the pinnaces and pinned the company in place. What are your orders, sir?"

Van Buren grimaced. "It makes sense for me to stay on board the pinnace and use the heavy weapons. I'm sure you're trained in their use, but I'm more experienced and probably a better choice.

"We'll move our prisoner to your pinnace, and the two of you will accompany the Imperial Security Services agents and the Marine Raider to kick in the front door of the facility. If our people are in a firefight down there, it's our job to make certain we give them the support they need.

"The Singularity cannot be allowed to escape with that formula, any of the equipment, or any prisoners. If any vehicles take off and run, I'm going to have to burn them down. If you see armed Singularity forces on the ground, shoot the hell out of them, and we'll sort out any prisoners when we're done. Understood?"

"Copy that, sir," Jerome said. "We'll take care of it. Reed, you're with me."

The two of them quickly boarded Kolstad's pinnace, and he made introductions. They then carried the portly CEO of Yi Holdings back to Van Buren's pinnace and secured him to one of the seats. Now when they went in, they wouldn't have to worry about leaving anyone on board the pinnace.

Since Reed was already armed and armored, they were ready to rock. Kolstad took off, and they raced toward the village at the valley's center. He'd have expected to see civilians going about their everyday lives, but the place seemed deserted. Not a good sign.

With directions from Paci, they brought the pinnace down in front of a warehouse that served as the primary entrance to the facility, dropping the ramp so all of them could race into the building.

The Marine Raider had locked the controls down, but she still hit a switch to seal the ramp as they headed for the building. The Singularity wouldn't be stealing her pinnace for their ride.

Their arrival did not go unnoticed. The pinnace had taken fire on the way in, and there were the sounds of shouting off in the distance as they disembarked. Enemy forces scattered throughout the village were responding to their unexpected appearance.

Which, of course, drew a response from Lieutenant Van Buren. He used their pinnace's weapons to fire into the village nearby, creating massive explosions and distracting the defenders' attention.

Jerome had no doubt that once he and his companions were down in the facility itself, if it looked like the entrance would be overrun by the enemy, the lieutenant would seal it up behind them. They had other ways to get out, so he'd keep the Singularity troops off their backs. They just needed to focus on the task ahead.

When they got into the warehouse, they found out why they hadn't seen any civilians. The Singularity had herded them all into the warehouse and executed them. Men, women, and children were piled high on one end of the space inside the long building.

The sight of their bodies filled Jerome with rage. Those bastards hadn't needed to do that. They'd just wanted to make sure that no witnesses remained to provide any clues that the Singularity had been here.

It was sickening, and they were going to pay for it.

The other side of the warehouse held an armored structure with an open hatch. It looked like the entrance wasn't so much hidden as merely concealed inside the building. Conveniently for them, the Singularity forces had left the door open when they'd gone inside, and all they had to do was follow them.

That didn't mean it was safe, however. As soon they got onto the stairway leading down, they found a number of troopers in nondescript armor at the bottom of the stairs firing at them. Jerome handled them by hurling a plasma grenade down the steps into their midst, where it went off like the end of the world.

Kolstad was over the crater in a flash, moving faster than anyone her age—or *any* age—had a right to move, shooting efficient bursts of flechettes into anything that still moved. After what he'd just seen in the warehouse, he couldn't and wouldn't blame her for it either.

Parada pointed at the leftmost of the two passages leading out of the room as soon as they were down the stairs. "That way leads toward the computer center and some of the research labs. My partner and I will go the other way and make certain the manufacturing and refining equipment is secure."

"Take Reed with you, and remember you can't leave the equipment intact. Good luck."

He and Kolstad ran down their assigned corridor. He had no idea what they were going to find, but somewhere ahead of them was one of his fire teams, and he was going to make sure they had all the support he could give them.

With any luck, they'd get there in time to make a difference, but even if they were too late, they'd avenge their comrades. This facility would not fall today.

* * *

"EVERYONE LISTEN UP," Diana shouted. "We're Imperial Marines, and we're going to get you out of here, but you need to do *exactly* as I say. Claudio, cover the door. If anyone comes our way, it's going to be your responsibility to handle them."

Her big blond friend crouched beside the door and used his rifle to cover the approaches outside the room. In his heightened state, she had no doubt he'd be able to spot any intruders before they got in a position to open fire on them.

"Everyone else, we need to get moving. We can't allow the enemy to take possession of these computers or any of their data. Are there backups?"

One of the men gestured helplessly toward the back of the room. "That woman took the backups. You can't destroy them, or we'll have lost everything."

"I'm not going to lecture you about how shortsighted it was to keep your backups right next to your computer," Diana said. "I think you've figured that out. We'll have to hope my companion stops the woman before she gets away and that she recovers your backups because I'm not going to leave these computers intact. Everyone line up by the door and get ready to run."

"No!" the man shouted. "This is our life's work! You can't destroy it!"

"I can, and I will," she said grimly. "The time to stop this from happening has passed. This facility is dead, and I'll do whatever it takes to protect the Empire from this data getting into enemy hands. Get a move on, or you're going to be left in here when I set off the plasma grenades."

The man kept yammering, but she stopped paying attention to him. She pulled three plasma grenades from her bandolier and set them to detonate remotely on her signal. The facility was still being jammed, but she was close enough to punch a signal through if she sent it from the corridor outside.

Diana put one grenade in with the data drives and the other two equidistant along the length of the computer console. The entire process took less than thirty seconds.

"Claudio, you have lead," she said when she was done. "We'll take them out the back way. Once we've got them in motion, you'll stay in front, and I'll bring up the rear."

When Claudio nodded and took off, Diana shouted for the scientists to follow at their best speed. It turned out that they could move pretty damned fast when their lives were on the line. Thankfully, the hidden supply chamber wasn't too distant.

As soon as she was safely in the corridor and far enough away, she triggered the plasma grenades, and the entire facility seemed to jump. One mission objective achieved.

Less than thirty seconds later, the floor under her feet jumped again from another explosion that was somewhere off in the direction of the manufacturing equipment, so she was hopeful that Campbell and his people had successfully cleared their area.

If so, they'd gone a long way toward protecting the Empire from the Singularity. If, of course, Andrea managed to catch up with Geller and stop her from escaping with the backups.

They were almost to the secret door when they ran headlong into two people in combat armor. Claudio almost opened fire but stopped himself in time.

The newcomers popped their helmets, and she found that they'd run into Sergeant Walker and an unknown older woman.

She was more than a bit surprised to see Walker because last she'd heard, he'd been trapped in the capital. She was glad the situation had changed.

"Status report," he commanded as he and the woman put their helmets back on and covered the approaches with their rifles.

"The computer center is destroyed, but Geller got away with the backups," Diana said. "Tolliver is trying to stop her. She ordered us to see to the security of the scientists and destroy the computer.

"I'm pretty sure the other explosion was the manufacturing

equipment going up. That would be Campbell and Fire Team One. We have one KIA, Corporal Buckman. His body is right around the corner ahead of us. We're planning on extracting him with us."

Walker grimaced but was snapping out orders as soon as she finished. "Good work. Make certain these people get out of here. They may be the only survivors left in the facility or the village above. The Singularity slaughtered everyone else."

"That's not all, Sergeant," Diana said after a moment's hesitation. "The storage room we're going through is in a hidden area of the base, and it's filled with portable cases containing single-dose vials of Panther.

"I injected the three of us with the drug. It allowed us to get an edge and take out almost a dozen of the Singularity troopers before they could return fire."

"It's a hoot, isn't it?" the woman asked. "That was good thinking and may just have kept you three alive."

Walker nodded. "If there's any trouble from doing that, I'll take the heat. Now, get these people out of here while we finish clearing this facility. Escort the civilians to the end of the tunnel and remain out of sight until the fighting is over. Go."

Diana gestured for Claudio to get moving, and they went around the corner. The presence of the two marines and the strange woman gave Diana hope that her friend would be able to get out of this alive, but a lot was going to depend on what happened over the next few minutes.

When they came to Buckman's body, she slung her rifle and picked him up with a grunt. They didn't leave other marines behind.

Once they arrived at the secret door, she was able to send it an implant command to open and could tell that its presence was something of a shock to everyone except the man who'd been wailing about the computer. He looked stunned that she'd been able to open it.

"How did you even know this was here?" he demanded. "This area was hidden well enough that no one should've been able to find it or the escape tunnels leading out of this facility."

"Looks like you didn't hide them as well as you thought. Your security systems could use a bit more work too. It's none of my business, but when you start building a new facility, I think you need to go over everything you did from the ground up because you've made a lot of mistakes.

"Geller and the Singularity have known about this place for at least a decade. You got complacent, and it cost a lot of people their lives. Do better next time."

The man grunted but didn't argue as Claudio led the way through the storage room and into the escape tunnel. Diana looked at all of the Panther around her as she closed the secret door. The stuff was amazing. It was a damned shame that only the Marine Raiders got to use it.

Once she had the security door secured behind her, she followed Claudio and the civilians. They'd get to the end of the tunnel, put Buckman into the lift, and wait. If everything turned out okay, they'd be able to leave the facility soon. If it didn't, they'd wait until dark and slip away.

She worried about her friend, but Andrea's fight with Geller was something she no longer had any ability to influence. All she could do was hope she'd given her friend enough of an edge to beat that bitch.

35

Andrea was in a bind. She needed to catch up with Geller, but if she rushed headlong after her, there was every chance the woman would ambush her. She was operating alone and had no idea where the woman might turn on her if that was her intention.

It was always possible there were more Singularity troops somewhere inside the underground facility, too, but it didn't seem likely. They'd have already put in an appearance if they'd been here.

If Geller got away, there was every chance she could make her way to the village above, where there were undoubtedly more Singularity forces and probably vehicles. If they were planning on taking a bunch of the equipment, then they'd have to have something there to haul it away in.

There had been two major explosions since Geller had tried to kill her. One of those would've been Diana destroying the computer system. The other was most likely Campbell and his people destroying the manufacturing equipment.

They'd almost stymied the Singularity, but now they had to finish the job, and that meant that she had to be on the top of her game.

Annoyingly, as prepared as she'd thought herself for an ambush,

Geller caught her by surprise anyway. She dropped out of the air vent almost on top of Andrea, kicking her rifle out of her hands almost before she even saw the movement and just about kneeing her in the helmet before she ducked.

If she hadn't had Panther in her system, the woman would've struck her cleanly on the side of the head, and that would've been deadly in a fight like this. It was apparent the other woman was thoroughly trained in hand-to-hand combat and was no slouch at it.

Evening up the odds, Andrea smashed the flechette pistol out of the other woman's hand moments before it could fire and sent it skittering down the corridor. She'd had to use her injured arm, which set it to throbbing again.

Geller returned the favor when Andrea drew her flechette pistol and tried to shoot her.

"You're pretty good," the woman said with a smirk. "Want to try getting that stunner out, or shall we go hand-to-hand? You're all armored up, but that slows you down. I can take you."

The combat armor did limit Andrea's range of motion, but it didn't really slow her down all that much. To be honest, her helmet was more of an impediment than her body armor.

"You want to go at it?" Andrea asked sweetly. "I'm not sure you can handle me, but I'm willing to give it a try. You're the one with the ticking clock. If you can't get out of here soon, you're not getting out at all."

"Yet you somehow got past all my people. There must be another way out that I didn't know about. I might just have to keep you alive so you can show it to me."

Andrea laughed and then drew her stunner, trying to get the drop on the other woman, but Geller kicked it out of her hand even as she was trying to bring it up. Even seeing the kick coming, the Panther didn't let her dodge the blow.

Damn, but the other woman was *fast*. So was she, but that seemingly only counted for so much in this particular fight.

Andrea had her concealed weapons on her, but they were under her armor and of no use at the moment. The only other weapon she had was her marine knife, but with Geller's speed, this was the wrong time to try to bring it into the fight.

She needed to shake the other woman up, and she knew just how to do that.

"You want to make me tell you how to get out of here? I don't think you can, but then again, I don't think you can beat me hand to hand either. Let's find out, shall we?"

Andrea took two steps back while reaching for her helmet, half expecting the other woman to attack while she pulled it off. Geller simply stood there smirking.

Her superior expression vanished the instant Andrea had her helmet off and had tossed it aside.

"That's impossible," Geller said harshly. "Who are you?"

"I think you know *exactly* who I am, other than my number," she said in the Tongue as she smiled coldly.

"I don't know how you got here or what game you're playing, but this is *my* mission, and I'm not going to let you screw it up," Geller replied in the same language.

She then pulled a long, thin, wickedly pointed knife from the small of her back and dropped into a fighting crouch, grinning cruelly. "You're going to bleed, little sister. Once this is done, you'll show me the way out of here, and we can go home and explain to leadership what you're doing here.

"Or maybe I'll just slit your throat and pretend we never met."

Andrea gave the woman another cold laugh and pulled her own shorter knife. Based on the other woman's confidence, her knife could punch through marine combat armor, so it was hull metal and had a monomolecular edge and point. She'd have to be careful, or she would die here.

Fei had never liked knife fights. She'd always said it was far too easy to get cut or killed, and no one walked away uninjured. Unless Andrea wanted to blow them both up with a plasma grenade, however, she didn't have a choice.

This time, Andrea was able to use the Panther as intended. This was no surprise attack out of the shadows. She could see Geller tensing to strike and was ready for her.

The other woman lunged, jabbing toward Andrea's face before driving her weapon down at Andrea's legs, no doubt assuming Andrea would attempt to block the weapon on the high feint.

Andrea had something far bloodier in mind.

She lashed out with her knife, using the monomolecular edge to chop Geller's right hand off at the wrist, sending it to slam against the wall with a meaty thump before it dropped to the floor.

That took the fight right out of the woman because she had no choice but to use her remaining hand to stanch the flow of blood as she screamed in horror and pain. All Geller seemed able to do was stare at her lost limb and scream. It was as if she'd forgotten Andrea was even there.

The woman's reaction shocked her. In Geller's place, she'd be kicking and biting if she had to. Geller was done. She hadn't been a warrior. She'd been a cruel assassin, and now she'd seemingly lost the will to fight.

Pathetic.

Andrea retrieved her stunner. "You think your genes make you superior. Well, here's a news flash. Regular humans are far better than you'll ever be.

"As for me, I'm an Imperial Marine, and I'll do everything in my power to bring the Singularity down. Suck on that for the rest of your miserable life while Imperial Intelligence has its way with you."

She shot Geller full in the face with her stunner. When the woman dropped, Andrea quickly stepped over and used the combat medkit at her wrist to tie off the spurting stump of Geller's wrist.

Regeneration could put the hand back in place if it didn't take too long to get to one, but it wouldn't bother Andrea if the woman had a permanent reminder of how badly she'd lost this fight.

She pulled the sheath from the woman's belt, retrieved the knife, and tucked it away. It was her souvenir of the fight. She'd leave the other weapons to be either recovered later or destroyed with the base.

She also searched her and smiled when she found the computer backups. Those would be helpful in reconstituting the facility, she was sure. She put them away and got ready to grab Geller and her hand. It was time to get the hell out of here.

"Well, I suppose you didn't need our help after all, did you, Tolliver?" a male voice asked from behind her.

Startled, Andrea spun and found two people in old-style combat armor standing in the corridor. Both had their helmets off, and she saw Sergeant Walker and an unknown woman.

A really old woman. Someone's great-grandmother. One who'd lost her walker somewhere.

"Sergeant Walker," she said, struggling to keep her voice level. "I'm glad to see you. Ah... how long have you been standing there?"

"We got here just before the knife fight but couldn't get a clean line of fire. In other words, we pretty much saw and heard everything."

He looked pointedly at Andrea's helmet on the floor as he walked up. "We can discuss the wisdom of getting rid of your helmet later, but I think the results speak for themselves. Well done, marine."

And with that, the noncom clapped his hand on her shoulder hard enough to send her staggering to the side. That set her injured arm to throbbing again, but she ignored it.

This was the first gesture of camaraderie she'd ever gotten from the man, and she almost grinned in response. Maybe things were going to be okay after all.

* * *

JEROME SAT in the small office he'd commandeered in the platoon area and focused on the unpleasant task ahead. He'd been too busy over the last week to finalize any kind of report while they tried to keep the Singularity raiding party from getting off the planet after they'd driven them off from Camp Pyramid.

They'd failed, but it wasn't really that big a surprise. Without any ships in orbit and only a single armed pinnace to contest the local space, there'd been no way to stop the raiding party from escaping.

There was talk that some of the Singularity troops had stayed behind, but he didn't buy that, even though they were prepared for another attack. The Singularity had failed in their primary mission and lost their commander. Even though they'd withdrawn in good order, it was still a retreat.

Anyone too hurt to fight had been killed by their Singularity comrades. They'd meant to keep the Empire from capturing anyone. Too bad Tolliver and her friends had captured two high-ranking Singularity personnel alive.

That would sting if they ever figured it.

It took a bit of trial and error to find an appropriate counter agent to remove the makeup that covered their tattoos, since it wasn't the same thing as Tolliver had been wearing that day, but they'd managed.

He'd already known the female prisoner was a member of the Andrea Line, but it turned out the man was a representative of one of their senior military lines. He wouldn't have been in command of the entire raid because he was socially inferior to Geller, but he'd undoubtedly been commanding the military side of things, in addition to being their lead interrogator.

Their loss would be a blow to the Singularity, not because Jerome expected either of them to crack under pressure but because their superiors couldn't be sure what their fate was. At the very least, they had to assume that the Empire now had their bodies as proof that the raid was sanctioned at the highest levels. Their worst case was that the Empire had them alive, which they did.

He hoped the thought kept the bastards awake at night.

Jerome knew this wasn't the way these raids usually worked. Deniability was key, even if neither side really believed the excuses. Singularity raids in the past used troops that didn't have tattoos and weren't genetically altered. Members of their so-called lower orders. That was undoubtedly what the troops they'd fought were.

Having two members of the senior lines this deep in Imperial space meant the raid had been damned important, and it had failed.

Tolliver had taken Geller down and recovered the computer backups. That had been a lucky break for the researchers because their facility had been completely and utterly trashed. The people Tolliver and the rest had rescued were the only survivors, including the head researcher they'd found in the mines.

Campbell and his people had killed some of the Singularity troops in the facility and recovered a massive bomb that had been intended to destroy everything. The Empire would've never believed it was anything other than an attack, but it would've made them wonder.

Lieutenant Van Buren had made the call not to waste the bomb. They'd evacuated the facility after the civilians had pulled out everything they could salvage. Then they'd made a big deal about the explosion over the unencrypted communications network to make the Singularity troops think their people had destroyed it—and perhaps themselves.

Who knew? Their leadership might even believe it.

Another wrinkle that had to be considered—which he'd expounded on in his report—was Tolliver's involvement. The Singularity didn't know she'd survived the raid that had rescued her—or so the Empire believed—but word of her presence would eventually make it to them.

Too many people knew of her existence now. It was only a matter of time.

If they also learned she'd been key in ruining their likely counterstrike for that raid—which he agreed with Reed that this could've been—they'd lose their little minds. They'd also come after Tolliver with everything they could bring to bear. Something else to keep an eye out for.

Still, that was above his pay grade. Best to focus on what was happening here and now, letting the officers look at the strategic end. He needed to wrap up his part of the work here.

The Empire would have to build a new facility somewhere on the planet so they could take advantage of the materials that only grew here, but it wasn't going to be up and running anytime soon.

That wasn't a problem for the Imperial Marines, though. They'd done what they'd been sent to do and stopped the supposed sabotage. The fact that it had never existed didn't really matter. They'd found what was causing the disruption, uncovered a plot that would've placed the entire Empire at risk, and stopped it.

The lieutenant had briefed them about what was going on with the CEO of Yi Holdings. Apparently, Geller had played the man like a fiddle, feeding him lies about what the Empire intended to do while also sending reports in his name that there was so much trouble and finally requesting Imperial intervention.

His credulity wasn't going to save him or his company in the end, though. Now that the corporation had proven itself a danger to Project Panther, Jerome had no doubt the Empire would rescind the company's ownership stake at a ruinous loss.

That would leave Schuster and Associates in control of the planet, including the mining operation. Since it was a front company used by the Empire, it meant that the Empire would be in direct control of the planet, even if that was not precisely the way it looked to outsiders.

He wouldn't be surprised if the actual governance was passed on to the citizens. That was what Craig Lindbergh had been pushing for, and he thought it was smart. Time would tell.

Jerome had no doubt that wherever they established the new Panther Project facility, it would be significantly better protected and much more concealed than the first time. Perhaps they'd only grow the raw materials here and ship them out to another location for processing. That was what he'd have done.

Still, that was above his pay grade, and he needed to focus on the things that were within his control. They were sending a report back to Seward on a civilian ship to request reinforcements and Fleet warships, and he needed to get his report written up before they left.

He set the portable recorder on his desk and assumed his most serious expression as he stared into its lens. Then he triggered it to record his report to Bashir.

"Major, I've finished the investigation you tasked me with and have a final report. Attached, you'll find records of all of the events here on Diorama that will sustain my conclusions.

"Private First Class Tolliver shows no indications of loyalty to the Singularity and has, in fact, caused them great harm by disrupting their operations on Diorama and capturing two very high-ranking members of their society.

"I have the highest confidence in Private First Class Tolliver, and I'm pleased to have her as a valued member of my squad. As you've instructed, I'll continue to observe her actions, but I don't believe I need to make any further reports on this matter. Her loyalty to the Empire is beyond question.

"Sergeant Jerome Walker, ending report."

He used his implants to encode the video and attached it to the rest of the reports being sent back on the civilian ship. Thank God that was finally done.

Jerome didn't expect his insights to go over well. Rather, he expected them to piss the man off, but he'd either get over it, or he'd find someone else to do his dirty work. Jerome was done doubting Tolliver.

He'd seen everything he'd needed to make up his mind. She was exactly what she'd portrayed herself as: a dedicated young marine determined to serve the Empire. End of story.

Jerome knew Lieutenant Van Buren had written a glowing report for the colonel and copied the major on it. It would have all the details of what Tolliver, Randall, and to a lesser extent Baker had done. No marine need ever doubt her commitment again.

He wasn't going to waste time worrying about it in any case. Not when he was in the first group heading to the Big L Ranch for what had been promoted as the biggest party this planet had ever seen.

For him, it wouldn't be about having a good time, though he had no doubt he would. It was to remember the dozens of marines who'd given their lives repelling the ambush by the Singularity raiders. It also helped that Craig Lindbergh's sister was overseeing the convalescence of all the injured marines at their big ranch house.

For them and his people, he'd put on a good face, but he was already planning the next stage of training the greenies. They might have proven themselves, but they had so much left to learn. And with the unexpected character they'd demonstrated, they might even enjoy the process.

He laughed at his own joke and stood. Time for barbecue.

36

Diana looked over the ranch yard and was stunned. What had been a frontier workplace with just a little bit of flair had turned into a party zone less than a week after she'd stayed there last.

That wasn't to say that it was overdone, by any means, but colorful paper bunting was *everywhere*. Tables had also been set up in the open yard. Those were groaning under the weight of food and drink. There were so many different things to try that she'd barely made any headway at all.

Some of the ranch hands were even giving the marines riding lessons. That was exciting when they occasionally demanded more adventurous mounts. When that happened, everybody cheered and whistled as the bold marines either hung on for dear life or were ignominiously tossed off.

Everyone seemed to be having a good time, and they more than deserved it.

Not all the marines were there, of course. While Lieutenant Van Buren was pretty sure they'd run the Singularity forces off the planet based on the number of unauthorized small craft taking off and rendezvousing with a now-departed merchant ship, they couldn't and wouldn't take that for granted.

That meant they'd left two platoons on duty back at Camp Pyramid to keep their base of operations secure. The plan had been to cycle each platoon through the party, letting them stay for about five hours.

Third Platoon held the position of honor, coming at the tail end so they could stay as long as the party lasted. Diana suspected it would go late into the night. She'd be shocked if any of them got back to Camp Pyramid before dawn.

Personally, she couldn't imagine how anyone could keep going that long, but it looked like the ranch hands were making a go of it. Maybe they were doing like the marines and swapping in replacements when no one was looking.

One of the biggest benefits of this spontaneous celebration was that it was in Andrea's honor. Well, technically, it was in honor of *all* the marines, but everyone knew the role Andrea had played, even if they didn't know the classified details.

That had done wonders in quashing any remaining uncertainty or antipathy toward her friend. Today, Andrea was the woman of the hour, and Diana couldn't be happier.

"They make pretty good barbecue, don't they?" the old woman next to Diane asked, startling her, since she hadn't heard her arrive. "I've lived most of my life here, and these guys really know how to cook meat."

Diana took a sip of her beer and turned her attention to the woman. "I'm not sure we've actually been introduced. Last time we saw each other, we were both a little busy to exchange names. I'm Diana Randall."

"Susan Kolstad," the woman said, not taking her eyes off the swirling crowd. "I'm a retired senior sergeant, formerly of the Marine Raiders."

The woman dropped that bomb in an even tone as if she was just passing along a bit of gossip. Marine Raiders were the boogeymen that went silently through the night, killing the Empire's enemies.

"You don't look like a Marine Raider."

Kolstad laughed. "Even Marine Raiders get old, kid. Doesn't mean I can't still do what's needed when called upon."

The woman turned her attention fully on Diana. "I'm not sure you realize the service you and your friends did for the Empire, but I've taken note of it. I wouldn't count on this actually bearing fruit, but I did send a report about the events to the Raiders. Don't be surprised if someone starts keeping an eye on you going forward."

Diana chuckled. "The Marine Raiders are *literally* the most exclusive club in the universe. Some days I question whether I actually have what it takes to be a marine and have to rededicate myself to doing better. I'm never going to make the cut for something like that."

Kolstad took a sip of her beer and shrugged slightly. "Their criteria might not be exactly what you think it is. And besides, just because you're not suitable right now doesn't mean that you won't be in ten or twenty years. The Raiders take a very long view when it comes to grooming potential recruits.

"Besides which, your group showed some intriguing traits that are bound to garner some interest. Of course, there's the obvious: your friend's enhanced genetics. I know you think her heritage would be an instant disqualifier, but I think she's done more than enough to put any lingering questions to rest. All she had to do to help the Singularity was fail to stop Gellei.

"She's more than proven her loyalty to the Empire at this point. As have you."

"Me?" Diana asked with a bit of a surprised smile. "All I did was my duty. Nothing special."

"Really?" Kolstad drew out the word as her smile grew. "Then how did you find the secret entrances to the facility? Once you did so, exactly how did you unlock the exits from the outside when they're programmed not to even respond to external signals? Then once inside the tunnels, how did you shut down the security systems?"

Before Diana could respond, the old woman held up a hand—not the one holding her beer—to stop her from speaking. "Let's not waste time with casual lies and misdirection to cover up what actually happened. You may not know it, but Marine Raiders have a suite of programs inside their implants that allow them to do a truly amazing number of things that aren't supposed to be possible.

"One of them is to access facilities they're not supposed to be able to get into. A little bit of checking on my part confirms that you used something similar to gain access to those tunnels.

"Hell, let's be honest, you knew about those tunnels before your friend even pointed them out. There were no anomalies. I double-checked using a different set of scanners, and no one could've seen those tunnels from the outside."

Diana smiled a bit brightly. "I must've gotten lucky. We managed to detect the entrances, and the security systems must have been somehow switched off during the attack on the facility."

"Uh-huh," Kolstad said, obviously unconvinced. "And you opened the secret door in front of the facility coordinator using your implants. Don't worry, by the way. I scrubbed that out of the official report. We wouldn't want anyone wondering where you got those hacking tools, would we?"

Diana was wondering how to respond when the old woman took a gulp of her beer, slid an arm around her shoulder, and gestured out toward the party around them with her glass.

"The answer isn't important. What matters is that you have unexpected depths that you're willing to use in defense of the Empire. You say you don't really have that much to offer an organization like the Marine Raiders, but I'm going to disagree.

"You've got grit and unexpected depth. Those two things in combination form a foundation I know my brothers and sisters in arms will be interested in."

Well, that was terrifying. How was she supposed to keep the secret databases in her head from becoming public knowledge if all it took was this one woman figuring out her deepest secrets based on this one mission? She was completely and utterly screwed.

"That's all very exciting, but I'd rather not talk about it tonight," she deflected. "This is a celebration about winning and mourning the losses we suffered doing so. I don't even want to think about some hypothetical recruitment effort by the Marine Raiders."

The old woman nodded. "Focusing on today is a lot more

important than worrying about what tomorrow will bring. For example, that young man over there has been eyeing you for the last fifteen or twenty minutes. I think he's waiting for a break so he can come over and whisk you away to somewhere a little bit more private."

Diana looked off in the direction Kolstad had gestured and spotted Claudio leaning against the ranch house steps. When he saw her looking in his direction, he smiled widely and saluted with his own mug of beer. Then he made a gesture toward the steps.

Considering how unsubtle Claudio usually was, that simple gesture spoke volumes without being pushy, and it almost made her laugh, imagining how many times he'd practiced it.

"If you'll excuse me, I should probably go talk with my friend," Diana said. "It was a pleasure meeting you, and on behalf of the Imperial Marines, I'd like to thank you for everything you did to help us. We appreciate it."

"It wasn't anything I'd have ever expected to do again, but it was my pleasure. Why don't you go see what your friend wants, and I'll check out the rest of the party. I doubt we'll meet again, but one never knows.

"One day—perhaps not even that long in the future—somebody very much like me might approach you with an offer. Wouldn't it be a hoot if it was me?"

Diana laughed, feeling a little spooked, and started to step away, but the older woman put a hand on her arm. "Oh, and before I forget, I stopped by your quarters at Camp Pyramid before I came over. Don't be shocked that I've confiscated your little souvenirs. I know they came in handy, but we can't let that kind of thing out in the wild. Be a good girl, and you'll get your own supply soon enough."

The old woman grinned and walked off into the crowd.

Well, it was probably best that she didn't have a highly classified drug stashed in her gear anyway. She'd thought she'd hidden the Panther pretty well, but obviously, Marine Raiders were much more capable of finding that kind of thing than ordinary people.

Oh, well. Such was life.

Diana sauntered toward the ranch house and saw Claudio perk up as she came closer, his smile widening. She knew what he hoped would happen tonight, and she'd already decided that it would. Everyone else could have their public celebration, but she had something a little bit more intimate in mind.

* * *

ANDREA WATCHED her friend walk up the ranch house steps with Claudio and shook her head. Life was about to get really complicated.

"I think they make a good couple," Craig said judiciously. "Not that I know much about the boy, but your friend isn't one to let somebody run over her. She's got spine."

"Oh, he's not too bad, I suppose," Andrea allowed. "I just don't want him to know that."

Her response made the man laugh. "I suppose that shouldn't surprise me. How is that supposed to work at your camp with everybody all around?"

"I have no idea, and thankfully, it's not my problem. If they start getting all googly-eyed, I'm heading somewhere else. There are some things in life that one just cannot unsee."

"Truth. And speaking of truth, did you enjoy the barbecue? The cooks went all out to make sure you and your friends had the best party we could arrange."

Andrea turned away from the ranch house and watched Third Platoon eating, dancing, and occasionally making fools out of themselves. "They're having the time of their lives. After a fight like they had, they deserve it."

Third Platoon had lost less than the other two platoons by a slight margin, but losing even one comrade was a blow. She hadn't known the dead or injured well. There just hadn't been enough time to become part of their lives. And they hadn't made up their minds whether to accept her at that point, and now they were gone.

There was a lesson to be learned from that: she'd have to make friends faster next time. Though she'd never been good at making friends, something had to change. She was done living her life apart from everyone around her.

Craig studied her for a few moments and then gestured toward the people in front of them. "I've been walking around listening to people all day. Maybe you haven't heard, but you're the center of conversation, and I'm not just talking about people from your platoon.

"Everyone I've heard mention your name respected what you've done and was listening to stories from the ranch hands about your adventures here. Let me tell you, the fight with the dire wolves has already gotten quite a bit of attention, and then there was the train escape."

She covered her eyes with her free hand. "Please tell me they haven't made it sound all crazy."

"Crazy is as crazy does, or so they say, but there *were* some embellishments. I won't get into the weeds of what my boys and girls added to the tales, but you can rest assured they know how to tell a good story. The trick is to keep from getting bogged down in facts."

Andrea pinched the bridge of her nose and shook her head. "You're not helping. I want to fit in with these people, not have them ridicule me."

"Oh, they weren't ridiculing you," he said with an easy grin. "I should also add that they were taking advantage of my people's storytelling expertise to enhance your fight with Geller. I wish I'd been a fly on the wall for that because it sounds like you're some kind of ninja."

This just kept getting better.

"How would they even know the details of my fight with Geller?" she demanded. "The only people there were Sergeant Walker and Susan Kolstad. Walker's not exactly the type to tell tales out of school, especially since Geller's identity is classified. Was it Kolstad?"

"Of course. Now, before you get all mad, she didn't share the information that the woman was the same as you genetically. Just that she was a bad guy. A *really* talented bad guy with a knife that almost took off your head before you whipped her ass. Oh, and I think there were some flying jump kicks too.

"Personally, the woman can tell a decent story, but she's a bit rough with the delivery. I could tell which parts were embellished and what she'd actually seen. My guess is they walked in right before you chopped Geller's hand off. The parts that she passed on about the fight beforehand—Get it? Beforehand?—sounded like she'd made them up."

Andrea let her breath out slowly. Maybe the story wouldn't gain much traction because of that.

"But don't worry about that," Craig continued. "The ranch hands took her story and massaged it real good before they passed it on to the marines. I think that might've been the plan all along, since no one inside your company really knew the details before the ranch hands started talking."

"This is an utter disaster," Andrea said tiredly. "They're going to think I somehow made all this up, and they're going to hold it against me."

The man put a hand on her shoulder. "That couldn't be further from the truth. Trust me when I say that I've heard the glee they responded to the stories with. There was pride in their voices that one of their own had done something like that.

"And make no mistake, young lady, that's what they consider you: one of their own. Whatever you were before your company came here, you only have to look around to see a bunch of men and women who would stand beside you against any threat or insult.

"You know who does that? Family. You've found your kin, Andrea Tolliver."

She tried to think about that, but he pressed on. "And speaking of homes and families, I know you already have a set, but you have a new home and family here on Diorama if you ever choose to come back. My family is your family, and my home is yours."

The words almost brought tears to her eyes before she saw Leroy and his sister Beatrice bearing down on her, holding something dark wadded up between them. She was still trying to figure out what it was when Craig grinned and turned to face the crowd.

"Everyone listen up! To show our appreciation for everything Andrea has done for me and my people, Leroy and Beatrice have created a gift from all of us to her. We thought long and hard to make sure it was something that would be appropriate for her heroic actions, and I think we've come up with the perfect gift. I didn't think they could get it ready in time for the party, but they pulled off a technological miracle."

Leroy and his sister shook out the thing, and Andrea finally realized what it was. It was a monstrously large dire wolf pelt. Based on the size, it had to be at least as large as the one she'd killed at the end of the fight.

Hell, it might be the very same one for all she knew.

"They took one of the smaller ones—which isn't really so small when you look at it—and put it in Diana Randall's room. I'm sure she's found it by now and will come up with something appropriate to use it for."

At least a third of the people out there in the crowd cheered and laughed, perhaps having seen Diana and Claudio heading into the ranch house earlier and making the correct assumption about what they'd be doing on that dire wolf pelt.

Under other circumstances, Andrea would've been embarrassed for her friend, but she was too busy being overwhelmed by the gift.

"I don't know what to say," she said almost too quietly to be heard. "Thank you."

When they handed her the pelt, it more than filled her arms, and she wondered where the hell she was supposed to put it. The tiny area she had to stay in during the deployment was far too small, but it wasn't exactly like she had a lot of space in the fire team's room when they got back to Seward either. The thing was *huge*.

She thought her embarrassment was over, but she was wrong.

Craig grabbed the pelt by the scruff of the neck and lifted its head high. "It's my understanding that marines love nicknames and that Andrea doesn't have one. I'd like to take a moment to suggest one for your consideration. Ladies and gentlemen, I give you the Empire's own Dire Wolf!"

There was a split second of silence, and then almost as if coordinated, virtually everyone threw their heads back and howled.

Andrea stood there, stunned so badly that she couldn't even think. She'd come to the Imperial Marines looking for a life where she could serve others and had instead found a camaraderie that almost made her heart beat out of her chest. She wouldn't have traded this moment for anything in the universe.

"Now, enough talking," Craig said. "I hear we've got another shipment of beer coming in, and I need some help drinking it. Who's with me?"

That got a roar out of both the marines and the ranch hands, and the crowd swept for the barn, literally picking Andrea up and carrying her along with them like the tide going out. It looked like the night was far from over, and she never wanted it to end.

She'd come home in almost every sense of the word.

* * *

WANT to get updates from Terry about new books and other general nonsense going on in his life? He promises there will be cats. Go to TerryMixon.com/Mailing-List and sign up.

DID YOU ENJOY THIS BOOK? Please leave a review on Amazon. It only takes a minute to dash off a few words and that kind of thing helps Terry make a living as a writer and gets you new books faster.

WANT MORE BOOKS BY TERRY? Flip to the next page and grab one.

VISIT TERRY'S Patreon page to find out how to get cool rewards and an early look at what he's working on at Patreon.com/TerryMixon.

ALSO BY TERRY MIXON

You can always find the most up to date listing of Terry's titles on his Amazon Author Page.

Note: the links below (ebook only, obviously) redirect you to my website where you can click a button to go to Amazon. This allows me to participate in Amazon's associates program and earn a little more. Sorry for any inconvenience.

Behind Enemy Lines

The Terra Gambit

Hidden Enemies

Race to Terra

Ruined Terra

Victory on Terra

When Luck Runs Out

Gunboat Diplomacy

The Imperial Marines Saga

Spoils of War

Imperial Recruit

Enemy Action

The Humanity Unlimited Saga

Liberty Station

Freedom Express

Tree of Liberty

Blood of Patriots

Single Novels

Scorched Earth

Storm Divers

The Vigilante Series with Glynn Stewart

Heart of Vengeance

Oath of Vengeance

Bound By Law

Bound By Honor

Bound By Blood

Box Sets

The Empire of Bones Saga Volume 1

The Empire of Bones Saga Volume 2

The Empire of Bones Saga Volume 3

The Empire of Bones Saga Volume 4

Humanity Unlimited Publisher's Pack 1

Humanity Unlimited Publisher's Pack 2

ABOUT TERRY

#1 Bestselling Military Science Fiction author Terry Mixon served as a non-commissioned officer in the United States Army 101st Airborne Division. He later worked alongside the flight controllers in the Mission Control Center at the NASA Johnson Space Center supporting the Space Shuttle, the International Space Station, and other human spaceflight projects.

He now writes full time while living in Texas with his lovely wife and a pounce of cats.

TerryMixon.com

a amazon.com/author/terrymixon

f facebook.com/TerryLMixon

patreon.com/TerryMixon

BB bookbub.com/authors/terry-mixon

g goodreads.com/TerryMixon